I0778651

love
LESSONS

Book Two of the Woodvale Series

KATIE CAWOOD

*For everyone who feels like
they're either too much
or not enough—*

Never settle for anyone who doesn't think you're just right.

Author's Note
& content warnings

Dear reader,

Thank you so much for picking up my book! After writing *Lesson Learned*, I decided Kendall's story needed to be told. After all, she deserves a happily ever after, too.

This story begins two school years after *Lesson Learned* took place. If you haven't read the first book, don't worry! You'll still be able to follow along. And if you have read it, I'm so excited for you to discover just how much Sarah and Owen appear in this book.

I do want to point out a couple of things about this book before you read. First of all, while there are a lot of laugh-out-loud moments and scenes that will give you the warm fuzzies, this book also has some raw, emotional moments. Parental abandonment is a major theme throughout this novel.

As you read, you'll come across multiple explicit sex scenes, mentions of alcohol and marijuana use, a whole lot of swearing, and heavy angst. It's also worth mentioning that Kendall, like me, has ADHD and struggles to manage it sometimes. Everyone handles ADHD differently, of course, but I modeled Kendall's experiences with it after mine.

I've included a full list of trigger warnings on my website at **www.authorkatiecawood.com/contentwarnings**. Please be advised, that page includes a little bit of a spoiler about a side character, so the choice to read through the list is entirely up to you.

Are you ready to meet your next book boyfriend, or what?

With love,
Katie

LOVE LESSONS

official playlist

"State of Grace" (Taylor's Version) – Taylor Swift

"Homesick" – Noah Kahan

"We're Going to Be Friends" – The White Stripes

"She Lit a Fire" – Lord Huron

"I Wanna Be Yours" – Arctic Monkeys

"Treacherous (Taylor's Version)" – Taylor Swift

"The Way I Am" – Ingrid Michaelson

"Sweater Weather" – The Neighbourhood

"could you love me while i hate myself?" – Zeph

"Fallin' All In You" – Shawn Mendes
(Mason & Kendall's song)

"Daughter" – Loudon Wainwright

chapter one
kendall

"Are you still in there taking nudes for Thor?"

Choosing to ignore my sister's latest Viking comment, I yanked my bra straps back up over my shoulders and grabbed the silk robe from the back of my bedroom door, tying it loosely around my waist. I pulled my door open to find Jamie just on the other side of it holding Titus, her girlfriend's crusty white dog. Titus immediately began yapping, just like he always did at the sight of me. Jamie tossed him onto the couch next to Daya, who scooped him up and held him to her chest.

"Can they receive nudes in Asgard?" Daya asked.

I lifted one eyebrow at her. "Um, what?"

Jamie rolled her eyes at her girlfriend. "She's not nerdy enough to understand your geeky references, babe." Turning back to me, she said, "The fry-cuterie board is done. Come and get 'em while they're still hot."

My phone buzzed in my hand, and I inhaled through my nose, almost too nervous to see what kind of response my latest sultry selfie had elicited. I'd put in the work for that one, using my mirror to get both my butt—barely covered by a thong—and boobs in the same shot. My long, blonde strands barely grazed my nipples. In my dark bedroom, only my pink neon heart light illuminated the contours of my body. I often lamented about my thunder thighs or belly pooch, but that night, I was really feeling myself, appreciating every curve.

And judging from the eggplant and water droplet emojis I'd just received, I wasn't the only one. I smiled down at the three little dots appearing on the screen—he was typing a second message.

"What's Kurt Cobain saying now?" Daya asked, stroking Titus between his ears.

I should have never shown my sister or her girlfriend a picture of Mason, the Tinder match I'd been texting for the last 48 hours. They couldn't handle his long, sandy blond hair or the flannel shirt he was wearing in his profile picture. Despite all their Fabio, Kurt Cobain, and Thor comments, however, they both admitted he was "pretty."

He was so pretty, in fact, I almost didn't swipe right on him. Guys like Mason with their icy blue eyes, muscular arms, and perfect hair knew how good-looking they were, and damn it, they were cocky about it. But as soon as we matched and started chatting, I got the impression he didn't do this kind of thing very often. He'd made at least two references to the fact he was a little rusty when it came to dating, and at least four self-deprecating jokes since we'd started texting. And he didn't even ask for my nudes like everyone else had—however, he respectfully and excitedly accepted my offer to send some.

"He's still not making a move," I said, slumping onto the couch next to Daya. Titus growled to show his discontent about my closeness. You'd think the little rat would have warmed up to having me as a roommate after four weeks.

"What's stopping *you* from making a move?" Jamie asked, sitting cross-legged on the floor in front of the latest fry-cuterie board on the coffee table. She and Daya had perfected the art of creating a fry-themed "charcuterie" board with a variety of French fries and sauces. It had become a weekend tradition—us filling the air fryer and oven simultaneously with four or five different kinds of fries or tater tots. It was only made complete with an assortment of dipping sauces, arranged in little bowls nestled perfectly along the edge of the board.

I dipped a waffle fry in ranch dressing. "I always had to make the first move with Heath," I said with a sigh, remembering the way I could literally sit on his lap buck naked and he'd still crane his neck to see the video game behind me. Yet, somehow, the models whose photos he liked on Instagram were still able to capture his attention. Amazing.

How I'd let *him* be the one to end things with *me,* I'd never understand. He told me I was putting too much pressure on him. I was too demanding, too high-maintenance. Too… everything.

Funny. For Owen Gardner, I wasn't enough. But for Heath, I was too much. Maybe one of these days, I'd find someone who thought I was just right? But for now, I just needed to get someone between the sheets. The sooner, the better.

"If this guy wants to see the goods in person, he's going to have to ask for it," I continued, watching Daya feed Titus a tater tot, which momentarily distracted him from glaring at me. "And so far, he's—"

My phone buzzed in my lap, causing me to lose my train of thought.

Mason: Very arty. 10/10. Really making me feel inadequate about my low-effort dick pic

Smiling to myself as I chewed, I quickly typed a response. Daya, curious to see my screen, leaned in so close that her smooth, dark hair dangled onto my shoulder. I angled my phone so she could get a better look. My attempt at breaking into the dating scene was a source of entertainment for her and my sister, which I was happy to provide.

After all, they were letting me stay with them rent-free after my break-up with Heath, only asking that I chip in with groceries sometimes. It was the least I could do.

Kendall: I assure you, you have nothing to feel
inadequate about

"Thor sent her a pic of his enormous hammer," Daya said, covering her eyes.

"Gross," was my sister's only response as she dipped a potato wedge in ketchup. I decided to ignore her comment, watching the three dots appear on my phone again.

I was starting to lose faith Mason would make any actual plans with me. Early in the conversation, we both established we were just after a hook-up, and I'd kept my Saturday night open in case he wanted to do this sooner rather than later.

Yet there I was, eating five different varieties of fried potatoes, nearly giving up on him. I wondered if he was just shy or feared rejection. Hadn't I been giving him all the right signals? Would I have to be the one to initiate this?

I sighed, distracted by the intricate details of the mandala tapestry hanging on the wall above the couch. A gift from Daya's aunt in India, it added a pop of color in an otherwise beige and brown room. My eyes traced the pink and purple pattern until my phone buzzed again.

Mason: So when are you going to sit on my face?

Oh my god.

I almost choked on my waffle fry, holding the back of my hand up to my mouth so I wouldn't spew food particles all over my sister. Once Daya saw Mason's response, she shook her head and covered her face. "I can't even say that out loud," she said, widening her eyes at Jamie as I frantically wrote my reply.

Kendall: I'm ready when you are.

Mason: Good. I think the aforementioned face-sitting should happen this coming Friday, if you're not busy

My entire body tingled with excitement. Friday was six days away—and that seemed like an eternity. However, I'd already gone a month without any sex whatsoever, and I was long overdue for a mind-shattering orgasm.

I'd be spending the week setting up my classroom, anyway, not to mention the professional development seminar, staff meeting, and meet-the-teacher night, all of which would be keeping me busy until then. Hopefully, it would all make the week pass by faster.

Mason and I continued our conversation, arranging to have drinks and shoot some pool at Poppy's Bar & Grill before "seeing where the night goes"—his words, not mine. Once we'd made our plans, I put my phone on the coffee table, smiling from ear to ear. "I need this so bad, you guys."

"Just be careful, Blondie," Jamie warned. I was the only blonde in the family, hence the nickname she'd given me. Her short hair was naturally pretty dark, though it was currently dyed a deep shade of blue. "This guy looks like a real heartbreaker."

"He's not even going to have the opportunity to break my heart," I assured her, reaching for a curly fry. I shook my head. "Neither of us want anything serious right now. Just sex. I barely know anything about him, and I'd like to keep it that way. It'll be nothing more than a one-night stand."

"Let me remind you Heath was supposed to be a one-night stand, and so was that Owen guy. You're gonna fall in love with this pretty boy."

"No I'm not," I responded, picking up my phone and navigating to his profile picture to gaze at it again. I bit my bottom lip, trying to suppress a smile, but it was no use.

Just six days.

chapter two

mason

I hated Sundays.

They were once my favorite day of the week, a day for relaxation with nowhere in particular I needed to be. No expectations. No commitments.

That was before I moved back in with my parents—before this stupid arrangement with Traci.

"Do you think she'll take me to McDonald's?" Finley asked from her booster seat in the back, staring me down in the rearview mirror.

I yawned. We'd been sitting at the back of this Wal-Mart parking lot, our usual meeting spot, for fifteen minutes. Traci was always late. "Probably," I answered. "You gonna get you a Big Mac?"

"Daddy! Little girls don't eat Big Macs."

"Oh, that's right. A filet-o-fish? Is that what you get there?"

She kicked the back of my seat. There was nothing I enjoyed more than making my daughter think I was a complete idiot. She threw her head back and laughed. "No, silly. What do I always get?"

I pretended not to remember, rubbing my bearded chin with my thumb and pointer finger. "Let's see, I don't think they have the McRib right now…"

"Chicken nuggets!" Finley squealed.

I smiled at her in the mirror. "You eat them so much, I think you *are* a chicken nugget."

"Nuh uh."

"Haven't you heard that phrase? 'You are what you eat'?"

"That's not true, because if it was, you'd be a big ol' burrito."

I nodded, yawning again as I stretched. It was getting close to 10:00 a.m., and Traci was going to be late for church if she didn't get here soon. Not that I cared. "I do eat a lot of burritos."

Finley made puking noises.

"You need to expand your palate, kid," I said.

"Huh?" She lifted one eyebrow, an ability she inherited from me—just like her stubborn streak and the tiny gap in her teeth. And though I was blonde and she had dark brown hair, everyone told us she was like my carbon copy, always mentioning our similar chins and noses. There was no denying this kid was mine.

I was momentarily distracted by a notification on my phone. It was from Kendall, a woman I matched with on Tinder, and I knew from our messaging history it was too risky to open this in front of my daughter. So I dropped my phone back into the center console and looked up at Finley in the rearview mirror.

Just as I opened my mouth to explain the words 'expand' and 'palate' to her, a white sedan pulled up beside my Jeep. My heart dropped to my stomach like it did every single time.

And when I heard Finley's disappointed moan, it sank even further. "There she is," I said, feigning a positive tone as I climbed out of the car. I made my way around to Finley's door. She could unbuckle herself from her high-back booster just fine, but it went a lot faster when she had help. When I reached her, though, she wasn't moving at all. "Can you go to church with us?" she whispered.

I was afraid she'd ask me that one of these days. Closing my eyes, I leaned against the doorframe. "I can't, kiddo. This is a you-and-Traci thing."

"Please?"

God, this was torturous. I hated telling her no. "Traci wants to spend some one-on-one time with you, okay? And church—well, it's not my thing." I leaned across her to unbuckle her seatbelt. She still didn't budge. "And you'll just be with her for a couple of hours."

"Okay," she said, sounding defeated.

I couldn't see Traci, but I could feel her looming behind me. I scooped Finley up in my arms and turned around. Sure enough, there the woman was—putting a cigarette out with her foot. "Hey there, Finley girl!"

Finley forced a smile. "Hi, Traci."

Traci's face fell. "What? When did you stop calling me Mamaw?" She coughed and turned to me. "Did you put her up to that?"

"Of course I didn't," I said, but Finley's sudden switch-up in the way she chose to address the woman didn't surprise me. The affection between them was almost entirely one-sided.

Ever since Finley's mother bolted down to Florida with her boyfriend and signed away her parenting rights, I had no obligation to let Traci take Finley to church with her on Sundays. But the woman had good intentions. She couldn't help it that her daughter was a complete fuck-up. Traci simply wanted to continue being part of Finley's life, so every Sunday morning, she took her to church and bought her lunch. This had been going on since the start of summer, just a couple months after Whitney's grand departure from Finley's life. When I moved back to Woodvale.

My apartment in Indianapolis wasn't suitable for a 5-year-old. Finley had outgrown her bedroom, which was about the same size as our walk-in closet now. The room had been big enough for her when she was smaller and only living with me on the weekends, but the twin-sized bed I'd bought her took up an entire wall. We needed more space. The girl also deserved a yard to run in, which my apartment complex didn't offer.

On top of all this, I needed my parents' support, as much as I hated to admit it. So after just a couple weeks of being a full-time dad, I found myself quitting my illustration job in the city and moving us into my parents' house in the Woodvale suburbs. The basement level of their home had two bedrooms, its own kitchenette, a living area, and a bathroom—and it was perfect for us.

For now, anyway.

My mom couldn't be happier to have us there. If it were up to her, both my sister and I and every last one of her grandchildren would be living under one roof with her. Permanently.

As for my dad, I was sure it was just another item on his "reasons why my son is an enormous disappointment" list. This was right up there with my voting record and the tattoos he couldn't stand to look at.

In fact, moving back home might even top choosing art school over following his footsteps in law school on that list.

I kissed Finley on the forehead after strapping her into her booster seat in Traci's car. "Be good and have fun, 'kay? Love you."

"Love you, Daddy."

I closed the door and took a deep breath, turning to Traci. "Hey, uh, can I talk to you about something?" My mouth felt dry. I hated confrontations, but when it came to my daughter, sometimes I had no choice but to have some awkward conversations. Traci squinted at me, waiting for me to continue. "Finley said you talked about Whitney last time she was with you…?"

She put her hands on her hips and released a long, drawn-out breath. "I'm sure I did. She's still my daughter. And even if she refuses to talk to me, her name is going to come up."

When Whitney escaped to Florida, she ceased all forms of contact with the rest of her family, too. She was determined to leave her life in Indiana behind completely and start over. I knew it was killing Traci, but it hurt Finley even more.

"Well, can you just, you know, tone it down?" I looked her in the eyes, trying to show her how serious this was. "Bringing up her mom all the time and stirring up her emotions about the situation… it's not helping."

Part of this deal with Traci was that she couldn't take Finley back to her house—I didn't want Finley to be surrounded by pictures of her mom or run into random relatives who might bring up her name. When Whitney signed her rights over to me, she insisted this was it for her—she wouldn't be returning. Cocoa Beach was calling her name, and she couldn't take Finley across state lines per our custody agreement.

So of course, she deemed the most rational course of action would be to give Finley up completely. Without the burden of parenthood holding her back, she and her boyfriend could live out their corn-dog-truck-owning dreams on the beach with virtually no worries.

It was unfathomable to me.

The first few weeks were hell. Whitney was as good as dead to Finley. Worse, actually—because the kid knew her mom was out there, somewhere, and that she could not see her. I found a therapist in Indianapolis for her to talk to, which was a tremendous help—and the spunky, goofy Finley I knew so well slowly began to resurface. I was beginning to feel a glimmer of hope she would someday heal from the trauma Whitney put her through.

But when we moved to Woodvale and Traci re-entered Finley's life, it was like all the work she'd done with her therapist vanished the second she saw portraits of her mom on the wall at Traci's house. It was a nightmare trying to console her after her first outing with Traci. That's when I made the difficult decision to shield Finley from conversations about Whitney as much as I could. There was no need to continuously reopen the wounds and force her to grieve her mom all over again.

If Finley mentioned her, that was one thing. But I wasn't about to let other people rub it in her face all the time.

Did I second-guess this choice sometimes? Absolutely. Doubt gnawed at me every single day. But for the time being, it was the only way I could think of to help Finley cope with losing her mom in such a way.

"Please respect my decision," I said, keeping my eyes locked on Traci's. I hoped she couldn't see the sweat on my forehead or detect the nervousness in my voice. "Don't mention Whitney unless she does first."

"Okay," she said, holding her hands up in surrender, but her voice was dripping with skepticism. "But if she asks about her, I'm not holding back."

That was still questionable, but I let it slide. I also resisted the urge to bring up my disapproval of the amount of gas station candy she'd been sending Finley home with each Sunday, deciding the Whitney comment was enough for now. I waved goodbye to Finley through the window and attempted to swallow the lump in my throat.

Fuck Sundays.

I sat in my Jeep and watched Traci's car until it disappeared from view. And then, deciding I couldn't wait any longer, I picked up my phone to see what kind of treat Kendall had in store for me now.

And when the picture loaded, I grinned from ear to ear. She was wearing pink lingerie with multiple criss-cross straps across the top of her breasts, overlapping in an X over both nipples. Trying to figure out how to remove such a garment would be like solving a very sexy puzzle, I imagined.

Kendall: Wish you were here ☺

Fuck me, I did too. This woman was gorgeous—angelic, almost—and the curves of her body absolutely *killed* me. And there was just something about those full lips and her big, brown eyes that made it impossible to look away.

She was almost too good to be true. Like me, she was just looking for a hook-up. She didn't ask many questions, so I didn't feel like I was deceiving her by not mentioning I had a daughter. This was one of the first things I'd done in the past several months that had absolutely nothing to do with Finley, and I preferred to keep it that way.

Mason: Wear that on Friday.

Kendall: Say please.

I put my phone down on my lap just to process this conversation for a couple of minutes. My day-to-day life typically consisted of making bologna sandwiches, playing with Barbies, and rewatching the jellyfish scene from *Finding Nemo* over and over—so this conversation with Kendall was a welcome change of pace.

Friday couldn't get here fast enough.

Mason: You'll be the one saying please.

chapter three
kendall

"Tell me you accidentally wrote down your students' grandparents' names and not their actual names," Jamie said, looking at the lollipops spread out on our kitchen table, each of them personalized with an attached card that read *"thanks for popping in!"* I planned to give them to each kindergartener who showed up for meet-the-teacher night. "Surely nobody is actually naming their kids Esther or Henry in this day and age?"

"You forgot Walter," I said, picking up the lollipop closest to me. Jamie's face fell, her amusement now replaced with disgust.

"WALTER?!" she yelled, loud enough that Titus barked a couple of times to show he was equally repulsed. Jamie rolled her eyes and moved some of the suckers around to get a better look. "Can someone revoke these parents' naming rights? At least *some* of them have normal names. Avery, Elijah, Fin—"

"I actually love the old-fashioned names," I interrupted. "Where's my laptop charger?" I was getting ready for a long day of setting up my classroom, making copies, and meeting my students and their families. Still in my jeans, I planned on getting dressed and doing my make-up in my classroom later. I was going to wear a white top tucked into a flowy, lavender skirt—it was no coincidence it matched the new pastel theme of my classroom, which I intended to finish decorating that day.

I spotted my laptop charger on the counter and dropped it in my tote bag before gathering up all the lollipops. I would have to hurry if I wanted to get to the good copier before anyone else. "I won't be home until around nine," I reminded Jamie, sliding the leftover suckers to her. She happily accepted, opening the watermelon one immediately. She was still in her pajamas, not having to go into work for a couple more hours. She was a pharmacy tech at Walgreens while going to school online to become a pharmacist herself. The kitchen had sort of become our shared workspace, hence the perpetual mess. "Is Daya cooking tonight?"

"Probably," Jamie said, pushing the sucker to one side of her mouth against her cheek. "Want us to save you a plate?"

"I wouldn't complain if you did," I said, slipping my phone into my back pocket. And I furrowed my brows as I tried to remember the last time either of them had asked for grocery money—yet the fridge and cabinets were fully stocked. "Don't I owe you guys money?"

Jamie shrugged with a dismissive wave of her hand. "You've done enough."

"I really haven't, though. I eat here, too. And Daya won't let me cook. So the least I can do is—"

Jamie laughed out loud. "That's because the last time you tried to cook, you almost blew up the house, Blondie."

I shook my head, trying not to seem too embarrassed. "It's not my fault I didn't know how gas stoves work."

"Leave the cooking to Daya and the grocery-shopping to me. We've got you covered, 'kay?"

I placed my hands on the back of the chair in front of me and stared down at Jamie's face, wondering why she still felt the need to protect me after all these years. When we were little, I would sneak across the hallway and sleep in her bed when our parents fought at night.

And at twenty-seven, I was still running to her. "I'm not going to mooch off you guys," I insisted, looking her in the eyes. "Like I said, I eat here, too. I use electricity. I use water. I—I take up space. And I might have been in a depressive slump there for a while, but I'm better now. If you don't let me contribute, I'm just going to move back in with Heath."

"Dear God, don't do that," Jamie blurted. She had to know I wasn't serious, but she nodded anyway, conceding. "Fine, I guess. But does your recent happiness have anything to do with the fact you're going to finally get some new dick in a few days?"

"Jamie!" I picked up my laminator from the counter and tucked it beneath one arm. "I'm just looking forward to the new school year, that's all. I finally have something to distract me."

"I'm sure Sarah will have a *lot* of little projects to distract you," Jamie said, rolling her eyes.

I smiled, shaking my head. I'd forgotten just how much I'd vented to Jamie last year about all the tasks that Sarah Lavely, the principal of Grissom Elementary, had assigned me. I'd somehow become her go-to person for every insane idea that popped into her head. "I'm sure she will. And you know what? I'm psyched about it."

Jamie pulled the sucker out of her mouth with a *pop!* "Yeah, say that again in like six weeks when she's got you cutting out a billion paper snowflakes or whatnot."

I shook my head, knowing her prediction probably wasn't far off. Sarah and I had become close over the past year or so, but I could barely keep up with her. When she became principal, it was like she felt she had something to prove to the community—and she took on entirely too many projects to improve our school. And, for some reason, I got looped into helping with every single one.

"Bye, Jamie."

* *

That afternoon, I stood in the center of my classroom with my hands on my hips, assessing my new décor theme. The muted pastels completely transformed the space, and I hoped it would instill a sense of calm within my students.

The rug beneath my feet was white with pink, lavender, and aqua stripes—I knew I'd be furiously hitting this thing with the carpet cleaner within a month, but at least it looked cute for now. My favorite area was the library corner, though, where I'd just placed four large, wooden letters spelling out the word "READ" on the wall, each of them painted a different pastel color. I'd also purchased matching pastel book totes and even a pink beanbag chair. My goal was to create a space I would have loved when I was five years old.

There was a gentle knock at my door. For a moment, I feared it was Heath—who was a third-grade-teacher here at Grissom—coming down to my room to pester me, so I was relieved to see Sarah poking her head through the doorway. "Hello!"

She was already dressed for tonight's open house event, it appeared, in a galaxy-print dress that reminded me of something Ms. Frizzle would wear—which is probably what she was going for, knowing her. She was carrying a manilla folder, which wasn't a good sign.

As she stepped into the room, her mouth dropped open. "Oh my god, Kendall?!" She walked over to me and clutched my arm. "You did all of this today?"

"I started yesterday."

She spun around in a circle to take it all in before her eyes found mine again. "This was more than a hundred and fifty dollars."

I shrugged. She was referring to the classroom budget I'd been given for the year. That all went toward the rug, and everything else she was looking at came straight out of my own pocket. "Everything was on sale," I lied, making her laugh.

"Well, the muted colors look fantastic," she said. "Can we sit?"

I led her over to my math center table beside my desk. I took the teacher's chair at the end, which was slightly bigger than the tiny chair Sarah sat in. I was the one with the bigger ass, so it was the logical choice. "I'm almost afraid to ask," I said, eyeing the manilla folder she placed in front of her.

"Don't be afraid," Sarah assured me with a laugh. "You can always say no to what I have in store."

"Right."

She took a deep breath. "It's fall festival time."

I nodded, knowing this was coming. Last year, Sarah, Vicki Santiago—a second grade teacher—and I organized a huge fall festival fundraiser in the school parking lot. The money earned was put into a field trip fund for all of our students. With a hayride, pumpkin carving contest, and bouncy castles, we drew a huge crowd last year, and it was an enormous success. Sarah vowed to make it an annual event. "You mean the 'Fucking Fun Fall Festival Fundraiser for Families'?" I asked, referring to the name Owen, Sarah's fiancé (and my ex-boyfriend), had given the event last year when he showed up to volunteer.

"I almost forgot about that. We should've put that on the shirts," she joked, opening her folder. She started thumbing through some of the papers in front of her, but she suddenly stopped and gave me a sheepish grin. "I'm just going to be totally upfront with you from the start, Kendall."

"Okay…"

"I can't lead this project. I'm going to be busy planning my wedding, and honestly, I need to be better about delegating projects like this instead of trying to take control of it all." I slowly nodded, and she continued. "And Vicki's going to be on maternity leave for the first four weeks of the school year, so most of the festival planning might fall on your shoulders. If you're up for it, that is."

I didn't say anything for a moment. I didn't feel capable of taking on such a project. I wasn't organized like Sarah, nor was I all that great at communicating with people—and planning this festival would require me to be proficient in both of those areas. "Are you sure you want *me* to take over?"

"Of course," she answered, tucking her hair behind her ears. "There's no one I would trust with this more than you. And since this is the second one, we can use the same vendors, same donors—most of the work is already done for you. This is going to be the PTO's main focus this semester, so you'll be able to lean on them for support."

I reached for her folder and pulled it toward me on the table. She was right—a lot of the hard work was already completed because we'd done it all before. She'd kept every receipt, every list, every bit of info—I practically had a step-by-step guide in my hands. "Okay," I said, looking up at her. "I'm in."

She clapped. "Good! I knew you would say yes."

As I rifled through the papers, I pulled out an off-white piece of cardstock, realizing a moment later it was a wedding invitation with Sarah and Owen's names on it in a swoopy, cursive font. My eyes lingered on Owen's name, and my mind flashed to the night he first kissed me outside of the Mexican restaurant at the staff Christmas party almost two years ago. The only reason he'd fallen into my arms in the first place was because Sarah had rejected him that night.

Look at them now, I thought. They were so disgustingly perfect for each other, it was impossible to feel bitter about being pushed aside so he could finally be with the woman he truly desired.

"Oh yeah," Sarah said, seeing the invitation in my hand. "I brought that in here for you. Your invitation was sent to your old address, because I printed the label before you guys broke up… and, well, I wasn't sure if Heath would have shared that with you."

"He didn't," I said, shaking my head. Of course he hadn't told me about it. If he hadn't been dating me at the time, they wouldn't have invited him at all. And though we were split up now, I could almost guarantee he would still go—meaning not one, but *two,* of my ex-boyfriends would be in attendance.

And one of them was the groom.

I could feel Sarah's eyes on me as I put the invitation down on the table. I heard the inhale, saw the way she shifted in her seat—and I knew the words that were about to come out of her mouth before she even uttered them. "I know I've said this before—"

"Don't," I said with a grin, shaking my head. "You're already said it twice."

"But I'm just so—"

"I know."

"And Owen's really—"

"Sorry," I finished for her. "I know. He told me, too. I promise my Owen-hating era only lasted, like, two weeks." This was mostly true—the sight of Owen and Sarah together stopped crushing my heart after about two months, but who's counting? "Let me be in my Heath-hating era now."

"I'm—shit, I almost said 'I'm sorry' again."

"I don't care if you're the principal, I'll kick you out of this room if you apologize to me one more time." I pointed at the door.

Sarah laughed, running her fingers through her dark hair. "Okay. I won't. Anyway, I wish I could uninvite Heath, but I sort of made it an open invitation to all the staff." She winced at me.

"Can I still bring another plus-one?" There was no way I could show up to this event alone. My mind shifted to Mason. Of course we'd both indicated our plans for this Friday night were just a one-time thing, but come November, maybe he'd be up for round two? I couldn't fight the grin spreading across my face.

And Sarah noticed. She raised both eyebrows and asked, "Why, do you have someone in mind?"

"No," I lied, but my smile grew even wider when I thought about some of the nasty things Mason had been expressing he desired to do to me. I could feel my cheeks starting to get hot, so I quickly attempted to change the subject. "I would just hate to show up to a wedding alone."

"Well, of course you can still bring a plus-one," she said, scooting her chair back. Just before she stood up, she elbowed me. "You can bring whoever's got you blushing like that, girl."

As Sarah turned to walk away, I laughed and hid my face with my hands. God. This man was turning me into a giggling schoolgirl, and I hadn't even met him yet.

chapter four

mason

Kendall: I'm not sure you can handle all this ass.

"Dad, have you seen my unicorn shoes?"

I blinked, looking up from my phone, trying to remember the last place in which I'd seen Finley's favorite pair of shoes. If she'd leave them in the basket by the bottom of the stairs like I constantly reminded her, this wouldn't be an issue. "Check under your bed," I mumbled, looking back at my phone. I glanced at the time—we had about ten minutes before we'd need to head out the door for meet-the-teacher night.

Mason: I'm up for the challenge.

"I already looked there," Finley whined, dramatically throwing herself down on the couch beside me. She rolled off the front of it, sliding onto the floor—a movement that ruined the tight ponytail I'd just pulled her hair into. Before I could open my mouth to tell her to get up off the floor, she turned to an imaginary camera and said, "Tune in next time for the unicorn shoe reveal, I guess."

I swallowed. For the past several weeks, Finley had been addressing a pretend camera as though she had a million YouTube subscribers watching her at all times. At first it was weird, and then it became annoying. We'd be in the middle of a meal at a restaurant with my parents and she'd say, "Leave a comment down below if you think I should put hot sauce on my mac and cheese!"

My parents were concerned, trying to convince me Finley had lost all sense of reality. Like it was a coping mechanism for the trauma she'd been through. And maybe it was? But by now, I'd accepted it, welcoming her invisible followers into our daily lives. Hosting an imaginary YouTube channel replaced her incessant begging to start a real one, so I decided to embrace it— sometimes participating in the shenanigans myself. "No, let's do the unicorn shoe reveal right now," I said, standing up from the couch. "Because if we don't find your shoes, you're not going to get to meet your teacher tonight."

Upon hearing this, she sprang into action. Nothing excited Finley more than starting kindergarten—we even had a paper chain countdown to mark the occasion. Finley's backpack was already packed with all of her school supplies and hanging in the foyer upstairs. The walk-in closet in our basement was full of all of Finley's new back-to-school clothes—she had a new outfit for the entire first month, which was the result of letting my mom take her to the mall. I should've known she'd spoil her.

In less than a week, our lives were going to change. Finley and I would no longer spend all hours of the day together, and I'd have a whole lot more time to take on more design clients. I'd been doing some freelancing since moving back to Woodvale, often getting most of my work done after Finley went to bed. Half of me looked forward to the quiet time I'd soon have.

The other half of me dreaded it so much it made me physically ill.

"Found them!" Finley yelled, crawling between the barstools and the counter in our kitchenette. She was wearing her shoes on her hands and whining like a puppy for some reason.

I glanced down at my phone, disappointed to see Kendall hadn't replied yet. Maybe she was busy. "Come on, Fin," I said. "Get 'em on. Let's go."

**

I hadn't set foot in Grissom Elementary School since my fifth-grade graduation fifteen years ago. It appeared not much had changed, from the statue of Gus Grissom in the vestibule to the mural of a rocket ship on the wall next to the front office.

And it smelled the same. As I walked through the main doorway into the front hallway, holding Finley's hand as she skipped, memories of my childhood flooded my mind. I swallowed, realizing Finley would be making memories in this building now.

My cousin Owen's fiancée, Sarah, was standing next to the office doors, greeting everyone. She smiled when she spotted us, giving Finley an enthusiastic wave. "Hi, Finley!" she said. "Are you excited about starting kindergarten?"

Finley raised one eyebrow at her. "Aren't you my aunt or something?"

"No, not your aunt—I'm your dad's cousin's fiancée, though," Sarah said, glancing at my face. "I guess that is a little confusing, isn't it? My name is Ms. Lavely, and I'm your new principal."

"Um, where's my classroom?" Finley clearly did not have time for this conversation.

Sarah laughed, and I glanced over my shoulder. "The kindergarten rooms are that way, right?" I asked, nodding down the hall. "We're looking for Ms. Devin's room."

"First door on the right," Sarah said. "Finley, you are going to absolutely love Ms. Devin. She's the sweetest, most fun teacher *ever*. You're so lucky!"

This made Finley's face light up, and she began pulling me in the direction of the kindergarten rooms. "See ya," I called over my shoulder as Finley yanked my arm even harder. "Tell Owen I said hey."

"I will, Mason. It was great seeing you both!"

Finley's classroom was the closest to the school office, and its proximity to the front entrance made me a little uneasy. My mind went to a dark place—if there was ever any kind of danger at the school, her classroom was an easy target. And in that moment, the vulnerability of sending a piece of my heart into the world hit me hard. With her here, I'd have no control over her safety—no way to protect her. For a few seconds, I considered turning right back around and homeschooling her instead. But the kid was smiling from ear-to-ear at the decorated bulletin board next to her classroom door, which made her stop in her tracks. "Daddy, look!" The display featured a giant beehive surrounded by twenty-something bees, each of them labeled with the kids' names. And right next to the hive itself was Finley's bumblebee. "I see my name!"

I squeezed her hand, feeling the worry begin to dissipate. She was going to be fine. "Are you the queen bee?"

"No, silly," Finley said, rolling her eyes at me like I was an idiot. "My teacher's the queen bee. Let's go meet her!" I let Finley lead me into the classroom behind another family. Upon entering, I realized it was the same kindergarten classroom I'd had myself. It had changed a lot—I remembered these horribly ugly alphabet plushies hanging on the wall that haunted my dreams, but thankfully, they were long gone. This room looked cozy, almost serene, with pink and purple accents everywhere. Right up Finley's alley.

She was momentarily speechless as she took it all in. I could tell she didn't know what to check out first. Finally, when she spotted a fuzzy pink beanbag chair in the corner, she gently tugged me in that direction. "Wow, Fin, look at all those books," I said, nodding toward the bookshelf. "Think you can read them all this year?"

She pulled a mermaid book out of a bin from the shelf and made herself at home in the beanbag chair with it. Chuckling at her, I turned to look around the room at all the other parents filtering in, wondering if I'd gone to school with any of these people. Woodvale was a small town, after all—I'd be shocked if Finley didn't have any of my former classmates' kids in her class.

My eyes stopped when I spotted a blonde woman in a purple skirt on the other side of the room.

And my heart stopped, too.

It was *Kendall.*

I spent the next three seconds scanning the area around her—which one of these kids belonged to her? That's when I noticed the lanyard hanging from her neck and heard the words coming from her mouth: "We're going to have *so* much fun this year," she was saying to the little boy in front of her. *Oh, fuck.*

At that exact moment, she lifted her eyes in my direction as she tucked her hair behind her ear. She immediately froze, her hand hovering near the side of her head. Though she quickly composed herself, the initial shock of seeing me was evident in the way her eyes darted from me to Finley and back to my face. Was her heart beating as fast as mine right now?

Swallowing, I whipped back around to look at Finley, who was deep into a book review for her fake YouTube audience. I heard her ask me a question, but the words didn't quite reach my brain. All I could think about was the sultry photo Kendall sent no more than one hour ago—*I'm not sure you can handle all this ass*—and now I realized she had definitely, absolutely, taken that photo somewhere in this school.

Ohmygodohmygodohmygod. Eventually, I was going to have to turn around and speak to this woman face-to-face, and that made me want to throw up.

As Finley made her way to a different section of the room, I watched Kendall in my peripheral vision. She was busy welcoming other kids and their parents and handing out papers. The longer we waited to approach her, the sweatier I got.

When Finley made her way over to the fish tank directly beside Kendall, I took a deep breath. *Here goes nothing*, I told myself. With my hands in my pockets, I joined Finley next to the fish tank within arms' reach of Kendall. The mom she was talking to wandered off, meaning she had no choice but to direct her attention toward us. Only the shelf holding the fish tank separated us.

"Here fishy, fishy, fishy," Finley was saying, pressing her face against the glass. I looked up from her at Kendall's face, meeting her gaze. I was taken aback by how big and bright her eyes were, momentarily getting lost in them until I remembered the predicament I was currently in.

"And who do we have here?" Kendall asked in a teacher-y voice, looking down at Finley. She held a stack of packets against her chest.

"Uh," I said, clearing my throat. My heart was going to explode right out of my chest any minute now. "This is Finley."

"Do you have any jellyfish?" Finley asked.

Kendall pulled her eyes away from mine to look down at Finley. "No, I'm sorry," she said with a little laugh. "I just have boring ol' goldfish. But guess what? You'll get a chance to feed them if you're the student of the day."

And much to my horror, Finley turned to an imaginary camera and said, "No jellyfish, guys, but be sure to subscribe so you don't miss the goldfish-feeding video!" Kendall turned to me with an inquisitive expression, both eyebrows raised. Because to her, it probably looked like Finley was speaking directly to the bookshelves beside her.

"She, um, watches a lot of YouTube," I explained with a nervous chuckle. Kendall kept her eyes locked on mine, and I had to be the one to break the eye contact because it was almost too intense—she was even more beautiful in person, and I simply could not bear it.

And it was slowly beginning to sink in that everything I had planned to do with her—to do *to* her—would never happen. Not now.

With some effort, I made myself look up at her again. She was observing the families on the other side of the room, all of them busy checking out the cubbies along the opposite wall. When Kendall turned back to me, my heart skipped a beat as she softly said, "I didn't know you had a daughter."

"Didn't know you were my daughter's teacher," I replied. Finley was tapping on the glass, so I gave her shoulder a gentle pat to make her stop.

"Obviously," Kendall said in this almost bratty tone that made it hard for me to breathe. My eyes dropped to her hips, and I couldn't help but envision all the pictures I possessed of this woman's naked body on the device in my pocket. Kendall's eyes darted from side to side. "And did you bring Finley… alone?"

"Yes, I did," I answered, pulling my hands out of my pockets. Was she looking for Finley's mom? I wiped my palms on my jeans, worried for a moment she thought I was a cheating husband. "It's just me and her."

Kendall nodded, seemingly satisfied with that answer. Finley, deciding she was bored with the fish, looked up at her teacher and asked, "So, where's my desk, anyway?" I stayed by the fish tank as Kendall led Finley to a table near the front of the room, pointing out a laminated nameplate with Finley's first and last name on it. She showed her all the other things laid out on her desk, including a stack of papers and a sucker—it took Finley a fraction of a second to rip the candy open.

After that, Kendall turned to greet another family that walked in—a mom, a dad, and a terrified-looking little boy. She put her hands on her knees, bending over as she spoke to him. I had to tear my eyes off her backside. *Don't make it obvious, idiot,* I told myself before joining Finley by her spot at the table. "Is this where you're going to sit, Fin?" I asked her.

"Yup! And look, my teacher gave me a sucker. I like her a lot, Dad."

"Yeah. She, uh—she seems pretty cool," I said, running my hands through my hair. As Finley knelt down to check out a shelf full of puzzles, I watched Kendall hand a packet to the mom she was speaking to.

"Here's the volunteer form for it—it has all the information you need."

"Thank you," the mom said, giving Kendall a nod before following her son to his table.

I approached Kendall from behind. "You wanna tell me about that packet you got there?"

She turned to me and blinked. "Oh, this?" She looked down at the papers in her hands. "It's… the Room Mom application form."

I took a step closer. "'Room Mom'?"

"Yeah, every year I get a couple of moms to volunteer in the classroom since I don't have an aide."

"Oh yeah?" I asked, stepping even closer to her. "And what kinds of things do these moms do?"

"Um," she started, glancing at the family that had just walked in the classroom door. "They just assist with general classroom needs. Whatever I need that day." She was still clutching the packets close to her chest. It appeared she wasn't going to give one up unless I asked.

"You gonna hand me one of those?" I asked, nodding toward the papers and taking yet another step closer to her.

She stared at me for a moment as if to assess whether I was serious or not before extending a packet toward me. "I highly doubt you'd be interested in something like this."

I took the packet from her. "You don't know me that well."

"Evidently not," she said with a quick glance in Finley's direction.

I grinned, skimming the form in my hands. "Let's see. Laminating, cutting, assisting children during small group time—yeah, this all sounds right up my alley. And look at that, it actually says 'Room Parent.' So you were just being a little sexist, huh?"

Kendall pressed her lips together, taking a moment before she replied. "I'm sorry, the terminology was changed a year ago when we got a new principal—and, well, I've never had a dad volunteer. Ever."

"Until now."

"You don't have a job during school hours to occupy your time?"

"I'm a freelancer," I said, side-eyeing Finley, who was introducing herself to another little girl. Good, she was talking to a real human being. Once I saw that she was still doing okay, I turned back to Kendall, who was already staring at me. The paper in my hand had gone limp, and with a smooth flick of my wrist, I made it taut again as I said, "I've got all the time in the world, baby."

Kendall blinked rapidly, and I could tell she was at a complete loss for words. I probably shouldn't have said "baby" just then, but it sort of slipped out. It had caught me off guard just as much as it had shocked her.

Finley skipped over toward us and slipped her hand in mine. "Daddy, can you show me the lunchroom now?"

"Sure. Tell Ms. Devin goodbye," I said, not taking my eyes off of Kendall.

"I'll see you next Monday, Finley," Kendall said, smiling down at her. And then she turned toward me, straightening a little. "It was nice meeting you both. Any and all communication with me from here on out should probably be initiated through e-mail or the classroom portal."

I understood exactly what she was implying with those words. She wanted the sexting to cease immediately, and that made perfect sense. I could respect that. And our date was off. That was a no-brainer.

Though it was a monumental disappointment, there was something about the twinkle in her eyes and the slight upturn at the corners of her mouth that gave me all the courage I needed to lean in close and say just loud enough for her to hear, "I could *definitely* handle it, by the way."

I was referring, of course, to her last text message—the one about her ass—but the statement was ambiguous enough that it might have seemed I was talking about the Room Parent gig.

Judging from the look of astonishment on her face, she understood exactly what I'd meant.

It was a real shame I'd never get to see that woman naked in person.

chapter five
kendall

"It was the most humiliating moment of my entire life."

I was hovering over the kitchen sink with a plate of reheated chicken lo mein in my hands, devouring it like—well, like someone who hadn't eaten in seven hours. I reached for the red wine with my free hand, taking a huge swig directly from the bottle. I didn't have time for a glass.

Behind me, Jamie and Daya were absolutely losing it at the kitchen table. And I couldn't blame them—what a sight I must have been. My curls had gone flat, my eye make-up was smeared, and I didn't care a single bit that I was slurping my noodles like a toddler. "He's even hotter in person, you guys," I said with my mouth full. "And seeing him interact with his daughter just about made my ovaries explode."

Jamie let out a dramatic sigh. "But you'll never get to touch his hammer."

"I'm not worthy," I said, shoveling more noodles into my mouth.

"Oh my god—did she just make a Thor reference?" Daya asked my sister, laughing even harder. "I'm so proud."

"If he actually signs up to volunteer in my classroom, I'll just die. I'm pretty sure he was just messing with me, but what if he follows through?" I set the plate down on the counter, picking up the wine bottle and turning to face the two of them. I wished there was something stronger to drink in this house, but we'd pretty much cleaned out the liquor cabinet the weekend after I moved in.

"If you guys hooked up, would you get fired?" Jamie asked as I took the seat across from her at our messy kitchen table. "Like, all awkwardness aside, what if you guys still boinked?"

"'Boinking' Mason would most assuredly get me fired if that got out," I told her, taking another long swig of the wine. "The policy very clearly forbids dating parents." I covered my eyes with my hand. "I can't believe one of my students' dads has my nudes. What if his daughter picks up his phone and sees them?"

"Oof, yikes," Daya said, giving Jamie a sideways glance. They both laughed at me again.

I shook my head, thinking some more about this. I couldn't risk Finley coming across those photos. Not only would they scar that poor child for life, it would be very difficult to explain. "He has to delete them," I said, reaching for my phone.

"You know he could just say he deleted them but secretly keep them in his special spank bank," Jamie said.

"Shut up," I told her, typing out my message.

Kendall: Would you mind deleting the photos I've sent you so they don't fall into the wrong hands? And never mention them to anyone else?

Kendall: Please.

Mason: You got it. You can check my phone next week at drop-off if you want. Also, I'm not that kind of guy. My lips are sealed.

Kendall: Thanks.

"It's done," I said. While I knew Jamie's assumption he was lying and he'd actually had the photos saved somewhere private was probably true, I still felt a little better about the situation.

Jamie got up to grab a beer from the fridge. "Hey, since I've got you both here," she began as she pulled the tab. She took a long swig as she made her way back to her chair. "I've got a bit of news to share. I added another class to my schedule for the upcoming semester, and it's... on campus."

Daya's back straightened, and she squinted at her. "What campus?"

"Uh," Jamie said, her eyes shifting back and forth. "Indianapolis? Where else would it be?"

"You're going to drive an hour to and from Indy? How many times a week are you going to do that?"

"Well," Jamie said, staring down at her beer. "The thing is— I don't have to drive back and forth. It's a Tuesday-Thursday class, and I've worked out a place to stay in the middle of the week."

"You have?" Daya hadn't moved at all since Jamie's initial announcement. She was frozen, keeping her eyes locked on my sister. Her stare was so intense that even I had to look away as I reached for the wine bottle. "With who?"

"Beth and Shelby. I've talked about them before. They're cool with me crashing at their place."

Daya was still stiff as a board and holding her stare, but now she wasn't even asking questions. So I took it upon myself to fill the silence. "What about your job?"

Jamie slowly turned from Daya to me. "Well, nothing's finalized, but it looks like I would be able to pick up some shifts at the Walgreens near campus while I'm staying there."

"Oh, good," I said, my voice coming out even more perky than I intended. I was trying to lighten the mood, but it didn't help to remove the tension from the room at all. I licked my lips. "I mean, it's just for a semester, right?"

Jamie didn't answer. She was just waiting for Daya to say something. After taking a moment to reflect, Daya leaned onto her elbows on the table and took a deep breath before asking, "Why did you decide all of this without me, James?"

"I didn't," Jamie said, shaking her head. "Nothing is finalized. I wanted to get everything in order before I even brought it up to you—either of you," she said, glancing at me for a second. "I knew you'd both have a bunch of questions, so I made sure I had answers for all of them before I shared anything. I don't have to do this—but, I mean, I *need* that class, and this seems like the only way I'm going to be able to take it."

It made sense. I knew Jamie's absence wouldn't affect my day-to-day that much, but Daya had worry etched all over her face. Their relationship had lasted longer than my last three combined, so I knew they could withstand a couple of days apart each week. Daya had nothing to worry about. "So, what class is it?" I asked, trying to ignore my phone buzzing on the table. Now wasn't the time.

The way I was attempting to divert Jamie's attention from Daya was taking me right back to my youth, when I would try to change the subject at the dinner table so my parents wouldn't fight. I was practically a pro.

"Pharmacokinetics," Jamie answered.

My face scrunched—I couldn't hide my disgust. "Sounds… fun."

"It is, actually," she said with a laugh. Jamie loved being a student. So much, in fact, she'd spent most of her twenties amassing student loan debt while exploring different college majors and programs. She thrived in academia.

We couldn't have been more different in that respect. ADHD combined with test anxiety made me glad to put my college years behind me. I much preferred being the teacher in the classroom.

"I have to get this class under my belt if I ever want to transfer to pharmacy school, so it's super necessary," she said, her eyes shifting to Daya again—she was saying this more for her sake than mine. She nodded toward my phone. "Anyway, what's Axl Rose up to now?"

I tried not to smile as I picked up my phone.

Mason: Told you you'd be the one saying please.

"Oh my god," I blurted, my phone slipping through my fingers and dropping to the table with a thud. I hid my eyes with my hands as though the text message wouldn't be real if I couldn't see it.

Jamie slid the phone toward her and Daya so they both could read the message.

My sister laughed, but Daya looked up in confusion. "What's that mean?"

"It means he wants her to beg for the D," Jamie answered.

I laid my head down on the table and moaned in agony. "You guys. This is the father of one of my students. What am I supposed to do now?" It was going to be one hell of an awkward year if Mason kept making comments like that. I knew exactly what he'd meant when he whispered in my ear before he and Finley left—he certainly wasn't talking about the Room Parent gig. He was still flirting.

Yet there was some finality to his previous messages—telling me he'd see me next week at drop-off made it clear he understood our date was canceled.

"Just play it by ear," Daya said just as Jamie muttered, "Maybe you should just fuck him anyway."

I laughed, but I shook my head to let both of them know I wasn't even entertaining the idea. "Believe me—I'd like to. He's…" I couldn't even finish the sentence. I knew very little about Mason so far, but something about him drew me in. In a way, I felt a bit of relief knowing we wouldn't hook up—because I knew those blue eyes of his would pull me under. And getting involved with a man with a kid? I couldn't see myself in that position. At all. "It's just not going to happen."

"So," Jamie said, tapping her fingertips on the table. "Is he, like, divorced? Where's the mom?"

"I don't know," I said, my thoughts drifting to the sweet way Mason interacted with his daughter that night. It was easy to tell they had a close bond. While it hadn't been the first time a father brought his child to an event alone, it wasn't very common.

Something about the way there was not a single mention of a mom in Finley's paperwork led me to believe there was a sad backstory there—and I was dying to find out what it was.

chapter six

mason

Since I'd moved away from Woodvale shortly after high school, the town had been making a lot of efforts in trying to be something it wasn't: a tourist city. The only thing it had going for it was being the home of an inn where Abraham Lincoln once stayed during his lawyer days. The city leaders milked that little factoid for all its worth, touting the town's connection to Lincoln at every opportunity. They made it seem like Woodvale was so charming, Lincoln just couldn't resist coming for a visit—when in reality, he was just passing through.

As I sat by the river on Sunday morning, answering some client emails on my phone while waiting on Finley, I couldn't help but sort of admire the new riverwalk. When I left Woodvale nine years ago, this was all just grass—a dead-end at the end of Main Street. Now there was a wide, winding path along the river with a bike lane, swinging benches, and, of course, a statue of ol' Abe himself.

It was all so new, it almost made me forget I was in the town I once couldn't wait to get away from.

I sat on one of the swings with my phone in my lap, trying to decipher the latest email from one of the most troublesome clients I'd had yet—and this man was just the latest in a string of picky, hard-to-please people who couldn't fully grasp the difference between illustration and graphic design.

I hated this work. Despised it. But for now, it was keeping me afloat and helping me build up a savings so I could get Finley and me out of my parents' house. Eventually.

Thoughts of Kendall kept pulling me away from my phone screen. Friday night, the night I'd been looking forward to, had come and gone, and we didn't get together. Because we couldn't.

It was probably for the best it worked out this way. Because after seeing her in person, I realized there was no chance—not in the slightest—I could have one night with Kendall and just move on from it. She didn't seem like the type of woman who'd be easy to forget. With those eyes, and that ass? I'd willingly let that woman shatter me into a million pieces and thank her afterwards. So maybe her being Finley's teacher was the universe's way of protecting my heart.

My last message to her was pushing it. She never responded, either—I was afraid I'd said too much. I hadn't meant to make her uncomfortable. It was all I could do not to text her again to assure her I was just kidding around and would stop the flirty comments, but I feared I would only make the situation worse. It was probably best to just drop it.

I was in the middle of responding to that annoying email when I heard someone ask, "Is that Mason?" I looked up to see Owen and Sarah walking my direction hand-in-hand. "It is," Owen said when he saw my face.

"In the flesh," I replied as they came closer. "What's up, guys?"

"Just out for our Sunday morning walk," Sarah said. They were both carrying coffee cups from the new café on the corner, and while most of the other walkers who passed were in gym clothes, Owen and Sarah were both in jeans. Something about going on a casual Sunday stroll by the river with the one you love seemed really sweet—and completely unattainable for me.

I was hit with a sudden pang of jealousy—these two seemed so perfect for each other. How was love like this even possible? I watched Sarah lift Owen's hand close to her face to look at his watch, and I struggled to remember the last time a woman had been that comfortable with me.

"Where's Finley?" Sarah asked.

"She's with her grandma. Her, uh—other grandma, that is."

"How's that working out?" Owen asked.

"It's…" I wasn't sure how to answer that question. My mom and Owen's mom talked on the phone a few times a week, so chances were, the drama had been passed along to Owen. He probably already knew what I'd been going through with Traci. I sat my phone on the bench beside me and stretched. "It keeps life interesting."

"Are you ready to send her off to kindergarten tomorrow?" Sarah asked, before taking a sip of her coffee.

"Oh, God no," I blurted, making both of them laugh. "I've been dreading the day all summer long."

"Aw, she'll be fine. She's going to love Ms. Devin. She's the sweetest. She was the most requested teacher this year—everyone wants her."

I lifted my hand to pull some hair away from my face. "Yeah, she seems great."

"When I was working on all the class rosters," Sarah said, "I just knew Ms. Devin would be the perfect fit for your little girl."

I met her eyes for a second—she had no idea, no idea at all, how that little decision she'd made had impacted me so much. "Thank you," I somehow managed to say. "Sounds like Finley's lucky to have her."

Owen glanced out at the river as he sipped his coffee, still holding Sarah's hand in his. He cleared his throat, turning back to me. "So, with Finley starting school, you'll have more time to take on clients now, won't you?"

"Looks like it, yeah," I said with a nod. "How's *STEM for the Win*?"

"Keeping me busy," Owen said. "Working on book number two."

"No shit?" I raised both eyebrows at him. This guy had been on a roll with his podcast. YouTube channel, and book lately. He went from being a teacher to an internet celebrity practically overnight—I would have hated him for it if he wasn't such a good guy. If anyone deserved this success, it was Owen Gardner. "I'm really proud of you, cuz."

"Thanks."

"I'm trying to get him to take an extra week off leading up to our wedding in November," Sarah said, shaking her head, "but I can't get this man to relax."

"Sounds like the Owen I know," I said, smiling up at them both.

Sarah tugged on his arm. "Did you ask him about the tux fitting?"

With a sheepish smile on his face, Owen turned to me and said, "I completely forgot—we got the groomsmen suits picked out, so you and the other guys have got to go get measured and all that. Maybe next weekend?"

Just weeks after I'd moved back to Woodvale, Owen asked me to be in his wedding. It came as a bit of a surprise, considering we hadn't kept in touch as much as we could've over the past few years. He was one of my favorite people growing up, though—always defending me against his brother, Jake, who used to torment me just because I was the baby of our family. Owen was also the only one of my cousins I was comfortable enough to ask to buy me alcohol when I was a teen—and he never said no.

He would forever be one of my favorite people, and as far as I could tell, the admiration was mutual.

"Yeah, just text me the details," I told him. The alarm on my phone went off just then, alerting me it was time to retrieve Finley from Traci. "Shit, I'm going to have to go get Fin—but it was great running into you guys. Oh, and have a good school year, Sarah." She wiggled the fingers around her coffee cup in a playful farewell gesture, and they were off. Owen slipped his arm around her waist as they walked away.

"I need to get fucking laid," I muttered as I gathered my things.

* *

Traci was fifteen minutes late getting Finley back to me. This wasn't completely out of the ordinary for her, but that didn't make it any less annoying. I exited my car the second I saw hers pull into the parking lot, propping myself against my door with my hands tucked in my pockets. This particular spot at the farthest edge of the lot, nestled against a chain-link fence, was exactly where Whitney and I used to meet for custody exchanges—the judge had recommended a neutral location. I'm not sure how either of us came to agree on the Wal-Mart parking lot, but it seemed to work. While it wasn't necessary to continue meeting Traci here, I preferred that over having her come all the way out to my parents' house in the suburbs. It gave me a sense of comfort to know Traci wasn't aware of Finley's precise address, anyway—she didn't need to be dropping in unexpectedly.

When Traci's car came to a stop beside me, I was immediately met with a very animated Finley in the backseat, pressing a phone up against the window. I couldn't quite make out what she was trying to show me on the screen because she was waving the phone around frantically, so I yanked open her door and leaned closer to see. "Hey, what is it?"

"It's mine!"

"What is?"

Traci twisted to face me. "Mason—"

"She gave me a phone!" Finley interrupted, smiling ear to ear. "My very own phone, Daddy!"

My eyes widened as she thrust the device toward my face, revealing the paused YouTube video on the screen. I cleared my throat and took a step back in an attempt to collect myself before the expletives on the tip of my tongue threatened to find their way out of my mouth.

"Mason," Traci said again, unbuckling. I pinched the bridge of my nose and closed my eyes as she continued. "Hear me out on this."

"Finley cannot have a phone," I said, barely moving my teeth.

Finley gasped. "Why not?"

"Now Mason, why are you so negative about it right from the start? Just let me explain this, okay?"

"Whatever reason you think you have for giving my daughter a phone, it doesn't matter. I'm her dad, and I say no." I jerked the phone out of Finley's hand. Her bottom lip quivered for a second, and then she launched into an eardrum-shattering sob. "Great," I muttered as I leaned over her to toss the phone in Traci's front seat. "She's five years old. Are you out of your mind?"

"How else is she going to communicate with me?" Traci's screeching had reached a high pitch that grated on my nerves. "I can't—"

"She communicates with you every Sunday morning," I mumbled, struggling to unbuckle Finley's seatbelt. I was trembling so much, I couldn't get a good grip. "Jesus. I can't believe you got her a phone without discussing it with me first."

"I did it this way because I knew you'd be against it. But I had no idea you'd rip the thing from the poor girl's hands like that. All I wanted was to give her a way to call Mamaw anytime she wants. It's on my phone plan, and you can control her apps if you want. What's the big deal?"

I ignored her, scooping Finley up into my arms. The crying didn't subside—in fact, she began sobbing even harder. I used the collar of my shirt to wipe the drool, snot, and tears from her face.

I hated Traci for putting me in this predicament.

The woman got out of her car and stood behind me as I strapped Finley into her booster seat. "Why don't you want her to talk to her family?"

"That's not what this is about," I said, shaking as I snapped Finley's buckle. I slammed the door once she was strapped in and turned to Traci with my arms crossed against my chest. "What the hell, Traci?"

"You're being so—"

"This is unacceptable." I could see right through her—didn't she know that? Couldn't she see how obvious it was she was trying to win Finley's affection with material things? "What's your endgame here?"

Traci let out a cold laugh. "There's no 'endgame.' I'm just a grandma who loves her grandbaby and wants her to be happy."

"You're about to lose the privilege of calling her that," I said, staring into her eyes. I knew those words were harsh, but maybe Traci needed to hear them. I had no obligation to keep letting her see Finley, and I was only doing so out of the kindness of my heart. I could stop anytime.

Traci scowled. "It doesn't have to be like this. You make this so difficult."

It was my turn to laugh. "You bought the kid a phone without clearing it with me first. She's not responsible enough to have one yet, and I don't want her glued to screens. Not yet. I have so many reasons—none of which I even need to explain to you. Now—" I sighed and shook my head, rubbing my eyes. "Now I have to deal with the most epic of temper tantrums."

"Well," Traci said, throwing her hands up, "that's not my fault."

I reached for my door handle. "Yes it is," I snapped. I glanced through the window at Finley, who was silently crying now—that was almost worse. When she cried like that, sometimes I had to remind her to take a breath. This wasn't going to be fun. Before I got in the car, I turned to Traci to say one more thing. "If you want to have a role in Finley's life, you have to respect my decisions as her father."

I expected her to snap back with a retort, but instead, she took a deep breath and said, "I'm sorry."

Nodding, I said, "Okay. We'll see you next week."

I'd been so close to telling her to fuck off and that we'd never see her again, but the apology—even if she didn't mean it—bought her another chance.

Finley cried the entire way home. I couldn't necessarily blame her, either. Getting caught in the middle of this wasn't fair. And being given something she'd been begging me for, only to have it taken away, had to crush her. "Fin, I'm sorry. You just don't understand. Sometimes dads have to make decisions that seem a little mean at first, but in the long run, I know what's best for you."

"No you don't!" More sobbing.

I looked at her in the rearview mirror. "Do you know how old I was when I got *my* first phone? I was fourteen. You're lucky I'm not as strict as Grandma and Grandpa were with me." There was no use in saying any of this—she wasn't listening.

Her crying had subdued by the time we got home, but her face was wet with tears as I unbuckled her. My heart sank. There was a tiny part of me that wanted to concede, wanted to call Traci and let her know I'd changed my mind—but I knew I had to stand firm in my convictions. If it meant Finley would spend our very last day of summer together being angry at me, I'd just have to deal with it.

As she hopped out of the car, I opened my mouth to further explain why I couldn't let her have a phone, but she stomped all the way down the driveway into the house. My mom, who was watering the flowers along the front porch, turned to me with her eyebrows raised. "What's that all about?"

"Traci gave her a phone and I wouldn't let her keep it." I sighed and ran my fingers through my hair. "Finley hates me."

"Well, if your kid hates you, that probably means you're doing something right."

"Guess so," I said, although I didn't completely agree.

Instead of going inside and dealing with Finley's wrath, I stayed on the front lawn with my mom, absentmindedly staring at the stream of water coming from the hose. "She'll get over it," my mom said, sweeping the hose back and forth over her roses. When I didn't answer, she turned the sprayer off and looked at me. "You seem stressed."

Yeah, mom, I'm a sexually frustrated twenty-six-year-old single father with an unfulfilling job who lives with his parents, and my one opportunity to get my rocks off just slipped through my fingers and the thought of Finley starting school tomorrow is literally making me feel sick. I'm fucking stressed. "I'm fine."

My phone buzzed in my pocket. I pulled it out to see a notification from the parent communication app I'd downloaded. There was a new message from Kendall.

Hello, parents!

I hope your kiddos are as excited as I am for the first day of kindergarten tomorrow! If you would like to volunteer to be a Room Parent, please bring your forms in ASAP, as a background check will need to be completed before you can begin.

Looking forward to a fantastic year ahead!

-Ms. Devin

"There's a smile," my mom said. "Let me guess. A woman?"

"What?" I glanced up at her face and back down at the phone in my hand. "No, it's Finley's teacher. I mean, she's a woman but—that's not—it's just a little welcome message, that's all." Smooth.

My mom raised an eyebrow at me before returning her attention to the flowers. I reread Kendall's note, considering the

Room Parent thing again. I was only half-serious when I told her I was interested, but when I thought about it, I wouldn't mind having the opportunity to spend time with Finley at school. It would make this transition a hell of a lot easier for both of us.

Getting to be around Ms. Devin would just be an added perk.

chapter seven
kendall

"Alexa, shuffle *Red, Taylor's Version.*"

I sat my water bottle and keys on my desk as "I Knew You Were Trouble" began playing on the speaker. Before long, my kindergarteners would be asking Alexa to make fart sounds—but right now, Taylor Swift was helping me mentally prepare for the first day of school.

I'd arrived early, giving myself plenty of time to make sure everything was in order. This was my third year of teaching—my third first day of school. I'd learned the hard way that doing any actual teaching the first week would be a waste of my time. Instead, I planned to spend this week establishing routines and getting to know these kids.

I made my way around the room, setting up morning stations—open-ended activities like magnetic tiles, LEGOs, and such. I was in the middle of dumping the pieces of a floor-sized dinosaur puzzle on the rug when there was a light knock at the door.

When I looked up and saw Heath, I couldn't help the way my face contorted into a grimace.

"Don't look so happy to see me."

"What do you need, Heath?"

He confidently strolled toward me, and the overwhelming smell of his cologne almost making me choke. "Just wanted to say I'm sorry we didn't get to chat after the staff meeting last week."

That was intentional. The second our meeting was over, I'd bolted out of the room to avoid him.

I carefully spread the gigantic puzzle pieces out with my foot and took a deep breath. "I don't really have anything to say to you, so—?"

He crossed his arms. "Look, I just came in here to talk real quick so we could start the year off on the right foot. It doesn't have to be all tense and awkward."

I rested my hands on my hips. "It's not."

"Okay, then." He looked around the room for a moment, his eyes eventually finding their way back to me. "I miss you."

"Don't," I said, holding up my right palm to signal for him to stop. "Don't you dare come in here and start that 'I miss you' bullshit with me. You broke up with *me*, remember? I'm trying to have a good first day, and I'm not about to let you ruin it."

"Kendall, just—"

"Nope. Get out of my classroom." I walked toward him with my hand still extended, expecting him to get the message and turn to go. But he remained frozen in the dead center of the room, so it appeared I was going to have to use physical force. With one hand on his arm and the other on his back, I nudged him toward the door.

"Are you serious right now?" He let out an annoyed laugh as I pushed him. His body was solid, but thankfully, he shuffled his feet toward the door.

"Have a good year, Heath."

He let out a defeated sigh once we reached the hallway, and I removed my hands. "Yep," he said, hanging his head. "You too."

As he disappeared down the hall, I cursed him under my breath for trying to ruin my morning. But I forced every thought of him from my mind, choosing instead to focus on getting things ready for the day. When I was finished, I had a couple minutes left to sip my coffee and listen to "State of Grace" in peace before the bell rang.

"Alexa, stop," I said, making sure my yellow-gold shirt was tucked perfectly into my plum dress pants as I walked across the room toward the door. This outfit was my subtle way of wearing the school colors—I'd even painted my fingernails the same shade of purple as my pants.

I stood just inside the room, awaiting the students' arrival. And just as I looked down to pick a dog hair off of my pants—that damn menace—I heard the first student approaching.

And it was Finley Reed, skipping into the room just ahead of her dad, who was carrying her backpack. Her dark hair was done up into two adorable buns, and the "KINDERGARTEN ROCKS" shirt she was wearing was almost the same shade of yellow as mine. I grinned. "Good morning, Finley! How are you?"

"Dad, look, Ms. Devin and I match," she hollered, planting her feet beside mine so Mason could get a good look at the two of us.

He held his lips together tight to suppress a smile as his eyes traveled up my body until they found mine. "That's right, you're both wearing yellow, aren't you?"

Finley put her hands on her hips and beamed up at me. "I know *all* the colors," she announced. "So you don't even have to waste your time teaching me that."

Mason and I laughed. "You sound really smart, Finley," I said. I turned to greet another parent walking in, a mom with a pale, redheaded boy whose name I couldn't remember from meet-the-teacher night. Mason helped Finley get her backpack into her cubby, and after a moment, she was getting started on the dinosaur puzzle on the rug. Mason stood nearby with one hand in his pocket, his other hand clutching a packet.

The Room Parent packet.

I opened my mouth to ask him if he had something to give me just as I heard the sound of sobbing near the doorway. I looked up to see a teary-eyed Elijah—at least, I thought that was his name—entering the room. The dark, springy curls on his head shone beneath the fluorescent lights—and even with tears streaming down his cheeks, he was adorable. His mom gave him a hug and looked over at me. "I'm so sorry about this," she said. "But I'm running late and can't stay to get him settled."

"Don't worry," I told her with a smile as I put my hand on Elijah's back to lead him toward his cubby. "Give him ten minutes, and he'll be having so much fun."

"Love you, buddy!" his mom hollered before ducking out. The sobbing stopped, but the tears still streaked down his cheeks. Finley popped up from her spot on the rug and made her way over to us.

"Hi, I'm Finley. What's your name?"

Elijah sniffled, leaving her question unanswered.

"You can tell me later. Wanna see the dinosaur puzzle?" She took him by the hand and pulled him over to the rug, where he warily knelt down and watched her put two pieces together. "Don't cry anymore, okay?" Finley told him in a perky voice. "We're in this together."

I looked up at Mason, who was watching this scene unfold while sucking on his bottom lip. He turned away from his daughter and cleared his throat, and if my assessment of his emotions was correct, he was holding back some tears himself.

I made my way over to him. "You getting a little emotional there?"

"A little bit, yeah," he said, letting out a little chuckle. "I always tell her that—'we're in this together.'"

"I guess it sunk in."

"Guess so," he said, turning to watch her again. She was telling Elijah all about her favorite dinosaurs, and though he didn't answer, he wasn't crying anymore at all. Mason took a deep, trembling breath. "This is so much harder on me than it is for her."

I stared at his face for a moment, watching him observe his daughter play. "Would it make you feel better if I gave you a little update later today? I could send you a picture."

"Yeah," he said, turning to look me in the eye. "You'd do that?"

"Of course."

"I would really appreciate that."

I crossed my arms against my chest. "No problem."

There was a silence between us that followed this exchange, and I wondered if he, too, was thinking about what could have been—what would have happened between us if Finley weren't in my class.

I'd be sending him a different kind of picture, that was certain.

After a moment, he finally looked down at the papers in his hands. "Oh, um… I filled out this Room Parent thing." He glanced over his shoulder at the parents on the other side of the room. "But before I turn it in, I wanted to make sure it wouldn't make you uncomfortable to have me… hanging around."

My lips parted, and I blinked, unsure of what to say. Hell yes, it would make me uncomfortable. To have him working in here with me a couple mornings a week, knowing he'd laid eyes on my nude body? Just thinking about it made me want to sink through the floor.

But despite every instinct urging me to say yes, there was something about Mason's twinkling blue eyes that made me blurt, "No, not at all. I'd appreciate the help."

"Good," he said, studying my face as though he was looking for any sign I might be lying about wanting him there. There was a hint of hesitancy in his voice when he held the packet toward me and said, "Here you go, then."

"Oh, thanks," I said, taking the papers from him. My mind was swirling with questions. What was the story with Finley's mother? How was he so available to volunteer in my classroom?

And why was his stare so intense? "Stop in the front office before you leave to get the info about the background check."

"Sounds good." He put his hands in his back pockets and looked down at Finley, who was talking a mile a minute to a still-silent Elijah. "Okay, Finley," Mason said. "I'm going to head out. Can I get a hug?"

She sprang up from the rug and lifted her skinny arms to hug him as he bent down. He kissed her on her temple and whispered, "I love you," in her ear as she clung to his neck.

"Love you, Daddy!"

I stared down at my shoes, overcome with feelings of attraction for this man. It was hard to even look at him. I only glanced up when he turned to speak to me. "Thanks, Ms. Devin."

"You're welcome," I said, tucking my hair behind my ear. His eyes lingered on mine for a moment before he turned to go, giving another parent a casual nod on his way out.

I shifted my attention to the other arriving students, but I had butterflies in my stomach all morning every time I thought of Mason. Allowing him to volunteer was a dangerous move. I didn't get the impression he was going to let me forget about the pictures I'd sent or all the naughty words we'd exchanged. As much as I wanted to believe he was doing this for Finley, a tiny part of me wondered if having the opportunity to flirt with me factored into his decision to fill out that form. What was he planning?

As anxious as it made me feel, I almost couldn't wait to find out.

That afternoon, while the kids were busy at work coloring their All About Me booklets, I squatted beside Finley's table. She raised one eyebrow at me in curiosity, and it struck me how much she looked like her father. "Hey Finley," I said sweetly, looking at the family portrait she'd drawn. There were four ovals on the paper, each with stick arms and legs poking out from them. It was easy to tell which one was meant to be Mason, with his blond hair drawn with a yellow crayon. "Who did you draw here?"

"Me and my daddy and grandma and grandpa."

"I love how everyone is smiling in this picture," I said, tapping the paper with my fingernail. "What kinds of things do you like to do with your grandparents?"

Finley tilted her head to the side and gave this some thought. "Eat spaghetti and play Candy Land."

I giggled. "That sounds perfect. Are you having a good first day of school?" Finley nodded, but I couldn't help but notice a frown forming on her face. "Is something wrong?"

She looked over her shoulder at Elijah, who was sitting several feet away. "I'm worried about Elijah."

"You are?" I adjusted my legs, dropping my knees to the ground to get more comfortable. "Why's that?"

"He has to ride the bus home, and he's afraid he's going to get on the wrong one, Ms. Devin. And then his mom won't be able to find him."

I stared at Finley and blinked. "Elijah... talked to you?" Finley nodded, and my mouth fell agape. Elijah's mom had alerted me in his registration papers that he may never speak out loud at school—he didn't talk to anyone besides his parents. He'd spent the entire morning quietly observing everyone else, so I was surprised Finley got him to open up so soon. "I'll make sure Elijah gets on the right bus. What else did he say?"

Finley picked up a purple crayon. "Um. He said he doesn't like The Wiggle Song."

I laughed. Unfortunately for Elijah, The Wiggle Song had been part of my morning routine since I'd started teaching, and it was the only way I knew to get my students warmed up and ready to learn. "Well, what about you, Finley? Besides worrying about Elijah, are you having a good day?"

She nodded. "I love school."

"Good!" I patted Finley's arm as I stood back up.. I let her get back to work, sneaking a picture of her as she colored to send to Mason in the parent portal. He replied almost immediately with a stream of heart emojis.

There was that ache in my ovaries again.

chapter eight

mason

"Daddy, what's wrong with your hands?"

I wiggled my black-tipped fingers at Finley in the seat beside her at Moretti's, her second-favorite restaurant in Woodvale. While it couldn't quite beat McDonald's level of cuisine, their spaghetti was one of Finley's favorite foods. And when she asked us to take her there for supper to celebrate the first day of school, we couldn't say no. Even my dad, who was normally against eating out on weeknights, was along for the ride.

"I had to get fingerprinted today to make sure I'm not a bad guy," I explained. I'd washed my hands at least three times since my background check that afternoon, but it did very little to remove the ink from my fingertips.

Finley raised her right eyebrow at me as she sipped her Sprite. It was noisy in that little restaurant—apparently we weren't the only family with this idea. Moretti's was a beloved institution in this town, and the sticky tables and grumpy servers were just part of the experience. Finley sat her Styrofoam cup on the table. "Does someone think you're a bad guy?"

"No, but they just want to make sure. It's for your school." I picked up my straw wrapper to play with it. "And guess why I had to do it?"

"Why?"

I glanced across the table at my dad before answering her. "I'm going to come help Ms. Devin in your classroom."

Finley's mouth dropped open and her eyes lit up as she said, "My *dad* gets to come to school with me?"

"Yup." I looked down at the table, feeling my father's disapproving glare. I knew exactly what he was thinking—this was unnecessary. A woman's job. I was hovering. He didn't have to say any of it out loud—his scowl told me enough.

My mom, on the other hand, already knew about it—and she was delighted. "I was a Room Mom when you were in kindergarten, remember? I helped at the Halloween party. The year you went as Woody."

I smiled down at my sweet tea. "How could I forget?" Just then, our server arrived with the food. Spaghetti for Finley, mushroom pizza for me, and fettuccine for both of my parents. The conversation died down for a few minutes as I cut Finley's spaghetti so she wouldn't slurp it and make a mess.

It was only a matter of time before my dad had to chime in with his opinion about my volunteering. "How are you going to get any work done if you're up at the school?"

I inhaled through my nose. "It's just a few hours a week."

"Well," he said, shaking his head as he swirled fettuccine noodles around his fork. "With her at school, you could probably get you a real job now."

There it was. He would never view my current situation as a "real job." To him, my work couldn't possibly be that serious if I was merely drawing on my iPad. I swallowed a bite of my pizza and attempted to ignore his comment. "So Fin, did that boy you were doing the puzzle with ever start talking?"

"Yup," she said, sucking a spaghetti noodle between her lips. "Except he only whispers. His name is Elijah, and his favorite dinosaur is a stegosaurus."

"Awesome. Did you and Elijah—"

"Is he your boyfriend?" my mom blurted, completely unprompted, as though this kind of unhinged assumption was normal.

"Mom," I snapped, my eyes widening at her. "She's five. Can you not?"

Thankfully, Finley stuck her tongue out in disgust and wiggled in a melodramatic shudder. "Ew, no," she protested, with spaghetti sauce in the corners of her mouth. "Boys are disgusting."

"Damn straight," I said, taking another bite. Finley gasped at the word choice, and I made a goofy face at her. Now I was feeling the judgment from both of my parents, but I didn't care. She was my daughter, not theirs.

The bells above the door of the restaurant jingled and Finley jumped to her feet, closely watching the group of people who stepped inside Moretti's. Her face went pale and I followed her gaze, trying to figure out how she might recognize these people.

"Is that someone from your school, Finley?"

Finley slowly sat back down and picked up her fork. "No, I thought I saw my mom. But it was somebody else."

I felt a sudden heaviness in my chest as I eyed the brunette woman standing by the hostess stand. She did resemble Whitney, in some ways—they were around the same size. I cleared my throat, catching both of my parents staring at me in my peripheral vision. "Finley, she's—you know your mom is in Florida, right?"

"I know. I just forgot," she said, forcing out a laugh to downplay her mistake.

I no longer felt like eating. Instead, I rested my chin on my hand and watched Finley finish her meal, not stopping her when she put a heaping mound of parmesan cheese on top of her spaghetti. I just let her go.

I swallowed, imagining what might happen if Whitney ever did decide to come back to Woodvale. What would I do then? How could I prevent Finley from seeing her? Would that even be the right thing to do?

When our meal was finished and my dad took Finley over to the claw machine to try to win a stuffed jellyfish, I brought up Whitney's Instagram profile on my phone. I liked keeping tabs on her just to make sure she was still in Florida, often scouring her captions and comments for any indication she might be visiting Indiana soon. I might not have a plan for her return, but I at least needed to be aware.

"Mason," my mom said, her voice low. I glanced up. "Does her teacher know about her situation? I mean, do you think Owen's fiancée filled her in on it?"

"Not that I know of. She's probably not allowed to, Mom. They have confidentiality rules about that sort of thing." I was fully aware I had nothing to base this on, but it sounded right.

"Maybe. But did you think to mention it in her registration papers?"

"No." I shifted in my seat, feeling like I'd screwed up yet again. "I didn't think it was anyone else's business. Too many people in this damn town already know her history."

"Well, her teacher probably needs to be aware. They do Muffins with Moms and all that stuff, you know. That woman needs to know Finley doesn't have one around."

I nodded, watching my dad stick another dollar in the claw machine for Finley, who clapped in delight. "Yeah. I'll mention it to her."

chapter nine
kendall

On the second Monday morning of the school year, I was surprised to see Daya was awake just as early as me. She shuffled into the kitchen and brewed herself a cup of coffee while I was packing my lunch. "You're up early," I noted.

"A beagle got hit by a car," she mumbled.

I clenched my eyes shut as I opened the fridge, trying not to picture it. Daya wasn't usually so blunt when it came to emergencies at the animal hospital, where she worked as a vet tech. Something was up. "Well—besides that, is everything okay?"

Despite living here for the last several weeks, she and I hadn't had many one-on-one conversations. And when we did, they were pretty casual in nature. To expect her to open up to me was a long shot. But to my surprise, she sat the package of coffee filters on the counter and looked up at the ceiling with a sigh. "Your sister."

"Oh no, what did Jamie do?"

She turned to face me. "She told me last night that I'm insecure."

"Oh," I said, pulling my aluminum water bottle out of the cabinet. "I'm sorry she said that."

"You don't think I'm insecure, do you?"

I stared at Daya for a moment. The fact she was asking this question all but confirmed it, didn't it? I couldn't tell her that, though. But I also couldn't lie to her. "Well, what made her say that?"

Daya crossed her arms. "I'm just really having a hard time with this whole Indianapolis thing. She's going to have this entire life without me there, and—it's not that I don't trust her. I do. It's just…"

I nodded, trying to understand. "It'll be different."

"Exactly."

"It's only a couple of days a week though," I reminded her, grabbing my phone from the island to look at the time. I would need to get dressed soon if I wanted to get to school on time. "And the semester will be over before you know it. It's going to be fine."

Daya nodded, although she didn't seem all that convinced. She turned around to face the coffeepot. "Yeah, maybe," she said, barely moving her lips. She looked up at my face. "Today's the day, isn't it?"

I nodded with a grin. "It is."

She was talking about Mason. This would be his first day volunteering in my classroom, something I'd talked about all weekend. And last night, he'd messaged me—within the parent app, as requested—to ask if he could speak to me face-to-face about Finley, promising me he had no ulterior motives. So we arranged for him to arrive twenty minutes sooner than I'd originally planned so we could talk while my students were in art class.

"I'm a little nervous," I told Daya as I filled my water bottle at the sink. "I've never had a man volunteer in my room."

"Let alone the fact that this particular man has sent you a picture of his… pee-pee."

I almost dropped my water bottle. Daya wasn't quite as blunt as my sister, but it was her word choice that got to me. "Daya! I'm trying to forget it."

"I mean," she said, reaching for a mug from the cabinet above. She half-shrugged, smiling from one side of her mouth. "I would be, too, but probably for a different reason."

"Uh huh."

Daya and I wrapped up our conversation, and I got dressed for school. As much as I wanted to tell myself I didn't care what Mason thought of my appearance, I may have set aside my most flattering outfit to wear on that particular day—a white and black striped A-line dress that was flowy enough to allow movement while still accentuating my waist.

And my butt.

I pushed every thought of Mason from my mind as I did my morning prep in the classroom and sat down in front of my work laptop to check my email. I had deleted my work email from my phone when Sarah took over as principal and the onslaught of "what do you think of this?" emails started flooding my inbox. She meant well—she really did—but some of us didn't think about this school 24/7.

So I wasn't surprised when I had not one, not two, but *three* emails from Sarah with information about the fall festival. The first one was an updated list of vendors, while the second one suggested that we should get t-shirts designed ASAP in order to start promoting this thing now.

And the third was an apology.

I apologize for all the emails. I promise not to email you again for a while. At least not until lunch. Have a terrific Monday! -Sarah

P.S. Do you think the hayride route should be longer?

I smiled down at my notebook as I added "figure out t-shirt design" to my to-do list. That woman drove me bonkers sometimes, but she was impossible to dislike. Sarah and I were polar opposites, which is why we worked so well together.

With a sigh, I slipped my lanyard over my neck. The first bell of the day rang, filling my stomach with butterflies. Mason would be arriving in fifty minutes.

"You're ridiculous," I whispered to myself as I double-checked my lipstick in the mirror inside the storage closet at the back of my classroom. Tempting Mason was a bad idea. If anything, I should have been making sure I looked my absolute worst. Scare him off, maybe.

Elijah was one of the first students to arrive, tears pooling in the corners of his eyes, just like every morning at drop-off. Parents weren't allowed to come back to the classroom after the first couple of days, which helped most of my students quickly get over their separation anxiety. But not Elijah.

"Oh my goodness, is that Charmander on your shirt?" I asked him as he hung his backpack in his cubby. He looked up, and though I knew he wouldn't respond verbally, he seemed pleased I recognized the Pokémon on his shirt. "He's my favorite."

Finley finished putting her backpack away a couple of cubbies down and skipped over to us. "Ms. Devin, look." She propped herself up against a cubby to lift her leg, showing off a Batman band-aid on her knee. "I fell off my scooter. Do you want to see the blood underneath?"

"No thank you, Finley. Let's keep the band-aid on, please." I laughed. "Batman, huh?"

Finley rolled her eyes. "Yeah, I let my dad pick out the band-aids this time. He says it's payback for the time he cut his finger and all we had were unicorn ones and all his friends made fun of him."

This was putting the most adorable mental image in my mind. As I tried to collect myself, Elijah leaned over and whispered something in Finley's ear. This kid wouldn't give me anything—barely even a head nod—but he was comfortable enough to share his whispered thoughts with Finley. After just a week, the two of them were practically attached at the hip.

"Ms. Devin, Elijah wants to know if we get to go to art class today."

"Yes, you do," I said, patting the soft curls atop Elijah's head. "I would love to hear that sweet little voice of yours sometime, too. But I'm so glad you have a friend like Finley you can talk to, buddy."

He lifted his shoulders and shrank into himself, looking down at his feet. Finley beamed at him like a proud mother hen.

"Elijah's like a little turtle, isn't he?" Finley giggled so hard she snorted. Elijah tried to fight it, but after a few seconds, he giggled out loud, too.

"What does that make you?" I put my hands on my hips and raised my eyebrows at Finley, like this was the most important question of the day. And at that moment, it was.

She put her index finger to her chin, thinking this over. "Can I be a jellyfish?"

"What is it with you and jellyfish, girl?"

Finley lifted her knee again to scratch the skin around her band-aid, saying, "I got to see real jellyfishes one time at the aquarium with my—" She stopped short and looked away, losing her train of thought for a moment.

Was she about to say "mom"? I inhaled, wondering if I should follow-up with another question or let her try to finish.

"—and they looked like ghosts," she finally said, skipping over any mention of whom she went to the aquarium with. I breathed out, forcing a chuckle. The room was filling up with more kids, many of them getting restless as they began the letter-tracing worksheets I'd laid out for them, so I'd have to cut this conversation short.

"That sounds really cool—just like you, Finley."

As I turned to give my attention to some kids on the other side of the room, I was caught off guard as she slammed into me with a tight hug around my legs. I rubbed her back with both hands, squeezing the best I could while towering over her. After a few seconds, her grip loosened, and she smiled up at me with a nervous laugh. Her face had gone completely red, too, like she was feeling embarrassed about this impromptu display of affection.

"My goodness," I said, swallowing. "I think you might be the best hugger ever."

"Well, you should try hugging my dad. His hugs are even better." And with that, she took off toward her spot at her table.

I'm sure they are, I thought to myself.

Later that morning, when the kids were off at art class, I found myself applying some roll-on perfume and popping a mint in my mouth just before Mason's scheduled time.

I'd met with countless parents face-to-face, sometimes in really tricky situations, but the way my stomach flipped when I heard Mason's gentle knock was unprecedented.

"Come in," I called out from my desk chair, and Mason appeared through the doorway across the room a second later. And as he approached, I choked on what remained of my mint, swallowing it whole.

I wasn't prepared for how sexy he'd look in dark jeans and a brown flannel shirt rolled up to his elbows. His hair was pulled back into an effortlessly sexy man-bun, a feat I only thought Jason Momoa was capable of. I was doing a pretty good job of pretending to be unfazed by all of this until he flashed his perfect smile at me and said, "Morning, Ms. Devin," as he strolled my direction with his thumbs tucked into his pockets.

I attempted to smile back in a way that didn't make it obvious I'd just been looking him up and down. "Good morning. Um," I looked over at the metal and yellow plastic chair several feet away from me, sitting against the whiteboard. "You can just pull up that chair if you want."

"Is this the time-out chair?" he asked, carrying it toward me. He didn't place it in front of my desk like I assumed he would, and instead sat it down just an arm's length away from mine. When I spun my chair to face him, our knees were merely inches apart.

"We don't do time-out here."

Mason crossed his arms against his chest. "They sure did when I went to kindergarten in this room. It was right over there," he said, nodding toward the corner behind me. "I remember it well."

"Did you find yourself in time-out a lot?"

"Oh yeah," he answered without a beat. "Pretty sure I forced my poor kindergarten teacher into early retirement."

"So, did you go to Woodvale High School?" We were similar in age, yet I couldn't remember seeing him back then.

"No." Mason touched the ID on his lanyard, idly twisting it around with his left hand. "I transferred to Woodvale Day School in sixth grade."

"Ah. The rich kids' school."

Mason grinned from one side of his mouth. "Is that what people call it?"

"That's what *my* people called it," I answered. This exchange was followed by a short lull, a moment in which we both stared silently at each other, each of us with a coy grin. In just a few sentences, we'd learned a lot about one another, which was not why we were here. I wondered if this was the kind of thing we would've talked about on that date that never happened.

"Well," Mason said, leaning back and crossing his hands behind his head. "This school's changed a lot since the early two-thousands. We didn't have a garden, that's for sure."

"Oh yeah, isn't that amazing? Our principal started that a couple years ago."

Mason nodded. "I should've known that was Sarah's doing."

I squinted at him, my curiosity piqued. "You're on a first-name basis with my principal?"

"Yeah, she's marrying my cousin."

My smile faded, and it took everything in me to hide my shock. I dropped my pen from my sweaty hand as I asked, "Owen Gardner is y-your cousin?"

Thankfully, Mason didn't catch my unease, at least not right away. He was still casually reclined, eyeing the word wall above my head. "Yeah, I used to run around in the creek behind his house and catch tadpoles with him and his brother. Best days of my life." After a moment, he lowered his eyes back to mine. "Why, do you know him?"

I just blinked. My cheeks felt hot, and I could feel myself beginning to sweat even more as I desperately tried to keep my composure. Damn this small town—I hated the way everyone knew each other here.

Still looking comfortable as ever with his fingers interlocked behind his head, a sly grin crept onto Mason's face. "Oh, you *know him,* know him." He couldn't hide his amusement. "Like, in the biblical sense."

"I didn't say that," I said, bending down to pick up my pen from the floor.

Mason shifted in his chair and leaned forward, pulling his phone from his back pocket. "That's fine, I can just call him up and ask him about it."

I froze. "Don't you dare."

"I won't," he said with a laugh as he slid his phone back into his pocket. "I was only kidding. I take it you won't be at their wedding?"

"Actually," I said, peering down at the notebook on my desk. We were wasting time. "Sarah is one of my good friends. So yes, I will be in attendance."

"Me too," he said. "Well, I'm actually one of the groomsmen. But I guess I'll… see you there." Though I wasn't looking up, I could feel his eyes on me. Concentrating. Assessing me. I did my best to appear calm and poised as I opened my notebook to a blank page.

"Aren't you here to discuss Finley?"

Mason cleared his throat. "Yeah." His playful demeanor faded as he leaned forward, resting his elbows on his knees. He stared down at his folded hands. "Sorry. This is something I don't like to talk about. Even when I… have to."

"It's okay," I said, taken aback by his sudden display of vulnerability. I searched for his eyes with mine, if only to give him a reassuring smile, but he didn't look up. A hundred scenarios ran through my mind, but in no way could I have predicted the next words to come out of his mouth.

"So… back in February, Finley's mother gave her up to move down to Florida and sell corn dogs out of a food truck at Cocoa Beach with her new boyfriend."

For a moment, I only blinked. "I'm sorry," I said, realizing I was taking too long to respond. "I'm just waiting for the punchline."

"There isn't one," Mason said, looking down at the floor. "Well, her mother is the punchline. She's the whole joke."

I had every intention of taking notes during this meeting, but instead, I held my blank notebook against my chest and stared at Mason's face, at the lines on his forehead that couldn't hide the worry and heartbreak this situation had put him through. "I don't understand how anyone could do that," I said, my mind briefly flashing to my dad, who probably would have cut Jamie and me off completely if he could've.

"Our custody agreement wouldn't allow her to move Finley across state lines, so she decided giving her up was the most logical solution," he said with a shrug. "Finley was just a burden to her."

"That's terrible," I said. "How is Finley coping with this? It was just six months ago, right?" I replayed all of my observations of Finley from last week in my head. You'd never guess that girl had experienced such trauma. She was ever-inquisitive, raising her hand at every opportunity, and constantly making sure every child around her was entertained. I had a hard time not laughing at her antics myself.

"The first couple of months were hell. I mean, how do you tell a little girl her mom doesn't want her?" I frowned in response, imagining how some of those early conversations might have gone. "It wasn't easy convincing her that it wasn't her fault, at first. But I also didn't want to trash-talk Whitney to her, you know? That didn't feel right. I struggled to find the words, but I ended up explaining to her that her mom wasn't able to take care of her anymore, so she was going to live with me now. And her grandparents."

I thought it was admirable that Mason didn't want to badmouth Finley's mom to her—that must have taken some strength. "She drew a portrait that included her grandparents last week. Do you still live with them?"

"Yeah. As embarrassing as that is to admit, I do." He chuckled at himself, glancing down at the ground. "It's temporary. But having them around has made this whole transition easier. Finley's doing so much better. She's incredibly resilient. So we're both just taking it one day at a time, now."

"I guess that's all you can do, huh?" I couldn't pretend to even begin to understand what he had been through. "Does Finley have a therapist?"

"Not anymore," he said, fiddling with his lanyard again. "She was seeing a psychologist in Indianapolis when this was all fresh, which helped—but it also..." His voice trailed off as he tried to find the words. He spoke with his hands, motioning like he was about to grasp something. "I almost feel like it's stunting the healing process for her, to keep having to talk about it. It irks the hell out of me when people force her to talk about her mom instead of just letting her move on. Does that make sense?"

"I think so. Sometimes, though…" I took a breath, choosing my next words carefully. I didn't want to overstep. "Talking about it is the only thing that heals. Once you get past that uncomfortable part, therapy can be really beneficial. Then again, I'm just speaking of my own experience here."

I looked up and found his eyes, taken aback by his sudden intense stare. Admitting I had a therapist didn't bother me— everyone I knew went to therapy—but I didn't enter into this conversation intending to reveal something so personal about myself. I felt more exposed before him now than I had when I sent him all those nudes.

I covered up my sudden disclosure with a chuckle. "Anyway, if you change your mind, she can always talk to our counselor here."

"I appreciate the offer," Mason said, giving me a warm smile. "It's just been a little tough to navigate this whole thing. I feel like I'm constantly making one bad decision after another."

"I'm guessing they don't write parenting books for this specific issue."

"No, they don't."

I lowered my notebook to my lap. "Well, from what I've observed in the last week, you're doing a terrific job with her. She's a great kid. So maybe you should give yourself a little grace."

"Thank you. Is she doing the whole YouTube thing here?"

I grinned. "I'm pretty sure I've been the star of many of her imaginary videos." We both laughed. "You need to get that girl a phone and let her start a real YouTube channel."

Mason's eyes widened at my suggestion, but before he could respond, my classroom door slowly pulled open. He and I turned our heads in unison to see who was about to walk in. And, with impeccably bad timing as always, Heath strolled into the room carrying my aqua Bluetooth speaker, the one I used to listen to in his bathroom while I showered. He hadn't even opened his mouth, and I already didn't like where this was going.

"Heath, I'm—"

"Been missing this?" he asked, not picking up on the vibe. He noticed Mason sitting there, but that didn't stop him from approaching my desk.

"Um," I said, giving Mason a quick glance. "I actually forgot about it. Just leave it on the table there. I'm in the middle of something right now."

"Sorry," he said, eyeing Mason again. He sat the speaker down on one of the student tables, but he didn't turn to go. Instead, he put his hands in his pockets and stood there with his feet planted firmly on the ground. "I think that's the last of your things. Unless you change your mind about the waffle maker."

I could have killed him. My back stiffened, and I glared at him, hoping he'd get the message. "I don't want it. Thank you." I widened my eyes slightly, praying he wouldn't start with his "I miss you" bullshit in front of Mason.

"You were the one who wanted us to get one, so—"

"I don't want it," I repeated, cringing at his inclusion of the word "us"—a detail I was sure wasn't lost on Mason. "Just keep it. Heath, I'm talking to a parent right now, and we don't have much time."

"Sorry, I won't keep you. We can just discuss it later."

God, why was it so hard for him to get the hint? "That won't be necessary, either."

Heath's shoulders sank, and I caught Mason shifting in his chair in my peripheral vision. He casually brought his hand to his mouth to conceal his smile as Heath whirled around to walk out my classroom door. "Well, enjoy your speaker, then. Bye."

I didn't return the farewell.

Beside me, Mason could barely contain himself. He was giving me a toothy smile, tracing his bottom lip with his pointer finger like there was some sarcastic comment on the tip of his tongue, threatening to spill out. I rolled my eyes. "What?"

He scooted forward in his chair until our knees were almost touching. I drew in a breath as he reached toward me and placed his fingers on the top of my notebook resting on my lap—just between my slightly parted knees. "Hey, can you do me a favor real quick?"

His thumb grazed the inside of my knee. "Um—sure, what is it?" I rasped.

His eyes twinkled with a hint of mischief as he gazed into mine. "Can you make me a list of the guys in Woodvale you *haven't* dated, because that might be easier for me to—"

Before Mason could finish, I jerked the notebook from his loose grasp and whacked the side of his arm with it. He cowered from me, laughing the entire time. And though I wanted to appear angry, I couldn't help but smile myself. "Fuck you."

He raised his eyebrows in feigned surprise. "Wow. That was vulgar." He had no idea what kind of vulgar thoughts he was putting in my head at that moment. "Is that what you do to your students when they talk back?"

"Five-year-olds don't generally talk back."

"Just wait until Finley gets to know you better, then." Mason looked down, pushing some hanging strands of hair away from his eyes. "Actually—I'm sorry for that list comment. It was a little out of pocket."

"I'd say it was," I muttered, hoping he could catch the playfulness in my tone as he glanced back up at my face. We didn't tear our eyes off of one another until the alarm on my phone went off, alerting me it was almost time for Mr. Woods to bring my students back from art. I shut the alarm off, sitting up a little straighter before turning back to Mason. "It's almost time for the kids to return. Did you have anything else you needed to share?"

Mason's smile began to fade, the mood in the room taking a somber turn. "It's just—Finley's really special, you know? And I know there's twenty-some other kids in your class whose parents would say the exact same thing. But she's been through so much, and…" He shook his head, letting his voice trail off.

It was all I could do not to touch Mason on the knee just then, to give him a reassuring pat. But I held back, choosing instead to lean back in my chair as I said, "I'll keep a close eye on her, Mason, and I'll let you know if I observe even the slightest shift in her mood. She's in good hands."

His eyes found mine again. "Good. I appreciate that. I appreciate—" He paused to swallow. For such a cocky guy, he was having trouble getting his last word out. "You."

Damn it. I could have melted before him. At that moment, I knew agreeing to let him volunteer in my room was a mistake—because my attraction to him had turned into a full-blown crush in just a ten-minute conversation. There was an ache deep within me—it started in my ovaries and crept up toward my heart.

It wasn't just that he was a good father that was making him more attractive to me. It was everything—from the way he smiled, the relaxed way he lounged in that tiny chair, and how he flirted—as inappropriate as his comments had been. Under any other circumstances, I'd be falling for this man hard and fast.

But I couldn't.

I swiveled my chair back around to set my notebook down on my oversized desk calendar. "Well," I said, reaching for a manilla folder containing that day's literacy printables. "Ready to hear about your Room Parent duties for the day?"

Mason sat up a little straighter in his chair and slapped his thighs to indicate just how ready he was. "Yup. Lay it on me, Ms. Devin."

chapter ten
mason

I'd never seen Finley act goofier than when she returned from art class and spotted me sitting in her classroom. She knew I would be there that day, but my presence still made her giddy. It took Ms. Devin five minutes to get everyone to quiet down and sit in their spots on the rug, but Finley was the antsiest of them all—giggling and cupping her hands over her mouth and whispering, "That's my dad."

When it seemed Finley's wiggling around wasn't about to die down, Kendall even had to ask her to sit on her hands as she went over the literacy activities for the morning. I wondered if she would have been sterner if I hadn't been sitting in the room. "Settle down," I mouthed to Finley, feeling a little embarrassed.

"So I'm going to put you in groups of four and we'll rotate, just like last week," Kendall was saying. "And Mr. Reed here—"

"Finley's dad!" The girl beside Finley pulled up to her knees, grinning at me.

"Yes, Avery," Kendall said, grinning in my direction as she tucked her hair behind her ears. "He's going to play a fun rhyming game with—"

"I want to play with Mr. Reed first!"

"He's *my* dad! I get to play with him first!"

Kendall shushed everyone, saying, "One-two-three, eyes on me!"

And the kids responded with, "One-two, eyes on you!" in unison before falling silent. Color me impressed.

"Listen, we're all going to get a chance to play with Mr. Reed." The second the last words left Ms. Devin's mouth, we caught each other's eyes again—and though she kept her composure, I could tell from the slight upturn at the corners of her mouth she was entertaining the same perverted thought as me.

Oh, how I'd love to play with her.

For the next forty minutes, I sat at a bright blue table and played a rhyming activity with four kids at a time—it reminded me of the memory game we had at home that Finley was obsessed with. Some of these kids were better at rhyming than others, and I found myself playfully roasting the ones who couldn't quite figure it out. "Bro, say that out loud—'man' and 'mat'? You're matching the beginning sounds!"

The kid before me slapped his forehead in defeat, but he was grinning from ear to ear. It seemed like every time I said the word "bro," these kids couldn't contain their giggles, so I kept doing it. And this particular redheaded boy—I think his name was Walter, for crying out loud—was so amused by my reaction every time he got a match wrong, he kept messing up on purpose.

At one point, Kendall walked over to my side of the room to remind Walter and the others to bring it down a notch. Her tone was gentle but authoritative, and as she spoke, she looked down at me. I swallowed, feeling like I was the one who'd been caught misbehaving. For a moment, I was worried she might be changing her mind about allowing me to volunteer—I was only getting these kids unnecessarily riled up and she'd ask me to never come back. I glanced across the table at Elijah, who was picking his nose, and awaited my punishment. But with her hand on the back of my chair, Kendall said, "I couldn't get them interested in this game at all last week, but they're so engaged with you. What's your secret?"

I found myself momentarily lost in the sweet vanilla fragrance that enveloped her, unable to answer right away. Her proximity overwhelmed me, her arm just grazing my back as she leaned over the table beside me to hand Elijah a tissue. I kept my eyes fixed on the cards in my hands, ignoring the fact that her breasts were inches from my face. I cleared my throat. "I think the magic ingredient is calling them 'bro," I answered, glancing at Walter, who nodded in agreement.

"Is that right?" Kendall asked, chuckling. Unable to avoid her gaze any longer, I finally looked up at her face only to immediately get lost in her eyes. The noise of the chattering kids began to fade, and for a second, it was as though we were the only two people in that classroom. All I could think about was the playful way she smiled in some of those nude photos she'd sent me, and how I wished I still had them.

"Well," Kendall continued after a moment, snapping me out of my daydream. "I'll leave you to it."

Her eyes lingered on mine for a second longer before she returned to her table on the other side of the room, where she had been doing some one-on-one assessments. I watched her walk away before lowering my eyes to Walter, who was wiggling his eyebrows at me.

"What?" He merely shot me a knowing stare like he was onto me. "Don't look at me like that, bro," I said, making every kid at that table giggle.

After a couple of center rotations, Kendall announced literacy time was over and everyone needed to find their seat. She gave me a job to do, too—she asked me to sit at her desk and cut some papers in half and staple them together to make rhyming booklets for all the students. I went to work as she taught at the front of the room, pointing at words on the smartboard and helping the kids sound them out. I was so distracted by the soothing sound of her voice and the way she giggled and clapped when her students correctly guessed a word I almost forgot she'd given me an assignment.

After that lesson, she allowed the kids to have a little free play before lunch. I swiveled the desk chair toward her and handed her the stack of completed rhyming booklets. "Here you are, ma'am."

"Perfect," she said, taking them from my hands. "You just saved me a ton of time." She thumbed through the booklets, as if double-checking I'd ordered the pages correctly. And then, seemingly satisfied with the work I'd done, she looked back up at me. "I'm sure you have work you need to get to, but you're welcome to stay for a few minutes if you want."

Finley, who was drawing at her table nearby, had overheard this. "Yeah, Daddy! Come color with us." She turned to the girl beside her and announced with a smug grin, "My dad's an artist."

How could I leave now?

I joined Finley and her friends at their table, accepting a blank piece of paper and a basket of markers that was scooted in my direction. "Draw something cute, Dad," Finley demanded.

"Like what?" I asked, taking the lid off of the black marker.

And before long, I found myself taking requests from all sides. Most of the kids in Kendall's class were gathered around me, craning their necks to see my paper as I drew a frog on a log—a little nod to Kendall's rhyming activity—and added details as the requests came in. "Give him a hat!" "Put mushrooms on the log!" "He needs a friend!"

The kids were enjoying this, but nobody was as impressed by my impromptu illustration as Kendall, who peered over my shoulder with her arms crossed against her chest. "Okay, so when you said you're a freelancer—please tell me it has something to do with art?"

"Kind of. I used to illustrate for a small publisher in Indy, but after moving here, I've just been taking on little commercial design jobs." I looked at Finley, who popped the lid off a green marker and began coloring in the frog I'd drawn. "I'm not exactly utilizing my creative talents anymore."

She studied my drawing a bit longer, smiling at the way Finley wasn't quite coloring inside the lines. "Would you consider creating something for the shirts for this fall festival I'm in charge of planning? I mean, it's not a paid gig, but it might allow you to put your creativity to use?"

"Absolutely."

"Really?"

"Sign me up." The silence that settled between us was only amplified by the noise level of the kids around us, many of them begging me to add more details to the background of the drawing.

I knew by agreeing to take on this additional project, it meant I was going to have to spend even more time with this woman who was tempting me with her soft lips, delicious scent, and perfect ass. Resisting the urge to speak every salacious thought that entered my mind would probably grow more difficult as time went on. But she wanted my help, and I couldn't tell her no.

When it was time for the kids to line up for lunch, some of them running over to their cubbies for their lunchboxes, Kendall stood beside me at the door and asked the kids to tell me goodbye. They all groaned when they realized I didn't get to go to lunch with them.

"We'll see Mr. Reed again on Wednesday," she announced as we stood by the door—and their whines turned into cheers. Kendall turned to me with a grin. "Um—there's a PTO meeting Thursday night. Do you think you could have a sketch of the fall festival shirt design by then?"

I nodded, distracted by Finley, who was swinging her arms like helicopter blades and coming dangerously close to knocking poor Elijah clean out with her lunchbox. "Yeah, I could probably have a mock-up for you by Wednesday."

"Perfect," Kendall said, and I redirected my focus back to her. How she dealt with these kids, especially mine, seven and a half hours a day was a feat I couldn't even begin to fathom. "I appreciate your help today."

"Yeah, you're welcome," I said, letting my hand rest on the doorknob. Behind her, the kids were getting antsier by the second. Her once-straight line was now zig-zagging across the back half of the classroom. Finley was clucking her arms like a chicken, much to the delight of the children closest to her. "Well, I should get going before these kids form a dance circle around my kid."

Kendall laughed as she tucked her hair behind one ear. "We're going to be making cinnamon playdough Wednesday morning. Think you can handle that?" I almost didn't catch it— the subtle crinkle in the corners of her eyes or the way she was pressing her lips together tight in an attempt to suppress a grin. But it was the mischievous glint in her eyes that confirmed the dirty undertone to what she was saying—another callback to our text exchange.

I smirked right back at her. "We'll see," I answered, shooting a quick glance in Finley's direction to return her goodbye wave. And as I made my way out the classroom door, pushing it open with my back, I gave Kendall a wink. "See you next time, Ms. Devin."

**

It was cloudless and eighty-degree day, which made the basement feel like a prison that afternoon. So I took my work outside, lounging in a deck chair while putting together a collection of marketing materials for an online boutique. There was minimal illustration involved with this project, and I found myself just plunking text and design elements together. They could've done this themselves, for crying out loud.

Feeling frustrated, I put my laptop down on the table beside me and reclined the deck chair, daydreaming about Kendall. And as luck would have it, that was the moment my father opened the sliding door and walked out onto the deck. Why couldn't he have gotten home just a few minutes sooner—he would've seen me hard at work instead of lounging around like he assumed I did all too often.

My father paced toward the deck railing and looked out at the trees behind our house, sticking his hands in the pockets of his slacks. He clearly had something to say.

"Was your hearing canceled?" I decided to initiate the conversation to keep the focus off of me.

He turned toward me and stared, looking from me to the laptop on the table next to me. "Yeah. Client accepted the plea deal at the last second. Saved us both some time."

"Looks like you've got the rest of the afternoon to enjoy this weather, then." I never knew what to say to my dad—it always came back to the weather.

"I don't have the luxury of lounging around. Too much work to do."

I took a deep breath, knowing this was a dig at me. I considered defending myself, letting him know I had a heavy workload myself, but there was no use. I ignored him instead, pulling my laptop back onto my lap. My dad turned on his heel and went back inside without another word. That man had a special talent for finding new creative yet subtle ways to cut me down, and after twenty-six years, I was used to it.

Someday, I'd stop letting his comments get under my skin.

chapter eleven
kendall

Sarah—
Mason Reed is working on a design for the fall festival t-shirts. He'll have a mock-up for us at the meeting Thursday night. By the way, he mentioned he's Owen's cousin. Small world, huh?
-Kendall
P.S. I think you're right about the hayride.

Kendall—
Oh my gosh, perfect! Owen and I are so fond of Mason, and he's an excellent artist. We visited his parents for Easter, and there's this enormous, breathtakingly beautiful painting of Finley above their fireplace. She's his little muse!
Can't wait to see his shirt design.
-Sarah

"Goddamn it," I muttered out loud, dropping my phone on the couch beside me. I knew better than to check my email at home, but I was waiting on a reply from Jerry Hagan, a local farmer I'd reached out to about buying some of his pumpkins at a discount. I should have known there'd be an email from Sarah waiting for me.

And of course. *Of course* Mason had a painting of Finley in his parents' house. *Of course* she was his muse.

Of course everything I learned about him just made me crush on him even harder.

"What's wrong?" Jamie asked. She was at the other end of the couch. Like me, her laptop was resting on her lap. She had her reading glasses on, and she'd been working on some homework while I was deep into fall festival planning.

I sighed. "He's too fucking cute, and it kills me."

"Who, Tamlin?"

I turned to her with furrowed brows. "What?"

"Never mind, you wouldn't get it. Mason. Are you talking about Mason again?"

I had already brought up his name three or four times that evening. I couldn't help it—thoughts of him flooded my mind all day long. His first volunteer session with me had gone better than I could have imagined, and he was easily the best Room Parent I'd ever had. He had the kids engaged. He didn't ask a bunch of questions. He knew exactly what my expectations were, and he followed through. And the kids loved him.

"You ever find out what's going on with the mom in that situation?"

I looked up from my laptop at my sister's face, watching her concentrate as she typed away. While my students' situations were confidential, I tended to share things with Jamie from time to time. But only because my students' problems often became my problems, too, and sometimes I just needed someone to vent to. Jamie could be trusted with any private information I chose to disclose. "She gave up custody and moved to Florida a few months ago."

Jamie looked up from her homework. "Seriously? Wow, that poor kid."

"Yeah. But Mason says she's really resilient." As I spoke the last word, I nearly cringed—because I knew the most "resilient" kids were often just putting on a good show for the adults around them who kept pointing out how strong they were.

Jamie stared across the couch at me, giving me a knowing look. People used to tell us how "strong" and "resilient" and "brave" we were after our parents divorced and Dad took off to start a new family. Jamie had to grow up faster than most other kids her age. Mom was the manager of a grocery store at the time, often getting home after dark, and Jamie took care of making sure I ate supper and completed my homework. It wasn't until years later that I grasped the enormity of what Jamie went through—she was essentially a kid herself while taking on all of those responsibilities.

So *resilient.*

As if Jamie could read my thoughts, she said, "At least Dad didn't run away to Florida."

"I almost wish he had," I blurted. I almost added, *instead of getting our hopes up with his false promises,* but it didn't need to be said. Jamie understood. Grabbing my notebook from the arm of the couch, I decided to change the subject. "So, you're heading to Indianapolis tomorrow?"

Jamie took off her glasses and rubbed her eyes. "Yeah. It's an afternoon class, so I'll head out around noon."

I thought about everything Daya said that morning, wondering how things were going between the two of them now. Daya was in their bedroom taking a nap, which wasn't entirely unusual for her on the days she had to go in early for an emergency, but the two of them did appear to be avoiding each other.

"Is Daya warming up to the idea?" I asked, though I already knew the answer.

"Not really. I don't know what she expected. She knew I'd eventually have to start attending some classes in person. This is just the beginning."

"Do you see yourself moving there? Eventually?"

She nodded. "I mean, I'm going to have to, aren't I?"

"Do you think Daya will move with you?" I asked, looking down at the list of food truck vendors in front of me. "I mean, her job—?"

Jamie just lifted one shoulder in a casual shrug, not even looking up from her work. I guess moving to Indianapolis meant Daya might get left behind.

She wasn't the only one.

I chewed my thumbnail, trying to imagine what my life might be like when Jamie made the inevitable move. Hopefully, I'd have my own place by then.

But I would feel so alone in this town without her. We fought like cats and dogs sometimes when we were teenagers, but adulthood brought us closer. Now that most of my old friends were married with kids or scattered across the state— wherever their jobs carried them—Jamie was my *person*. Even before we were living together, we spoke nearly every day. We would still be able to do that, I supposed, but the distance would pull us apart in more ways than one.

With Jamie gone, all I would have left to focus on was my work.　I guess that gave me even more reason to pour my heart into this fall festival project, to impress Sarah. I went back to work, deciding not to press the moving issue. Or the Daya issue.

I was studying a map of the school grounds Sarah had given me when my phone buzzed on the arm of the couch beside me.

Mason: Working on this sketch and I've got a few questions. Might be easier to just talk on the phone. Is it ok to call?

Mason: I promise to keep it professional.

Rather than tell Jamie, I showed her the messages on my screen. She shook her head and grinned. "He's just looking for an excuse to talk to you."

I held my phone against my chin, trying not to smile. "Probably." I sent Mason a quick message to let him know it was ok to call and excused myself to my room—I knew better than to talk to him with Jamie so close. She'd probably make moaning noises to ensure I was good and embarrassed.

He called the second my bedroom door closed.

"Sorry, I know it's a little late. I just put Finley to bed and wanted to get started on this."

"It's fine," I said. "I'm working on fall festival stuff right now myself." I sat on my bed and pulled my knees up to my chest.

"So, first question." He cleared his throat. "I need an idea of what exactly this fall festival entails. Are we talking carnival rides and games, or like—bobbing for apples and shit?"

I grinned down at my knees, amused that "shit" still made it into his vernacular when he was trying to keep it professional. "Something in between. There will be a hayride and bouncy castles and games and pumpkin carving. Oh, and a pumpkin slingshot—that was kind of a big deal last year." I lay on my back and stared up at the popcorn ceiling. "No bobbing for apples, but there *will* be a caramel apple booth, which is hands-down the best part."

"Wait, wait, wait," Mason said. I thought for a second I'd been talking too fast and he was about to ask me to repeat myself, but he let out a little chuckle and said, "You're telling me there's a pumpkin slingshot, but the *caramel apples* are the best part?"

"Well, yeah. I mean, it's *my* favorite part, anyway."

"Even better than a hayride?"

"I didn't get to participate in that stuff last year because I was too busy volunteering. So maybe I'm a little biased—but the caramel apples are literally the only part I'm looking forward to, personally."

"So what I'm hearing is that there'd better be a damn caramel apple in this t-shirt design, is that correct?"

"Correct."

"Gotcha." I could hear the sound of his pen on the paper as he took notes. He asked me a couple more questions—did I want a full-color design, what were the details of the event. Et cetera. There were pauses here and there as he took time to write down everything I told him. "So you've got a little more than four weeks to plan this thing, huh?"

"Yeah," I said with a sigh, rolling over onto my stomach. "Sarah asked me to take over this year—she's busy planning her wedding, so I'm just... going to do my best not to screw it up."

"You're not going to screw it up," he said. "I guarantee a couple of things will go wrong, because that's life, but as long as there's a bouncy castle, every kid in attendance is going to be more than happy."

"I hope you're right."

"I *know* I'm right. It doesn't take much to make kids happy. I mean—Finley spent an hour playing with the cardboard box my mom's new dishwasher came in tonight. So—got any extra boxes?"

I smiled. "Forget the pumpkin slingshot. I'll just set out a bunch of boxes and let them go to town."

"See? That's all you need," Mason said with a laugh. "Well, that and caramel apples."

"Obviously."

For a moment, neither of us said anything—and I wondered if his smile was as big as the one currently stretching across my face. I bit my bottom lip, thankful he couldn't see how dorky I looked at that moment. And then, after a few more seconds, he said, "Hey." His voice had shifted to a low, serious tone, sending the butterflies in my stomach into a frenzy. "I'm sorry, again, about that comment I made earlier today... about the list of the men you haven't dated. That wasn't any of my business."

I could tell this had been eating at him all day—which was kind of sweet. "I'm sorry for slapping you with my notebook, then," I said. "But I'm even more sorry that you had to witness my ex-boyfriend's douchebaggery."

Silence.

"Hello?"

"I'm—just—I'm trying really hard to be respectful after just apologizing to you, but the 'douchebaggery' comment is making it difficult." His voice sounded a little strained, like he was holding in a laugh.

"If you have anything disrespectful to say right now, you get a free pass."

"Oh, really?"

Assuming he would have something to say about Heath, I urged, "By all means, say whatever's on your mind."

"I think," he began, pausing to take a deep breath mid-sentence, "you looked really pretty in that dress today."

My heart leapt from my chest to my throat, and I knew he heard the gasp that escaped my lips. My brain turned to mush, and I struggled to form words. "I meant—that's—you think calling someone pretty is disrespectful?"

"In our case? Probably. Borderline sexual harassment, at best."

"Then why'd you say it?"

"You gave me a free pass."

"Because I thought you were going to say something about my ex!" I laughed.

"And waste my free pass on him? No. But—if I upset you by saying that, I'm sorry, again." He let out an exasperated groan and I could almost hear him cringing when he said, "Fuck. Please forget I said that."

"Well, you can't take it back *now*," I said, keeping my tone playful so he'd know I wasn't offended. I sat up in the center of my bed and crossed my legs. "I've already let it get to my head. And… I would be lying if I said I wasn't thinking about you when I put on that dress this morning."

I could hear him breathing—the tiniest expulsion of air from his mouth before he said, "Weird, most women tell me they think about me when they *un*-dress."

The giggle that erupted from my mouth just then was borderline embarrassing. My cheeks, sore from smiling, were getting warm. I could have told him that I thought about him when I undressed, too, but I bit down on my lip to prevent those words from escaping. I wouldn't be able to look him in the eyes ever again if I said them.

"Well." Mason cleared his throat. "I'd say this conversation has taken an unprofessional turn. Sorry."

"That's just as much my fault as it is yours."

A pause. And then he said, "I'm going to guess there's something in your school policy that frowns upon certain types of relationships between parents and teachers, huh?"

"Yes. I may have actually reread that particular clause recently. And it's not just frowned upon. It's strictly prohibited." As I lay on my back again, there was more silence on his end, though it was safe to assume we were thinking the same thing. "But," I said, trying to sound hopeful, "there's nothing in there against being friends."

"Great." I heard him suck air in through his teeth. "That came out more sarcastic than I intended. Friends—that's fine. I can do friendship with you."

I couldn't hold in my laughter, amused by his awkward phrasing. "Okay. Let's *do* friendship, then."

"*Friend, gooood!*" he grunted, his voice quivering dramatically.

I blinked. "What was that?"

"Don't tell me you haven't seen *Bride of Frankenstein*."

"I have not seen *Bride of Frankenstein*," I admitted. "Read the book in high school, though."

"Aw, they had books at the poor kids' school? That's good."

"Oh, wow," I said, switching my phone to the other ear. "You go from complimenting me to insulting me. Nice."

"Had to balance it out."

"I guess that's what friends do."

"Yeah. I—" He stopped, and his voice sounded distant when he said, "What are you doing up?" He told me to hold on, and I waited as he talked to Finley. It sounded like she got closer, and then there was a grunt like he was picking her up. "Guess who I'm talking to?"

I bit my lip as Finley said, "Who is it, Daddy?"

"Your teacher."

She gasped. "Let me see."

"Not on FaceTime, goofball." And then, to me, he said, "Sorry, Kendall—Finley's still awake, apparently."

"I'm sorry. I should let you go so you can—"

"Uh, actually, she wants to say hi."

Before I had a chance to respond, there was a breathy giggle on the other end. "Ms. Devin!"

I smiled. "Hi, Finley. Isn't it past your bedtime?"

"Why are you talking to my dad?"

Wow. She didn't waste any time getting right down to business. "Your dad is designing a t-shirt for school, and he had some questions. He's a good artist, isn't he?"

"Are you at school?"

"Nope, I'm at my house."

"Do you live with a husband?"

"No… I live with my sister and her girlfriend." I almost said *friend*, fearing this would lead to an awkward conversation for Mason, but it didn't feel right to edit the truth. I kept talking so her curiosity wouldn't linger. "And we have a grumpy, old dog named Titus."

"Does he bite?"

"Sometimes," I said, laughing. "He really hates me."

"Can I see him sometime? I bet he'd like me."

"Um—maybe," I said. "I bet he'd like you, too." I could hear Mason murmur something to Finley in the background.

"Dad says I have to go to bed," Finley whined. "See you tomorrow, Ms. Devin."

"Goodnight, Finley."

I heard Mason tell her, "Go in there and pick out a book. A *short* one this time. I'll be there in two minutes." And then, to me, he said, "Sorry about that. She insisted."

"No, don't apologize. That was really sweet."

"She really likes you," he said. "She wants to be a teacher when she grows up because of you, which is a relief, because previously, she had her heart set on being a unicorn trainer."

"I'm sure there's more money in that."

He chuckled, and then we were both silent for a moment. I wished I were there with him, next to him—taking in his scent and feeling the warmth of his touch. When I closed my eyes, I could almost see his face—his sweet grin and the twinkle in his ocean blue eyes. And—fuck me—that *magnificent* hair.

Finally, he broke the silence, saying, "All right, well, I've got to go read *Go Dog Go* for the ninetieth time, probably."

"I've got a copy of that in the classroom, too—I'll set it aside for you to read to the kids Wednesday."

"Don't you dare."

I laughed as I said, "Goodnight, Mason."

"Goodnight, Kendall."

God, I wanted him.

chapter twelve
mason

When Kendall asked me to delete her naked pictures from my phone, I followed her orders. Her fears that Finley might see them could safely subside.

But those pictures were forever etched in my mind, especially the one she'd taken in front of the mirror with all the roundest, softest parts of her on full display.

I couldn't forget it.

It was such a persistent thought, in fact, I felt compelled to reach for my iPad and sketch that photo from memory the morning after we spoke on the phone. I pushed all of my freelance work aside, even forgetting about her fall festival t-shirt design for a while, and focused only on my illustration of Kendall. With each stroke of my Apple Pencil, I carefully duplicated every curve of her body, the subtle smirk on her lips, and the way her hair fell over the tops of her breasts.

When I zoomed out to admire the entire illustration, I felt myself getting hard as my eyes scanned every detail. This wasn't quite as satisfying as the photo she'd sent me, and if I had it my way, I'd get to see the real deal in person. But this would suffice.

No more than three seconds after my hand slid down the front of my pants, I heard the horrifyingly familiar squeak of the door opening at the top of the stairs. The only other person home was my mother. Fucking great.

When my sister moved out for college, my parents let me move down to the basement and claim it as my space. At sixteen, I was living my best life—smoking weed undetected, inviting my friends over to jam in *my* living room, and sneaking girls in through the door that led to the patio. We all called it my "apartment" because, essentially, that's what it was. I loved every aspect of living down there—except for one thing.

The basement door didn't lock.

And there I was, ten years later, encountering the same problem: a door without a lock and a mom with no boundaries.

I was in my bedroom, but the door to the living area was open. "Mason?" I threw a blanket over myself as my mom began descending the stairs.

"I'm a little busy," I hollered back, flipping the cover of my iPad shut. I reached for my laptop at the foot of the bed to pull it toward me. "Can we talk later?"

"I'm bringing some of Finley's toys down!" More footsteps. "I nearly broke my neck tripping over the toys she left on the dining room rug, Mase. You've got to have that girl pick up after herself."

I sighed. "Just throw them in the—"

I heard the sound of the toys being dropped into Finley's toy box in the living room. I assumed that would be the end of our conversation, but my mom continued, saying, "You're lucky I picked those up before the housekeeper got here." And then she appeared at my doorway. "You know how I hate it when there's still clutter out when she arrives."

"Yeah, how humiliating."

"If that girl drags toys out in the morning, you've gotta make sure she picks them up before school," my mom said, putting one hand on her hip and looking around my bedroom, which was still mostly bare. Many of my possessions—my books, keepsakes, and winter clothes—remained in boxes in the closet, because this living arrangement was meant to be more temporary than this. Before Finley and I moved in, this was a guest bedroom—vacant for 51 weeks out of the year, only occupied by my sister and her family when they stayed at Christmastime. And though Finley and I had been there for a few months, it looked nearly the same, aside from a few of my belongings collecting on the bedside table.

And it was neat, just like our living area and kitchenette. I did my best to clean up after myself and teach Finley the same standards. Surely my mom could see that as she looked around? I wanted to call her out for nitpicking, but in an attempt to cut this interaction short, I said, "Sorry—I'll make sure she picks up next time."

Both hands were on her hips now. "You look like you just woke up. What'd you do, fall asleep after you dropped Fin off at school?"

I inhaled. "Yeah. She had a rough time getting to sleep last night. And look, I really need to—"

"Your Aunt Michelle said Owen's up every day at seven, hitting the gym before he starts writing. He's working on his second book, did you know that? I still need him to sign the first one for me. Think I could take it to their wedding for him to sign?" She stopped talking to laugh at her own joke, finally giving me a chance to speak.

"I could probably write a book, too, if I weren't constantly interrupted." I held my mom's gaze so she would get the point.

She rolled her eyes and held up her hands in defeat. "I'm sorry, I'll leave you to it." She turned to go, but I caught her eyeing my hair—and she got in one last dig. "My hairdresser takes walk-ins on Wednesdays, if you ever want to do something about that hair."

"I will certainly keep that in mind," I said, running my fingers through my hair, which could stand to be a bit longer, in my opinion. "Better go… make sure it doesn't look like anyone lives here before the housekeeper shows up."

"You're *so* funny," she said, making her way out the door. She was still murmuring as she walked up the stairs, something about how I just didn't "get it." I waited until the door at the top of the stairs closed before letting out a heavy sigh, cursing Owen's name under my breath.

Not that he deserved it. I was just in the same place I was ten years ago, living in my parents' basement and getting off to the image of a woman I could never have. Kendall was about as available to me now as Lara Croft had been then.

The only difference between the man I'd become and the clueless teenager I once was lay in the fact I now had another human being to support—and I was doing a piss-poor job of it.

* *

By Wednesday, my mood had improved, though that probably had a lot to do with seeing Kendall—and getting out of that house.

After dropping Finley off at school, I headed to the new café downtown—the one every single old friend insisted I visit upon my return, but hadn't had a chance to explore. It was the one I'd seen Sarah and Owen carrying coffee cups from— Riverside Coffee Company.

It seemed cozy with its mismatched wooden furnishings, a wall of old books that were likely only touched by the most pretentious of customers, and a single, enormous bay window facing the street. Hozier's voice crooned over the speakers, one of his quieter, mellower songs. And the café was nearly vacant, aside from a thirty-something woman typing on a laptop at a table in the corner, oblivious to the world around her.

Immediately, I could envision this becoming a potential workspace for me—as long as their coffee passed the test. The young, lavender-haired barista greeted me with a smile, saying, "Welcome in! Today's a special day—we just launched our pumpkin spice lattes for the season!"

"Fuck yes," I blurted, making her laugh. I wasn't about to pretend I wanted anything different. I ordered a medium before settling into a barstool near the window with my iPad. I had a little bit of time to finish up the fall festival t-shirt sketch before showing it to Kendall.

The nude illustration of her was carefully hidden in a secure, private folder—there was no chance in hell I'd let her accidentally swipe to that one.

I pulled up the file in my illustration app. I'd decided on going with a vintage-inspired design, choosing a bold but whimsical serif font for the words FALL FESTIVAL that reminded me of some of my grandparents' vinyl album covers from the 60s. Peeking out from behind the letters, I added as many details from what Kendall described as I could in order to capture the essence of the festival—the hayride wagon, a jack-o'-lantern, a scarecrow, a vintage-looking ticket, and, of course, Kendall's caramel apple. All of these details were surrounded by fall leaves, which cascaded over the letters below.

I reworked some of the details on the scarecrow's face as I took my first sip of coffee—relieved to know I could indeed return to this café to get some work done in the future. The drink was perfection.

A thought occurred to me as I reached the bottom of my drink and closed the cover of my iPad. Teachers loved coffee, didn't they? And—maybe—Kendall would appreciate a mid-morning pick-me-up?

I debated it in my head for a full minute before approaching the counter again. "That may have been the best pumpkin spice latte ever made—I'm going to need another one to take to a friend."

"Uh huh," the barista said as she rang me up. "You're just using that as an excuse to drink a second one, aren't you?"

"You caught me," I teased, pulling my wallet out of my pocket.

As I watched the girl make the drink, humming along to the music as she worked, I almost told her never mind. And on my way out, I even considered throwing it in the trashcan on the sidewalk. What kind of message would I be sending by buying Kendall a coffee? I wanted it to say, "you deserve this for having to put up with my kid," not, "I want to fuck you."

The latter was the reason I left it in my cupholder and walked away from my car in the school parking lot, locking my car behind me. What a stupid idea.

I made it halfway across the lot before jogging back for it. Nope, nope, nope—the stupid thing would be to waste a five dollar drink that purple-haired barista so lovingly made. And no matter how Kendall perceived the gesture, it wasn't like she would be wrong either way.

chapter thirteen
kendall

On Wednesday morning, I had to pull out my very first "I'm going to sit here and wait until everyone's quiet" of the year and nearly died in my rocking chair at the front of the rug before the kids were silent. The wiggliest and noisiest of them all was Finley, who was yet again antsy because she knew her dad would be there soon. She repeatedly cupped her hands over her mouth, though, like she truly could not help her outbursts.

I saw so much of myself in her. And that's part of the reason why I kept my tone gentle when I said, "Finley, can you find your listening ears for me?"

She pretended to pull her "listening ears" out of her pocket and put them over her real ears—and due to some miracle, she only interrupted the Johnny Appleseed book I was reading once more before it was time for me to walk them to the library.

Once I was alone in my classroom, I sat at my desk and rubbed my temples, wishing I would have had time to make myself a coffee that morning. So when Mason ambled in holding a coffee cup in his outstretched hand, saying, "Apparently it's officially pumpkin spice season," I could have hugged him.

I reached across my desk to accept the cup. "This is for me?"

Mason shoved one hand in his pocket, the other clutching an iPad with a black leather cover against his chest. With a slow nod, he said, "I was at Riverside this morning and… they made this by accident, so they gave it to me for free."

"Oh—lucky me."

A smile slowly crept onto Mason's face, and he shook his head. "Every single word I just told you was a lie."

I let out a breathy giggle as I took my first sip. "What do you mean?"

He rolled his eyes at himself. "I bought it for you because mine was so good, I needed someone else to experience it with me."

"Well," I said, sensing a comforting warmth spreading through my body that wasn't just from the coffee. "It *is* delicious. So… thank you."

"Welcome. Wasn't sure if you were a pumpkin spice girl, or…" He barely opened his mouth as he spoke, staring down at my desk.

I shrugged one shoulder. "Caramel macchiatos are my usual go-to from that place, but I'll happily accept a PSL anytime."

His eyes met mine again as he lightly tapped his fingers on the back of his iPad. "So. Wanna see your shirt design?"

I gasped. "Oh my gosh, of course."

Mason made his way around to my side of the desk, grabbing the same chair he'd sat in on Monday and scooting it beside mine—closer this time. He flipped the cover off his iPad and tapped the screen a few times before turning it around to show me his design.

I gasped and took the iPad from his hands. I wasn't sure he even intended to pass the device to me, but he had no choice. "Mason," I said in a whisper, gazing down at the retro design—it was so detailed. With a warm mixture of reds, browns, and yellows, he'd managed to perfectly capture the essence of everything I'd described to him over the phone.

And there was the caramel apple, prominently situated on the edge of the design.

"Is it too much?" he asked, and I realized I'd been staring at it for a while, only uttering his name.

"What?" I looked up from the design at his worried face. "No, it's perfect. I—I can't believe you got this done in a day."

He reached over to swipe right on the iPad. "There's a blackline version, too, see? Wasn't sure what your t-shirt budget was."

"You did all of this by hand?"

"Apart from the lettering… yeah." Mason leaned forward, bracing his forearms on his knees. And with a quick, subtle glance at my thighs, he said, "It's what I do."

I put his iPad down on my desk in front of me, but I still stared down at the design that exceeded every one of my expectations. "What is it you were doing, exactly, before you moved back here?" I lifted my chin to look at him to find he was already staring at my face.

He cleared his throat. "Uh—I was the in-house illustrator at a small publisher."

"Any books I'd know?" I asked him.

"Doubt it," he said with a soft chuckle. "It was a lot of non-fiction. Very niche stuff. Although—you know that HGTV show, *Flipping Fabulous?*"

"Oh, yeah!" I answered a little too enthusiastically, tucking my hair behind my ear. "They're based out of Indy, right? I once made my ex take me up there and look for some of the houses they flipped on the show."

Mason grinned. "Did you find any?"

"I sure did. I was sort of hoping I'd run into the couple from the show. But… no luck."

There was a gleam in his eyes when he said, "I might have a connection there." I lifted my eyebrows in question as he continued. "They've got a book coming out this fall, and I did the cover and all the interior illustrations for it last spring. A bunch of simple doodles of, like, porches and kitchen cabinets—but it was hands-down my favorite project I've ever worked on."

"Did you get to meet them?"

"Sure did," he said, crossing his arms against his chest. "Met with them multiple times to go over their designs. That publishing house was real big on the hands-on, face-to-face meetings—which is why they refused to allow me to work remotely when I left the city."

My heart sank. It was clear Mason loved that job, and it was a shame he had to leave it behind. I tapped the screen of his iPad to make his shirt design reappear. Just as I opened my mouth to compliment him again, I heard the unmistakable sound of approaching five-year-olds—quickly followed by Ms. Sterling, the librarian, reminding them, "Your voices should still be at level one, guys."

I walked to the door to greet my students, motioning for them to sit on the rug. Ms. Sterling hesitated in the hallway, waving at the last couple of stragglers as they made their way past us. "Hey," she said, her voice low. "Sarah recruited me for your fall festival thing."

Abigail Sterling was one of the new hires this year, replacing Mrs. Hawley, who had been the school's librarian since the dawn of time. And she was Mrs. Hawley's opposite in every way— coming into the building every morning carrying a tote bag that said "READ BANNED BOOKS" with a bisexual flag enamel pin on the strap. Her first order of business was to purchase more diverse books for the library—which Sarah enthusiastically approved.

Abigail tucked her fire-engine red hair behind her ears and continued, saying, "I was thinking of hosting a used book drive the same night... maybe?"

"Oh—that's actually a great idea," I said, giving Mason a sideways glance—he was standing at the edge of the rug and high-fiving a few kids while Finley clung to his legs in a melodramatic fashion. If I didn't hurry, he was going to have these kids so riled up they wouldn't be able to listen to my instructions for our next activity. "Thanks, Abigail. Can you come to the meeting tomorrow night?"

"I'll be there," she replied, shooting a glance in Mason's direction—he was now teaching Walter some kind of special handshake, and nobody was sitting where they were supposed to. "Well, I'll let you handle—that."

She turned to walk toward the library and I closed the door behind her, bracing myself for the chaos behind me. I made my way over to the rug clapping rhythmically to get everyone's attention, which only a few of them repeated. Mason caught on quickly, though, and the second time I clapped five times—he followed suit, sitting cross-legged right in the center of the kids—all of whom immediately copied him.

"Let's see what Ms. Devin has to say, okay, guys?" He pretended to zip his lips before gazing up at me with an adorable grin—an expression I got lost in for a few seconds before remembering I had twenty-five five-year-olds staring at me, too.

The morning went by fast, with the kids assisting me in making cinnamon playdough for apple week—and then Mason worked with four of them at a time, using the letter stampers to stamp their names and sight words into the playdough. Afterwards, he cut out laminated apple flashcards for me while I led the group literacy lesson. And just like Monday, we finished off the morning with some free time, and every single kid gathered around the table where Mason took their art requests.

This time, they had him drawing Johnny Appleseed, proving at least some of them were paying attention to this week's lessons. I pinned his illustration to the bulletin board behind my desk beside his frog picture as the kids lined up for lunch.

With both hands in his pockets, Mason stepped toward me with a low, "Hey." I held my breath, taken aback by his sudden closeness. "I'm pretty sure Elijah ate, like, a *considerable* amount of that playdough."

I laughed, glancing at Elijah, who was rubbing his belly in line. "Great."

"I tried to stop him."

"Well, I mean—it *is* edible," I murmured over my shoulder as I rearranged some of the other artwork on the bulletin board to accommodate Mason's. I turned to face him, standing just inches from his body. A fresh pine scent emanated from him, combining with the cinnamon from the playdough that was no doubt clinging to his hands. "You were great again today, by the way."

He leaned sideways to reach for his iPad from my desk, and as he straightened up again, he was even closer to me than before. "I'm honestly really enjoying it," he said, glancing over at Finley. "Gives me an excuse to be a helicopter dad—and a reason to get out of the house."

It took everything in me not to invite him to join me every day. "Thanks again for the coffee, too. That was really sweet."

He glanced at my empty latte cup on my desk. "You're welcome. I almost didn't bring it in."

"Why?"

His eyes found mine again. "Wasn't sure how you'd take that gesture."

"Is that why you tried to lie at first?"

"Maybe."

"Friends get each other coffee all the time," I said, adjusting my lanyard and flipping my hair over my shoulder. "And you can bring me a caramel macchiato next time."

Mason grinned and sucked in his bottom lip, an expression I knew meant he was fighting the urge to say something that would unquestionably cross the line. Finally, his lips slowly parted and he said, "And what are you going to do for me, Ms. Devin?"

I prayed he wouldn't notice the way his words—and his husky voice—sent goosebumps down both my arms. He waited for me to answer, his gaze bouncing from my eyes to my lips. I swallowed. "Teach your daughter how to read." It came out with a little more sass than I intended, but it made him smile even bigger.

"I guess we're even."

He was still staring at me like he wanted to kiss me or perhaps undress me—like if we weren't standing in a room full of children, he would. I was the one to break eye contact to look at the clock—there was less than a minute before the lunch bell.

And as Mason made his way over to the kids for their final high-fives and one last hug from Finley, all I could think about was how badly I wanted that man to kiss me, to undress me—to do all the things he once expressed he would do to my body in those texts we exchanged.

None of which could ever happen.

* *

"I have some big news about the festival, and I'm not sure how you're going to take it."

These were the first words I heard upon entering the teacher's lounge for lunch. Sarah waved me over to her end of the long table—unlike Principal Cates, she ate her lunch in here a lot because she said it made her more approachable. One of us.

"I'm almost scared to ask," I said, taking the seat across from her. Heath was sitting a few seats away on the opposite side, and though he was engaged in a conversation with Mr. Woods, he glanced in my direction.

Sarah smiled sheepishly as she said, "I swear it's a good thing, and it's all going to work out in the end."

"Just tell me," I said, pulling my hummus out of my lunchbox.

"Okay." She opened the binder in front of her and took a deep breath. "It's something I tried to do a year ago, but we didn't have the budget for it. And now... well, *STEM for the Win* has agreed to donate enough money to cover the rental of two carnival rides."

My mouth fell open. "Owen's donating... carnival rides?"

"Yes—and I'm taking care of arranging everything with the company that will be delivering them. They sent me a digital catalog—we can all vote on which rides we want at the meeting."

I just blinked at her in wonderment. Carnival rides? I remembered her mentioning them last year, but it was a financial impossibility at the time. "Do we have the *room*? And what about the liability?"

"We'll have to expand into the southern parking lot," she said, glancing down at the paper in front of her. "And as far as liability, we're covered in the ride company's insurance—I already had Delgado go over their contract to ensure it wouldn't be a risk." She'd already gone to the superintendent about this, so it looked like it was pretty much a done deal. "This is going to be bigger than just the Grissom community, Kendall—let's get all of Woodvale there."

Great.

No pressure or anything.

And as if she could read the overwhelm on my face, she reached across the table to rest her hand on my wrist. "I know this gives you more work to do, as far as logistical planning goes, but you're not alone in it—I'm not going to sit back and watch you struggle, okay?" She paused to give me a warm smile, squeezing my wrist before she pulled her hand away. "I'm going to do everything I can to help you recruit more volunteers."

As if he were personally beckoned, Heath cleared his throat, turning to us. "Let me help."

We both whipped our heads his direction, and Sarah quickly turned back to me, assessing my reaction. "I doubt you'd have time for all this," I said, my mouth dry.

He shrugged. "But I always help with projects like these, don't I?" He looked at Sarah, who shot the tiniest wince in my direction before she nodded in agreement. Selfish as he was, Heath was one of her usual recruits. "What can I do?"

I wanted to tell him to fuck off, but I couldn't say that in front of our boss—even if she was my friend. Inhaling, I tapped my phone and brought up the document that contained my to-do list, trying to find a task that was suitable for Heath. And finally, I saw it. I'd written "bathrooms??" near the bottom of the list.

"Well, now that we'll be drawing a bigger crowd," I started, tapping my fingernails on the table, "I doubt we can have all those people using the student bathrooms by the gym. I think we're going to need portable toilets, right?"

I looked at Sarah for confirmation, and she nodded, saying, "I had the very same thought."

Turning to Heath, I said, "That would take a huge load off my shoulders—if you could track down a portable toilet company and have them delivered the night before."

Heath's jaw clenched. "So you're… putting me in charge of where people shit, huh?"

There were a couple giggles at the other end of the table. I stared at Heath, ignoring them. "I mean, it's something I need help with—if you're not up for the task, Heath, just say it."

Whatever it was Heath wanted to say, he couldn't—not in front of Sarah. He was seething. Finally, he ended our stare-down and rolled his eyes. "Whatever. I can do it."

Across from me, I caught a glimmer of a smile on Sarah's lips as she jotted something down in her planner. And that subtle look of amusement on her face was exactly why we were friends.

Even if I did sort of want to kill her sometimes.

chapter fourteen
mason

"Why can't I go with you?"

Finley was seated on my parents' living room floor surrounded by all of her Barbies, which, from the looks of it, had just suffered a brutal dinosaur attack. Her oversized t-rex was lying sideways in the midst of the pile of toys. "Because this meeting is for grown-ups."

"Like grandma's meeting?"

"Yup," I said, running a hand through my hair. I glanced over at my dad, seated in his recliner, so enthralled by whatever they were spewing on Fox News that I was concerned leaving right now might not be the best idea.

My mom was at one of her weekly church meetings—women's bible study or something. Her meeting just so happened to coincide with the PTO meeting on Thursday night, which meant Finley was stuck with Grandpa. Luckily for her, she thought his grumpiness was amusing—and she often egged it on to the point he couldn't help but laugh with her.

"Fin, make sure you pick all of these toys up before Grandma gets home," I told her, checking the time on my phone. I had plenty of time, but I wanted to be early—if anything for an excuse to talk to Kendall a bit longer.

Finley was already too distracted by her toys to answer. "Finley," my dad's voice boomed. "Your father just spoke to you. Acknowledge him."

Finley looked up, glancing from my father to me. "Okay, Dad."

My dad looked up at me. "What's this you're doing, anyway?"

I shook my keys in my hand as I reached for my iPad from the coffee table. "PTO meeting at Finley's school," I mumbled, barely opening my mouth.

"You know," he started, and I closed my eyes for a second, bracing myself for the judgment. "If you weren't doing all this stuff at the school, you might have time to get out there and look for a real job."

I squeezed my keys in my fist. "I've been putting applications in, Dad," I said, which wasn't a lie—since June, I'd been applying to some illustration jobs here and there. Was I being picky? Yes. But I knew my worth, and I also knew that if I held out, the right job would come along.

At least I hoped.

My dad shook his head. "What you need to do is take your resumé and hand it to the managers of these companies in person—shake their hands, look 'em in the eye. Make yourself stand out."

"If I want to make myself stand out as a sociopath, I'll be sure to do that, Dad," I said. "They just want people to follow the damn directions and submit their applications online."

"And how's that working out for you?"

I let out an exasperated sigh because I didn't have a comeback for that one—which led my dad to believe he'd won. With a smug look on his face, he interlocked his fingers behind his head and said, "You're just—stagnant. And I hate to see it."

I swallowed as I bent over to kiss the top of Finley's head, deciding it was probably in the best interest of everyone in this room if I kept my rage to myself.

However, I leaned in close to Finley's ear and said, "Be good. And hey, you ought to see if Grandpa wants to play Candy Land. It's funny when he loses, isn't it?"

She let out an excited gasp, and I turned to leave, fully aware of the chaos I'd just unleashed. My dad despised Candy Land, but Finley always managed to talk him into it, anyway. It often resulted in him flipping the board and accusing Finley of cheating. And Finley would throw her head back in laughter until my dad was so frustrated he removed his glasses and pinched the bridge of his nose, cursing under his breath.

I was sad I wouldn't be able to witness it this time.

* *

"You're going to hate me."

Those were the words Kendall greeted me with when I entered the gym to find her and Sarah unfolding a lunch table from its pocket in the wall. I was momentarily lost in the memory of helping my P.E. teacher put the tables up when I had gone to school here all those years ago.

Once the table was down and secured, Kendall turned to me with a sheepish smile, both hands on her cheeks like she was scared to tell me—whatever it was she was about to tell me. "Hate you? Impossible," I said, holding my iPad under my arm. I greeted Sarah with a little nod.

"Well," Kendall said, "you're probably going to have to make some adjustments to your design."

"Oh yeah? Why's that?"

"Your *cousin*—" she started, but Sarah joined her at her side.

"Carnival rides!" Sarah sang out in a playful voice, like she was Oprah announcing free cars for everyone in her audience. She clapped her hands together. "We have the budget for a couple of carnival rides now, and—"

"Thanks to Owen, huh?" I asked with a grin, catching the wary look in Kendall's eyes.

"Thanks to *STEM for the Win*," Sarah corrected, like she was trying to downplay Owen's wealth. "And we're going to vote on rides tonight. Poor Kendall here—" she said, putting her hands on Kendall's shoulders, "—is feeling *slightly* overwhelmed, but I keep telling her she's got this."

"Course she does," I agreed. I was tempted to wink at Kendall, but it probably wasn't a good idea to do anything of the sort right in front of her boss.

"You're putting way too much trust in me," Kendall said over her shoulder at Sarah. "It's going to be a disaster."

Sarah leaned closer to Kendall as she softly said, "Well, if it is, just blame it on Heath," before pulling away to greet the other people entering the gym.

Kendall shook her head and smiled. I wasn't entirely sure who Heath was, but I had an inkling he was the guy who'd asked her about the waffle maker.

For a moment, she and I stood facing each other as others started entering the gym. Eventually, she turned to greet some of them—other teachers and parents she knew. I found a seat on the bench near the end of the table, and though I pretended to be looking over the t-shirt design on my iPad, I was taking in every detail of Kendall's appearance—her yellow skirt, the striped blouse that hugged her chest—and the charm bracelet that slid down her arm every time she brushed her long bangs away from her eyes. The sweet, nervous chuckle she gave when someone said to her, "They put you in charge of this whole thing, huh?"

She was so beautiful, and it was like she didn't even know it.

Sarah and Kendall sat in metal folding chairs, angling them so everyone could see them. And while it was obvious Sarah was eager to speak, she allowed Kendall to take over—even urging her to make the announcement about the carnival rides herself. "This of course gives us a little more work to do," Kendall said, shooting Sarah a sly grin. "But I think if we all pull together, it's possible."

First on the agenda was to choose two rides. After some heavy debate—and a few people going off on tangents about the fall festivals of their youth—the group ultimately decided on a Ferris wheel and merry-go-round. The classics.

I picked up my stylus and immediately went to work on my new design as they carried on, talking about tickets, concessions, a book drive, and parking. Someone asked about t-shirts, and Kendall's eyes found mine as she said, "We've got a parent working on the design right now, actually."

I lifted my left hand in a casual wave, keeping my stylus on the screen as I worked on the intricate details of the horses on the merry-go-round. A few people around me leaned in closer to see what I had so far, and they seemed to exchange impressed glances in my peripheral vision.

Halfway through the meeting, Sarah announced she needed to go, which left Kendall fully in charge. There was a shift in Kendall's demeanor once Sarah was gone, her discomfort apparent in the way she crossed and uncrossed her legs repeatedly. She could no longer look at Sarah to answer questions for her—this was all her.

I stopped drawing for a while so I could pay closer attention. From several feet away, Kendall's eyes found mine as she spoke, and though her words were directed at the woman who'd just asked her a question, her gaze remained fixed on me. I didn't pick up my stylus again for the rest of the meeting. I got the sense she was pretending she was speaking only to me as a way to calm her nerves, so I gave her my full attention.

When it came time to discuss advertising, the redhead seated across from me—if I recalled correctly, she was the librarian—spoke up. "My friend Xander works for the paper, and I bet he could do a little write-up about it."

"That would be great, Abigail," Kendall said, jotting down something in her notebook.

Just behind me, someone cleared their throat. "Actually," Lori, the school receptionist, said, "Meghan Dobson is our contact at the Woodvale Times. She always covers school events. And they gave us a half-page last year. Not just a 'write-up.'"

Kendall looked up at her and blinked. "Oh, okay. I'll reach out to her, then." I watched her closely as she fidgeted with the charms on her bracelet, momentarily distracted by Lori's interruption. Her eyes scanned the notebook on her lap, and I could tell she'd lost her train of thought. And her confidence.

"Want me to work on an ad design?" I asked.

Her eyes found mine. "Yes, that would be perfect, Mason—thank you." We exchanged subtle smiles before she sat up a little straighter and addressed the whole crowd, saying, "So, moving on, we should form sub-committees…"

Atta girl.

Sub-committees were formed. Tasks were assigned. Follow-up meetings were planned. After an hour and fifteen minutes, the meeting adjourned, and everyone scattered to engage in separate conversations. I got up from the table so we could push it back into the wall. People began filtering out to get home for dinner or pick their kids up from practice, but Kendall was talking to Abigail, Heath, and another teacher in the corner.

I remained a few feet away, leaning over my iPad on the edge of the stage at the front of the gym. I was half-listening to Kendall assure Heath she didn't need more help from him as I fine-tuned some more details on the t-shirt design. It was getting late—I'd need to get home to get Finley's bath and bedtime routine started soon, but I couldn't fight the urge to stay, hoping I'd have the chance to talk to Kendall alone.

After what seemed like an eternity, Heath finally left, with Abigail not far behind. And Kendall made her way over to the stage toward a *Pete the Cat* tote bag and slipped her notebook inside it. She zipped the bag but didn't reach for it, instead bringing both of her hands to her temples to rub them.

I slid the iPad down the stage closer to her and sidled up beside her. "So who do you hate more, Lori or Heath?"

"Right now? That's a toss-up."

I tucked the stylus into my iPad cover and closed it, crossing my arms against my chest. "I'm dying to know what Heath did to you to get stuck with porta-potty duty."

She turned around, facing the gym with her back against the stage. "I'd rather not talk about him."

"Then I've got some questions about Owen Gardner..."

Kendall shook her head, but she was smiling from one corner of her mouth. "I think it's time we talk about some of your exes instead."

I tilted my head backward with a groan. "How much time do you got?"

"I take it you've dated a lot of women?"

"No, I could count on one hand the number of women I've dated in the last three years. What I mean is I've got some interesting stories. Some humorous, some traumatic. Depends on what you want to hear."

Kendall pivoted to fully face me. "Would you think I'm weird if I said I'd rather hear the traumatic stories than the funny ones?"

"No. I think that's only natural."

"How did you meet Finley's mom?" Kendall asked, pressing her hip against the edge of the stage. It wasn't a story I usually disclosed, but something about the innocence in Kendall's big, brown eyes encouraged me to open up.

"Whitney was a one-night stand."

Kendall's eyebrows lifted. "Oh."

"I was home from college for the summer. It was my twenty-first birthday, and I was I-don't-know-how-many birthday shots deep. Whitney was just—I don't know—*there*. And my dumbass friends invited her and her friends to bar-hop with us a little bit. She ended up coming home with me, and..." I stopped to swallow, the details of that night blurring together like a supercut from a movie. "Well, anyway, I didn't hear from her again for eleven months."

Kendall reacted appropriately—her mouth dropping open, eyes blinking. "Wait—what?"

"Yeah, you heard me right." I ran my fingers through my hair and crossed my arms. "She was just not going to tell me. And I don't think she ever would have if this other guy she was seeing hadn't demanded a paternity test."

"So you… you weren't there when she was born?"

"By no choice of my own, no. And after that, it became an intentional choice. I—"

I chewed on my bottom lip, knowing this next part would be difficult. And I wasn't entirely sure how she'd take it or that she'd even signed up to hear all of this. She merely wanted to get me talking about my exes so I'd stop pestering her about hers. But her eyes were still locked on my face. Concentrating. Waiting.

So I hoisted myself up onto the stage, and I continued, leaning back onto my hands.

"I was young and stupid when she was an infant. I loved that girl from the first second I finally held her in my hands. But for the first year, I didn't exactly fight to see her as much as I should have. I didn't know what the hell to do with a baby. Whitney had her the majority of the time back then.

"I still had a year of college left, and as much as I'd like to blame my absence on that, it's not an excuse. I missed out on a lot of firsts. And then, when Finley was almost two, there was… an incident."

"What happened?"

I inhaled. "Whitney was taking a nap, and Finley wandered over to the neighbor's house wearing nothing but a soggy diaper. And it took—" I swallowed, struggling to find my voice. "It took the police three hours to figure out who she was, where she lived. And I guess their home was in such disarray that they decided to remove Finley, temporarily.

"She came to me in the middle of the night. They took her from her mother and brought her to my clueless ass. I was not prepared for that."

"What did you do?"

I rolled my eyes at myself. "Called my mom, what else?" Kendall smiled warmly as I continued. "She stayed with us for the first week. Helped me pick out everything Finley would need. Helped me... console her. She tried to convince me to move back to Woodvale then, but I'd just gotten hired at the publishing house and couldn't leave.

"I had Finley full-time for ten weeks while Whitney got her shit together. In the meantime, Traci—Whitney's mom—had her a couple days out of the week while I worked. I had a girlfriend watch her the other days."

Kendall pulled herself onto the stage with a grunt to sit beside me. "Well. It sounds like you had a big support system."

"I did. Still do. Minus the girlfriend," I said with a small chuckle. "But after that incident, after my brief time being Finley's full-time dad, it was hard to go back to the way things were—to barely seeing her. So that's when I stepped the fuck up and fought to see her more often. With my dad's help—he's a lawyer—I was able to get the courts to agree to let me have her every other weekend. And then Whitney actually wanted me to take her more and more, so I did. I finally did what I should have done in the first place, and I became the dad she needed me to be. A year and a half too late."

"But look at all you've done for her now," Kendall said. I felt her hand on my arm, her fingers curling around my elbow. "She is so lucky to have you, Mason."

"Maybe. But I will never forgive myself for not being there for her. Sometimes I'm grateful she was too young to remember that I wasn't there—she doesn't know. But I'll spend the rest of my life making it up to her."

I folded my hands between my legs and looked down, deciding I'd said enough now. I became aware of just how dark it had become in that gym now that the sun was beginning to set—there was an almost-eerie, orange glow cast on the gym floor at center court. I could still feel Kendall's hand touching my arm through the flannel fabric, her fingers tucked between my bicep and torso.

I turned to face her, my heart skipping a beat when I saw her face. The corners of her eyebrows lifted in a sad expression, and her eyes were welling up with tears. "Fuck, I'm sorry," I said, my words coming out in an involuntary whisper. I pulled my elbow back, the one she'd been clinging to, and placed my palm against her back. "I didn't mean to unload all of that on you right now."

"No, Mason, I'm glad you did."

A single tear dropped from her eye, and it took everything in me to keep my hands exactly where they were—one still on her back, the other fidgeting with the frayed denim around my knee.

Kendall lifted her hand to her face to wipe the tear away herself, a faint smile gradually spreading across her lips. With the sweetest chuckle, she said, "Think you could call my dad and teach him a thing or two?"

I held her gaze, wanting to ask her to open up to me like I just had with her—but I didn't want to cause her tears to flow any more than they already had. As Kendall stared back at me in silence, my heart threatened to pound right out of my chest. All I could think about was how good she smelled, how soft her lips looked—and how much I wanted to kiss her and put my hands in her hair.

So I leaned in, closing the distance between us, and did exactly that.

chapter fifteen
kendall

Mason Reed is kissing me.

Those were the words repeating in my head again and again—the only thought I was capable of producing as Mason's mouth met mine and his palm rested against my cheek. I let out a soft gasp against his lips, parting mine for him as his hand made its way to the back of my neck. His fingers were entangled in my hair, his other hand sliding lower down my back. *Mason Reed is kissing me.*

I reached out for something to hold onto, settling for the open front of his flannel shirt to pull his body closer. An involuntary moan escaped from somewhere in the back of my throat when he slipped his tongue into my mouth. *I'm kissing Mason Reed.*

And then another thought slammed into me like a speeding school bus: *I'm kissing Finley's dad.*

With a gentle tug, I pulled my mouth from his and let go of his shirt. "Mason," I rasped. He pressed his forehead against mine, lowering the hand that had just been tugging on my hair to rest on the side of my neck. "We can't."

Like me, he was out of breath. "I know," he said in this sweet, defeated way, like a student who'd just been caught misbehaving. He clamped his eyes shut and cursed under his breath. "I should—I shouldn't volunteer anymore."

Logic told me to agree, that having him so close was playing a dangerous game. But I found myself saying, "No, Finley needs you."

With his head still leaning against mine, both of his hands holding onto my upper arms, Mason snickered and scrunched his nose. "No she doesn't."

I giggled right back at him. "Okay, she doesn't—but the other kids do. And I don't want you to stop."

He pulled far enough away that he could look into my eyes, and said nothing.

With a hopeful grin, I said, "'Friend, good,' remember?"

He returned the smile and let go of me, twisting his body away from mine so he was facing the gym again. "I'd hate to disappoint… Walter."

"You can't let him down," I joked. "And I think you and I have a good system going. Just, you know…" I looked at his face. "Promise you won't kiss me again."

Nothing. No reply, just a smirk.

"Mason!"

"Okay, okay, I promise. I can do that, as long as you promise to stop—" His voice cut off as he studied my face, and his smile gradually faded into a stoic stare.

"Stop what?"

Mason shook his head. "Stop everything. Everything you do drives me wild."

"Oh." My cheeks flushed, and I felt a tingle between my legs.

I couldn't look at him. So I turned away, glancing up at the windows at the top of the wall. It was getting darker by the minute. Just as I opened my mouth to suggest we should probably go, the doors at the other end of the gym opened and Russell, the custodian, walked in with a dust mop. I could feel Mason scooting away as Russell looked our direction. "Hello," he bellowed, pushing the mop along the gym wall. "Thought I heard voices in here."

"Sorry, Russell—we'll get out of your way," I said, leaning to grab my tote bag. Mason slid off the stage and reached for my hand to help me down. As we walked out of the gym, Russel gave us a casual wave, whistling as he swept the gym floor.

We were silent the entire way to the front double doors. My mind raced with thoughts of a younger Mason trying to grapple with his newfound parenthood while finishing college and the guilt he was now carrying in his heart for not being around when Finley was a baby. If he could see himself from my perspective, he'd know he was the type of father every little girl deserved.

Outside, the air was brisk, a reminder that fall was almost officially here. When we reached the halfway point of the wide sidewalk leading to the parking lot, Mason suddenly stopped, bending over.

It took a moment for me to realize he was picking up acorns from the edge of the mulched landscape. I laughed. "What are you doing?"

"Collecting acorns for Finley," he said without looking up. He dropped a few of them into the front pocket of his flannel shirt—a gesture so annoyingly cute I had to shake my head.

It almost made me wish I hadn't just made him promise not to kiss me.

I sighed. "Stop it."

Mason straightened. "What? Should I not be stealing acorns?" He looked genuinely concerned that he'd just committed a crime. "We just like to paint little faces on them."

I rolled my eyes with a grin. "Don't say another adorable fucking word," I muttered, walking away from him. He let out a deep laugh and jogged to catch up with me at the end of the sidewalk. My car was in the staff parking lot to the right; his, I assumed, was the Jeep to our left. We had no choice but to party\ ways now, but neither of us made an attempt to turn away.

Mason dropped the rest of the acorns in his shirt pocket. After patting the plaid fabric to make sure they were secure, he ran his fingers through his hair and locked eyes with me. Though the corners of his lips lifted in a smile, there was sadness in his eyes as he said, "You being Finley's teacher is the best thing that could happen for her… and the most devastating thing to ever happen to me."

My heart ached in agreement. I felt it, too—the cruel truth of our situation. The knowledge that any sort of romantic involvement between the two of us was impossible. Forbidden. I fought the urge to reach out for some kind of goodbye embrace, his words in the gym echoing in my head: *everything you do drives me wild, Kendall.* Would he have enough restraint to keep the hug platonic? Would I?

I opted for a whispered, "See you tomorrow, Mason," before I turned and walked away.

When I got home, I looked for Jamie, knowing she'd want the details. However, I only found Daya, curled up on the couch with Titus and in the middle of an episode of *The Office.* She paused it when I came in.

"Where's Jamie?"

"Working a late shift at the Walgreens in Indy," Daya answered, scratching a growling Titus between his ears. "She said she might stay there another night depending on how tired she feels after." Daya barely opened her mouth as she spoke, and I considered sitting down beside her to ask if she wanted to talk about it. But she unpaused her show, giving it her full attention—so I bid her goodnight.

After a shower, I slipped into some silk pajamas and got under my covers—but not to sleep. I opened my text conversation with Mason, scrolling through the flirty messages he'd sent and lingered on some of my favorites—like the one in which he'd ask me to sit on his face and the text assuring me he'd know how to handle my ass. I slid my hand down the front of my underwear. My anxiety medication often made it difficult for me to get myself off manually, but when I imagined it was Mason's fingers touching me instead, I came in record time.

chapter sixteen
mason

Kissing Kendall felt like an out-of-body experience. My senses were overwhelmed—the sweet taste of her lips, the way her hands fisted the front of my shirt to pull me closer, and the soft moan that escaped from her mouth when my tongue found hers—it was dizzying. Intoxicating. She made me feel like a teenager kissing his first love.

But knowing I could never do it again—it was like being abruptly awoken from the most delightful dream. It wasn't fair.

Finley was coloring at the dining room table with my mom when I got home—and when I pulled a handful of acorns out of my pocket and placed them in front of her, she insisted on painting them immediately.

"Mason." My mom watched Finley drag out her little containers of acrylics from the cabinet in the dining room, humming as she laid everything out for us. "Shouldn't she get a bath and get ready for bed?"

I shrugged. "She had a bath last night. She's fine."

"Isn't it part of her bedtime routine, though? She needs a more consistent nighttime ritual to set the tone for bedtime, don't you think?"

"Kids don't need a bath every night. It's not good for their skin." I thought I'd read that somewhere once, at least.

My mother sighed as she pushed in her chair. "You always had a bath every single night growing up."

I wasn't in the mood for a debate, so I decided ignoring her was the better option. I sat in the chair next to Finley and crossed my arms, watching her get to work. She knew to lay out newspaper beneath her work area after we'd learned the hard way that summer just how irate my mom could get when a speck of paint tarnished her table.

She should've seen our kitchen table in our apartment in Indy—we'd turned it into a mini artist's studio.

I allowed Finley to paint for about twenty minutes, knowing my mom was half-right and she'd need to start getting ready for bed soon. Otherwise, it'd be impossible to get her out of bed on time in the morning. She showed me her favorite painted acorns—one of them represented her with blushing pink cheeks, and another one was meant to look like me, with a blond beard, delicately painted on with the finest, most precise paintbrush we owned.

There was a third acorn sitting on the newspaper alongside the other two—and this one had well-defined eyelashes. I turned it to face me, careful not to smear Finley's paint job. "So if that's me and you, is this one grandma?"

"Nope!" Finley snapped her paint set closed with one hand, swirling her paint brush around in a little jar of water with the other. "That's the mommy one."

Oh.

It felt like something heavy had been placed upon my chest, forcing every bit of air from my lungs with an exhale. *The mommy one.* She'd said it so casually, too, like I was a complete idiot for not understanding it right away. She whistled as she hopped down from the table to put her paint set away in the cabinet, leaving me to sit there staring at her little family of acorns with my chin in my hand.

Was she imagining it was Whitney?

The question was on the tip of my tongue, but I couldn't make myself say her name out loud. Not now. Not when Finley was literally skipping as she put away her art supplies.

"Uh oh, Dad," she said, twisting her arm around so I could see she was covered in purple and yellow splotches. "Looks like I'm gonna need a bath."

I rubbed my eyes. "Let's make it a quick one, okay?"

She just raised an eyebrow at me, a gesture I returned. We both knew there was no such thing as a "quick" bath.

By the time Finley was tucked in, it was forty-five minutes past her usual bedtime. As for me, I tossed and turned all night, my mind swirling with thoughts of kissing Kendall—by 3:00 a.m., I almost had myself convinced I'd dreamt the entire thing. Imagined it.

And when I finally shook her out of my mind, I kept hearing Finley's words again and again. *The mommy one.* Those three little words were just another painful reminder of what was missing from our lives.

* *

"Careful," my cousin Jake warned from the platform facing mine at the formal menswear shop downtown. The seamstress preparing to measure my pantleg glanced over her shoulder at him. Jake smirked at me. "That's the closest a woman's ever come to his junk—there's no telling what might happen."

I gave Jake the finger as he cackled at his own joke. "Ignore him," I told the poor seamstress, who shook her head, trying to suppress a smile as she whipped out her measuring tape.

"You think that's the first time I've heard that one? It's the same thing every time we get a group of boys like you in here. At least be original."

Over on the loveseat facing the platform where Jake and I were both getting our measurements taken sat Owen—whose suit was already tailored and hanging in his closet—and his college friend, Xander, whose laugh was even louder than Jake's. We'd only been here for twenty minutes, and it appeared Jake and Xander were having an unspoken contest to out-asshole each other.

"Don't make me call Sarah up and tell her I'm firing half of our wedding party," Owen said.

I remained still as the seamstress stretched her measuring tape from the crotch of my pants to the hem. "You'd better not take away my chance of hooking up with a bridesmaid," Xander said, resting a foot on the driftwood coffee table in front of him. He nudged a menswear catalog out of the way with his black boot.

"All of Sarah's bridesmaids are married women," Owen said.

Xander shrugged like this was a trivial detail he could work around.

Owen sighed. "I promise there will be plenty of single women there. Loads of teachers. Sarah literally made it an open invitation to her entire staff."

As I watched Xander's eyebrows raise in curiosity, I thought to myself—*I've got to keep this guy away from Kendall.* Though I was quite secure in my heterosexuality, I couldn't deny Xander had that whole "tall, dark, and handsome" thing going on. He was a real charismatic asshole, and wasn't that exactly what women tripped over themselves for?

Damn it.

But maybe I could steer him in another direction. Shift his focus elsewhere.

"Hey, wait," I said, holding still as the seamstress measured my waist. "Are you the Xander that—shit, I can't remember her name. The redheaded librarian, I think she mentioned you."

"Yeah?" he answered, putting his foot back on the floor. He rocked his knee from side to side, concentrating on my face. "What'd she say?"

"Oh, nothing. Just that she knew you."

"Fascinating story, my guy," he said. Jake shook with laughter, and the seamstress measuring his arms asked him to hold still.

I sighed, getting annoyed. I really hated this guy. "I mean, she was smiling when she talked about you. Is she just a friend, or—?"

Xander shook his head, glancing at Owen. "She's just—Abigail."

Hearing that name made Owen's eyes widen. "Oh, right. I should've known when he mentioned the red hair." He pushed against Xander's shoulder with his closed fist. "I mean, she's single right now, isn't she?"

"Think so," Xander answered, turning back to me. "And she's *all* yours."

"Oh, I'm not interested in—" I paused as the seamstress measured my chest, her head a little close to mine. "That's not why I was asking." Clearly, there was some kind of history between Xander and that librarian, but he wasn't going to share it with the class.

He rolled his eyes. "Anyway, who else? I'm gonna start looking these babes up on the school website. Grissom, right?"

Owen and I exchanged glances as Xander pulled out his phone.

"Those teachers like to get dirty, from what I hear," Jake said, winking at his brother. Owen inhaled, glaring at Jake—he was getting closer and closer to firing his wedding party every second, it appeared.

A second later, it dawned on me Jake might have been talking about Kendall—not Sarah. Maybe both. Either way, Owen would know.

I was struggling to push that thought out of my mind when Xander sat up a little straighter. "Here we go. Lookie there, it's Principal Lavely—soon to be Principal Gardner." He lifted his eyebrows at Owen. "And—*holy shit*, is this kindergarten teacher going to be there?"

He didn't have to say anything—I already knew. And Owen's blank stare when Xander flipped his phone around to show him confirmed it—he was talking about Kendall. Xander must not have been aware of Owen's past with her, so it couldn't have been very serious. Still, there was some hesitancy in Owen's eyes as he said, "Well—"

"Ms. Kendall Devin," Xander interrupted, turning his screen back around and zooming in on her headshot. "She is..." Instead of finishing the sentence, he let out a low whistle and flashed the "okay" sign, punctuating the gesture with a click of his tongue.

Both of my hands were clenched into fists. "Relax your arms, baby," the seamstress told me.

"She'll definitely be there," Owen said. "Just—please—don't."

"Oh, I most certainly will," Xander said.

"You sound pretty damn sure of yourself," I blurted, every word tinged with disdain. My eyes locked on his, but I could see Jake and Owen turning toward me in the corner of my eye.

Xander lowered his phone to his lap, returning my cold stare. "I *am* sure of myself."

Neither of us looked away. The seamstress circled around me, tugging at the bottom of my suit jacket and muttering something to herself, but I barely registered her presence because I was busy strangling Xander with my eyes.

At last, Owen broke the awkward silence by clearing his throat and saying, "So, Mason here—his daughter is in Kendall's class, and he volunteers in there sometimes."

Xander was the first to break eye contact, bringing his phone closer to his face to get a better look at Kendall. "I mean, if my kid's teacher looked like that, I'd be volunteering, too. *Damn.*"

I sucked in a breath. "Got any kids, Xander?"

Rather than answer me, he just laughed at the absurdity of that notion. Jake spoke for him. "Xander probably has at least a dozen illegitimate children out in the world. We try not to think about it."

With his eyes back on me, Xander said, "I'm tryin' to add a little blonde one to the roster after this wedding."

The seamstress pulled away to jot my chest measurements down in a tiny notebook. "Well," I said, running my hands down the length of the open suit jacket. "I've gotta say, watching Kendall Devin reject you just might be the highlight of that wedding for me, *'my guy.'*"

All at once, Jake, Owen, and both seamstresses burst into laughter, and the initial scowl on Xander's face eventually softened into a grin. "You just wait and see. Wait and see."

I looked forward to it.

Once our suits were fitted, ordered, and paid for, Owen and I stood between our cars in the parking lot as the other two drove off. He returned Jake's middle finger as he pulled out of the lot into the street before turning to me, shaking his head in amusement. He and his brother couldn't be more different.

"How's *STEM for the Win* going?" I asked him, crossing my arms. "What's next for you?"

Owen inhaled. "Well—a lot. Finishing the second book. Adding some new merch to the shop. Got a speaking gig in Atlanta in December."

"You just never stop, do you?"

He grinned. "No. Sarah says I need to slow down. But what about you? How's working for yourself going?" He never liked talking about himself or his accomplishments, so his attempt to shift the focus to me wasn't surprising. "I don't know if I said this to you before, but I think it's pretty impressive that you decided to quit your job and freelance. I know firsthand that takes guts."

I swallowed. Guts? What I was doing didn't take guts. I'd made the switch out of necessity because I was so desperate for help with Finley. My current earnings were a small fraction of my old salary, and I was putting in minimal effort.

I was nothing like him.

"It's—I love the flexibility. But it's the stability that I miss," I admitted. "I mean, I'm raising a kid in my parents' basement. Alone. I'm not exactly thriving."

Owen stared at me for a good while, carefully considering his next words. "You're just laying the foundation for something greater, that's all. This part is just temporary."

I just shrugged. I wanted to believe him—and deep down, I knew this situation wasn't forever. I just didn't know if I had the gumption to pull myself out of it. I'd been looking for the motivation to move onto something better since we got here four months ago, and I still hadn't found it.

I was exactly what my dad said I was—stagnant.

* *

I spent the majority of Sunday night tossing and turning yet again, anticipating having to face Kendall after kissing her. 7:00 a.m. came too quickly, and I was dragging the entire time I got Finley ready for school. Her braid that day was sloppy, but it was good enough. I prayed the extra espresso shot in my coffee at Riverside would jolt me awake before I got to the school.

But Kendall's reaction to the caramel macchiato I brought her energized me more than any latte could—she accepted it graciously and held it with two hands as she took her first sip, closing her eyes because it was just that good—and the little sound that emitted from her throat was so similar to the one she'd made when my tongue was in her mouth that it momentarily took my breath away.

The perverted comment on the tip of my tongue threatened to spill out, but I somehow mustered up the strength to keep it inside, choosing instead to pull out my iPad and show her the updated t-shirt design. She approved it, choosing the color version—and had me email it to her.

And that morning, we only talked about the festival until the kids arrived. Neither of us mentioned the kiss.

We were professional. Mature. I did what she asked me to do, playing the rhyming game from the previous week, and then she sent me to the hallway to staple the kids' apple writing crafts to a bulletin board. I grinned at Finley's: *My name is FINLEY and I like GREEN apples the best.*

Anyone watching Kendall and me interact that morning would have never guessed we'd kissed just days earlier—would never be able to tell how badly I wanted her when I returned the stapler to her desk and sat in her chair to observe the end of her lesson.

But they might have noticed the way Kendall praised Finley when she was first to sound out the word "zip," how she told her "you're so smart!" and glanced my direction for half a second before returning to her lesson with a playful grin. And they might have observed the way I crossed my ankle over my knee and folded my hands on my stomach, too distracted by her phonics lesson to remember she'd left some laminated apple cards for me to cut out on her desk.

At the end of her lesson, she asked the children to find a quiet, independent activity until lunch and walked over to her desk. "My name is Mason, and I like red apples the best," I said, spinning in her desk chair to face her.

Kendall flashed a smile my direction as she set her notebook down on her desk. She had on a pair of black pants that hugged her ass in the most remarkable way—it took some effort to keep my eyes on her face as she leaned over the side of her desk to reach for her coffee.

"Are you prepared for Wednesday?" she asked.

I blinked up at her in confusion until she tapped the stack of permission slips on the corner of her desk—one of which I'd signed last week. "Oh, right. Apple orchard day."

She took a sip before saying, "I hope you're ready for the chaos that is apple-picking with twenty-five feral kindergarteners."

"I'm sure it'll be—" I stopped talking when I spotted a painted acorn propped up against a pencil holder, hidden behind her coffee a moment ago.

It was the one with the eyelashes—the "mommy" one.

Kendall followed my gaze. "Oh, Finley brought me that this morning," she said with a little laugh. "She says it looks like me."

The words that had crushed my heart last week repeated in my mind now as I watched Kendall adjust that same acorn on her desk, wedging it between her pencil cup and a folder tray so it stood upright.

I cleared my throat as I looked up at her face, her long eyelashes more noticeable from this angle. "I mean, the resemblance *is* uncanny—you just need a French beret."

She let out a sweet laugh and fiddled with her lanyard between two fingers, glancing down at her coffee to avoid my stare, which was no doubt intense. And when some boys on the other side of the room began to get a bit rowdy, and she had to set her coffee down and take care of the situation, I was still unable to tear my eyes off of her.

That woman had no idea—no idea at all—the impact she'd had on my daughter in just two weeks of knowing her.

And the effect she'd had on me was even stronger. I was already under her spell. Entranced. Obsessed. But the sight of that little painted acorn on her desk, and the knowledge of what it symbolized to Finley, set my heart on fire in an unprecedented way.

chapter seventeen
kendall

We signed up for the painting class at the winery weeks ago, when I was nearing the end of my post-Heath depressive slump and Jamie insisted I find a new hobby.

Now, as Daya, Jamie, and I sat before our canvases on a balcony overlooking a vineyard on a Monday evening, I was regretting this decision. My painting of a moonlit pumpkin patch bore no resemblance to the teacher's example—it didn't even come close. The instructions were pretty straightforward—a curved line here, long, sweeping strokes there—yet I managed to mess up every single step. My lines were sloppy, my pumpkins lopsided. It looked pathetic.

In fact, the painting was so comically awful that I snapped a photo of it and sent it to Mason, to which he immediately replied: *Well, it's a good thing you don't teach art.*

My giggling caught Jamie's attention. First she looked at me, and then at my canvas. "Dude. What happened?"

"Maybe we should've done the pottery class instead," I whispered, hiding my face behind my hands.

"You think you'd be any better at *pottery*?" Jamie shook her head. "You'd be sitting there sculpting a dick while the rest of us were making vases."

Maybe it was all the wine samples they'd given us—or it could have been the sight of my horrible painting—but the laughing fit that followed Jamie's words could not be stopped. I buried my face in my smock, ignoring the instructor's commentary that "someone back there might be having a little too much fun."

Around us, everyone was working on their finishing touches, adding highlights and shadows, but I decided I'd done enough damage. I traded my paintbrush for my wine glass and watched Jamie and Daya finish instead.

I stared at my phone, wondering how I might reply to Mason's text—or if I even should. It didn't feel right to flirt and lead him on, but it was hard to resist temptation. I smiled down at my screen, contemplating sharing Jamie's dick-sculpting comment with him. Before I could think of a response, he messaged me again.

Mason: Here's what I'm working on. Doodled this while listening to Owen's podcast.

I'd hardly call the drawing he'd just sent a "doodle." I gasped when it loaded. It was a digital illustration of the most adorable fox—a girl, I assumed, based on her long eyelashes and the little purple bow—and she was wearing a lab coat and holding a beaker.

Kendall: That is the cutest thing I have ever seen.

Kendall: Please tell me you're going to send that to Owen? I bet he'd share it with his followers.

Mason: I don't care about Owen's followers. This right here is a Kendall Devin exclusive.

"You know," Jamie said, clearing her throat. I snapped out of my Mason-induced trance, but my grin remained. "You haven't stopped smiling ever since James from *Twilight* kissed you."

I winced—that might have been her worst nickname for Mason yet. "Jesus, can you just call him by his actual name?"

"Wait, they kissed?" Daya leaned forward so she could see me. "You *kissed?*"

"It was nothing."

Jamie crossed her arms. "Who were you just texting?"

"Mom...?"

Jamie and Daya laughed.

"Well, what are you going to do now?" Daya asked. Around us, some of the women were finishing up, cleaning out their brushes and removing their smocks, while others were still working on adding more details to their paintings.

"Nothing," I answered, pulling my smock over my head. "I'm going to do nothing."

"Ooh," Jamie said, perking up. "You could use his dick pic as inspo if we ever take that pottery class." Without giving it a second thought, I picked up my paintbrush and flicked pale yellow paint at her. Most of it splattered on her smock, but a small speck landed in her hair. "You little—" she started, and she dipped her fingers in her jar of paint water. I covered my face, narrowly escaping her retaliatory splash.

Daya stood up to remove her smock, dropping it onto her chair. "Play nice, you two—I'm going to go talk to the instructor for a minute."

Jamie watched Daya walk away. "What's that about?" I asked.

"She said she's going to sign up for the next few classes."

"Oh," I said, pulling my smock over my head. "Are you going to join her?"

"I don't think so." Jamie used her smock to wipe the paint from her hair. "Might be good for her to have something to focus on besides work and... me."

They were only spending four or five evenings together a week as it was. I hoped, if just for Daya's sake, that whole absence-makes-the-heart-grow-fonder thing was true.

My sister eyed my painting again, shaking her head. "That monstrosity is going up in our living room."

**

On Wednesday morning, Mason showed up for the apple orchard field trip in dark denim overalls—cuffed at the hems—and a black t-shirt with black high-top Chuck Taylors. No flannel in sight. I never would've guessed a man in overalls could be so sexy, but it was really doing something for me. I kept my flirty thoughts to myself, though, considering he wasn't the only volunteer that day. Elijah's mom, Cara, and Trinity's dad, Noah, were also chaperoning.

Noah Sherman was on the school board, and though he'd been nothing but kind since Meet-the-Teacher night, there was still an aura of authority around him that made me uneasy. It didn't help that he was wearing a suit that day.

"He's here to negotiate a contract with Johnny Appleseed," Mason whispered in my ear while I counted children as they made their way to the bus that morning.

I covered my laughter with a forced cough. "Stop. He's on the school board," I warned, my voice low enough no one would overhear. "So be on your best behavior."

Mason smirked, squeezing Finley's hand as she pulled him toward the bus. "Hmm." He rubbed his chin in mock contemplation. "But there's so much I could tell him about you."

I rolled my eyes, but my smile gave away my true mood. "Just get on the bus."

How many kids had I just counted? Once again, I'd let Mason Reed distract me—and I had to completely start over.

The apple orchard was a ten-minute drive east of Woodvale. I kept my eye on the sky as the bus turned off the highway—though it was currently sunny and 70 degrees, the clouds in the eastern sky were dark and ominous. I prayed the storm would hold off.

When we stepped off the bus, we were greeted by Mr. and Mrs. Howard, the apple orchard owners. They introduced us to their calico cat, Braeburn, who didn't seem to mind being crowded and petted by a dozen pairs of hands at once. I supposed she was accustomed to this kind of attention. She even rolled onto her back like a dog, allowing the kids to pet her belly.

"We normally start with a slide show inside," Mr. Howard said, before motioning toward the sky. "But let's go ahead and start with apple-picking, shall we? See if we can beat the rain."

The old man went over a few basic rules—each child could pick one apple, only from the designated trees. Don't touch any tools that might have been left out. Stick together. And so on.

We began our walk up the hill between the rows of trees. I had assigned six children to each chaperone, but we mainly stuck together as a group as we listened to Mr. and Mrs. Howard talk about the different apple varieties and everything they made with them.

The air was thick with the scent of rotting apples, which the honeybees seemed to be enjoying. The kids were excited to see Braeburn had followed us the entire way, some of us—myself included—too busy watching the cat chase grasshoppers to pay much attention to Mr. Howard's apple lecture.

We made our way up and over hills, through rows of Granny Smith, golden delicious, and Fuji apple trees, stopping often so the kids could choose one to pick. I watched Mason pull a red delicious apple from a tree, wipe it on the front of his overalls, and take a bite. "You're supposed to wait," I told him.

He responded by taking another bite inches from my face, smirking as he chewed. And then something behind me caught his eye. "It looks like all hell's about to break loose," he said, nodding his head forward. I turned around to see the darkening sky, now contrasted with a wall of white clouds at its forefront.

The farther we got from the bus and the main building, the more I began to internally panic. But the Howards didn't seem concerned—they just kept walking and talking. I tried to bring up the radar on my phone, but the service out there wasn't the greatest. It never loaded.

Mason and I brought up the rear of the group. It was easy for me to keep an eye on all of the kids that way, to make sure there weren't any stragglers. As we made our way down the well-trodden dirt path between the trees, Finley ran up to her dad and grabbed him by the hand.

Then, after shoving her little Granny Smith apple down into Mason's pocket, she slipped her other hand into mine, walking between us with the biggest grin on her face. I looked over at Mason, and it appeared he was fighting the urge to smile, too, staring down at the ground as we walked. It felt a little funny, especially when Cara turned to look at us, but Finley couldn't have been happier about it. "Are you having fun, Finley?" I asked her.

"Uh huh," she said. We continued walking hand in hand, the three of us, until Finley spotted Elijah struggling to reach a yellow apple on a tree. She ran up ahead to pull the branch down so Elijah could pick the apple himself.

"She, uh, gets her height from her mom's side," Mason said quietly, making me giggle. He wasn't exactly what I'd call short—but he wasn't that tall, either. That was probably where some of the cockiness came from.

"She gets her kindness from you," I said, watching Finley walk side-by-side with Elijah, the boy she'd decided to take under her wing the very moment she met him. I'd never known a more compassionate kindergartener. I opened my mouth to praise Mason on his parenting skills when my phone rang in my pocket.

It was the school. "Hello?"

"Finally!" It was Sarah on the other end, and she sounded panicked. "I haven't been able to get through to you. Are you still at the orchard?"

"Yes. Why?"

"Are you indoors?"

I turned around to assess how far we'd walked. The bus looked like a matchbox car from where we stood. "We're in the middle of the orchard now. What's going on?"

"There's a severe thunderstorm warning. Vincennes just got pelted with hail, and it's all heading your way. Fast. Is there a safe place to go nearby?"

"Um." I spun around. There were no buildings in sight, and it started sprinkling. "Not exactly. But we'll head for shelter right now."

"Okay. Hanging up so you can take care of it. Text me when it's all clear."

Up ahead, Mr. Howard was in the middle of showing the students an apple-grabbing tool. Either he couldn't tell it was starting to sprinkle, or he didn't care.

"Mr. Howard," I interrupted, walking up to him. "I hate to cut this tour short, but my principal just let me know there's a severe storm heading toward us. We're going to need to head back."

Thunder rumbled in the distance. "Probably fast," Mason added.

Mrs. Howard turned to her husband, her eyes wide. "Should you send Richie for the wagon?"

Mr. Howard nodded. "You kids wanna go on a hayride?"

Of course they did. All around us, the children erupted into cheers. Mr. Howard pulled a walkie talkie from his pocket and asked someone—Richie, apparently—to come pick us up with the wagon. "Sit tight for a couple of minutes, kiddos. My son's going to take us on a ride in just a couple of minutes."

The lack of urgency was sending my anxiety through the roof. Mason must have been able to see the panic on my face, because he touched me on the back of the arm and said, "We'll make it."

By the time Richie made it to us with a rickety wagon pulled behind an ancient blue tractor, the sprinkling turned into a drizzle. We all began grabbing kids and lifting them onto the wagon, which was in no way prepared for a hayride. For starters, there was no hay—instead, this wagon was full of tools and ropes. Everything was covered in a layer of dirt that would soon become mud. It was enough to make me consider having us all run down to the building instead, but half of the kids were already seated and chanting, "Hay-ride! Hay-ride!"

A streak of lightning flashed in the distant sky, immediately followed by twenty or so high-pitched screams. I grasped Noah Sherman's extended hand as I pulled myself onto the wagon, relying on his support to steady myself. There wasn't much room left on this wagon for all of the adults to sit, so Noah and Mason decided at the last second they would instead run down the hill and meet us there.

"Show-offs," Cara said with a chuckle, rolling her eyes as the wagon lurched forward. I forced out a laugh, squeezing between Finley and Walter.

"I hope my daddy's okay," Finley worried aloud. She was squeezing Elijah's hand. The men were fast—and the sight of Noah Sherman trailing behind Mason in his gray suit was almost enough to make my anxiety subside.

Almost.

The whole way back, I devised a plan in my head. At the bottom of that hill, I'd be dealing with twenty-five wet kids, all of whom would be trying to jump off of this wagon at the same time. "Listen, friends," I announced as loudly as I could. "When this wagon comes to a stop, we're going to play the freeze game.

Nobody jumps down by themselves. Wait for Mr. Reed or Mr. Sherman to help you down. Does everyone understand?"

There were a few "yeahs," but the kids were mostly distracted by the rain, some of them trying to catch it in their mouths. To my relief, most of them listened when the wagon pulled up to the porch at the front of the Howards' main building. Mason and Noah leapt into action, hoisting kids from the wagon and setting them down on the covered porch, where Cara and Mrs. Howard corralled them all. I helped pass the kids to the men, a clap of thunder spurring us all to pick up the pace. It was raining harder now, soaking us to the bone as we hurried to get the children to safety.

As Noah lifted the very last child from the wagon, her feet swung out in my direction. I attempted to take a step backwards in order to avoid being kicked in the stomach. And just as I did, Mason's eyes widened. "Watch out for the—"

But it was too late. Before he could finish his warning, I was already tripping backwards over a pile of rusty chains I had forgotten was there. With nothing to grab onto to catch myself, I was falling.

One second I was standing in that wagon, and the next, I was in Mason's arms.

If he hadn't been there to catch me, I would have fallen into the puddle below, perhaps even hitting my head on the planter of mums on the way down.

Instinctively, I threw my arms around Mason's neck and hung on for dear life. The rain and wind had picked up, but we were half-covered by the porch's overhang. The absence of chattering voices let me know the kids had safely been escorted inside. Mason kept his eyes locked on mine—and with one arm around my back and the other tucked beneath my thighs, he didn't let go.

"I've got you," he said, his voice barely audible over the sound of the rain hitting the tin roof.

Noah laughed and murmured something that sounded like "that was a close one" before he jogged ahead to join everyone inside. The door swung shut behind him, and Mason and I were alone.

I blinked up at his face. All of the words he couldn't say out loud were written in the depths of his cerulean eyes, concentrating on my face. "Thank you," I choked out. I licked my lips, remembering I was still the person in charge here, despite my clumsiness, and needed to manage the chaos that was likely ensuing on the other side of that door. "You can put me down now, Mason."

"Sorry," he said, chuckling to cover up the awkwardness as he carefully set me down on the porch. His hands steadied my hips until I found my footing, and then he let go.

The entire interaction couldn't have lasted more than thirty seconds, yet the warmth of his touch lingered in every spot his body had made contact with mine. Even as I hurried inside, I could still feel his hand on my thigh, his arm cradling my back. His solid body propping mine up so I wouldn't meet my demise on the ground below.

I felt him everywhere.

As Cara, Noah, and I passed out applesauce pouches to the children, I caught a glimpse of Mason through the window—he was standing at the edge of the porch, staring out at the rain falling on the apple trees with his arms dangling at his sides. When I bent down to help Avery unscrew the top of her applesauce beside the window, I witnessed Mason flex both of his hands—like the memory of my touch was lingering there for him, too.

chapter eighteen
mason

I remained alone on that rain-slicked porch for only a minute or two—just long enough to gather my thoughts and allow my heart to return to a tempo that didn't threaten to outpace the steady raindrops hitting the tin roof.

I felt as though I could still feel Kendall there in my arms, even after she'd gone inside. She was the perfect fit, yet entirely out of reach. The universe had quite literally dropped the most amazing woman into my arms while simultaneously dictating I could never have her. Not in the way I hoped.

The sound of hail pelting against metal alerted me it was time to join the others inside. As I helped distribute cups filled with freshly pressed apple cider, I made a conscious effort to avoid meeting Kendall's gaze.

I just couldn't look at her.

After the kids finished their snacks, Mr. Howard ushered everyone into a different room to show how they sorted and packaged all the apples. The kids were a little mystified to discover they had to give up the apples they'd picked themselves to be sorted, even after Mr. Howard promised to send their teacher back to school with a bag of fresh apples.

Finley scowled for the remainder of the tour.

For the last segment of the field trip, Mr. and Mrs. Howard led the children into a room with rows of metal chairs facing a white projector screen. "Let's hope the power doesn't go out," Noah muttered as we stood at the back of the room with Kendall and Cara.

"That'd be just our luck," Cara said, crossing her arms.

Noah shook his head. "It couldn't be more clear they weren't ready for us today. What a mess." And then, pointing toward me, he added, "And this guy saved them from a lawsuit."

Cara's brows furrowed. "What do you mean?"

Noah nodded toward Kendall. "We almost lost our teacher here. She fell out of the wagon, and if he hadn't been there to catch her…?" He let his voice trail off and raised his eyebrows. "I tell you what, this day would be going very differently."

Cara let out an astonished chuckle as she turned to face me. "Wow. Good on you for catching her."

I eyed Kendall, whose hands were tucked delicately into her skirt pockets beside me. She chewed her lip and stared ahead at the kids, all of them enthralled with the apple life cycle film. I gave Cara a casual shrug, saying, "I was merely in the right place at the right time."

"I'd say you were," Noah said. "And they're lucky, too. I think I might make a complaint. They never should have led us that far into the orchard when there was a storm approaching."

"Nope," Cara agreed.

The two of them continued to complain about the Howards while Kendall and I remained quiet. There was some discussion of writing to the Woodvale Times and posting about it on the Concerned Citizens of Woodvale Facebook page—those two were determined to drag the poor Howards down by any means necessary. It all seemed a bit over the top to me. The kids were fine, and so was their teacher.

I wanted to interject, to tell them they were overreacting, but I kept my mouth shut for Kendall's sake. The last thing she needed right now was an argument between chaperones in the middle of an already chaotic field trip. So I stood back and watched the film without saying a word.

That is, until Noah Sherman decided to put his hand on Kendall's lower back and lean in close to tell her she still seemed a little shaken up.

"Oh, I'm okay," Kendall said, letting out a nervous chuckle.

I glared at Noah's hand—and if my eyes weren't deceiving me, it was sliding even lower down Kendall's backside. Her arms clung tightly to her sides as she shifted her weight from one foot to the other, leaning ever-so-slightly away from him. She wanted his hand off. But there it remained as he leaned in a second time, as though he didn't want Cara or me to overhear him say, "Your clothes are soaked. I hope you've got something dry to change into at the school." His eyes darted to her chest.

Fuck this guy.

Kendall tucked her damp hair behind her ear. "I—"

"Maybe you could run home and grab some of your wife's clothes for her to borrow," I suggested.

Noah and Kendall turned to me in unison, both of their mouths falling open.

Before he had the chance to muster up some shitty explanation for touching her, I kept going. "Speaking of your wife—let me see that ring. Is that diamond-encrusted?" I crossed my arms and nodded toward his left ring finger, which was still resting just above Kendall's butt.

"Uh—" Noah slowly pulled his hand away from Kendall's body and glanced down at his gold wedding band. "Yes. It is."

I tucked my thumbs under the straps of my overalls. "Wow. That is some ring. Kendall—I'm sorry, Ms. Devin—did you see it?"

Kendall looked more uncomfortable now than she had before I opened my stupid mouth. Her face was pale, and while she ever-so-slightly shook her head, the rest of her body was tense and rigid. Her eyes were focused on the projector screen at the front of the room. "Let's just learn about the apple life cycle, shall we?"

At that exact second, lightning illuminated the entire room—immediately followed by an enormous crack of thunder. The lights went out, the film came to a stop, and the kids erupted into screams, some of them jumping to their feet. And without any hesitation at all, Kendall stepped forward and her voice carried over their heads: "Everyone stay exactly where you are. Do not get up. We're safe." Despite the floor-to-ceiling windows along the wall, the room was so dark I could just barely make out Finley putting her arm around Elijah's shoulders. The kids' screaming turned into giggles as Kendall repeated, "We're safe right where we are."

Mr. Howard walked over to one of the windows with his hands in his pockets and stared out at his orchard. "It's a good thing we did the apple-picking first, huh?" He turned to us with a laugh.

Kendall made her way around to the front of the room to lead the kids in a few songs while we waited out the storm. Meanwhile, Noah and I stood shoulder-to-shoulder. He didn't look my direction once, though I was practically daring him to with my eyes.

When the power finally came back on, it was too late to do anything else. The children needed to get back to school in time for lunch, Kendall explained. On our way out, she turned to Mrs. Howard and said, "Thank you, again, for everything. I'll see you at the Fall Festival."

Mrs. Howard slapped her hand against her forehead. "Oh good heavens, I forgot to let you know. We're not going to be able to set up our caramel apple stand. Bob's having back surgery that Thursday."

I could see the devastation on Kendall's face as she replied, "Oh no, I'm so sorry to hear that. I hope his surgery goes well."

Her "oh no" had nothing to do with Bob's injured back and everything to do with caramel apples.

I half-listened to Mrs. Howard prattle on about her husband's surgeries and his numerous ailments to Kendall, who did her best not to appear bored, as we led the line of kids to the bus. The rain had mostly subsided, reduced to a misty drizzle.

There were puddles everywhere, which some of the kids couldn't resist stomping in on their way to the bus.

Finally, Kendall shook hands with the Howards and stepped down off the porch to join us. When we reached the door of the bus, I turned to face her. "Hey," I said, keeping my voice low as Walter walked between us to step up onto the bus.

Kendall looked up at me, holding a paper bag full of apples against her chest with one arm, the other waving for the last few kids to hurry up the steps.

"Sorry for butting in earlier," I said. "But—he was sexually harassing you."

"And you're the only one of my students' fathers allowed to do *that*," she snapped, her eyes locked on mine as she gently nudged the last child up the bus steps.

Shit. She had every right to say what she'd just said, but still—her words stung. I swallowed and looked down at my muddy Chucks, knowing I probably deserved to be called out like this. "I—I'm sorry," I said, my voice almost drowned out by the rhythmic sweep of the bus's windshield wipers.

"No," Kendall said, clutching my bicep. She pulled me toward her, bringing my ear to her mouth so she could whisper, "I wasn't being sarcastic. I was letting you know."

Oh.

Kendall shoved the bag of apples in my arms without another word and stepped up onto the bus. A subtle, flirtatious smile played upon her lips, leaving me momentarily speechless in her wake.

That woman absolutely killed me.

* *

Back at school, Finley was having a hard time letting go.
Literally.

143

She clung to my legs at the classroom door, tears streaming down her red cheeks, begging me to stay. I looked up at Kendall in desperation as the rest of the kids lined up for lunch. "I don't know why she's doing this. I'm so sorry."

The more I tried to pull her hands off my calves, the tighter she held on.

"Finley, come on. I got to be with you longer today than most other days." I grunted as I pried one of her hands off of me, only for her to immediately clutch onto my leg in a different spot.

"That might be the problem," Kendall said as she crouched beside Finley, her skirt pooling on the floor around her. She rubbed Finley's back. "It's hard to come back to school after a really exciting morning, isn't it?"

Finley sniffled. Listening, but not responding.

"The day's already halfway over, Finley. And you know what else? We could get out the apple playdough again this afternoon. Won't that be fun?"

Finley nodded, and much to my relief, she let go of my legs and fell against her teacher's chest instead, almost knocking her off balance. "There you go," Kendall said with a laugh, returning the hug. She stood up with Finley in her arms and looked at me. "She's going to be just fine, Daddy."

Don't react to her calling you daddy don't react to her calling you daddy don't react to her—

I avoided Kendall's stare as I leaned in to kiss Finley on the temple, a mere four inches from her teacher's face. "Be a good girl for Ms. Devin, okay?" And then, after a quick glance at Kendall's tight-lipped smile, I added, "And tell Ms. Devin she needs to be a good girl, too."

This elicited some giggles from them both.

I pulled away, pausing for a moment to savor the sight of my daughter's arms around Kendall's neck. And, after a wink that carried different meanings for each of them, I turned and left.

The second I stepped out of the main door into the cool, misty air, I pulled my phone out of my pocket and started making calls. Bakeries, candy stores, local farmer's markets. One by one, I called every business I could think of that might make caramel apples, my hopes sinking with each refusal. They all pointed me in the same direction—the apple orchard. None of these people had the capacity to make and sell as many caramel apples as we'd need.

I was feeling discouraged about this, still trying to come up with a solution for Kendall in the back of my mind as I worked on some graphics for a client back home. Not even a request for an interview from one of the companies I'd applied to could get Kendall's caramel apples off my mind. I saved the email—I'd come back to it later when I had better focus.

After being rejected by the apple orchard in the next county over, I was starting to accept I'd run out of options. This idea, this grand gesture I wanted to perform just to make Kendall smile, wasn't within the realm of possibility.

But as I helped my mom unpack her grocery delivery later that afternoon, I noticed a bag of apples nestled in one of the sacks, and another idea sprang to mind.

"How much do you love me, Mom?" I asked, taking one of the apples out and rinsing it in the sink. She peered over her glasses at me as I pulled myself up onto the kitchen counter and took a bite.

"Oh boy. What do you want, Masey?"

I grinned, deciding to let that "Masey" comment slide right now. "Wouldn't you love to make a few dozen caramel apples for Finley's school?"

She tilted her chin down and glared at me as she dropped one of the grocery sacks into the recycling. "Um, no. I would not *love* to do that. I have about a billion other things on my plate right now."

No she didn't. "Ask your church lady friends to help. Oh, you know what?" I snapped my fingers and pointed at her. "You guys could set up a booth at the fall festival to sell them and hand out flyers for your church's trunk-or-treat thing. Every kid in Woodvale will be at this event."

She leaned on the counter without saying a word. But the wheels were turning.

"It's for a good cause?" I offered. "I'll get the apples and everything you need. Just make the things and show up and sell them." *And make sure Finley's teacher gets one.*

She crossed her arms and shook her head, but I knew it wasn't really a "no." I was still going to have to pull the grandparent card. "It would make Finley so happy."

"Good Lord," she said, rolling her eyes. "These caramel apples must be really important to you. And I'll tell you what— I'll talk to the fellowship committee about it. They'll all need to agree."

With my mouth full of apple, I mumbled, "Thanks. I knew you'd make the right decision." I narrowly avoided the empty grocery sack she hurled at my head.

I shook my head at myself, taking one last bite of the apple in my hands. Hopping down from the counter to help my mom put her groceries away, I smiled as I imagined how Kendall would react to the news she'd be getting her caramel apple stand after all.

chapter nineteen
kendall

"That's not how we did it last year" was becoming my new least-favorite phrase. I heard it every week, sometimes two or three times, as the fall festival grew closer. Lori, in particular, made it her personal goal to berate me at every opportunity. "You haven't posted the entertainment schedule yet?"

No, Lori, I don't even have all the entertainment blocks filled yet.

Each time Sarah checked in on my progress, I assured her everything was coming together. However, a new problem presented itself every day. I kept encountering little snags or issues I hadn't considered before, and by the time festival week came around, my sloppily written to-do list was two notebook pages long. I was on the verge of throwing in the towel and admitting to Sarah I couldn't do this after all.

The caramel apple vendor pulling out was just another setback I didn't have time to dwell on. I'd never be able to find a replacement with such short notice, which meant I had to shift all the food vendors around on my festival map.

My map looked like a kindergartener had drawn it, but Sarah was still impressed. And though she squinted at it and rotated it again and again in order to comprehend it, she didn't have a single negative thing to say. "Look at how much this has grown since last year."

"Well, yeah," I said with a nonchalant shrug in one of her leather office chairs. "You said you wanted all of Woodvale there. I mean, they can't just ride the Ferris wheel the whole time." I chuckled to let her know I wasn't mad—just overwhelmed.

"But thirty-six vendors?" Sarah looked up from my terribly drawn map in astonishment. "The used book drive? The petting zoo? How are you not losing your mind right now?"

I was. "Copious amounts of coffee."

Sarah lifted her eyebrows as she slid the festival map across her desk toward me. "Aha, you're a girl after my own heart." With a glance at her smartwatch, a birthday gift from Owen, she said, "By the way, I recruited Owen to help us with the lanterns."

Sarah had invited me over to her house Friday evening to assemble sixteen mason jar lanterns to illuminate the eating area by the food trucks. She had the jars already—she planned to use them for her wedding—but we needed to fix them up with electric tealights, faux leaves, and little craft pumpkins. "Oh, good." I said, uncrossing my legs. "That'll make it go faster."

Her eyes lingered on my face for a moment. I'd begun to recognize that look, so I prepared myself for what would now be the fourth apology. "Are you sure that's okay?"

"Why wouldn't it be?" I challenged.

She blinked. "I just don't want to be that person that's like, 'my boyfriend will be joining us' when it was supposed to be a girls' night."

Maybe I had misread her. "No, I'm glad he's helping. Maybe we can con him into doing all the work while we… get drunk and play with his robots."

"Perfect," Sarah said with a laugh, flipping her dark hair off her shoulders. No awkward apology after the mention of Owen's name this time. Every conversation we had brought us closer to becoming actual friends—something I wanted more than I was willing to admit to myself.

* *

My desk was as messy as my mind that week. It was so cluttered, in fact, that it took me five minutes to find the laminated leaves I wanted Mason to help me cut out. "I swear they're here somewhere," I told him, a little embarrassed that he was seeing me like this. Not that I ever held any illusion of having it all together. "I'm sorry, I'm a mess this week. Oh, look—"

Beneath a stack of phonics worksheets, I found three fall festival t-shirts—Mason's, Finley's, and mine.

"These came in yesterday afternoon," I said, holding up Finley's little shirt.

"Aww," Mason responded, taking the shirt from my hands so he could get a better look at the design. "This looks pretty good, if I do say so myself."

"They're perfect."

Mason folded the shirt back up, dropping it on the little table behind him. And he turned back to me with expectant eyes—looking from me to my desk and back to me.

"What?"

"Weren't you... looking for something?"

"Oh, yeah. ADHD strikes again," I said, giggling nervously. As I moved some of the mess around on my desk, I noticed Mason smiling in my peripheral vision. Finally, I came across the laminated sheets of leaves featuring all of our recent sight words—I was going to tape them around the walls in the hallway and let the kids go on a "leaf hunt," writing down all the words they could find. There were forty leaves total, and cutting them out was going to be a pain in the ass—which is why I wasn't going to make Mason do them all himself.

I handed him half of the stack and a pair of scissors, and he sat in his chair and got to work. He made do with the tiny, uncluttered former of my desk without complaining. "So, just making an observation here—you seem a little stressed."

I lowered myself into my desk chair and pulled my hair back in a claw clip. "A little?" I slid the trashcan out from beneath my desk and placed it between us so I wouldn't have little cut-up pieces of laminating sheets all over my floor. "I feel like I'm on the brink of a major failure. This event is getting so much exposure that I truly believe all of Woodvale is actually going to be present—and it's going to be a huge letdown."

Mason furrowed his brows as he cut a yellow maple leaf featuring the word *see*. "Yeah, the sight of that enormous Ferris wheel is really going to… bum people out."

"Shut up, you know what I mean," I said, trying not to smile. "I just—I'm honestly ready for this event to be over with so I can stop thinking about it."

Mason took a deep breath. "Okay, I get that—but promise me something."

"What?"

He continued concentrating on his cutting, going around each point of the maple leaf with care. "Promise me you'll enjoy yourself Saturday. I know you'll be busy and stressing that night—but you have to at least allow yourself to have a little bit of fun while it's happening."

I slowly shook my head. "I don't think I can promise that. My anxiety doesn't allow me to have fun, sometimes."

Mason's eyes flitted up to mine, and there was something whimsical in the upturned corners of his lips as he said, "Does your anxiety allow you to enjoy caramel apples?"

I blinked. "Yes—but there won't be any. I thought you knew that?"

He was full-on grinning now, cutting his leaf without saying a word.

"What?"

"Woodvale Methodist is going to be there, and they're going to have your caramel apples, Ms. Devin."

I tilted my head to the side and stared at him. "What are you talking about? They're not one of my vendors."

"Oh, but they're one of *my* vendors," he said, picking up another leaf to cut. "I got one of my mom's church committees to agree to do it. They're making them Friday night—it's all taken care of."

I couldn't fully grasp what he was telling me. I stared at him with my mouth wide open for ten seconds—maybe more—trying to comprehend this… this gesture. "But—how? Where'd they get the apples? Are they—are they—"

"Don't worry about it," Mason interrupted. "Just give them a spot to set up, and that's all you have to do."

"But do they have receipts? I mean, I have to—"

"You don't have to do a single thing." He eyed my sloppy map, which was sitting in the center of my desk. "Just draw another rectangle on your little map there."

"But—"

"Listen," Mason said, a hint of authority in his voice. He leaned forward in his chair, holding his scissors between his knees. "If Owen Gardner can buy a couple of damn carnival rides, I can take care of a few apples. Okay?"

I wanted to tell him no.

I wanted to tell him that he was only wasting his time by doing this gesture for me because I couldn't give him anything in return. I wanted to say I didn't deserve it and to tell his mom and her church group to forget about it. But I made myself say, "Okay. Thank you."

Mason smirked as he leaned back, returning to his leaf-cutting. "You're welcome. And actually—there is one condition."

"What's that?"

He looked up at me in mock frustration. "I get to cut out these perfect little rounded leaves. You get all the annoyingly pointy maple ones."

I laughed. "Deal." We worked in silence for a while, cutting out leaves over the trash can between us. I muttered "a few apples" under my breath, which brought another smile to his lips. I would have loved to have told him that this act of his would have bought him a VIP ticket to my panties if he weren't one of my students' fathers, but I kept that thought to myself.

"Finley's getting excited for the festival," Mason said after a couple of minutes, cutting away at an orange leaf. "We actually have a paper-chain countdown for it. She has me make one for every holiday. Every event. It helps her grasp the concept of time a little bit better."

"That's so sweet," I said, imagining the two of them doing crafts together at home. "So, if you don't mind me asking, how has Finley been coping with everything?"

He glanced up at me with a hint of confusion in his eyes, as though he wasn't sure what I could be referring to. Afraid I might have overstepped, I opened my mouth to apologize—but Mason said, "She's fine."

There was something about the confidence in his tone that filled me with doubt. I cut another leaf in silence, carefully considering a follow-up question. I hoped Mason would say more, but he didn't.

And then I found myself mentioning something that had been in the back of my mind since the second I'd learned of Finley's situation. "You know, when I was a kid, sometimes I would pretend to be okay when I wasn't—just because I thought that's what the adults around me needed to hear."

Mason's cutting slowed, and he glanced up toward my face. "But you weren't okay?"

I took a deep breath, dropping a finished leaf onto my desk before picking up another. "No, not really. I could tell I was just upsetting my mom even more with all of my worries, so I just kept them to myself."

Mason leaned forward to put his scissors down on the edge of my desk and crossed his ankle over his knee. I had his full attention. Maybe I'd said too much—he came here to help me with classroom duties, not to listen to me tell him how *not okay* his daughter was.

And what did I know, anyway?

"So you've always been a worrier," he observed.

"I guess you could say that."

"What kinds of things did you worry about back then?"

I inhaled, realizing I'd somehow made this about me, which wasn't my intention. But it was too late to take it back. "I worried that it might have been my fault that my dad left, because my sister and I fought all the time. We drove him crazy. And I just thought—if only I could have listened better and been quieter when he was trying to take a nap, maybe he would still be around."

Mason was quiet, so I continued.

"I worried my dad loved my new half-sisters more than me and Jamie. And I worried about my mom, working all these late hours just to keep food on the table. I was one stressed out little kid, and my mom had no clue."

Mason's gaze was too intense, so I chose to look at his shoe instead, the one propped up on his knee. He absentmindedly ran his finger through the loop of his shoestring and said, "I wish you would have had someone to tell you back then that it wasn't your fault."

"I wouldn't have believed them if they had," I replied, meeting his gaze again.

He nodded. "Do you—do you think Finley might be pretending to be okay for my sake?"

I studied his face, trying to decipher whether he was ready to hear this or not—and debating whether I was the right person to say it. "I don't know, Mason. I just know that it takes more than a few months to get over a parent who abandons you."

He fiddled with his shoestring some more, scratching his chin with his other hand. Neither of us were cutting out leaves now. I had no idea what time it was—but I could guess it was almost time for the kids to return from music class. Mason seemed like he might have been on the brink of saying something, so I didn't dare turn to look at the clock. Not now. "Thank you," he finally said, looking up at my face. "For sharing your perspective, I mean."

"I don't want to step on your toes."

"You're not," he quickly said. "Please, I have so many people trying to tell me what to do with Finley, and you're someone whose opinion I actually respect. So I—" He paused, his Adam's apple bobbing. "I just appreciate you opening up like that."

"It's good to talk about it sometimes."

Mason pulled out his phone, distracted by a notification—an email, it looked like. "Hmm," he said.

"What is it?"

"Got a job interview," he mumbled into his fisted hand. "But I might not go through with it."

"Why not?"

He sighed. "It's a remote position for an app developer on the West Coast?" Mason's voice pitched upward in a question, like he was really unsure about this. "It's not what I envisioned myself doing. They're just the first company that's actually responded to my application."

"What's the harm in doing the interview?"

He shrugged. "I'm afraid I'm going to end up saying yes when I really want to say no."

My eyes widened. "I know exactly what you mean."

"That's how you ended up doing this fall festival thing, isn't it?" he asked, nodding toward my chaotic festival map.

"Exactly." I turned my chair toward my desk and grabbed a pencil, looking for a place on the map for the caramel apple stand. I still couldn't believe he'd managed to find someone to sell them—I'd have to remember to thank his mom, too. I kept smiling as I erased and redrew a couple of rectangles, making space for my new vendor. "You know, most teachers are traditionally given just a single apple. Not an entire caramel apple stand."

"Most teachers don't—" Mason stopped abruptly, shaking his head.

"What?"

He ignored me.

"Say it," I urged with a laugh, putting my pencil down.

"No."

"I want you to say it, Mason."

"No you don't," he assured me with a husky chuckle.

Well, now he was just irking me. "Don't tell me what I want or don't want to hear. You don't—"

Before I could finish my sentence, Mason kicked the trashcan out of the way and grabbed the seat of my chair, spinning it so that I was facing him. In the same motion, he pulled the chair toward him, spreading his legs so that my knees were between both of his. And, with his hands clamped down on either side of me—his forearms pressing into my thighs—he said, "*Most* teachers don't make me think about what they look like naked every moment we're together, either."

Oh.

I couldn't breathe. Mason kept his eyes on mine, gauging my reaction. And when I slowly began to grin and he could see I wasn't pissed, he smiled, too. There was relief in his eyes. I could sense him leaning closer—so subtly, so slowly that concentrating on the shrinking distance between us was making me dizzy. Was my classroom getting smaller, too? Both of his hands slid forward on the seat of the chair, inching toward my butt as he brought his upper body even closer to mine.

It was a good thing the sound of approaching children filled the hallway outside the classroom door, because I felt like I was on the verge of fainting. Mason released me, nudging my chair away from his. I turned back toward my desk and rose to my feet in one fluid motion, readying myself to greet the kids. I held onto the edge of my desk, still feeling the dizzying effect of Mason's closeness as the kids burst into the room.

For the rest of the morning, I could hardly look at him.

One of two things would soon happen: either Mason would have to stop volunteering in my classroom, or we were going to sleep together.

And I sure as hell didn't want him to stop volunteering.

chapter twenty
mason

My mom had told me at least half a dozen times to find a back-up baby-sitter. "I have a life, too, you know," she kept telling me, begging me not to always rely on her and my dad to watch Finley when I made plans. And I repeatedly assured her I'd find someone—but I hadn't. Not yet, anyway.

So when the company I was interviewing for wanted to talk to me on Friday evening, I found myself in a bit of a tricky situation. It was a video interview, but I knew better than to have Finley under the same roof. For some reason, anytime I said, "be quiet, I'm in a Zoom meeting," she heard: "ever think about acting out a one-girl circus? Now's a good time."

My mom was at the church kitchen making caramel apples, and my dad was bowling that night. Finley wanted to join her grandpa, but he was just going to give her a handful of quarters and send her to the arcade unsupervised—and my mind filled up with several tragic scenarios. Kids had gone missing from Woodvale before, and I wasn't about to let Finley be the next one.

Traci would have watched her in a heartbeat. But that would mean Finley would be in her house, where pictures of Whitney and other memorabilia relating to her were in every room—and that was another tragic scenario in itself.

And of course I considered asking Kendall. Finley would shit if she got to spend a Friday night with her teacher, and I wouldn't have minded seeing her, either. But there was no telling where that might lead, and I was coming on a little too strong for someone who promised not to kiss her again. The caramel apple stand was one thing. Accosting her in her desk chair? That was probably out of line.

Though she didn't seem to mind—which was exactly the problem. The two of us would only continue to tempt each other, so avoiding Kendall outside the classroom as much as possible would probably be for the best.

So that's how I found myself pulling up behind Owen's Volvo in his driveway on Friday evening. He and Sarah watched their nieces and nephews all the time, so they were more than happy to take Finley off my hands for a little while. And when Finley heard Owen had actual working robots—she put on her shoes at lightning speed. "I'm going to make a YouTube video about this!"

Owen and Sarah lived in Meadowbrook Heights, a new development on the edge of town. Their modern, gray house with its white shutters stood tall at the end of a cul-de-sac surrounded by other, smaller gray houses with white shutters.

"STEM for the Fucking Win," I muttered under my breath as Finley and I walked up their driveway hand-in-hand.

Sarah was already standing at the door. "Hey, Finley! Guess what?"

Finley dropped my hand and bounded up the porch steps. "My dad already told me about the robots. Where are they?"

I laughed as I stepped up onto the porch. "She's a little excited, if you can't tell."

"Something even better than robots is going to be here," Sarah told her, bending down to her level. Her eyes widened. "Your teacher."

Finley gasped. "Ms. Devin's coming?"

I had a similar—albeit internal—reaction.

"Uh huh," Sarah said, holding the door open for both of us to let us into the foyer. I exchanged a nod with Owen, who was standing just behind her at the bottom of their stairwell. "Finley, what would you rather do first—play with Owen's robots or meet our new puppy?"

This question made Finley pause. It was a tough decision, after all. She looked around their foyer in wonderment, taking it all in as she weighed her options. On the wall above the console table, there was an enormous wooden sign featuring the words *better together* artfully off-center in a typewriter font—which seemed so very… them. Finley's eyes zeroed in on the colorful leash and harness hanging from a bone-shaped hook rack, however. "I want to see the puppy first," she said, so Sarah led her through the kitchen to the back of the house.

Owen leaned against the banister with his hands in his pockets. "So, you ready for this interview?"

I nodded, mimicking his pose. "I guess so."

"Sounds like you're not that enthused about it."

"It's a job," I said with a shrug. "We'll see how it goes." I didn't want to talk about that, though. I tugged on my earlobe, pretending to scratch it in an attempt to appear as casual as possible. "So Ms. Devin's coming over tonight, huh? What's that all about?"

A knowing smile spread across Owen's face. "She's helping Sarah with some festival prep stuff." He nodded toward something behind me, and I turned around to see their dining room table covered with jars, faux leaves, and a whole mess of other random objects. "It's gonna take them a while. I'm sure she'll still be here when you get back."

I turned back toward Owen as I reached for the door handle. "Doesn't affect me one way or another."

He crossed his arms, studying my face. "'Kay. Well, good luck with this interview. You'll have to let us know how it goes."

I held his gaze for a moment, trying to decide whether or not I should defend myself against what he was obviously implying—but doing so would only make it more obvious. My grin probably said enough. "Thanks, cuz. Good luck watching my kid."

I couldn't see Finley, but I could hear her having a barking contest with the puppy a couple rooms away. When I tried to tell her goodbye, she didn't even look up—she was in the middle of a game of tug-of-war with the dog.

It was time to shift into job interview mode. Back at home, I propped my laptop up on the counter and joined the meeting five minutes early, reading about the company online as I waited for the interviewer to join. This company specialized in creating apps for pet owners—one that simplified tracking pet medications and another that helped connect pet owners with local vets.

I wasn't exactly sure where my skills would come in—until the interview, anyway. A man and a woman, whose names I couldn't remember thirty seconds after they'd said them, took turns questioning me about my experience and familiarity with their apps. They wanted someone to help them completely overhaul their branding. "We're looking for a less 'corporate' look, and we instead want to go for something playful and whimsical," the woman said. "That's where your illustrations could come in."

"Your work is impressive." The middle-aged man beside her was swiping through my portfolio on an iPad. "And not just that, it looks like you're capable of adapting to different styles."

I cleared my throat. "Well, I've had the opportunity to work with a range of clients, each with a unique vision and their own style preferences. So I always collaborate with them to deliver exactly what they envision."

The two of them turned to each other, exchanging impressed nods. The rest of the interview continued a lot like this—with them asking me exactly the kinds of questions I'd anticipated, and me telling them precisely what I knew they wanted to hear.

And as far as I could tell, I was nailing this interview—these people liked me. And the longer we spoke, the more I realized I might actually be pretty comfortable working for them. If anything, just for the consistency. I wouldn't be designing a logo for a photographer one day and slapping together a holiday promo for an online boutique the next.

This job would be challenging—in all the right ways.

"Tell us about your availability, Mason," the woman said, looking down at the clipboard in her hand. "When would you be able to start?"

Tomorrow? "I would need one week to wrap things up with my freelance clients," I said, not wanting to sound too eager. "But after that, I'm all yours."

She smiled and wrote something down. "Good. And as you know, we're located on the West Coast, so your workday might start a little later than you're used to."

"Which means you get to sleep in," the guy interjected.

"I like the sound of that." Finley's schedule would never allow me to sleep in—but I couldn't pass up the opportunity to make another joke. And, as anticipated, it made both of them laugh.

"But I also want to be clear—we're on Pacific time," the woman said, looking up from her clipboard. "Which means that we *will* need you to be available between the hours of nine and five, which, if I'm correct, is twelve and eight there in Indiana?"

I opened my mouth to speak, only to slowly bring my lips together again. 8:00. Finley's bedtime. "Um…" I would miss dinner. I'd miss picking her up from school. I'd miss talking to her during her after-school snack and listening to her read her sight words aloud. Essentially, 3:00 to 8:00 was the only time I spent with Finley on weekdays at all. If I were to take this job, that meant I would miss… everything.

I let out a heavy sigh, trying to come up with a tactful way to back out of this as the realization this job wasn't right for me sank in. "I guess I was under the impression the hours were a bit more flexible."

"I'm afraid not," the woman said. "While the majority of our employees are remote, we need everyone to be, you know, logged in and available for meetings between those set hours. We're still a team."

"I'm a single dad," I said with an awkward laugh. I had hoped that would elicit some sympathy, but the two of them just exchanged uncomfortable glances, neither wanting to be the one to deliver the rejecting words. So I beat them to the punch. "Well, it sounds like I'm just wasting your time now." And they were wasting mine.

"We do, unfortunately, have other candidates with better availability," the male interviewer said.

"Yup," I said, already navigating to the 'end meeting' button. "Thank you for the opportunity, anyway." I waited for them to tell me goodbye, not wanting to appear rude—and then I was out.

I closed my laptop and rested my forehead on my palm, allowing myself a few minutes to sulk over this. It was becoming more and more apparent I was never going to find any kind of "dream" job. Not while living in Woodvale, Indiana, anyway.

Not if I wanted to keep putting Finley first.

Sighing, I slid off the barstool and grabbed my keys from the end of the counter. My enthusiasm for potentially seeing Kendall that night had waned some—I was afraid I couldn't hide my bad mood, and she'd catch a glimpse of the real me. Real Fucking Depressed Mason.

And they were all going to ask questions. *"How'd your interview go, Mason?"* I wasn't prepared for their disappointed stares. Most of all, I was going to disappoint Finley, who had made me a GOOD LUCK card that afternoon.

("GUD LUKE", actually. But it was close enough—and I saved it so I could tease her about it in a few years.)

I parked behind Kendall's car in Owen and Sarah's driveway before slipping through their front door unnoticed. As I crouched down to scratch the ears of the golden retriever puppy that greeted me, I smiled when I saw what was happening in the dining room to my right. Kendall and Finley were both doing headstands against the wall—a talent I wasn't even aware Finley possessed.

She couldn't see me because her shirt was hanging over her face, but Kendall immediately dropped her feet to the ground and said, "There's your dad, Fin." That was the nickname my family had given her—Kendall must have heard me say it at some point.

I liked hearing her say it.

As Finley squealed and ran toward me to hug my legs, Kendall pulled her own shirt down to cover her midriff and smiled. Her face was red from hanging upside down—or maybe I'd caught her off guard.

I stood beneath the arched doorway as I half-hugged Finley back. I opened my mouth to ask Kendall where Sarah and Owen were, but Finley spoke first. "Dad, can I join a tumbling class?"

"Tumbling?"

"Yeah," she said, and I grunted as I picked her up to hold her on my hip. "Ms. Devin taught me how to do a somersault and a headstand and a backbend."

"Wow, you learned all of that while I was gone?"

"She's a natural," Kendall said, combing her fingers through her hair as she walked over to us. She was wearing jeans and a loose-fitting t-shirt, and her feet were bare. I'd never seen her look so… casual. She tugged on the back of Finley's shirt to pull it down and said, "We'll have to try cartwheels again some other time."

With both arms around Finley's middle, I tightened my grip on her. "So Ms. Devin's got you wanting to do some tumbling, huh? I'll have to—"

"Oh, you're back!" Sarah said behind me. I turned around to see her holding a tall glass full of a frozen red substance. "That didn't take long. How did it go?" She was speaking a lot louder than necessary, which made sense once I smelled the alcohol in her glass.

"Wow," I said with a laugh, ignoring her question. "Drinking while you're supposed to be supervising my kid, huh?"

"I just made this, I promise," she said with a laugh, pausing to take a sip through a bendy straw. "Do you want one? We just got a new margarita maker."

"Blender," Owen corrected, coming up behind Sarah. He crossed his arms against his chest and shook his head at me. "We got a new blender."

I let out a little chuckle, watching him maneuver away from her as she tried to jab him in the side. "Wish I could have a drink, but…" I lifted Finley in my arms and nodded toward her, knowing that was enough of an answer. I couldn't remember the last time I'd had drinks with friends. Not since getting full custody of Finley, that's for sure. "And she needs to go home and get a bath. So maybe another time. How's the festival prep going?"

Their dining room table looked a lot like it did when I'd left. "We got a little distracted by the puppy. Leia tends to steal the show," Sarah said. Of course those nerds named their dog Leia. "So between the dog and an impromptu tumbling lesson, we didn't get much done."

Kendall tucked her hair behind her ears and gave Sarah a sheepish grin. "Sorry. I just can't say no to her."

"Well, my dad tells me 'no' all the time," Finley said, sliding down my hip until I put her down. Everyone laughed, but Finley rolled her eyes. "It's like his favorite word."

"That's a load of crap," I said, giving the kid a playful shove. "You know you can talk me into pretty much anything."

She looked up at me and blinked with her puppy dog eyes. "Then can we stay for a little bit, Daddy? Please?"

What a manipulative little thing she was. She was good—too good. My mouth was ready to form the word 'no', but instead, I just looked down at her puppy dog eyes and grinned, feeling everyone else watching me. "Do you think I should stay and help these guys?"

Finley nodded, her eyes widening in anticipation of my answer.

"Then *yes*," I said, though I shook my head. "We can stay, you little manipulator." She clapped her hands together and skipped around the dining room table—with Leia following her every step.

As I watched her go around and around, my eyes stopped on Kendall, who was already looking at me. I swallowed, knowing it might be a little easier to refrain from flirting with her when her boss, her ex, and my kid were in the room.

"Is that all it takes to get you to fold?" Kendall asked, putting one hand on her hip. "Just a little bit of begging?"

Oh, fuck—she had no idea. I blinked, feeling Owen's eyes on me. "It's usually the puppy dog eyes that do it for me, actually."

Kendall bit her bottom lip, and all I could think about was how much I wished it were *me* biting it.

Sarah cleared her throat beside me, perhaps picking up on the tension in the room. She looked from me to Kendall as she stirred her drink and asked, "So… should we get started?"

"Yup," Kendall and I said in unison. It looked like we were finally going to get to spend a Friday night together, after all.

chapter twenty-one
kendall

Having Mason stay was such a relief.

His presence eased some of the awkwardness of being in Sarah and Owen's house. While Owen seemed pretty relaxed—offering me a bottle of water and making his usual stupid jokes—Sarah was very much on edge. I was the one who encouraged her to go make herself that drink so she'd stop treating me like I was an egg about to crack. Someday she'd believe I was over Owen, but not yet, apparently.

It didn't help that when she asked me if I had found a date for her wedding, I stared at her like a deer in headlights before admitting that no, I had zero prospects. And then she and Owen got into a playful argument about how she never told him Heath and I ended things, despite her swearing up and down she'd mentioned it—which is how the tumbling lesson with Finley got started in the first place. Their arguing turned into a tickle fight, which I was happy to ignore while showing Finley how to do a headstand.

Not only did Mason's presence ease my nerves, having a fourth set of hands for our project made it go a lot faster. Sarah had bought some miniature fairy lights to wrap around each mason jar, which turned out to be a more complicated task than it seemed—and there were so many.

Sarah made a margarita for me—twice as strong as any drink I'd ever had at La Cocina—and the four of us got to work assembling lanterns. Finley played with Leia beneath the table, both of them wriggling beneath chairs and weaving in between our legs. Mason and I mostly kept to ourselves, occasionally looking up to eye each other across the table as Sarah and Owen swapped stories about the dog. It was like sitting in on one of Owen's podcasts, and Sarah was his esteemed guest. And while their stories were entertaining enough, I was finding it difficult to listen, too distracted by Mason's hands as he wrapped the wires of lights around each jar.

When there was a lull in the conversation taking place beside us, I picked up my drink and took a long sip, staring across the table at Mason. "So, Mason," I said, and he froze for a second, the sudden attention catching him off guard. "You haven't told us how your interview went."

His shoulders slumped as he sat a finished jar on the table between him and Owen. "It went really well—until it didn't."

"Uh oh," Owen said, tucking faux leaves in between the wires around the jar exactly the way Sarah showed him.

"Yeah, they wanted me to be available in the evenings, which is a no-go for me. For obvious reasons." Mason nodded in Finley's direction, just in case it wasn't that obvious. "Pretty sure they were going to hire me, too."

"Sounds like it wasn't meant to be," Sarah said.

Mason shook his head. "I guess not."

He stared down at his hands as he opened another package of mini fairy lights, and I could tell he was feeling pretty down. He wasn't his usual perky, flirty self. Maybe I could cheer him up. "So that means I get to keep you a little bit longer."

His eyes lifted to meet mine, and he gave me a half smile. "Yeah, it looks like you're not going to be able to get rid of me just yet, Ms. Devin."

I picked up my glass, taking another big sip through the straw. Mason was watching my lips closely when I said, "I'm going to run out of space for your drawings on my bulletin board."

"You've been drawing pictures in the kindergarten room, huh?" Owen teased.

"Every week," Mason answered.

I glanced across the table at Owen, who was seated diagonally from me. "He draws the cutest little woodland animals. Oh!" I turned back to Mason. "You should show him that fox."

Mason just raised an eyebrow at me, shaking his head. "It was just a doodle."

"Shut up—you said it was inspired by the podcast, right?"

"Owen's podcast?" Sarah asked, looking up from the jar in her hands. "I want to see it."

Mason just shrugged like it wasn't a big deal. "It's just a little fox… scientist… girl. It was nothing."

"Mason." I slapped the table in frustration, realizing then I was starting to feel a little bit of a buzz. I reached for my phone in my back pocket. "Would you totally hate me right now if I showed them?" I hoped he wouldn't say no—but if he did, I wouldn't insist on it. I'd hate to put him on the spot, especially when he was already having a bad day. But I caught a hint of a smile on his lips and the playful way he glanced to the side—indicating he might actually like this attention—so I threw in a soft, "Please?"

He stared across the table into my puppy dog eyes. "You just had to say that, didn't you?"

I grinned, unlocking my phone. "Finley's taught me the inner workings of manipulating you."

"Show them if you want—but it's not very good."

"He's lying," I said to Owen and Sarah, navigating to the fox photo in our message history—taking extra care not to scroll too far back. It didn't take me long to find the illustration. "There she is."

I turned my screen toward Owen and Sarah. Immediately, Owen let out a pleased gasp, reaching across the table to take the phone from my hand. "Oh wow," he said, giving Mason a quick side glance before studying the illustration more closely. "This is—this is really, really good."

Mason shifted in his chair, his eyes widening slightly as his gaze drifted from me to Owen's hands on my phone. At first I thought his unease might be from all the attention he was receiving, but it occurred to me he might be concerned about something else. If Owen accidentally swiped right—

"Wait, let me see something," Mason said, holding out his hand to take the phone from Owen. He held it close to his face, squinting to get a closer look. "Yeah, those lines are so sloppy." And the next thing I knew, he was smoothly passing the phone back to me.

An effortless save.

It'd been a year and a half since Owen Gardner had laid eyes on a nude photo of me, and I would have been mortified if he saw one now. Not only that—he'd know who I'd been sending them to. And Mason understood all of that without me saying a single word. I thanked him with a silent grin from across the table, and he responded with the slightest nod, imperceivable to everyone else.

"Mason, that's not sloppy at all," Sarah said, slapping the table. She was craning her neck to see it, so I tilted the screen toward her. "I mean it—you are remarkably talented. The company that didn't hire you today doesn't know what they're missing."

Owen sat with his arms folded against his chest, turning to Mason. "Could you send that to me?"

Mason turned to him and blinked. "Uh—yeah, I guess?"

"Not to use without your permission or anything. I'd just love to look at it some more, maybe show it to my team."

"Yeah, sure," Mason said, sitting up a little straighter. "I'll email it to you."

"Good," Owen said, looking across the table at Sarah. Mason turned and looked at me in the same manner, raising his eyebrows slightly. The room was silent for a moment and the four of us got back to work. That is, until Finley sprang up from beneath the table shouting my name, "Ms. Devin!" On her way up, she hit her head on the edge of the table with a loud *thump* that made all of us gasp.

The tears came immediately. And since I was closest, she lunged toward my lap and planted her face against my knees, sobbing. "Oh no, sweetie," I said, rubbing the top of her head. "That sounded like it hurt."

Mason rose to his feet across the table, but when I pulled Finley up to my lap, he hesitated—waiting to see how this would play out. I hugged Finley against my chest, her crying turning into shaking, silent sobs that were somehow even more pitiful. I frowned at Mason, who was still standing up with his hands on the table. Concerned, but letting me handle it.

Sarah got up and made her way over to the refrigerator, returning with a frozen bag of peas. "I'm sorry, I don't think we have an actual ice pack," she said. I accepted the bag of peas, pressing it against the top of Finley's head.

She sniffled, reaching up to hold the bag in place. "What is that?"

"Frozen peas," I told her. "Maybe when you're all better, we can eat them."

With tears streaming down both of her cheeks, she made a retching sound. "I hate peas."

I giggled. "Me too."

Mason slowly lowered himself back to his chair and scooted up to the table. "You going to be alright, Fin?" She nodded in response. "We need to get them a jellyfish ice pack like ours, don't we?" Another nod.

"You'd think we'd have a real ice pack," Owen said, "considering our nieces and nephews are always over here knocking their heads together." He and Sarah turned to each other and laughed, as if they were both remembering some specific incident.

"So—do you guys think you might have kids of your own anytime soon?" Mason asked. Sarah and Owen's laughter trailed off until the room got quiet, and the energy around us shifted. It was subtle, but I couldn't help but notice the way Sarah reached for her drink, tipping it back to finish it off—and Owen stared at his hands on the table.

"One day," he said, glancing up at Sarah. "We'll have to do a lot of baby-proofing around here first, that's for sure. Lots of... choking hazards."

"And stupid tables," Finley muttered against my chest, unknowingly rescuing us from the awkwardness. We all laughed.

"You are absolutely right. We'll get rid of this stupid table first," Owen told her, drumming on the edge of it.

Sarah refilled both of our drinks and the four of us continued to assemble the mason jar lanterns, working into the night. Only now, I had the added challenge of completing the task with a sleepy kid in my arms. Mason asked me to check her pupils to make sure she didn't have a concussion—and then I let her fall asleep. I had a sinking suspicion she was drooling on my shirt, but I didn't mind. As I reached for a faux maple leaf, careful not to jostle Finley too much, I glanced across the table at Mason. His eyes were fixed on Finley's face, nestled against my chest. Unaware I was watching him, the corners of his mouth lifted in a lazy smile as he wrapped fairy lights around the very last mason jar.

When the lanterns were finished, we carefully packed them into boxes—designating Owen as the person who'd bring them up to the school the following afternoon. And, attempting to take a limp Finley from my arms, Mason said, "I need to get her to bed."

Finley clung to me even tighter as her dad tried to pull her away. I smiled up at him over the top of her head. "Do you want me to carry her out?"

"I'm not sure you have a choice."

Mason held the front door for me and followed me down the driveway toward his Jeep. I didn't realize how much I was buzzing until the chilly night air hit my face and I became a little lightheaded. I tightened my grip on Finley, willing myself not to trip and hurt us both. "This kid is sleeping hard," I told Mason, walking toward his Jeep with my bare feet.

He opened the car door. "She's going to wake up in her bed and have no idea how she got there," he said as I bent down to put Finley in her booster seat. Her eyes opened for a couple of seconds, but by the time I was finished buckling her in, she was back to sleep.

I closed the door and turned to face Mason, who was standing next to the Jeep with his hands in his pockets. He looked a little tired himself. "I'm glad you stayed," I said.

He lifted his chin to look up at my face. "Me too."

It was the quiet moments like this, in which we stood impossibly close and alone—or almost alone—that I wished I'd never asked him to make that promise. Because if he tried to kiss me now, I wouldn't pull away. I'd let him. I'd let Mason Reed do anything he wanted to me.

But he knew better.

Mason took a deep breath, saying, "I'll see you tom—"

"Did you keep those pictures I sent you?" I didn't know what made me blurt those words—it was probably the extra tequila Sarah had added to our second round of drinks combined with my nagging curiosity. The question had been in the back of my mind ever since Owen held my phone in his hands. The photos were *right there*, but did Mason still have them, too? Did he ever look at them?

A sleepy grin spread across his face. "I deleted them just like you asked me to."

"You didn't keep them in a private spank bank?"

His smile grew. "'Spank bank'? Is that what it's called?"

"You can call it whatever you want."

Mason looked up at the night sky and exhaled, and I knew he was about to crack. It was a clear night, and the moon overhead was almost full. We both stood silently and stared at it for a moment as I waited for his admission. Finally, he turned back to me and pulled his hands from his pockets, letting his arms dangle loosely at his sides. "I deleted them. Every last one. And that's the honest-to-God truth." His stare was so intense, I believed every word. "But."

Of course there was a "but."

Mason watched me closely as he spoke. "What if I told you I… drew one from memory?"

"You… drew one of them?" He nodded in confirmation as I nervously played with the charms on my bracelet. "W-which photo?"

I absentmindedly moved closer to him, awaiting his next words. If we stood any closer, he might even hear the way my heart was ready to pound right out of my chest. "It was based on that one of you in the mirror with those neon lights," Mason said. "Because it shows off all your—" He swallowed and glanced down at my hips, slowly bringing his eyes back up to my face. "Everything."

Fuck me. I tried to hold back a smile, but there was no use. I was already giggling like a goddamn schoolgirl. I really shouldn't have downed that second margarita so quickly. "I want to see it," I blurted.

He reached for his door handle and turned to get into the Jeep. "Welp. Goodnight."

My hand flew up to the top of the door to prevent him from leaving. "Nope, you're not getting out of this now. Too late. I want to see this sketch of yours. It's only fair."

Mason scratched his forehead with his thumb, smiling down at the ground between us. The creases in the corners of his eyes became more prominent as he said, "Boy oh boy, am I praying you're so drunk you'll forget this tomorrow…"

"Not a chance. This conversation will forever be etched in my memory, Mason Reed." I leaned closer to him, my hand still on the car. "And you're going to show me that drawing."

"Am I?" His eyes were still locked on mine. "I don't have it with me."

"That's okay. You can send it to me later."

Mason shook his head and licked his lips, trying not to smile. "You don't think I'm a pervert for drawing you in nothing but a thong?"

I pressed my lips together, fighting a smile myself. "You're a modern-day Jack Dawson."

He grinned down at his feet, signaling he'd understood my *Titanic* reference. In the quiet moment that followed, we both turned to look at Finley, who was still fast asleep with her mouth hanging open.

Mason cleared his throat. "You going to be okay to get home?"

"Yeah—I'll either wait until I sober up or have Owen take me," I said with a shrug. I hadn't really thought about it, but I knew Sarah and Owen would make sure I made it home safe.

Something about my answer made Mason's face fall and his body tense up. "Go get your stuff."

The sudden shift in his mood threw me. "Excuse me?"

"Get your stuff," he repeated, nodding toward the house. "I'll take you home."

I didn't like the way he'd just decided this for me. "No."

"Come on," he said with a subtle eyeroll. "Don't have Owen take you."

"What's it matter to you?" I crossed my arms with a scowl. This wasn't the first time Mason had shown me his possessive side, and it was more unnecessary now than it had been at the apple orchard that day.

"It doesn't. I—" He stopped, lifting his hand to his forehead in frustration. "Damn it, I'm sorry. My jealousy of Owen just manifested itself in a really ugly way, and I wish I could take that back—among everything else I've said tonight."

"Jealousy of Owen?"

"Well, yeah. I mean, look at this house. He's got the six-figure business. The Volvo. The fiancée. The fucking… golden retriever." He really emphasized the dog comment, which would have made me laugh if he hadn't seemed so distressed about it. He shook his head, eyeing Finley in the backseat before turning back to me. "And once upon a time… he even had you."

Now I could laugh. "Barely. He *barely* had me, Mason."

His hand returned to the door handle. I tried to get him to look at me, but he was suddenly afraid of making eye contact. "Look, I'm sorry, Kendall. I didn't mean to sound all possessive a minute ago. I had no right. This isn't my proudest moment."

I searched for a way to let him know there was no comparison. None at all. He'd already shown me more attention than Owen Gardner ever had, and he couldn't even call me his.

I wished he could.

"'Kay, well, I'm going to go put Finley to bed before I dig this hole even deeper," he mumbled, lifting up his door handle. But the second the door opened, I reached up again to close it, a motion so sudden it finally got him to look at me. I knew what I wanted to say.

"Would a goodnight hug be totally out of the question?"

Mason inhaled, giving this careful consideration. "You're so drunk." But he turned his body toward mine and held his arms out to the side to accept my embrace. I wrapped my arms around his middle, attempting to pull him into me—but his feet were planted firmly on the ground. He was resisting this, either because he thought I was too drunk to realize what I was doing or because he didn't want to be tempted. I couldn't be sure. Either way, his body was as stiff as a board. Since he wasn't budging, I'd have to come to him. I pulled myself against his chest, shuffling my feet forward, and I waited for him to relax. For him to give me more than this bullshit, half-hearted, half-embrace.

After a few seconds, he delicately placed his hands on my back like I was something he might break if he applied too much pressure. I felt his body loosen as he exhaled, finally surrendering to the hug. Surrendering to me. He wrapped his arms all the way around my body, bowing his head forward over my shoulder. *There you go.* He wanted this as much as I did.

One of his hands slid up my back, getting entangled in my hair at the base of my neck. I knew I was running out of time to say what I wanted for it still to be relevant. I pulled back from him slightly, holding onto his arms as I pressed my mouth up to his ear, our cheeks barely touching. I almost couldn't say the words.

What was the number one thing men compared?

"At least your dick is bigger," I whispered.

And then I released him, stepping back far enough that I could see his entire face. And what a sight that was. His jaw dropped, and he stared straight ahead, fixating on the shrubbery behind me as he processed my words. His hands remained in the exact position they were in when we hugged, frozen in midair. I'd broken him. At the very least, my words had rendered the man completely speechless.

I had to give him *something*. Even if I couldn't be sure it was true, it only mattered that he thought it was.

Tucking my hair behind my ears, I paused to enjoy Mason's shocked and perplexed expression for a few more seconds before I turned to go. "Anyway, goodnight!" I left him with that thought and ran up the driveway in my bare feet without looking back.

chapter twenty-two
kendall

I woke up the morning of the fall festival with a stomachache. It could have just been my nerves, or it could have been the Taco Bell Sarah and I insisted on having Owen get for us late the night before. I had a vague, blurry memory of Sarah holding both of my hands in Owen's backseat, tearing up as she told me, "I should've asked you to be in my wedding, but I didn't want you to feel weird."

And Owen, annoyed and exhausted in the driver's seat, glanced over his shoulder and said, "Pretty sure you're making her feel weird right now, babe."

I pulled my blanket up to my chin and rolled over, reaching for my phone on my nightstand. I opened it up to see an unsent message to Mason.

Kendall: I may need a new pic to make sure that was an accurate statement

"Oh my god," I said, sitting up. Thank God I hadn't sent it. I couldn't believe I'd even typed it in the first place! I quickly backspaced so there was no chance I'd accidentally send it to him, and that's when I saw what he'd texted me around midnight:

Mason: Let me know when you've made it home safe.

But just above that, there was another message—a photo. I tapped on it to get the full view.

It was the naked illustration of me. I held my breath the second it loaded, stunned at how accurately he'd captured my features. If he hadn't mentioned drawing it from memory, I would've sworn he'd used the actual photo as a side-by-side reference. It looked exactly like me.

What struck me the most was the way he'd drawn my belly. He hadn't attempted to minimize it, which would have been insulting. The roll I often tried desperately to conceal with Spanx was on full display, yet it somehow looked… cute? Maybe even… sexy?

I swallowed, taking in this very precise detail. It was just an extra line, a tiny detail that he could've left out entirely. But his inclusion of it made me believe he thought it was sexy, too.

I grinned at my phone, chewing my thumbnail as I typed a response.

Kendall: I'm alive. And falling in love with myself because of the way you drew me. I could cry.

Mason: Good to know you're alive. And I hope those are tears of happiness… because your body is incredible.

Mason: Probably shouldn't have said that.

Mason: Anyway, are you psyched for today?

Kendall: Psyched? No. Anxious? Yes.

Mason: Everything's going to be fine. People are going to have a blast and the PTO's going to make a buttload of money. You've done all you can. Might as well let yourself have some fun today.

Kendall: Thanks. I can't wait to see you and Finley.

I couldn't stop smiling as I got dressed that morning, tying my fall festival t-shirt in a knot in the front and pairing it with a long, black skirt. I grabbed a yellow cardigan before I headed out, knowing it was going to be cold by nightfall.

Jamie and Daya were raking leaves in the front yard together that morning as I left, which I took as a good sign they were getting along. "I'm telling you," Daya was saying, "we're destroying the ecosystem right now. Do you know how many helpless little critters are losing their homes?"

"Tell that to the landlord, 'cause it's gonna be us losing our home next. He's been breathing down my neck about these leaves since the first sign of fall," Jamie said, stopping for a vape break as I walked past. "You headed up to the school already, Blondie?"

"Someone's got to be there to show everyone where to set up."

"Can't Legolas do it?"

I grinned, knowing there was no use in fighting her on this anymore. "No, Mason won't be there until later. Will you two be coming by?"

"Doubt it," Jamie said, leaning on the end of her rake. "FYI—when you get home, there may be, like, eight or nine lesbians in our living room."

"Um. Thanks for the warning, I guess?"

"It's a lesbian book club," Daya explained, dragging her rake across the front walk. I had to admit, our yard was already looking better. "We're going to read a sapphic romance novel every month and discuss it over beer and a fry-cuterie board."

"Are there… a lot of sapphic romance novels?" I asked, raising my eyebrows in question.

Jamie shook her head at Daya. "We so need to educate her." Then she turned to me, holding her vape pen up to her lips. "Anyway, we're not going to be able to come to your festival. But good luck with all that."

"Thanks, I'll need it."

But it would appear luck was not on my side.

There had been some miscommunication, apparently, about where the carnival ride people were meant to set up. They beat me to the school, too, so they decided to go ahead and set up where they felt best—which just so happened to be exactly where I'd planned for the petting zoo to go. I panicked for a solid ten minutes until I worked everything out—only to get a call from one of the food truck vendors saying they were pulling out. They'd double-booked themselves and decided the other event was more worthy of their time.

More shifting. More adjusting.

By mid-afternoon, many of the volunteers had shown up, which eased my nerves a little since I was able to delegate some of my worries. Together, we raced against the clock to get everything ready. Setting up tables. Showing vendors where to go. Putting out hay bales. Stringing up lights.

All afternoon, volunteers approached me with questions. Some I could answer, some I couldn't. I felt dread in my stomach every time someone approached me. Even worse than the questions, however, was the way everyone kept handing me things. A roll of tickets here, a package of food-safe gloves there. I was running out of pockets and hands.

Mason arrived at some point, but other than a quick wave from across the lot, we didn't get a chance to interact. He and Owen were tackling another problem: a bouncy castle that wouldn't stay inflated.

This thing hadn't even started yet, and it was already a disaster.

"What's wrong?"

I closed my eyes, recognizing the voice behind me even before I saw his face. "Everything, Heath. Everything's wrong."

"Anything I can help with?" He stood before me with his hands on his hips in front of the merry-go-round as the ride workers assembled the last horse.

I was tempted to respond with something sassy, like telling him to stay out of my way. Instead, I sighed, admitting, "Yeah, can you give these tickets to Lori?"

"Sure." He took the roll of tickets from me, but he didn't leave my side. I should have known it wouldn't be that easy to get rid of him. "By the way, I keep forgetting to ask you something."

I could tell from Heath's cautious tone and the way he wiped his palm on his jeans I wasn't going to like this question. "Ask me what?"

"Do you have a date to Owen and Sarah's wedding?"

"Yes," I lied, looking him directly in the eyes. He blinked a few times and nodded, turning to look up at the Ferris wheel, which was finally starting to turn. I studied Heath's face, struggling to remember what it was that made me fall for him in the first place.

"Figured you probably did," he muttered. "I've got a date, too—I was just making sure you had someone. Didn't want to leave you hanging."

Right. "Just—go give those to Lori at the ticket booth, okay?" I was glad to get away from him. I'd be happy to never speak with him again, but I knew I wouldn't be that lucky. I spent the rest of the set-up time hiding from him, avoiding his questions. I almost felt guilty about the way he followed Sarah like a lost puppy, but she seemed to be handling it fine.

As the food vendors started arriving and setting up, the air filled with a decadent combination of smells—funnel cakes, cotton candy, and popcorn. All of these foods, combined with the exhaust fumes from the carnival rides, were making me nostalgic for all the summers my dad took Jamie and me to the county fair when we were little. Our mom couldn't stand the July heat, so he took us alone, letting us ride the Tornado until we were both ready to barf up all the fried treats he'd splurged on.

I wondered if he ever took his new daughters to the fair.

The smell of caramel distracted me from my daydreaming. I turned around to see a petite woman with short blonde hair arranging trays of caramel apples on a flimsy card table. I would have recognized her as Mason's mom even if I hadn't stalked her online—the resemblance was uncanny.

"Excuse me," I said, walking right up to her. "I don't think we've met—I'm Finley's teacher, Ms. Devin."

She put her tray down and smiled, extending her hand to shake mine. "Christine Reed. I have heard *all* about you," she said with a laugh. She had kind eyes, just like her son. "Finley just thinks the world of you."

"It's mutual."

"I hope she behaves for you. She can get hyperactive at times. That little girl talks my ear off."

I smiled warmly. "She's definitely a little chatterbox."

"Her dad was, too—he gave all his teachers a run for their money. And I guess my son's pestering *you* twice a week now, huh?"

"It's easy to see where Finley gets her antics," I joked. "Anyway, I need to check on the other vendors, but I just wanted to thank you for jumping in at the last minute. Mason could tell how devastated I was when the other vendor backed out, and I'm so glad you guys made this possible."

When I said this, Christine gave me a funny look, and I swore she looked me up and down for a second—like she was trying to figure something out. There was a hint of amusement in her voice when she said, "Well, it's my pleasure to be able to help out, hon. What'd you say your first name was?"

I hadn't. "Kendall."

"Kendall," she repeated as we shook hands again. "It was wonderful to finally meet you."

"You too." Christine had a warm, welcoming presence about her—very mom-like. I felt like I could have stayed and chatted with her longer, but we were twenty minutes from the official start time, and families were beginning to arrive, from the looks of it. There was just something about a Ferris wheel popping up in the middle of town that caught everyone's attention. I felt my anxiety building as the festival filled up with people—were we ready for this? Were all the vendors here? Why was the DJ I'd hired playing "Thriller" on repeat? Had I thought of everything?

I had to push my panicked thoughts aside to talk to Meghan from the Woodvale Times in front of the merry-go-round. That was one task I would have loved to have delegated to Sarah—she was much better at this kind of thing—but she was nowhere to be found. I had no choice but to do the interview myself.

"Feel free to paraphrase my awkward ramblings," I told Meghan when we finished.

She sighed as she put her recorder away, muttering, "Don't worry. Nobody reads the fucking paper, anyway."

I barely had time to react to this frank declaration before Jillian Taylor from WWTV approached me for an interview for the seven o'clock news. It felt like meeting a celebrity—she was on all the billboards around town, and her make-up and blonde bob were just as flawless in person. I hadn't even reached out to WWTV, but the festival must have caught their attention.

"I'm not really sure what to say," I admitted to Jillian, trying to comb my hair with my fingers.

"You'll do fine. Just pretend the camera isn't there and talk to me. We'll keep it casual—it'll be like talking to a friend." Jillian did have a comforting presence about her, and I felt some of my anxiety melt away. When the camera started rolling, we talked about everything from the fundraising aspect of the festival to what kind of food was being served in the food trucks behind us. "If only you could smell through your TV screens, folks," Jillian said to the camera, and I mustered up my best fake laugh. It didn't sound as believable as hers—but then again, she was a pro at this.

Throughout our talk, I imagined I was Sarah—I said all the things I assumed she would probably say. Whatever I could to make Grissom look good. "We're just hoping everyone in the community can come out and have a good time while supporting a good cause," I said. The second those words left my mouth, I heard the unmistakable sound of the bouncy castle deflating once again—and this time it was followed by the shrieks of horrified kids. The camera was still pointed at me, so I did my best to keep a smile plastered on my face and pretended like there wasn't chaos unfolding thirty feet from us.

"Oh, the humanity," the cameraman joked, referencing the Hindenburg disaster.

"We'll edit out the screams," Jillian deadpanned, and I wanted to die.

By the time the interview was over and WWTV packed up and left, the space around me had filled up with people. My hands were getting shaky, and my head was killing me—and suddenly, it dawned on me that not only had I forgotten to eat anything that day, I'd also left my anxiety medication at home.

"Isn't this amazing?" I heard Sarah before I saw her. She gripped my arm from behind and came in for a side-hug between the merry-go-round and the slowly reinflating bouncy castle. "Look, it all turned out so well."

"It's a shit show."

"What are you talking about?" Sarah laughed. "Everyone's already having so much fun. You did it, Kendall."

Owen came up on her other side, interlocking his fingers on top of his backwards Cubs hat. "We can't figure out why the bouncy castle keeps shorting out. But the good news is, the kids all think it's hilarious when it starts to deflate. Their parents—not so much."

I put one of my hands over my eyes as though the chaos would fade away if I couldn't see it. "Great. We're so going to get sued." Logically, I knew everything was going to be okay—but I still felt like I was on the verge of tears. Even Sarah's reassuring pats on my back weren't helping.

"She's feeling a little stressed out," I heard her tell Owen. I half-listened to them have a conversation about me that somehow turned into a joke about Sarah needing to give me a raise and her reminding him that was out of her control.

With my forehead still resting on my palm, I sensed someone approaching, their body eclipsing the sun to cast a shadow over my face. "You're terrible at following directions," a husky voice said.

I looked up to see Mason smirking at me, his wild hair blowing in the breeze. No force in the world could have prevented the goofy grin from forming on my face. "What are you talking about?"

"Did I or did I not ask you to enjoy yourself? And you're just standing here commiserating with these guys?" He nodded at Sarah and Owen and clicked his tongue. "Shame."

"I'm just overwhelmed."

"Will this help?" It was then that I noticed he was holding a caramel apple—he must have been hiding it behind his back. "These are selling fast, and there's a long line. So I may have just cut in front of them all and stolen this from my mom."

Owen laughed. "Aunt Christine let that happen?"

I accepted the caramel apple from Mason, no longer able to ignore my growling stomach. My fingers grazed his before he let go of the stick. "Oh my gosh, thank you."

I could tell it took him some effort to tear his eyes from mine to answer Owen. "Christine's in a good mood today."

"Your mom is the sweetest," I said, eagerly taking a bite. I swallowed quickly. "We had the best chat earlier."

Mason licked his lips, watching me eat. "You met my mom, did you?" I nodded, my mouth too full of chewy caramel to respond with anything more than a nod. "If you're lucky, you might get to meet my dad, too. Finley's dragging him all over this place. She's had him on the merry-go-round at least twice."

I wiped my mouth with the back of my hand, regretting my decision to eat this caramel apple so fast. "That's a good grandpa."

Mason maneuvered to stand beside me to get out of the way of the people walking behind him. Once they passed, though, he remained by my side, his shoulder grazing mine. In the corner of my eye, I saw Owen tug on Sarah's shirt sleeve to pull her away, leaving Mason and me to stand there alone at the center of the festival.

"Good to know this DJ does, in fact, have other songs in his repertoire besides 'Thriller'," Mason said, squinting up at the Ferris wheel in the setting sun. I stood still and listened—it was difficult to hear "I Put a Spell On You" playing over the sounds of the carnival rides and all the screaming kids. I opened my mouth to make a joke about wondering if he could play Taylor Swift, but Mason leaned in close and said, "You're giving me some disrespectful thoughts with the way you're eating that caramel apple, Ms. Devin."

"Mason!" I gave his arm a playful shove. "Thanks a lot, now I'm going to be self-conscious about it."

Just then, Elijah ran past us clutching a corn dog in one hand and a fistful of pink cotton candy in the other, his face painted like Spider-man. He threw his head back in maniacal laughter as he ran, and his exhausted-looking mom wasn't far behind. Mason and I turned to each other and laughed. "I think that's the first time I've heard that kid's voice," Mason said.

Laughing at Elijah had somehow brought our bodies even closer, and his arm was fully smashed against mine now. I could feel Mason's eyes lingering on me, so I lifted the caramel apple to my mouth to take a slow, deliberate bite, letting out the slightest, softest moan of pleasure that only he could hear. Maybe it was teasing. Perhaps it was even cruel. But when Mason cleared his throat and shifted his weight on his feet, I knew I'd achieved the desired effect.

"Yeah, you're *real* self-conscious about it," he mumbled, crossing his arms.

"I don't know what you're talking about." I handed him what was left of the apple on the stick while licking the caramel from my lips. I needed to make my rounds and ensure everything was operating how it should and everyone was in their place. I turned to walk away, but he grabbed my wrist, deciding he'd be the one to have the last word this time.

"What?"

"Just thinking that I might have to bring you a corn dog next."

chapter twenty-three
mason

As the evening went on and the sun dipped below the horizon, the festival crowd appeared to triple in size. Kendall's fear that half of Woodvale would be in attendance was coming true. I found my dad and Finley in the midst of the insanity and reminded him to keep a good eye on her. "Don't let her out of your sight." We established a meeting place—the merry-go-round—just in case she got separated from him.

Which was likely, considering he was having a hard time keeping up with her.

I joined them in the games area for a while and wasted eighteen dollars to win Finley a jellyfish plushie at a ring toss. Her excitement when it was handed to her made it all worth it, though. Her day was made.

"You won that for me, right?" Owen came up behind us and pretended to take the jellyfish from Finley, who scowled at him and clung onto it even tighter.

"There's our family celebrity," my dad said, clamping his hand on Owen's shoulder. The man actually smiled for the first time that day. "I heard you funded this whole thing."

Owen put his hands in his pockets and looked down at the rock he was lazily kicking between his feet on the pavement. "No, just the rides. There are other donors who—"

"How's that second book coming along?"

Owen gave me a side glance before answering. "It's getting there. Wedding plans are taking precedence right now, though."

"I imagine. This is a big year for you, huh?" Already, my dad was having a longer conversation with his favorite nephew than he'd had with me since I'd moved back home. He continued to ask Owen questions about his business, praising him with every other statement. He was completely oblivious to the way Owen kept attempting to steer the conversation a different direction.

As they spoke, I absentmindedly twirled Finley (and her jellyfish) around while scanning the crowd for Kendall. The last time I'd seen her, she was manning the hot cocoa booth so the vendor could take a bathroom break—and that was a half hour ago.

"Grandpa, I'm bored," Finley whined, letting go of my hand to tug on her grandpa's arm instead. "Can we ride the merry-go-round again?"

My dad sighed, pulling his eyes away from Owen to acknowledge her. "We've already been on it four times, sweetheart. Why don't I just watch you ride it this time?"

"No, you have to ride the blue horsey again! He misses you!"

"That's a pretty compelling argument, Uncle Mitch," Owen said as Finley began to pull her grandpa away. My dad groaned, but he gave in to her anyway—just like usual.

I shook my head, watching them get in line for the ride. "She's going to sleep good tonight."

Owen chuckled. "That's a plus. Hey—before I forget." He pulled out his phone and glanced down at the screen. "My team is loving your little illustration."

"Oh, are they?"

"Yeah. I forwarded it to them earlier. My PA's trying to convince me to use it in some of our marketing." I nodded, trying not to fixate on his choice of words. What did he mean they were trying to "convince" him? Did that mean he needed convincing? It bothered me that it wasn't the other way around—why wasn't he the one convincing them? "So are you going to let me buy it from you?"

I looked up at his face. Maybe he *was* interested. "I'm sure we could work something out."

"And we could discuss having you draw a whole crew of characters. Maybe a… raccoon with a microscope," he said with a grin. I wanted to believe he wasn't being disingenuous, and that he really wanted to hire me to do some custom illustrations for him, but it sounded so silly. I was grateful my dad wasn't around to overhear this conversation.

"Yeah, I could come up with some ideas for you," I said, surprised he didn't already have an employee for this kind of thing. "So how many people do you have working for you, anyway?"

"Five, right now."

"What all do they do for you?"

Owen furrowed his brows in concentration. "Uh, bookkeeping, producing, social media, curriculum development, and a general personal assistant of sorts. Why?"

With a shrug, I answered, "I was just curious." I couldn't help but notice some untapped opportunities there, especially on the creative end of things. Maybe if this character illustration gig worked out, I could make Owen one of my regular clients. The wheels in my brain started to turn, but before I could offer up another idea to him, I spotted Kendall through the crowd. She was standing by the book drive table talking to Abigail as she pulled on a yellow cardigan. I half-listened to Owen talk while watching her—and the second she stepped away from Abigail, I saw an opportunity. "Sorry," I interrupted Owen. "I have something I need to take care of."

I offered no explanation. I just walked away, knowing he'd probably understand once he saw me approach Kendall. I was about 90% sure he was onto us, anyway.

Kendall was walking fast—I had to sprint to catch up to her. I waited until we were walking shoulder-to-shoulder to get her attention. "Hey, you."

She put her hand over her heart and came to an abrupt halt, turning to me with wide eyes. "Oh my god, you scared me."

I chuckled. "Sorry. Where you headed?"

"I was going to see if some of the vendors needed to take a break to grab something to eat."

"When do *you* get a break?"

She just grinned at me from one side of her mouth before looking down at her shoes.

"When's the last time you sat down?"

"Um…" We both knew it had probably been hours.

I reached for her arm, gently tugging her in the direction of the Ferris wheel. "Come on. Why don't we go ride the Ferris wheel while the line is short?"

She scoffed in protest as I pulled her along. "Mason, I have a dozen things I need to do right now."

"Can't they wait?" I maneuvered through the crowd of people waiting to get their kids' faces painted and past the petting zoo area to the line for the Ferris wheel, which was the shortest I'd seen it all evening. I dropped her arm once we reached the back of the line. "I mean, if you'd rather ride the merry-go-round, just tell me."

Kendall put her hands in the pockets of her cardigan and gave me a playful eyeroll. "No, this is fine." I knew I'd get her to give in. She looked over her shoulder in the direction of Noah Sherman and his family, who were in line at the cotton candy cart, and I worried she might be feeling nervous about what people would think about seeing us together.

"I promise to keep my hands to myself," I said, immediately wanting to kick myself for making yet another promise I wasn't sure I was strong enough to keep.

Kendall looked up with a grin that told me she didn't quite believe me. Fuck, she looked so pretty under the glow of the Ferris wheel lights. I put my hands in my back pockets as we stepped forward in line and looked up at the gondolas above—

just how much did they conceal, anyway? What might I be able to get away with up there?

I was imagining how this ride might go when I felt something—or someone—tugging on the back of my shirt. I whipped around to see Finley standing there chewing on the end of one of her jellyfish's tentacles. After a quick glance around, I realized my dad was nowhere in sight. "Fin, where's Grandpa?"

"The merry-go-round made him dizzy, so he had to sit down. He told me to stick with you for a little while." It took everything I had to hide the disappointment in my face. I slowly inhaled as Finley slipped her hand in mine and waved her jellyfish in the air in front of Kendall. "Look what my daddy won for me!"

"Your favorite animal!" Kendall replied. If she was disappointed, she was doing a better job than me of not letting it show. "Are you going to ride the Ferris wheel with us?"

"Yup."

I turned to Kendall and whispered, "I'm sorry."

"It's fine," she said, tucking her hair behind her ears with a smile. "The more the merrier, right?"

Right. Kendall seemed so happy that Finley had joined us that I began to feel a little guilty—what was I hoping would happen, anyway? I gave Finley's hand a squeeze, accepting that I might as well embrace it. As far as I knew, Finley had never been on a Ferris wheel before. And her presence there could serve as a buffer of sorts between me and Kendall. We needed that.

When it was our turn to get on, Kendall slid into our seat first. Finley and her jellyfish sat between us. As we started to rise into the air, Kendall inhaled and her body went stiff.

"Are you okay?"

"I actually might be a little scared of heights."

"And why didn't you tell me that before I practically forced you to get on this thing?"

"I don't know?" She laughed at herself, but her eyes darted around as she gripped the metal door in front of us. The ride jerked and rocked more than any Ferris wheel I'd ever been on, which wasn't helping the situation. Finley was giggling with excitement as we rose higher and higher, but Kendall's body was still tense as she peered over the side of the gondola.

"Hey, look at me," I said, resting my arm on the back of the seat behind her and Finley. She turned to face me. "Do you hear that?"

"Hear what?"

"What song is the DJ playing?" I asked, pausing so she could listen more closely. I tried not to smile as the realization hit her face—because the song that was playing was "Never Gonna Give You Up" by Rick Astley.

Kendall's mouth dropped open. "Did you just—did you just Rick Roll me?"

"What's that mean?" Finley asked.

"Too hard to explain," I answered, giving her knee a squeeze before looking back up at Kendall, who was shaking her head in amusement. I was pleased my method of distraction worked. We were at the top of the Ferris wheel now, which gave us a perfect view of the festival. I could see the lights from the lanterns we'd assembled the night before down on the tables below, and the aroma from the cotton candy cart was wafting all the way to us. I could hear the kids shrieking and laughing in the bouncy castle below—it hadn't spontaneously deflated in the past hour. It seemed we were in the clear.

I hoped Kendall realized none of this would have been possible if it weren't for her. "You know, aside from the world's worst DJ, this festival is really somethin' else," I said. "You did an amazing job planning it."

"Yeah. Right." She shook her head.

"Finley, what do you think of this festival?"

"It's the best!" she yelled, holding her jellyfish high above her head.

"See?" I raised my eyebrows at Kendall over the top of Finley's head. "I'm gonna ask Elijah next."

"If you can catch him," she said with a laugh. We were back at the bottom now, which might have been helping her relax. Without giving it much thought, I lowered my arm just enough for my wrist to graze her upper back as we began to ascend to the top again.

"Just admit you pulled it off," I said. "ADHD and anxiety be damned."

Finley gasped as though she hadn't heard me say that word a thousand times. Kendall giggled. "I'm just glad I don't have to worry about it anymore after tonight. And I'm praying Sarah doesn't ask me to do this ever—" The ride jerked as it came to a halt to unload people at the bottom. We were near the top again, and Kendall clenched her eyes shut.

My distracting her could only work for so long—I was running out of things to say. This time, however, it was Finley who came to her rescue. She stared up at Kendall's frightened expression for a few seconds before reaching for her teacher's hand. "Don't worry, Ms. Devin," she said in a perky, reassuring tone. "We're safe right where we are."

Kendall opened her eyes. "You're right," she said, giving Finley's hand a squeeze. I looked down at my lap and smiled, instinctively letting my hand drop to Kendall's shoulder. I hoped she would perceive it as a comforting gesture, not just me trying to make a move. As we started moving again, I thought I caught the corners of her lips lifting in a smile as she stared down at her hand holding Finley's.

I swallowed. The three of us together like this—it was exactly the kind of connection I had been longing for. If only our circumstances were a little different. My mind swirled with thoughts of a future with Kendall, a future I knew was impossible. Or almost impossible.

I'd made that promise all those weeks ago, but if Kendall showed me just the tiniest inclination she'd changed her mind about it—I'd seize the opportunity without giving it a second thought.

I scanned her face for some kind of signal that she wanted to move forward—that she was willing to give this a try. Be it a secret relationship or a one-night thing just to get it out of our systems—I'd give her whatever she wanted.

Even if what she wanted was for me to leave her alone.

"Thanks for making sure I got a break," she said. Her eyes lingered on mine, and for a moment, it was like Finley wasn't sitting between us.

"You're welcome."

We were playing chicken with our gaze—who would be the first to tear their eyes away? Neither of us budged until Finley announced, "I hope this ride ends soon, 'cause I'm about to pee my pants."

That'll do it.

＊＊

Just after nine o'clock, the rides came to a halt and their lights were shut off, and the crowd began to dissipate. The DJ played "Closing Time" just before shutting down and packing up for the night, along with all the vendors. My mom had been out of caramel apples for the past hour, and she and my dad dragged a tearful Finley to their car. It was well past her bedtime. "If you're going to stay and clean up, she can sleep on the cot in our room tonight," my mom had said, carrying Finley on her hip. My dad couldn't hide his annoyance—we all knew Finley was going to end up in the bed between her grandparents.

Owen and I carried tables and chairs into the school, and then we loaded the cotton candy cart into a storage room at the back of the kitchen. The rest of the clean-up mostly involved picking up trash—it was everywhere. It took a group of ten or so volunteers almost an hour to get the school parking lot to look like—well, a parking lot—again.

Sarah, Owen, Kendall, and I were the last four to remain at the end of the night. "Everything we can do tonight is done," Sarah said as she approached us on the sidewalk between the parking lot and the schoolyard. "The ride company and bouncy castle people are coming tomorrow morning to disassemble everything."

"Do you need me here for that?" Kendall asked.

"No, you've done enough already. More than enough." Sarah pulled Kendall in for a hug. "Now go get some rest."

Owen gave me a goodbye nod. "See you, cuz." And as the two of them made their way to Owen's car parked down the street, he spontaneously picked her up by the legs and threw her over his shoulder. Sarah's shrieking laughter echoed across the school grounds as he carried her off. We waved goodbye to them as they drove away. Only two cars remained in the side lot—mine and hers. Beneath the glow of the twinkle lights strung from the awning, we were completely alone.

"You didn't have to stay so late," Kendall said, pulling her cardigan together in the front. The temperature had dipped a bit since the sun went down. "I'm sure you need to get home to Finley."

"She's my parents' problem right now."

Kendall smiled. "She had a lot of fun tonight, didn't she?"

"Yeah, she did." I loosely crossed my arms and licked my lips, glancing from Kendall's eyes to her mouth and back to her eyes. "Did you?"

She merely nodded.

"Good."

"Thanks to you," she added.

"Oh, you mean when I unwittingly gave you exposure therapy for your fear of heights? Yeah, I'm sure that was—"

"The highlight of my night," she finished. The intensity of her stare made my heart skip a beat. And her lips looked so welcoming, so… inviting.

But I promised.

"You know," I said, taking a step toward her. "I promised I wouldn't kiss you again, and I intend to keep that promise. But I'm warning you—if you were to initiate a kiss, I wouldn't hold back. And I can't guarantee I'd be able to stop."

I'd given her a fair warning. She tried not to look at me as I dared her to kiss me with my eyes. Her hesitation didn't worry me—the desire was right there. I could almost taste it. But would she give in?

Kendall let out a heavy sigh of defeat before yanking on the front of my flannel shirt to pull my body toward hers. I took the smallest, tumbling step forward as she brought her lips up to meet mine. I let her initiate it, but the second our mouths touched, I took control, holding her face in both of my hands. Her tongue tasted like caramel and cotton candy and risk and possibility. As her hands slid around my midsection, I dropped my own hands to cup her ass in them—turns out it was a little more than I could handle, after all. I grunted against her mouth before pulling away with a gentle tug, feeling myself go hard against her abdomen. I took a few short breaths, resting my forehead against hers.

"What's wrong?"

"Just taking the time to appreciate you," I said, giving her ass a hard squeeze that made her grin. I lowered my hands to that delicious spot at the top of her thighs. "All of you."

I moved my lips to her neck, kissing and sucking on her skin. "Take me to your place," I whispered, hooking two of my fingers beneath the waistband of her skirt.

"Can't," she said breathlessly. "Lesbian book club."

I didn't ask for an explanation. I needn't explain why we couldn't go back to my house, either. Though Finley would be sleeping two floors above me, it was still too risky. "Fuck," I said before kissing her lips again. There was nowhere for us to go. I feared that if I didn't fuck this woman very soon, we'd both come to our senses and the moment would forever be lost.

That was when we both turned to the still-inflated bouncy castle in unison. It was in the grassy area near the school entrance, half-hidden from the view of passing cars by the Ferris wheel.

I turned back to Kendall and raised an eyebrow at her in question. Surely we couldn't—?

Her eyes twinkled.

Oh, yes.

Yes we could.

chapter twenty-four
kendall

"Are we actually doing this right now?" Mason crawled between the flaps of the bouncy castle behind me, not laughing about this nearly as much as I was. We'd tossed our shoes on the ground outside—because we were rule followers, obviously.

"Don't change your mind on me now," I told him as we slid backwards against the vinyl toward the middle of the bouncy castle.

"Believe me, I'm not," he said with a husky chuckle before pulling me down on top of him. I straddled his lap, a knee on either side of him, making a point not to sit on my skirt to give him easier access—an effort that was immediately rewarded. With his lips on mine and one hand cradling the back of my neck, his other hand slid up my thigh beneath my skirt. His fingers wasted no time at all slipping beneath the back of my panties, too, and he pressed his whole palm against my butt, squeezing me so hard he was probably going to leave five little fingertip-shaped bruises. It took my breath away. "I love watching your ass jiggle when you walk in the classroom," he said in a low, growl-like voice.

I threw my head back to laugh, which he took as an invitation to kiss the front of my throat. It made me shiver. I brought my chin back down and focused on his eyes. His brows furrowed with worry. "Kendall," he said, his throat bobbing. "I don't—I don't have anything on me."

"I'm on birth control."

He nodded, but the look of concern didn't fade.

"We don't have to do this, Mason."

"No," he said, moving both of his hands to my thighs. He kissed me again. "I want to. And this might be a really unsexy thing to say right now, but I just want to tell you—I got tested not that long ago. Over the summer. And I'm good."

I grinned. "I did too—after Heath. All good here, too. And that's not unsexy at all." Come to think of it, Mason was the first man to ever take the time to mention such a thing to me, and I couldn't think of anything sexier at the moment. I kissed him more tenderly after that exchange, and he matched my pace, returning his hands to my cheeks to hold my face as he kissed me back. With one hand, he brushed some of my hair out of my eyes before tucking it behind my ear. Slowly, he removed my cardigan, dropping it to the side before kissing my forehead. I wasn't expecting this gentleness from him, this slowness—but I liked it.

"Are you cold?" he asked me.

I shook my head against his forehead. And before it even registered that his hand was inching up the back of my t-shirt, my bra was unfastened—and that same warm hand was already sliding to the front of my body. I tried not to think about how many bras Mason must have unhooked in his life to become so skilled at it, choosing instead to concentrate on the sensation of his fingers finding their way to one of my nipples. I removed my bra through one of my sleeves to make it easier on him, tossing it out of the way. If I had known I'd have Mason Reed undressing me that night, I might have worn something sexier than a plain white bra, but he was more interested in what was underneath, anyway.

He put both of his hands under my shirt, kissing me as he ran his thumbs over my nipples. "The things I want to do to you," he whispered.

"The way I want to let you," I rasped against his ear. And, understanding I was giving him permission to not be so gentle, he pinched both of my nipples between his thumbs and forefingers. I let out a soft moan against his cheek as he nuzzled against my ear.

Mason's hands dropped down to my hips just before he slid me off his lap, laying me down on the cool vinyl. I tugged on the bottom of his t-shirt until he got the message, removing both of his shirts and throwing them into the growing pile of discarded garments beside us. I gasped at the sight of the tattoo that covered half of his chest. It was an old-fashioned looking clock with Finley's name on it in the spot where the clock's brand was usually printed—and the hands were pointed to the two and the seven—likely representing the time of Finley's birth. I traced the tattoo with my fingers, taking in every detail of the illustration on the face of the clock, where there was a silhouette of a father holding a little girl's hand before a starlit sky.

"Are you still with me?" Mason asked, hovering above me.

"I'm sorry—I'm a little distracted."

"I drew that."

My lips parted in surprise. "It's beautiful." I was silently cursing myself for slowing us down and letting my tendency to get distracted ruin the moment, but his face softened into a smile as he lowered himself all the way onto me.

"You're beautiful," he said, brushing his lips against mine. He maneuvered to the side of me just enough to give himself room to slide his hand between my thighs under my skirt again. When his thumb reached the top of my legs, he brushed it against my underwear in a delicate, sweeping motion. Then he pressed down harder, rubbing my clit with his thumb over the cotton fabric. His lips pulled up into a smile. "Your pussy's already so wet for me, princess," he said. I closed my eyes, the sudden dirty talk completely undoing me. That last word stuck in my mind, though.

"Princess?" I asked as Mason's fingers inched toward the waistband of my underwear.

"We're in a castle, aren't we?"

I couldn't answer him—because his hand was sliding beneath the fabric now. I wanted to warn him I hadn't had time to shave lately—and the words were on the tip of my tongue—but I willed myself to forget about it as his fingers sank even further down. His glassy-eyed smile let me know he didn't care about what he found there—if anything, he was enjoying himself. I turned my head more to kiss him, but he pulled just far enough away that my lips couldn't reach his. I thought it was cruel until I realized he wanted to see the expression on my face when his hand brushed against the most sensitive part of me. He applied gentle pressure with his middle and pointer fingers, alternating curling movements on either side of my clit.

Bless the woman who came before me that taught him this.

I scrunched up my face, feeling my cheeks get warm as he watched me enjoy the magic he was working with his fingers. "I want to hear you say my name," he said.

My eyes clenched shut. "Mmmm," was the only sound I was able to make. It was hard to speak when he was playing me like a piano. I felt like I was sinking further and further into the vinyl, my body relaxing more and more with every breath I exhaled.

Mason brought his mouth to my ear, slowing his fingers down. "Tell me, princess—who's got your cheeks flushed right now?"

"Mason," I whimpered.

"That's it," he said. And without warning, he pulled his hand back to reach for the top of my panties—pulling up to kneel beside me as he yanked them off with both hands. Then he repositioned himself by my feet, pushing my legs apart. With my knees in the air, my skirt slid down my thighs to my waist, exposing me to him.

My mind raced with a million thoughts and worries—I wanted to let him know that thanks to my anxiety pills, I might not finish, especially if my mind wandered like it sometimes did in situations like this.

"Mason," I said as he laid down between my legs, his whiskers brushing against my thighs. I pulled up onto my elbows so I could see his face better. "I want to make you feel good."

"You're about to," he said. And with no further commentary, he forced my thighs farther apart and began devouring me like I was his last meal. Like some kind of wild animal consuming his prey.

Like he was somehow enjoying this even more than me.

As much as I loved what he was doing with his lips and his tongue, his hands were driving me wild—one was splayed across the back of my thigh, his fingertips sinking into my skin—and the other was pressing onto my lower abdomen just above my pubic bone. The pressure he applied there made this whole experience even more mind-numbingly pleasurable.

He stopped long enough to say, "Fuck, you taste so good," before diving face-first into me again, using two fingers to spread me apart so he could thrust his tongue just inside.

I slid my hands across the smooth vinyl, wishing I had a headboard to grab on to or at least some sheets to grip. To my surprise, one of Mason's hands found mine—and he wrapped his fingers around my palm, squeezing it tight.

"Mmmm." Mason's lips vibrated against my clit. "God, I could live down here."

I lifted my head to peer down at him, finding him staring back at me as his tongue flicked over my clit again and again. This level of intimacy was entirely new to me—I'd never been able to make eye contact with a man who was going down on me. It always made me anxious, taking me right out of the moment. But the way Mason blinked slowly and blissfully as he stared into my eyes sent me right to the edge. "Oh God, oh fuck," I whined, arching my back as I felt my release coming. I tugged on his hair as I began to shake, squeezing his hand so hard I feared I might break his bones. Pleasure rippled through me and the pressure built and built until I almost couldn't stand it anymore. I arched my back more, lifting from the vinyl—and I may have screamed his name, but my head was spinning so much I was hardly aware of my own existence. As I gasped for air, I felt Mason slap the side of my thigh as he continued to lick me through every wave of pleasure until my knees fell to the side and I finally relaxed.

He pulled up beside me and lifted a few sweaty strands of hair off my forehead. "You probably don't want to kiss me now, do you?"

Without hesitation, I put my palm against his glistening cheek and brought his face closer to mine. I didn't mind tasting myself on his lips. He growled against my mouth, aggressively kissing me back before pulling up to straddle me again. I put my hands on his waistband, tucking my fingers beneath his jeans. "Let me return the favor."

"Oh, I'm not done with you yet," he said, rolling over to tear off the rest of his clothes. His already erect cock sprang from his boxers and I couldn't hold my gasp. I only had a second to react to the size of it before he was climbing atop me again, grabbing me by the backs of my knees to fold my legs over my body. On the surface, I was still twitching and pulsating from the orgasm he'd just given me as I felt him slide inside of me. He leaned over my body, folding me in half, and gripped my chin in his hand to force me to look at him. "Do you want more?"

I nodded, my eyes widening as he eased himself into me even further. His hand slid down to my neck. At first he didn't apply pressure—but I clasped my hand around his and showed him exactly what I wanted. He followed directions well, clamping his hand tighter around my throat as he thrusted.

"Naughty Ms. Devin," Mason said, his voice sounding deeper and huskier than it ever had. His grip tightened and he smiled devilishly. "All this time I thought you were a good girl," he said as pushed into me with a grunt, "but I was so wrong about you."

I struggled to make a sound, to retort with something sassy, but all I could manage was a strained gasp. I was completely and utterly under his control. Having Mason's hand clamped around my throat might have been the hottest thing I'd ever experienced.

"God, your pussy feels amazing," he said, leaning forward to kiss my lips. I let out a sad moan when he pulled his hand from my throat, but my disappointment was short-lived—because he used both hands to hold up my legs as he slammed his hips against mine with even deeper thrusts.

I could hear the sound of a car on gravel in the distance—the gravel lot at the back of the school. Someone was here. Mason heard it, too—but instead of stopping, he lowered his body against mine. He shushed me and then covered my mouth with his to keep me quiet.

My heart pounded in my chest. The idea of someone catching us was kind of a thrill.

I could be fired.

I could be arrested for public indecency.

This was so *wrong*.

I could feel myself inching toward another orgasm. I moaned, tilting my head backwards against the vinyl. "Can you come for me again, princess?" Mason growled against my ear.

I looked into his eyes—and, like last time, it was that level of intimacy that made me explode from the inside. I ran my fingernails down his back, clenching around his cock with a deeper orgasm ten times more powerful than the last. I moaned until he clamped a hand over my mouth, and I bit his hand—not hard enough for him to hurt, but enough for him to really feel it. Mason pressed his face into my collarbone as he sank into me again and again, faster now. His hand slid off my mouth as he twitched on top of me. "Fuck—Kendall," he groaned, his entire body shuddering as he came inside of me.

I ran my hands up and down his sweaty back as he quivered above me, his face still buried in my neck. As soon as he rolled off, I pulled down my skirt to catch the semen oozing out of me—the less mess we had to clean up, the better. Mason put an arm around my waist, sliding his other one behind my head. I nestled against his armpit, totally breathless. He turned to me and smiled before planting a kiss on my sweaty forehead. We lay there in silence for a moment, both of us listening—was someone else still here?

Somewhere nearby, a car door slammed, followed by the sound of tires on gravel again. They were leaving. "I think we're in the clear now," Mason said.

"Good."

He gazed into my eyes as he stroked my arm with his thumb. "That was incredible."

"My legs are still shaking."

That made him smile proudly. He could probably feel how much I was still trembling all over—it wasn't just my legs. And as smug as he might have felt about it, he still stroked my hair and said, "You've never looked more beautiful than you do right now."

I laughed. "I'm a mess."

"Yeah, and I like it." He touched my chin and kissed me. The cool breeze flowing through the screens of the bouncy castle made me shiver. Mason sat up to pull on his boxers, but in a matter of seconds, he was back by my side. "I know we probably should get out of here before we get caught," he said, putting his arm around me, "but can I hold you first?"

I turned so my back was against his chest, giving him my silent answer. He wanted to *hold* me. I'd never felt safer or more cared for than I did in the arms of Mason Reed.

And despite the nagging awareness that this wasn't supposed to happen and probably never would again, I shut my eyes, savoring this moment for as long as I could.

chapter twenty-five
mason

We were lucky the bouncy castle began deflating as we slept—otherwise, we might have awoken to a crew of amused carnival ride disassemblers in the morning. We scrambled to gather our discarded clothes and crawled out before it could fully collapse on us, only to have to re-inflate it because I'd lost my phone in there. Not only that, but we thought it might be respectful to clean up after ourselves.

I was still smiling as I tiptoed into the dark house, quietly locking the door behind me. I was thinking about how we parted in the parking lot—the way we embraced for the longest time because we were either too sleepy to move or simply unwilling to let go. And when I leaned in for one last kiss, she shoved her underwear in my pocket.

I rested my tired body against the front door, holding Kendall's underwear against my chin. How I would look at her with a straight face on Monday, I wasn't sure. I couldn't. I wouldn't.

Even after I washed my face and brushed my teeth, Kendall's taste lingered in my memory. I never wanted to forget the feeling of being between her thighs or the way my name sounded when she screamed it. Sighing, I dried my face with a hand towel and trudged to my bedroom.

The second I opened my dresser drawer to hide Kendall's panties away, I heard a quiet, squeaking cry come from my bed. "Jesus Christ," I muttered, flipping on the light. I turned around to see Finley curled into the fetal position on my bed, half-covered by the comforter and clutching her new jellyfish. She clamped her eyes shut, bothered by the overhead light. "Finley, what the hell? You're supposed to be up in Grandma's room."

She inhaled. "I was looking for you, and you weren't here!"

I sat on the bed beside her, nudging her feet out of my way. "Fin, you knew I had to stay and clean up."

"But not for fifteen hours!"

Her math wasn't quite adding up. I smiled and reached for her shoulder. "Sweetie, I wasn't gone for fifteen hours."

She shirked away from me and sniffled. "I needed to—I needed to hug you and you were gone."

"Does Grandma know where you are?" I rubbed her arm, awaiting some kind of explanation, but she ignored me. "Hey. What's wrong? Why did you need me so badly? Why are you so upset?"

"Because!" She widened her eyes at me like I was impossibly stupid for not figuring this out. "I don't like it when Grandma and Grandpa put me to bed. I get really sad. I get a cry stuck right here." She touched the front of her throat. "I was scared that you weren't coming home ever again."

"Finley." I couldn't help but chuckle at the absurdity of it. She scowled at me. "I'm sorry, but why wouldn't I come home? Why would you even think I—?"

I stopped and swallowed, pressing my lips together. I knew exactly why. And though she resisted, I scooped her up onto my lap and held her against my chest. Thankfully, she clung to me tight and let me hold her. I kissed the top of her head and rubbed her back.

"Finley," I whispered, pulling her hair off her shoulders. "I'll always come home."

"Not if you die."

Fuck.

"I'm not going to die." I held her a little tighter and began to rock my body from side to side with a soothing rhythm. "I'm not going to leave you. I'll always be here for you, okay?"

She sniffled against my chest and used my flannel shirt as a tissue. I didn't mind. I continued rocking her back and forth, unsure of what else to say—it was hard to find the words when my heart was breaking. It was everything I could do not to cry, too, but I had to keep it together. For her.

"I'm the only kid in my class who doesn't have a mom." This was the first time she'd ever spoken of her mom in such a way—the first time she'd ever said she didn't have one. Before, it was always, *"My mom lives far away."* This was new.

"Oh, Fin," I said, "I'm sure you're not the only one."

"Yuh-huh. I asked everyone at recess the 'nother day. Everybody has a mom. Emma even has two moms."

"Well." I cleared my throat—she had me there. "I bet Emma doesn't have a cool dad."

"Emma has two moms *and* a dad."

That's what I got for making an assumption. "Okay, I'm obviously not aware of Emma's… familial situation. But what I'm saying is that all families are different. And while you don't have a mom… here, with you… you've got me and Grandma and Grandpa. And you've got the best aunt who loves you so much, even if she does live far away." I took a deep breath. "And you have Traci, too. There are so many people in your life who love you. Even—even Ms. Devin."

I felt Finley nod against my chest. "Ms. Devin is really pretty and nice," she said, playing with the buttons on my shirt.

"You're right. She is." I took a deep breath, squeezing her closer to my chest. She was quiet for a couple of minutes, and I thought she might have been drifting off to sleep, but she lifted her hand to twist my hair around her fingers the way she always did when she was smaller. I peered down at her open eyes—she was staring blankly at the wall. Lost in thought.

And then she asked me a question that nearly stopped my heart from beating in my chest.

"Do you think if my old mom could see that I'm a really good girl now, she'd come back?"

All the air escaped from my lungs. I brought my hand to my eyes, wishing like hell there was a script for this kind of thing. What could I possibly say to this child to comfort her? How could I even begin to explain? "Finley," I whispered, my voice cracking. "She didn't leave because of you. She left because there was something wrong with her, okay? It was never, ever, your fault." I had told Finley all of this months ago, but evidently she didn't believe me then. And she probably wasn't believing me now.

I needed help.

"Hey." I shifted her body in my arms so I could see her face better. "Finley, do you remember Dr. Janelle in Indianapolis?" She nodded. "What if I found someone like that here in Woodvale that you could talk to?"

"With a Lite Brite?"

I forced myself to smile. "I can't guarantee they'll have a Lite Brite in their office like Dr. Janelle, but people like her—they're called therapists. I've talked to one before, and Grandma has one. They can help you figure out feelings that are really confusing. And all the feelings you have right now, they're a little confusing, right?"

"Sometimes my feelings are all jumbled up like this—" She wiggled her entire body and wagged her tongue, making a goofy noise. I waited patiently for her to stop.

"Exactly. Sometimes I can help you with those jumbled-up feelings, but a therapist—that's their *job*, Finley. They make it all fit together like a puzzle. They don't magically make the sadness go away, but they can, like, give you some strategies to make it a little easier to handle. Wouldn't that be great?"

"I guess so. I want to see Dr. Janelle, though."

"You can't, she's—" I stopped. Why couldn't she? Indianapolis wasn't that far away. If the kid had to miss a half day of school every now and then to talk to a therapist, who the fuck cared? "You know what? I'll see if she still has a slot for us."

"Yay!"

I already felt a sense of relief about the situation, and I'd given the kid something to look forward to. Hopefully, I could talk to the therapist one-on-one about how to better handle this.

I had Finley cover her eyes with the blanket as I changed into sweats. "You can sleep in my bed tonight," I told her as I flipped off the light and slid into the bed next to her. Finley was smiling from ear to ear—she knew I usually didn't allow this. She always ended up kicking me in the ribs or stealing the blanket. But tonight, I could deal with all of that.

Kendall was right. Finley was not okay.

That night, as she snored beside me, I stared up at the ceiling for what felt like an hour—maybe even longer. My daughter was monumentally traumatized by what her mother had done to her, and I'd spent the last couple of months pretending like everything was okay.

And that night, I'd watched my parents drag a crying Finley away from the festival grounds and simply brushed it off. Dismissed it. At the time, my brain could only focus on one thing: getting more time with Kendall. If I had just been paying closer attention, maybe I would have noticed how genuine her tears were.

The guilt kept me awake well into the early morning hours. As I watched Finley sleep, I stroked the side of her cheek, deciding I'd never again put my desires before her needs.

chapter twenty-six
kendall

On Sunday morning, I threw myself headfirst into a new hobby: baking.

Normally, I spent Sunday mornings curled under a blanket devouring smutty romance novels—often cover-to-cover. But that morning, I was so full of nervous energy, I felt the need to do something with my hands. So I baked some banana nut muffins from a mix I found in the pantry. Surely I could handle this.

As I whisked the mixture in the bowl, I closed my eyes and imagined Mason looking up at me, the whiskers on his chin glistening from my arousal. I felt him on top of me, inside of me. I smelled his cinnamon-y, musky scent mixing with the aroma of funnel cakes, which lingered in the air well after the festival was over. I heard the way he called me "princess" and the sounds his mouth made when he was licking me.

None of it could ever happen again. It shouldn't have happened to begin with—why had I kissed him in the first place, knowing where it would lead? He'd practically spelled it out for me. If I had known just how good it could be, maybe I would have resisted. Now I knew what it felt like to be close to Mason Reed, and my mind and body were forever changed.

"So stupid," I muttered to myself, sloppily pouring the banana-scented mixture into the muffin pan. I popped it into the oven before grabbing my book and a blanket, taking them to the porch as though a change of scenery might distract me.

And maybe it would have if my phone hadn't lit up with a "good morning" text from Mason—immediately followed by a picture of him lying down with Finley's feet next to his head, captioned "how I slept."

It made me giddy. I covered my face with the blanket and screamed into it, realizing this made it two mornings in a row now that he'd texted me. Boyfriend behavior.

I thought carefully about how to reply, but I couldn't hold myself back from responding to that photo with a bunch of heart emojis. *Real subtle, Kendall.*

We texted back and forth for five minutes, just talking about Finley and how her tiny body took up 90% of Mason's bed. I only put my phone down when Jamie's car pulled up to the curb at the end of her night shift at the pharmacy. She strolled up to the porch, pulled her vape out of her pocket, and sat next to me on the swing.

"How'd your book club thing go last night?"

She raised her eyebrows. "It was fun. We're definitely going to make it a regular thing." She zipped up her jacket with a shiver, so I draped the blanket over her back. Tugging the corner of it over her shoulder, she added, "Would've been a lot better if Daya hadn't gone to her room an hour into it."

"Oh, did something happen?"

"No. She just—" Jamie shook her head, sucking on her vape. "She just wasn't vibing with my friends, I guess. It's hard not to take it personal."

"Well, Daya's a little shy. Maybe it's hard for her to socialize with a big group of people like that?"

"I know. You're not wrong. But the thing is, I'm constantly giving up doing social things for the sake of her comfort. We stay home all the time now, and we don't talk to people. I thought that by inviting people to *us*, into the comfort of our own home, it would make a difference. But I guess not. She couldn't just make an effort for a few hours?"

I could see her point.

"We're just so different," Jamie said, sticking her vape into her jacket pocket. I nodded. Perhaps they were *too* different, I thought. "Anyway, how'd that festival go?"

I turned my head toward her, a grin creeping onto my lips.

Jamie squinted at me, sliding closer to me so the blanket could cover her better. "What? Why are you smiling like a weirdo?"

My smile grew until my cheeks hurt. "I don't know," I lied.

"Oh my god." Her mouth fell open. "You had sex with that Hanson brother, didn't you?"

I laughed. "What? How could you possibly know that?"

"Because I've known you your whole fucking life. And you're giving me that 'I just got my socks knocked off' look. So go on, spill. Did you do it on the Ferris wheel, or what?"

I covered my face. "The bouncy castle, actually."

"The bouncy—Kendall! I was joking! Are you serious right now?" She squeezed my knee. "You dirty whore."

I let out an elongated sigh. "I just don't know what to do now, Jamie. It was perfect—everything about it was just—ugh." I couldn't even find the words. "He was amazing. But it was such a risk. I slept with one of my students' parents. I could get fired if this got out."

"No one needs to find out. It's not like you haven't done the whole 'forbidden relationship' thing before."

"But it's different this time. Not just because it's my job that's on the line this time, but—he's got a *daughter*. What am I thinking messing around with a guy with a kid? I could never be some kind of—" I almost said "maternal figure," but I couldn't make my mouth form the words.

"You're worrying about this way too much. Just have some more meaningless sex with the guy and relax. You don't have to go catching feelings."

The sex I had with Mason was anything but meaningless, but I didn't mention that. Before I could say anything at all, Jamie sniffed the air with a confused look on her face. "Is something burning?"

Shit.

* *

On Monday morning, I was determined to act completely normal when Mason arrived. Due to an ear infection, Elijah had to stay inside during an outdoor PE activity, but I was somewhat grateful for his presence. Maybe it could ease the tension a little.

But when Mason "Two Orgasms" Reed walked into my classroom, my stomach fluttered and a warmth spread through my cheeks. Clutching two coffees against his chest, he halted when he saw Elijah coloring a picture at his desk. "Uh oh. What's going on, buddy?"

"He's got an ear infection," I explained. "His mom doesn't want him going outside."

"You sure felt fine Saturday night, dude," Mason said, standing directly in front of him. Elijah looked up at him with wide eyes. "Uh huh, I saw you. Double-fisting snacks and giving the bouncy castle supervisors a run for their money. Our regular ol' shy Elijah was nowhere in sight. Now—which one is the real you?" Mason bent down and raised a curious eyebrow at the child, like he was trying to crack the code or something. Elijah quietly giggled in response.

Mason approached me with a shrug. "At least I tried." He held my coffee toward me. "Here you are, princess."

His eyes lingered on my flushed cheeks as I accepted the coffee from his hand. "Thanks." The image of him looking up at me from between my legs flashed before my eyes, and I had to force myself to look down at my cup as I took a drink.

Mason remained standing in front of my desk, sipping his own coffee as he eyed Elijah. If I had to guess, he was probably a little annoyed by Elijah's presence—it meant he'd have to censor himself. "So," he said, turning back to me. "What do you have for me today, Ms. Devin?"

I picked up a stack of the kids' Halloween crafts from Friday afternoon. "I could use some help taping bats to the back of the door," I said.

Mason sat his coffee down on the corner of my desk—the only part of it not covered by clutter—and clapped his hands together. "All right, let's do it."

I pulled two rolls of masking tape from my desk drawer, handing one of them to Mason—along with half of the bats. As he followed me toward the classroom door, all I could think about was what he said about watching my ass jiggle when I walked. I was wearing a brown corduroy pinafore over a crème top with crème tights that day—and I had no idea what I looked like from behind. The grin he was failing to suppress when I turned around, though, confirmed my suspicion he was checking me out. "Is something amusing?" I asked.

He put his stack of bats on the shelf by the door and tore off a piece of tape. "Just thinking about how much fun that festival was."

I glanced over my shoulder at Elijah as I rolled my own piece of tape. He was picking his nose and watching us closely. We couldn't have this conversation—not now. "Yeah, all the kids really enjoyed that pumpkin slingshot."

Mason pressed the first bat against the door. "I was actually thinking that bouncy castles are way more fun than I remembered."

I smiled from one side of my mouth as I stood on my tiptoes to tape a bat near the top of the door. "Well. You're not wrong about that," I mumbled.

Mason bit into his tape to tear off a piece, which was somewhat unnecessary—but hot. He glanced over at Elijah, tossing his head to get his hair out of his eyes. And, with his voice low, he stepped a little closer to me to say, "I just—I don't know what—I'm not sure if—" Whatever he wanted to say to me, he sure was having a hard time spitting it out. Finally, he took a deep breath and started over. "I wanted to see how you were feeling about what happened."

"Well." I eyed the bats we'd already taped to the door, contemplating where to hang the next one. "I think it was a huge risk. And we're really lucky we weren't caught."

"Right," he said quickly, nodding in agreement. "It was a little bit stupid. Having said that, though, I'm glad we got it out of our systems."

"That we did."

"I also think… that it probably wouldn't be a good idea for us to—" He brought his eyes up to mine when he said, "Do that again."

I blinked, unsure if the air that escaped from my lips was a sigh of relief or disappointment. Maybe both. "Probably not." Though I meant those words, it pained me to say them. His eyes were still laser-focused on mine, reading me, so I added, "That kills me a little, to tell you that, but it's probably for the best if we just… don't."

Mason nodded slowly. "Yeah. I know." He glanced down at the bat in his hands before taping it to the door. "Things just got really tough with Finley, too, and I need to focus on that."

"They did? What do you mean?"

He sighed. "She had a rough weekend." He paused, glancing over his shoulder at Elijah, who had gone back to coloring. He could have still been listening, though, so Mason lowered his voice when he said, "She had a little bit of a mental breakdown Saturday night when I got back. So I called her old therapist this morning—she's going to start seeing her regularly again."

"Oh, that's good. The therapist part. Not the mental breakdown part." I held my hand over my heart. "What prompted this to happen?"

"I wasn't home, and she panicked. She started talking about her mom and she even brought up my mortality and—" He shook his head. "It was rough, Kendall."

"I'm sure it was. What about you—are you okay?"

"I'll be fine." He shrugged and pulled his eyes away, turning back to our project. But I grabbed his arm and made him look at me again.

"Just saying that you're fine doesn't make it true."

"I know." He stared down at my fingers wrapped around his muscular forearm. Feeling awkward about this gesture now, I slid my hand down to his wrist and squeezed him there before letting go.

"Maybe you should talk to someone, too," I said.

"Maybe." He held up the bat in his hands—this one had particularly large pupils, much bigger than all the other bats. "Look, this one has seen some shit."

"Mason." I waited for him to look at me again before I continued. "Promise me you'll talk to someone."

He could have made another joke. And I could tell from the way his lips parted before closing again that he almost did. Instead, he turned away and said, "Okay. I promise."

We continued taping bats for a few more minutes without speaking to each other. Mason talked to Elijah, cracking jokes at him in an attempt to get the kid to laugh the way he did at the festival, but he had no luck. "I'm onto you, mister," Mason warned him. Finally, a tiny giggle.

When it was almost time for the rest of the children to return from PE, Mason and I sat down by my desk and drank our coffee. He leaned forward, resting his elbows on his knees. "So, are we going to be able to bounce back from this? I can keep volunteering and it won't be weird?"

I slowly shook my head. "I don't know. I don't think it'll be that weird. I don't want you to stop." There. An honest answer.

"Okay. Can I still bring you coffee?"

"Absolutely."

He rubbed his beard. "Do you want me to return that—thing—you gave me?"

"No, Mason. Those are yours to keep."

"Like a… fall festival souvenir."

"Sure," I said with a laugh.

We smiled at each other as the hallway outside my door filled with the kids' excited voices. Maybe we really could go back to normal. We got all of that sexual frustration and tension out of our systems and we could leave it in the past. Do the responsible thing and move on.

It would be fine.

chapter twenty-seven
mason

All I could think about was how badly I wanted to bend that woman over her desk and fuck her from behind.

But that was probably frowned upon.

Especially after the conversation we'd just had. We'd reached a mutual agreement—what happened between us was a one-time thing, never to occur again. We both had our reasons. I understood hers, and she seemed to accept mine.

I didn't need anything distracting me from putting Finley first.

After that day, we went right back to our usual friendly—but flirty—banter. It was almost effortless, the way we both pretended like nothing had happened between us. We playfully roasted each other in front of the kids—I teased her about her terrible drawing skills during one of her lessons, and she dragged me for telling cheesy dad jokes during small group time. And as the days passed, we further nailed our routine, sometimes communicating across the classroom without saying a word at all.

And it was like we now had an understanding—*this is all we are. This is all we ever can be together.*

But there was something different, just beneath the surface. Those stares that lingered a few seconds longer than they would have before. The knowledge that I'd made her come twice—it wasn't like either of us could just forget it. I thought about it every time her fingers grazed my arm. Daydreamed about it when she slipped her foot out of her boot to perch it on the opposite thigh like a flamingo at the front of the room. I knew now just how flexible she really was—how far those legs could bend toward her body.

At least I got to have her once.

******

The walls in Dr. Janelle Lyons' office were painted a peaceful, muted shade of blue, and in lieu of fluorescents, there were a couple of lamps providing a calming warm light. The walls were decorated with colorful canvas photographs of rainforest animals and framed children's artwork displayed in a gallery-like manner. The room didn't feel the least bit sterile or clinical—Dr. Lyons did everything she could to make her young clients feel comfortable.

I sat in a cushy leather chair facing her desk while Finley played with a Lite Brite in the adjacent room, separated by a soundproof window. Dr. Lyons often spoke to me first, and then spent some time with the two of us together before having some one-on-one time with Finley.

"Go ahead and update me on what's happened in your lives in the past few months," she said, folding her hands on her desk. Dr. Lyons' hair was styled into a natural afro, and she was wearing a button-up shirt with vertical black and white stripes. Her pink glasses added a playful touch to her professional appearance. "She started kindergarten, right?"

"Yeah, she did. She's loving it, too—she's made a lot of friends."

"That's good to hear. Do you know who she talks to or plays with the most?" Dr. Lyons picked up a pen and pulled a yellow notepad close to her.

"Elijah, probably," I answered. "He's, um—he's selectively mute, I guess? But Finley talks enough for the both of them."

Dr. Lyons chuckled as she wrote something down. "I bet she does. And what about her teacher—does Finley like them?" My stomach fluttered.

"Yeah, she does. Finley adores Ms. Devin—that's her name. She's…" I shook my head to get my hair out of my eyes and gazed up at the photograph of a toucan on the wall. I pictured Kendall's smile and the way her eyes sparkled when I said something stupid. "I couldn't have handpicked a better teacher for her."

"That's wonderful. Is she aware of Finley's situation?"

"Yes."

"Good." Dr. Lyons wrote down something else. She took a deep breath before looking up at me again. "So, I'm guessing there's a reason you're here. I know you moved back home, and it probably took some effort to make it here today. What prompted you to make this appointment?"

I sat up a little straighter and folded my hands between my knees. "I just came to the realization that I'm not handling this very well, and I thought that she was okay—that she was starting to get over it—but I think I've been unintentionally forcing her to suppress her emotions. I saw the way she never mentioned her mom as a good thing, but now I know I was wrong. So wrong. Because it all sort of spilled out at once."

Dr. Lyons nodded. "Like a volcano of emotions."

"Yes, exactly. It was all bubbling just beneath the surface, and I—" I stopped to take a breath, turning to watch Finley build a LEGO house through the soundproof window. "I couldn't even see it. I assumed she was fine. I've been failing her." I stared down at my lap.

"It takes a lot to acknowledge we're struggling as parents. And struggling isn't failing, Mason. You recognized she was having some challenges, and now you're here. That's a significant first step. You're doing a great job."

I chewed on my lip, allowing that validation to sink in. She said it all with so much confidence, I almost believed her.

"Can you remember what Finley said during this volcano of emotions?"

I nodded, and then I relayed the entire conversation Finley and I had in my room the night I came home from the festival, even mentioning Finley's fear that I could die. I told Dr. Lyons how Finley was still blaming herself for her mother's abandonment. "I hate Whitney so much for putting her through this." I'd never spoken those words out loud, like I wasn't allowed to say them. But that thought had been brewing just beneath the surface for some time, much like Finley's worries and fears.

"It's completely natural to feel angry and resentful. Whitney's actions have undoubtedly caused a lot of pain in both of your lives." I picked at the seam of my jeans as she spoke. She put her pen down on the notepad and leaned back. "It can be difficult to navigate these conversations when they come up, but the most important thing is to reassure her how loved she is by the adults surrounding her now."

This was even more validating—because that's exactly what I had done. I ran my pointer finger along my bottom lip and nodded, watching Finley again. It looked like she was singing to herself as she played. And as though she somehow knew I was watching her, she turned toward the window and froze for a second before making a silly face. I made one right back at her.

Dr. Lyons laughed. "Should we bring her in now?"

"Sure."

She retrieved Finley from the playroom and brought her in. Finley sat on my lap, and Dr. Lyons talked to us together, keeping the conversation casual the entire time. She asked about school and Elijah and Ms. Devin. She let Finley talk about what she was going to be for Halloween—a jellyfish—and listened to her carry on about the fall festival. I could tell the goal was to get reacquainted with Finley after not speaking with her for five months, and I was somewhat relieved she didn't dive into the deeper stuff right away.

"We're running out of time now," Dr. Lyons said, looking at her watch, "but we'll get to talk and do an activity by ourselves next time, okay, Finley?"

Finley slid off of my lap. "What kind of activity?"

"It's a surprise," Dr. Lyons answered with a wink.

I stood up, taking Finley by the hand. "Thank you for everything. This has been more helpful than you know." Dr. Lyons smiled with her eyes like she did know, though, as we shook hands and said goodbye.

When we got outside, I scooped Finley up in my arms and held her on the sidewalk, separated from the busy street by a row of trees with yellowing leaves. Dr. Lyons' office was connected to the hospital on the north side of downtown Indianapolis, and the city was bustling with activity on that late Friday afternoon. "Did you like talking to Dr. Janelle?" I asked.

"Yeah. But I really liked playing with the toys."

I laughed. "I hope you picked up that room when you were done in there."

Finley bit her bottom lip. "Umm…"

I kissed her on the temple. "What do you say we find something fun to do in Indy before we head home?"

**

Finley somehow convinced me to navigate to the nearest McDonald's, despite my begging her to try something new—or literally anything else. After we ate, we headed to her favorite bookstore, clear on the other side of the city on Mass Avenue. She loved it because the children's section was enclosed in a playhouse at the back of the store, and I liked it because the used books were often marked down to a dollar. The kid could leave with an armload of books and think I'd won the lottery or something.

"You can pick out ten books this time," I told her as she made her way to the back of the store when we arrived. "I'll be wandering around up here."

As I sipped my McDonald's Coke and meandered through the limited selection of new releases, I stopped in my tracks when I saw the last project I'd completed at my old job—the *Flipping Fabulous* book. I'd completely missed its release date.

I sat my drink down on the shelf and picked up the book, flipping to the copyright page to find my name. It felt like so long ago that I'd worked on that project. I inhaled through my nose, thinking about how different my life was before I became a full-time dad—when I still lived and worked in the city.

That felt like a completely different lifetime.

I put the book back on the shelf—only to pick it right back up and tuck it under my armpit, remembering Kendall was a fan of the show. I might not be allowed to touch her anymore, but I could still give her a gift. As a friend, or whatever.

When I grabbed my Coke and turned around, I saw Owen's *STEM for the Win* book on display beneath a chalkboard that said *SIGNED BY THE AUTHOR!* We already had two copies of this book at my parents' house, but admittedly, I hadn't thumbed through it since the summer when Finley and I conducted one of Owen's science experiments.

After making sure Finley was still content at the other side of the store, I grabbed the book and casually flipped through the pages. It was a self-published book, and Owen prided himself on doing a lot of the work himself. The page layouts were sleek and modern, but they seemed a bit too straightforward—too basic—for the lively and sometimes whimsical tone of Owen's writing.

Suddenly, an idea occurred to me.

I should get Owen to hire me.

And not just for a single project. If I played my cards right, I could persuade him to bring me on as a full-time employee. He was probably planning his budget for the upcoming fiscal year, and if he was going to bring in a new member for his team, the time was now. I could get away from doing meaningless, tedious work for people I'd never met and work for my cousin instead, giving all of his projects the creative flair they were missing.

No more sitting around, waiting for an opportunity to come knocking. It was time for me to seize control and create one for myself.

Finley emerged from the playhouse at the back of the store, struggling to carry a stack of what looked like a bit more than ten books. "Daddy, I really, really need all of these books."

"Okay."

Her mouth dropped open. "Really?"

I placed the *Flipping Fabulous* book atop Finley's bookstack and chuckled at the way she grunted under the weight. Then, lifting the whole stack from her arms, I said, "Yes, really. Under one condition."

"What?"

"Next time we come up here for an appointment, I choose where we eat."

chapter twenty-eight
kendall

I probably should have specified that students only needed to bring one item for Show and Tell. Because it was Letter B week, and Finley Reed unloaded seventeen books from her backpack at the center of the rug.

Seventeen.

I kept thinking she was finished, only for her to say, "Wait, there's still more!" and pull out another one like she was Mary Poppins.

It just so happened to be observation day, and Sarah was seated at the back of my classroom with a clipboard—which she covered her face with to laugh when Finley said, "That's it for today! Make sure to like and subscribe!"

"Thank you, Finley," I said when she finished showing her books to her classmates—and her pretend subscribers. "As you put all those books back in your bag, why don't you choose one for me to read this afternoon?"

Her face lit up with joy, and she knelt on the rug to make her selection. The classmates sitting closest to her scooted in to help her decide, and I turned to Sarah and shook my head with a chuckle.

Having Sarah in my room to observe my lessons didn't make me anxious—not like it did when Cates came in the room. He was the principal before Sarah, and although he was perfectly nice and seemed to like me all right, I couldn't quite relax with him staring me down as he stood at the back of the room. I was in constant fear one of my students would start acting out. And his feedback, as constructive as it was, always made me want to cry.

But with Sarah, I knew that even if everything went wrong, she'd simply jump in and help rather than pull me aside and tell me how I could have handled it differently.

She stayed for the entirety of my morning math lesson, even lingering at the back of the room as they lined up to go to art. She was still there when I returned to the classroom. "Show and Tell exhausts me," I said, collapsing into my desk chair.

Sarah walked over to the chair that Mason usually sat in, scooting it closer to me. "I don't know how you do it," she said, writing down some more notes. "I could never teach kindergarten."

"I could never teach those mouthy fifth-graders." That was the grade Sarah taught before she became principal. "I'll take Finley Reed's antics over their drama any day."

Sarah smiled from one corner of her mouth. "That kid is so funny. When does her dad usually get here, anyway?"

I reached for my phone and looked at the time. "Anytime now. Soon, I hope—I need some copies made."

"He's like your personal secretary."

"That he is."

"Owen said he's meeting with him today," Sarah said, crossing her legs. "I wonder what that's about?"

She was looking at me as though I'd have some sort of clue about it. "Oh—I don't know. Weird."

She held her clipboard against her chest and grinned at me. There was something about the mischievous look in her eyes that made me a little uneasy. She always looked like this when she was up to something. Normally it indicated she was about to drop some bombshell announcement that only she was excited about, like new recycling bins or a team-building retreat. But this time, her amused stare scared me a little. "He's pretty cute, isn't he?"

I blinked. "Mason? I don't know."

"Yeah you do," she said, a hint of feistiness in her voice. It felt like she was peering into my soul.

I tucked my hair behind my ears with a nervous laugh. "I haven't really thought about him that way. But I mean, he's a little easy on the eyes, I guess." The man was a fucking god.

"I think he's got a thing for you."

You have no idea. My cheeks began to get warm as I thought about the night Mason and I spent together after the fall festival. That was over two weeks ago, and not a day had passed that I hadn't replayed every moment in my mind. I never wanted to forget how he made me feel. Not that I ever could. "A 'thing' for me? I really doubt that."

"No, I think he does. I'm picking up on a vibe there," she said, gesturing in a circular motion with one of her hands. "And I'm not the only one."

I shook my head in protest. "There's no vibe. Mason's just a volunteer, and I'd never—" At that exact moment, Mason entered the room carrying a caramel macchiato in one hand and a book in the other. He momentarily paused when he spotted Sarah in his usual spot, his eyes darting from me to her before he made his way over to us.

"Speak of the devil," Sarah said, and I couldn't make myself look at her. For the love of God, I hoped she wouldn't make this awkward. "I was just teasing Kendall about you being her secretary."

Mason sat on one of the students' tables, setting my coffee down beside him. I could only assume he didn't want to make a show out of giving it to me in front of Sarah. He glanced at me as he said, "That's better than 'Room Mom,' I guess."

Sarah and I laughed. She nodded toward the book he was now holding on his lap. "Going to do some reading? Or did you bring a book for Show and Tell, like your daughter?"

"I guess you could say it's Show and Tell. I was going to, uh, show Kendall that this was the last book I worked on at my old job." He stepped forward to hand it to me. It was the *Flipping Fabulous* book he'd mentioned weeks ago, with that couple from Indianapolis on the cover.

I gasped and flipped through the pages, looking for Mason's drawings. They were scattered throughout the book—little doodles of floor plans, hammers and nails, ceiling fans, and kitchen cabinets—the sketches were simple, but they were all so whimsical and fun. I looked up at Mason's face. "It's so wild to me that you did all of this—these are *your* drawings in a published book." I stared down at the book again, turning the pages in awe at his illustrations. "You should be so proud."

Mason shrugged, backing up to sit on the table again. He opened his mouth to speak, and I expected him to say something humble or downplay his skills, but he stopped and took a breath. And then, with a glance toward Sarah, he said, "That was honestly a blast to work on. You'd be surprised at how much research I had to do just for those little doodles—but it was worth it, because they were over the moon about it." And then, after a beat, he turned to Sarah again. "By the way, I saw Owen's book at a shop in Indy."

"The one on Mass Ave?"

He nodded. "Yeah. Finley and I went there after her therapy appointment on Friday. And I'm sorry she brought a million books for Show and Tell." He turned back to me with a chuckle. "I tried to talk her out of it."

I closed the *Flipping Fabulous* book and pushed it toward the edge of my desk, but Mason didn't take it back from me. "How did therapy go?" I wouldn't have asked in front of Sarah if he hadn't brought it up so casually to begin with. Besides that, she was about to become family to him—she was well aware of Finley's issues.

Mason relaxed his shoulders. "It was great. Really glad we went. I think it might have been more of a therapy session for me than her, and I'm not entirely sure that's how it's supposed to work—?" He paused and looked down at his feet with a quiet laugh. "But the psychologist had some good advice."

I could see the relief on his face. If Sarah hadn't been sitting there, I might have walked over and hugged him. "I'm so happy for both of you, Mason," I said. When he lifted his head, our eyes met—and I hoped he could tell I wanted to say more but couldn't.

Sarah smiled up at him, hugging her clipboard. "Owen and I are really impressed with how well you're raising Finley, especially given your circumstances. That girl is so lucky to have a dad like you." Sarah's voice trembled as the last couple of words came out—almost like she was on the verge of tears. "Well, I need to get going. Thanks for welcoming me into your classroom this morning, Kendall."

"Of course."

Mason waited until Sarah was all the way out of the room before picking up the coffee and setting it down on the desk in front of me. "This is yours—and so is that book."

I grinned. "I wondered. Thank you—I love it." I opened it again, turning to the copyright page. There was his name. "Will you sign it for me?"

He laughed. "You're joking, right? I didn't write the thing."

"I don't care." I handed him a pen. "I want you to sign it."

"You're ridiculous," he said, taking the pen from me. He took the book to his chair and sat down. I expected him to scribble a signature and hand the book back to me, but he just kept writing. And writing. Mason was composing an entire paragraph on the copyright page, and the longer he wrote, the more eager I became to read it.

He closed the book and clicked the pen. "Don't read that until I leave, okay?"

I giggled nervously as he leaned forward to hand me the book. "Okay." And for the very first time, I couldn't wait for Mason to leave, imagining all the perverted things he could have written. I leaned back in my chair, sipping my coffee. "So, Sarah suspects you have a 'thing' for me."

He snickered, crossing his arms. "Gross."

Staring into his eyes, I felt the echoes of his touch, and my mind couldn't escape the imprint his body had left on mine. His eyes traveled down to my corduroy pants, tight around my thighs, only confirming he was thinking about the same thing.

Not wanting to risk any further flirtation, I grabbed the assessment packet I needed him to copy. "I've got an exciting job for you today. The main copier is down—so you're going to have to use Bertha."

He raised an eyebrow at me. "Bertha who?"

Right—he didn't know about the old copier in the prep room. I wasn't really sure why everyone called it Bertha, but the name seemed fitting. The thing was a beast. I was going to have to show Mason how to load the paper just right to avoid a Bertha meltdown. "Come on," I said, standing up and nodding for him to follow me.

The prep room was small—it could have been a storage closet at some point. "Meet Bertha," I said, leading him into the room. The door swung shut behind him. "She's a temperamental bitch. You've got to push her buttons just right."

Mason nodded, glancing around at all the cabinets before turning to me. "Well, luckily I'm really good at pushing women's buttons."

"Uh huh," I agreed, sliding the papers into the loading tray.

"Do I push your buttons sometimes?" He was using that deep husky tone, the one that drove me absolutely wild. He knew it, too. Not fair.

I tried not to smile as I looked down at the copier screen. "Just the one time."

Mason's eyes widened and a little chuckle escaped from his mouth. "I wasn't going to go there, but if you want to get technical—it was actually twice."

I threw my head back and laughed like a dork. He laughed, too, leaning against the copier to get a better look at my face so he could fully enjoy my embarrassment. "Stop distracting me," I said. "I'm trying to show you how to use this thing."

He crossed his arms, refusing to take his eyes off of me. "Put paper in, push big green button. Seems pretty self-explanatory."

"Yeah, but—sometimes the paper in the bottom tray gets stuck and—" I bent over to check the lower tray, unintentionally pushing my butt against his thigh. "I'm sorry," I said, straightening back up.

He was gazing innocently up at the ceiling now. "You're good."

If I tried to tell him it was an accident, he'd never believe me—so I didn't waste my breath. I pushed the lower tray closed with my leg, not wanting to risk brushing my ass against him again. Jesus, was it hot in this room?

I tapped one of the arrow buttons on the copier. "So—um, this is how you change the amount."

"Mmm-hmm." He leaned closer to see the little screen.

"And you have to—" I swallowed. He was standing so close, I could feel his body heat. "—select color or grayscale."

"Gotcha."

I turned my head to look into his eyes. "And then you can push the big green button."

He pushed the button himself without even tearing his eyes off my face. "Is that it?"

"That's all there is to it." Once the copier started printing, I twisted my body to face him. He was still leaning on the copier with one hand, resting it next to my waist. I stood with my back against the machine as he moved closer, lifting his other hand to place it on the other side of the copier, caging me in. But he made no attempt to touch me. He wouldn't. Not without my consent.

His eyes shifted to the door handle. "I just noticed that door locks."

I had mere seconds to decide what would happen next. I should've turned away—should've asked him to give me some space. But instead, I licked my lips and said, "Lock it, then."

Mason stretched to lock the door with one hand, touching my waist with the other—keeping his eyes on mine the whole time. Once the door was secured, he wrapped both of his arms around my body. Still, he waited—he was giving me one more chance to change my mind. Or maybe he wasn't all that sure about this himself. Just in case he was the one needing some coaxing, I whispered, "Kiss me already."

The corners of his mouth lifted in a smile before he leaned in for a kiss, bending my body over the copier. I brought both of my hands to his chest. The hum of the machine faded into the background as I melted beneath the weight of his warm body, letting out a soft moan into his open mouth. He responded with a growl-like sound, kissing me harder and ramming his tongue farther into my mouth. One of his hands slid around to my front, slipping up beneath my sweater. As his palm ran over the thin fabric of my bra, he whispered, "Fuck, I think I'm addicted to you."

I held Mason's face in my hands and gazed into his eyes, so close to mine. "I've been going through withdrawals myself." I knew we shouldn't be touching like this, but when Mason was this close to me, all reasoning flew right out the window. His hands persuaded me to let my guard down, while his lips made a pretty compelling argument themselves, convincing me I needed him more than I needed to follow the rules. Why were we resisting this, anyway? As he lowered his mouth to my neck, I couldn't even remember.

Just as Mason gripped my butt with both of his hands, the door handle jiggled and we jerked away from one another. I yanked my sweater down to cover my midriff and unlocked the door before pulling it open. Lori stood just on the other side, holding a milk crate full of file folders. "What the—? Why on earth does this door lock from the inside?" Of all the people to need to be in this room right now, of course it would be the school's biggest gossip. Her eyes darted back and forth between us as she adjusted the crate in her arms. "Sorry to interrupt."

"I was just… showing him where everything was."

She pursed her lips together, letting the door close behind her. There wasn't much room for the three of us to stand in that cramped space, but Lori didn't seem bothered. "I'm sure you were," she said, inching between us to put the crate down beside the paper cutter on the counter at the back of the room.

I turned to face Mason, who looked like he wanted to melt through the floor. "Um, will you just bring the rest of the copies back to the classroom when they're finished printing?"

"Yes ma'am," he said with wide eyes.

I followed Lori into the hallway without giving Mason another glance. The second the door closed behind me, I cleared my throat and said, "Whatever you think was happening in there—it wasn't."

Lori laughed snarkily as we walked side by side. "Please. I know you can't help yourself, honey."

"What's that supposed to mean?"

"It's kind of your thing, isn't it?" Lori's tone was deceivably sweet and friendly. "I think you've had your little escapades in every corner of this school by now—first it was Owen Gardner, and then Heath—and now one of our parent aides?" She paused to chuckle. "I'm not judging you for it, hon—but you're not as sneaky as you think."

What a bitch. I gripped her arm, forcing her to stop walking. "You don't know what you're talking about. Yes, you stumbled upon a private moment—but Mason was sharing something personal about his daughter with me. That's why the door was locked." I was a little proud of myself for thinking so quick on my feet, yet Lori's judgmental sneer only worsened. She wasn't buying it.

"Well. Forgive me for assuming you were—"

"Lori, you can take whatever assumptions you have about me and shove them up your ass."

Her mouth fell open, and the fifth-grader carrying a bathroom pass at the end of the hallway gasped. I let go of Lori's arm and turned on my heel to walk the other direction without another word. My legs were trembling.

How could we have been so reckless?

Stupid, stupid, stupid.

chapter twenty-nine
mason

Kendall couldn't even look at me when I returned to the classroom with her copies. The kids were already back from whatever special class they had that day, and she just motioned for me to join the group playing a literacy game on the rug. "Thank you, Mr. Reed," she said, keeping her eyes on Walter, who was reading aloud to her. So formal.

Look what you're doing to her, I told myself. Kissing her here, inside this school? How stupid and reckless. I should've just left her alone, but now I had her completely and utterly freaked out. I'd done nothing for this woman except give her another problem to be anxious about.

And she hadn't even read what I'd written in that book yet.

I considered stealing it off her desk before I left, but ultimately, I decided the damage was already done. My feelings for her weren't exactly a mystery. The words I'd written inside that book would only confirm what she already knew.

When I left that day, my goodbye felt more final—because I wasn't sure I should return at all. The only way to kick this addiction we both had was to put some space between us, right? We clearly couldn't keep our hands to ourselves. "I'm sorry," I said, lingering in the doorway between her classroom and the hall.

"It's fine," she assured me—but her faux smile said it was anything but.

It was time to let this die.

* *

"Oh. My. God. Finding out the art guy knows the STEM guy is the best thing that has happened to me all day."

My favorite purple-haired barista, whose name I still didn't know despite becoming an essential part of my morning routine, was completely beside herself when Owen and I walked into Riverside Coffee together. "We're actually cousins," I informed her as I pulled my wallet out of my back pocket.

Her mouth dropped open. "Mind. Blown." She put her hands up to the side of her head and theatrically mimicked an explosion. "My two favorite customers are *cousins*? I am so not okay right now. It's like two worlds colliding."

Owen and I laughed, and then I turned to him, saying, "Hey, let me get your coffee, since this meeting was my idea."

Surprisingly, he didn't fight me on this. "All right," he said, stepping aside so I could pay for our drinks. He had no idea why we were here, and when he saw me step out of the Jeep with a folder under my arm, he raised his eyebrows in confusion. I had my father's voice inside my head—all of those little tidbits of old-school advice he'd given me years ago when I first entered the workforce. *Don't let them pay. Take the lead. Control the conversation. Wear a tie.*

Using those tactics on my cousin felt a little dirty, but I'd spent all weekend formulating the perfect plan for mine and Finley's lives—and a lot of that banked on how well this meeting went.

I was not, however, wearing a tie.

We sat at a table in the corner. "I come here some afternoons just to be around other humans for a little bit," Owen said as he sat down. "Entrepreneurship can be a little isolating."

Perfect segue. "Agreed. So, is most of your team remote, then?"

"Yeah. Mostly. That seems to work better for everyone." He held his coffee cup with both hands and looked down at the folder in front of me. "So whatcha got there, cuz?"

I took a deep breath. "I have a few ideas I want to share with you. And just—I promise there's a point to all of it, okay?" I waited for him to nod before continuing, opening the folder as I spoke. "I've spent the last few days learning everything I can about *STEM for the Win.* I've scoured all the content you're putting out there across all the platforms. And there are a few areas you're not tapping into that I think you could be."

Owen's eyebrows raised and he sat up a little straighter, glancing at the papers in front of me. "Okay," he said, nodding with a grin. "Let's hear them."

"Right. So, first of all, look at this," I said, handing him the sheet that broke down one of my ideas. "I think you can offer teachers a database of STEM clip art and stock photos via a monthly subscription. This is something I could work on for you—your content would be one hundred percent original."

Owen looked over the sheet of paper I'd given him that broke this project idea down into three columns. "Oh—wow. I hadn't thought of something like that."

"I know my way around a DSLR camera, and obviously I could provide you with unique clip art. Something like this can consistently bring in extra income for you each month."

"You're right about that," he said, glancing up at my face. "You officially have my attention."

"Good," I said, sliding another paper across the table. "Because there's more ideas where that came from." I spent the next fifteen minutes or so revealing to Owen all the information I'd spent all weekend outlining—custom character illustrations, SFTW merch designs, a better and more unique website, and ways to incorporate art into his STEM projects. "You know a lot of schools are calling it STEAM now?"

Owen nodded. "Yeah, I've been looking for ways to add art into the mix—that's not exactly my area of expertise."

"Well," I said, glancing at the barista, who was half-hidden behind the register to watch a video on her phone. I turned back to him. "Every STEM guy needs an art guy, right?"

Owen smiled at me for a long time. "Mason, this is…" He inhaled, flipping the pages in front of him with his thumb. "This is all really amazing stuff."

"You like my ideas?"

He nodded emphatically. "Yeah, every single one of them."

"Good," I said, leaning slightly forward as I prepared myself to get to the point. "I want to be the one to integrate all of these things."

"It's going to be a lot of work," he said, scratching his cheek as he skimmed the page about the clip art database. "I'd be stealing you away from your other clients."

"That's the thing," I said. "I don't want you to be a client. I want you to add me to your team as a full-time employee."

Owen lifted his eyes from the paper to stare at me, his expression unreadable. I fought the urge to say more, fearing overexplaining would reduce the impact of my words. I needed him to see how serious I was. I didn't break eye contact, and neither did he when he said, "You want to work for me… permanently?"

"Yeah. Yeah, I do. I can be the creative driving force behind these projects, to bring them all to life. You need me." I only half-believed what I was saying. "But I want you to hire me because you see me as an asset to your business. Not out of pity or because I'm your cousin. If the answer is no, I can handle it."

Owen rested his chin on his fist and pored over the papers I'd given him, carefully reading every word. I drank my coffee and stared out the window at Main Street—there wasn't much to look at out there besides the occasional pedestrian strolling in front of the long-abandoned storefronts.

After what seemed like a couple of minutes, Owen laid the papers flat on the table and leaned back in his chair. "I can't make a decision right away," he said, tracing his coffee lid with one finger. "I'll need to talk to my accountant and look at the numbers."

"Understandable. I knew this wouldn't be a decision you'd make lightly."

A grin began to spread across Owen's face. "This is really impressive, cuz. Sarah asked me what I thought you wanted to talk about this morning, and I told her I had no clue. She was afraid it had something to do with our wedding—but that's sort of all she thinks about these days."

I chuckled, taking a drink. "You guys have less than a month now. How are you feeling about that?"

Owen took a deep breath, glancing out the window. "Everything's coming together—but I'm just eager for it to *be here*, you know? I'm so ready to just be married. Call her my wife." He looked down at his hands, clutching his cup. "Start a family."

"I get it. All the focus is on the big day when that's not really what it's about."

"Right." We both sipped our coffees, and Owen leaned onto his arms on the table. "What about you? Have you dated since you've been back in town?"

I sighed. "Uh, not much. It's a little hard to put myself out there when I've got Finley." It wasn't a total lie.

"I bet," Owen said with a nod. "So—*totally* off topic here—how's volunteering in Finley's classroom going?" His not-so-subtle subject change wasn't lost on me, and neither was his knowing smile.

I shook my head, trying not to grin. "It's fine." I didn't want to talk about that for two reasons. One, I wouldn't be able to talk about Kendall with a straight face. And two, I was pretty sure I'd just volunteered for the very last time. "All Finley cares about right now is Halloween. It's all she can talk about."

"Oh, you'll have to make sure to bring her by our house. Sarah's heart will be broken if we don't get a lot of trick or treaters."

"Will do," I said.

This would be my very first time taking Finley trick-or-treating. She'd spent all of her previous Halloweens with Whitney—even if she was meant to be with me for the weekend. I was looking forward to it almost as much as she was.

And we had coordinating costumes.

Before Owen and I parted ways that morning, I thanked him for meeting with me and gave him a firm handshake. "Give me some time to figure this all out," he said, which left me feeling optimistic. I tried not to allow myself to get too excited about it just yet—for all I knew, his accountant could strongly advise against this.

But Owen had the final say—and I just hoped I made a convincing enough argument that he needed me.

* *

"Hey, Fin. Guess what?" I asked Finley the second she climbed into the backseat of the Jeep in the school pick-up line.

"What?"

I turned around to make sure she buckled up before I pulled away from the curb. After I heard the click, I said, "We're going trick-or-treating at Owen and Sarah's on Halloween."

She gasped. "Will I get to pet Leia?"

"I don't know, maybe? They might have her put up that night."

Finley gave this some thought as I drove on. I dreamed about the day I could get this girl a dog. When we had our own place, it would be first on my agenda.

"I've got something else to tell you about, too," I said, lowering the music. I glanced at her in the rearview mirror to make sure she was listening. "I don't think I'm going to volunteer in your classroom anymore."

"What? Why not?"

"I've got some new projects I'm working on, and I'm just not going to have the time. I'm sorry, kiddo." She was silent for a minute or so. I waited until I pulled up to a stop sign before turning around to look at her. "Did you hear me?"

To my utter astonishment, her bottom lip was sticking out in a pout, and her eyes were welling up with tears. She sniffled. "You can't stop."

I let out a silent laugh. "Finley—you barely acknowledge me when I'm there. I think I talk to Walter more than I talk to you. You'll be fine. What's up with this reaction, kiddo?"

"You *have* to keep coming." Her voice quivered—she was on the verge of sobbing. "We're having the Halloween party on Wednesday. You can't miss it. We're going to match and look so cute together, Daddy. I want all my friends to see us. And Ms. Devin."

Fuuuuck. I gripped the steering wheel hard and sighed. I guessed it wouldn't do much harm if I went in one more time. Surely Kendall and I could keep things friendly for one day. I shook my head as I drove, realizing I was letting this kid manipulate my emotions again. She had me wrapped around her little finger, didn't she? "All right," I said with a sigh, and she clapped.

I hadn't realized my presence in her classroom mattered to her so much. And maybe it didn't. But when that bottom lip poked out and she gave me those puppy dog eyes, I would do whatever she said. Maybe I could endure working beside Kendall a little longer.

For all I knew, Kendall might have been on the verge of asking me to stop volunteering herself. When my phone lit up with a text message from her as we pulled into the driveway, I assumed the worst. She was probably about to ask me to back off, saying it would be for the best for both of us.

But she'd sent me a photo of one of the illustrations inside the book—it was a sketch of some decorative baskets in a kids' playroom, and I'd labeled one of them *FINLEY*.

Kendall: I see what you did there.

I smiled, having completely forgotten about that detail. At the time, I assumed it wouldn't have passed the first round of edits, but the creators loved it. I'd have to get a copy of the book myself to show Finley later—she'd be delighted to see her name in a real book. I turned around to tell her about it when my phone buzzed again.

Kendall: And I read your note.

Kendall: It's the best thing that's ever happened to me, too.

chapter thirty
kendall

Kendall-

You being Finley's teacher is the <u>best thing</u> to ever happen to both of us. You somehow make living in Woodvale bearable—and I'll never regret swiping right on you.

I feel like I'm supposed to throw in a pun here about how "flipping fabulous" you are, but I think "fucking phenomenal" is more accurate.

-Mason

I read Mason's note the second my students left for lunch that day, and I'd read it twenty times since. At least. Jamie and Daya read it, too, each of them offering different but equally valid opinions.

"Aww! You know he's falling in love with you, right?"
(Daya.)
"He's just spitting game to get in your pants again."
(Jamie.)

There was probably some truth in both of their theories. I feared we were past the point of no return now. What was meant to be some one-night thing was turning into something more. Our connection was more than just physical—and I knew he was feeling it too, especially after reading those words.

Mason made me weak in the knees in a way no other man had before. And even after that confrontation with Lori, I was edging closer to throwing in the towel, saying "fuck it," and telling him I wanted to keep sneaking around.

But to ask him to do such a thing would be unfair, wouldn't it? I'd been in that position before, and it's not all it's cracked up to be. Mason was so family-oriented, too—he clearly loved his mom, and his cousin was his best friend, for Christ's sake. He wouldn't want to date someone he couldn't even bring around his family.

And Finley, the center of Mason's entire universe, deserved some stability and some semblance of a family—two things I wasn't entirely sure I could offer. I wouldn't let myself be the reason for any more disruption in her or Mason's lives.

If it wouldn't have been for the Halloween party on Wednesday, I might have asked Mason to stop volunteering. I could see he was nearing that conclusion himself, so it seemed like the right thing to do. But I wasn't about to wrangle twenty-five sugared-up kindergarteners in costumes for an entire day by myself. I needed his help.

He strolled into the classroom on Halloween wearing snorkeling gear and a homemade oxygen tank he'd fashioned out of a couple of two-liter bottles. As ridiculous as it all was, I melted when I saw him—because Finley had shown up that day in a jellyfish costume.

They matched.

He swaggered up to my desk with the goofiest grin, like he was completely aware of what this adorable display was doing to me. He wasn't the least bit embarrassed about it—in fact, he looked quite the opposite. Proud. Smug. And then, eyeing my costume, he pulled off his snorkeling gear and said, "Oh no."

"What?" Every year, I went for a costume inspired by a book character my students would recognize. This year, I opted for the mouse from *If You Give a Mouse a Cookie*—and I was wearing mouse ears and overalls over a white t-shirt. An oversized chocolate chip cookie made out of cardboard hung from my neck, and I'd even taken the time to draw a little mouse nose and whiskers on my face that morning.

"What happens if you give a mouse a caramel macchiato?" Mason asked, setting my drink down on my desk.

"She might ask you to help her assemble twenty-five Halloween treat bags."

I winced up at him, expecting him to jokingly turn around and walk away. But he removed the rest of his costume and, after setting it on the floor beside my desk, said, "Okay." No silly argument or negotiation tactic this time.

I put the treat bags on the round table and handed Mason a sack of plastic spider rings. "Why don't we go around the table in a circle with each of the items?" I asked him before opening a bag of witch fingers with my teeth.

"Yes ma'am," he said, looking down at the rings. And we got to work, making our way around the table to pass out each of the Halloween party favors. Rings, witch fingers, bubbles, Skittles, and little containers of slime. I used my left hand to distribute the witch fingers, making my charm bracelet jingle with every movement. Mason was quieter than normal, making a few comments about the party favors here and there, but otherwise holding back from flirting with me. I understood his reasoning, but it still made my heart sink.

"Hey," I said after a couple of minutes. "I wanted to let you know—you don't have to keep bringing me coffee every day."

He touched his chest in mock surprise. "Wait, you thought I was doing that for you? I'm just trying to support a local business."

"Right," I said, rolling my eyes at him with a smile.

"And the barista said Owen and I tie for her favorite customer, so I can't let her down."

"Oh, that's right—you met with him the other day, didn't you? What was that all about?"

He inhaled, reaching down to open the bag of Halloween-themed bubbles. "I, uh, asked him for a job, actually."

"A job?" I stopped.

"Yeah, I told him to add me to his team. Full time. He hasn't given me an answer yet, but we'll see."

I couldn't imagine how difficult it must have been for him to approach Owen with that, given that he was obviously jealous of the man and made no attempt to hide it. And it was probably just as hard for him to admit to me that he'd asked my ex for a job.

His poor ego.

"He'd be stupid not to hire you."

"You think so?" he asked, dropping a ring into a treat bag.

"Of course. But does this mean I'm going to lose you as a volunteer?"

He stared at my face for a moment, like he didn't want to give me the answer. "I'm sure he'd be flexible with me on that," he finally said.

"Good." I turned back to the treat bags, struggling to remember where I'd left off. Someone might end up with an extra witch finger, and I hoped it wouldn't cause drama.

Mason hesitated for a moment before he, too, returned to the job at hand. When he jumped back in, he took a deep breath and said, "Question."

"What?" I turned to him.

"Do you ever take that bracelet off?"

I laughed, shaking my wrist in his direction to make the charms jangle a few extra times before I opened the bag of slime containers. "Only when I sleep and shower," I answered. "My sister and I got matching charm bracelets in Gatlinburg when we were little, and even though I've replaced just about every charm and even the bracelet itself, I've worn it ever since even though technically it's not even the same bracelet anymore and *wow*—I am rambling." I laughed and covered my face.

Mason grinned like he wanted to laugh at me, too, but he held back. "You're fine. I'm guessing all the charms mean something special to you?"

"Would it make me sound incredibly lame if I admitted they're mostly meaningless?"

He sidled up beside me with that warm smile of his that had become so familiar to me—the one that made the corners of his eyes crinkle—and he lifted my wrist to get a better look at the charms. "You're going to tell me—" He squinted to get a better look. "Pizza's meaningless?"

"I would *never*. Pizza's my favorite food."

"Noted. And the pencil is—?"

"Because I'm a teacher."

"Makes sense." He dropped the bag of spider rings on the table, taking my wrist in both of his hands so he could look at each and every charm. "And a disco ball."

"Mirrorball. It's for Taylor Swift."

He blinked at me a couple of times. "I'll have to take your word for it," he said before moving onto the next charm. "Let's see. We've got mountains…"

I hesitated a moment before explaining that one. I'd had the mountain charm the longest—in fact, it was the only charm I'd never replaced. It wasn't as shiny as the other charms on my wrist, and the peaks and valleys of the miniature mountain range—once pointy and defined—were now curved and dull. I swallowed. "For the aesthetic." I hurriedly moved onto the next one, holding it between two fingers. "And this is my zodiac sign. Cancer."

Something about that made Mason grin. "Cancer, huh? Are you into astrology?"

I yanked my wrist away from his hands. "Maybe. Got a problem with that?" Heath was constantly teasing me about my fascination with astrology, and Owen had been pretty skeptical about it, too—he tended to believe in things that were a little more… concrete.

I was no stranger to men dismissing my interest in astrology.

"No, I don't." Mason shook his head, but a hint of a smile remained on his lips when he asked, "What sign do you think I am?"

I stared into his kind, blue eyes and accepted he wasn't teasing me about this. He seemed genuinely curious to see if I'd be able to nail down his zodiac sign. Pisces would have been my first guess if I hadn't already known his birthday was in the summer. "Gemini?"

Mason's smile grew. "You already knew, didn't you?"

"I swear I didn't."

He took a deep breath and picked up the bag of mini bubbles. "I'm a Gemini sun, a Pisces moon and... Scorpio rising, I think?"

I rested a hand on my hip. "Okay. What's her name?"

Mason turned to me and froze. "Who?"

"The girl who did your birth chart. Who is she?"

Mason's eyes danced in amusement. He dropped a container of bubbles into one of the treat bags, saying, "Lesley. Her name is Lesley."

"I knew it," I said with a laugh. "I knew there had to be a—"

"And she's my sister."

I clamped my mouth shut, feeling a little embarrassed as I stared down at the mess of Halloween treat bags on the table in front of me. "Oh."

Mason scooted closer to me—as near as he could get without touching me—and said in a low whisper, "I think you just got a little jealous there, Ms. Devin."

His eyes were fixed on mine like he was daring me to be the first to look away. But I wouldn't. "Do we really want to talk about jealousy right now?" I asked, keeping my tone playful.

He swallowed and looked down. "Ah—no, we probably don't."

"Then get back to work, Mr. Reed," I said, turning away from him. We were about to run out of time. When the kids returned, it would be time for their Halloween party, and we still had a lot to do. As I circled the table distributing slime containers in the rest of the treat bags, I couldn't help but steal a few glances over my shoulder at Mason—he was still grinning.

It was becoming less and less of a possibility that Mason and I could ever have a normal interaction without flirting with one another. His inquisition about my bracelet was innocent enough, but it felt like it may have just been an excuse to get close to me. To touch me.

I tried my best not to think about it as we finished distributing slime and Skittles and set out the snacks for the party. My classroom was quiet—the calm before the storm. Mason had no idea what he was in for. Halloween parties were second only to the yearly Christmas party for the most chaotic event of the school year, and I had learned the hard way that my usual whatever-goes approach wouldn't cut it. I had my party management tactics down to a science now, and I was in the middle of explaining some of them to Mason when the kids barged back into the room. Fairies, superheroes, witches, and football players found their spot on the rug, but stealing the spotlight in the center of them all was the cutest jellyfish I'd ever seen—whipping her head around so the tentacles on her costume swung back and forth. One of them whacked Elijah in the face, but he didn't seem to mind—he merely let out a silent giggle and watched his best friend twist and fling her entire body around until half of the kids were laughing and the other half were scowling at her for hitting them with her flailing tentacles.

"Finley," Mason said, adjusting the pretend oxygen tank on his back. "If your tentacles were actually poisonous, I'm pretty sure your classmates would be in bad shape right now. Can you not?"

Getting Finley to settle down was just one of our challenges that morning. I asked Mason to read *Room on the Broom* to the kids in hopes of getting them to calm down, but they were all too antsy about the party to listen—despite Mason's best efforts to mimic the old witch in the book.

After story time, we moved on to the party games—a mummy-wrapping contest, Halloween bingo, and a pumpkin ring toss. They annihilated their treat bags, and it wasn't long before Elijah was using one of the witch fingers to pick his nose. I tried not to laugh at the panicked, desperate look in Mason's wide eyes as he stood at the center of all the chaos. I should have warned him just how out of control kindergarten parties could get, but then again, he might not have shown up at all if I had.

"'Kay, I'm going to go take a nap now," he said once the party was over and the kids were lining up for lunch. "And I might even treat myself to a stiff drink."

"Drink one for me," I said, adjusting the claw clip in my hair with a wink. As Mason lingered by the door, he watched me pull a few strands out of my messy updo so that they framed my face. I was becoming familiar with that look of longing in his eyes. And it usually occurred when I was doing the most mundane thing. Fixing my hair. Stretching. Bending over to pick up a scrap of paper from the floor. "What?" I asked, prompting him to snap out of it.

He shook his head and ran his fingers through his hair. I could tell from the way he sighed and looked down at the floor there was something he wanted to say, but either he couldn't speak it in the presence of children or he chickened out. "Nothin'. Good luck with these monsters the rest of the day," he said, motioning toward the kids—some of whom responded by putting their hands on their hips and saying, "Hey!" He laughed on his way out the door without uttering another word.

The pang of sadness I usually felt after Mason's departure was stronger that morning. To be this aware of how someone felt about me—and to know there was nothing I could do about it—left me with a cruel, lingering ache in my heart.

For the remainder of the day, I was about as focused as the kids with their Skittle-induced hyperactivity and insistence to mess with each other's costumes. To attempt to teach anything would be futile. So I let them watch the *Room on the Broom* movie on the smartboard, which I wasn't sure was more of a treat for me or them.

I was making my way around the room to pick up the mess they'd left behind from the party when I heard sniffling. Finley was laying her head down on her desk. "Ms. Devin? Finley's crying," Walter said.

"I see that." I made my way to Finley's seat. "Finley, what's the matter?"

She lifted her head and looked up at me, tears sliding down her cheeks. "One of my tentacles broke off and now my costume is ruined."

I tilted my head to the side. "Do you think that may have been because you were dancing around and whacking people with your tentacles?"

She frowned.

I took the loose jellyfish tentacle from Finley's hand and inspected it, eyeing the hat to see how I might be able to reattach it. "You know what?" I asked, squatting to get on her level. I placed my hand on her back. "I bet I can hot glue this and you'll be good to go. Should I try that?"

She nodded enthusiastically. "Uh huh."

I had to fumble through my desk drawer to find my hot glue gun and dig even further to find the glue sticks. One of these days I'd have to organize this desk.

Just not today.

When I turned around to plug the hot glue gun into the wall behind my desk, I was astonished to find Finley at my heels. "Can I help you with it, Ms. Devin?"

"Gosh, you scared me." I placed my hand on my heart as Finley giggled. "I don't want you to get burned, but you could keep me company back here if you promise not to get too close."

She nodded in response. As we waited for the hot glue gun to heat up, I sat in my desk chair and motioned for her to come closer to me. She misunderstood the gesture, though, and climbed right up onto my lap. Under normal circumstances, I wouldn't hold one of my students like this—because if I did it for one, they'd all line up to be next. But the rest of the class was enthralled by the movie, and something about holding that girl on my lap made my heart soar. "I like your costume," she whispered, tracing her finger around the edge of the giant cookie.

"Thank you. And I love yours. Are you going trick-or-treating tonight?"

She nodded, keeping her eyes on the cookie. "Yup. My dad's taking me to *two* trunk-or-treats. And Principal Sarah's house." Suddenly, her face lit up with a smile. "And then we're coming to your house."

I blinked. "Um. What?"

"What kind of candy do you got?"

"I haven't bought any yet. Finley, when did your dad say this?"

She shrugged like it wasn't a big deal. "Earlier today. He told me to get your address. So yeah, if you can just write that down for me, that'd be great. Got a post-it?"

I wasn't sure whether to laugh at the way she was talking like a little adult or panic over this new revelation. Mason was coming to my house? Why wouldn't he have told me this?

Or was she just making this up?

"Why don't I just message him my address instead?"

"Okay. I just hope you got Kit Kats."

There was something in her smile that reminded me of the way her dad smirked when he gave me a hard time. I lightly rubbed her back and said, "Your smile looks just like your daddy's."

"Everyone tells me that," she said with an eyeroll, reaching up to play with the clip at the back of my head. "But I don't have blonde hair like him. Or you. You have blonde hair, too."

"That's right. My sister calls me Blondie."

"That's funny. Will your sister be there tonight? And the dog?"

"Yes. Do you want to meet Titus?"

She nodded. "Is he going to like me?"

"Well, Titus doesn't like most people. But he might tolerate you if you give him a treat."

This made her eyes grow wide. And then she turned to the hot glue gun, which now had a glowing red light on it to indicate it was ready. "Can you fix my costume now?"

"Sure, sweetie. But you're going to have to get down so you don't accidentally get—" I had to stop talking because she leaned forward to squeeze me, locking me into the tightest hug of my life. I inhaled, hugging her back just as hard. And when Finley slid down off my lap to go back to her seat, I sat there frozen with a lump in my throat.

How could anyone ever willingly walk away from that girl?

I fought back tears as I mended Finley's costume, a curse for her biological mother in the back of my mind.

* *

When I got home that afternoon, Daya and Jamie were on the porch getting ready to carve pumpkins. They had all the tools laid out on the edge of the porch beside them, both of them using large kitchen spoons to scoop out the stringy pumpkin guts. As I strolled up the walkway, Jamie lifted a third pumpkin by its long, skinny stem and said, "We got you a pumpkin to carve, Blondie."

I sat on the bottom step and dropped my heavy tote bag to the ground. "Do you really trust me with a knife?"

The two of them exchanged glances. "I'd say she could paint hers instead, but that could be just as disastrous," Jamie said.

"These tools aren't that sharp. You'll be fine." Daya dropped an enormous spoonful of pumpkin pulp into a metal mixing bowl between her and Jamie. As for my sister, she laid her spoon on the porch and began scooping the pumpkin guts out with her bare hand. Just thinking about the texture of it made me shudder.

Since I couldn't watch her anymore, I picked up my phone to text Mason.

Kendall: Guess you need my address for trick or treating? 1215 Chestnut St.

Mason: 👍

Mason: Finley showed me how you fixed her costume. Thank you

Kendall: Of course. So are you really stopping by tonight?

Mason: Let's just say she hasn't stopped talking about meeting your dog since I picked her up. So... yeah

The sensation of pumpkin guts splattering onto my wrist jolted me away from my conversation. I shrieked and flung it off of me only to realize that there was more flying past me—Jamie and Daya were fully engaged in a pumpkin guts war, both of them picking it up with their bare hands and chucking it at each other. Daya had pumpkin seeds stuck in her hair. "You just got some on your sister, you butthole," she said, picking up another handful. Jamie dodged it just in time, throwing her head back and cackling with laughter.

"You started it," she said, attempting to smash some of the stringy pulp on Daya's face. Daya smacked my sister's hand away, grinning. Jamie shook her head and leaned forward to pluck the seeds from Daya's hair. I hugged my knees against my chest, quietly observing the way they stared into each other's eyes with mirrored intensity. Jamie's movements slowed, and when she pulled out the last pumpkin seed, she delicately tucked Daya's hair behind her ear—a romantic gesture that evoked the same emotions I felt as a child in those rare moments when my parents got along. When my mom wasn't slamming cabinet doors and my dad wasn't peeling out of our driveway to disappear for hours at a time. *Please make this last*, I thought, just how I had back then.

Jamie wiped her hands on her jeans. "Um. I'm going to head to the store in a little bit for some tealights for these babies."

"I'll give you some cash if you grab a bag of Kit Kats," I said, pulling my pumpkin toward me. "And can you grab some apple pie filling? I want to try baking something again."

"Oh, great," Jamie said, looking alarmed. "And we should wait until all the Halloween candy is half-off tomorrow for that."

"Well," I said, blowing the loose strands of hair away from my face as I reached for a carving knife. "I had a special request from a VIP trick-or-treater."

"Who?"

I glanced up with a grin. "You guys ready to meet Thor and his daughter?"

chapter thirty-one
mason

"And you're sure Ms. Devin seemed like she really wanted us to come to her house?"

"Yup!"

I sat on the bench in front of the window in my parents' bedroom, watching my mom apply Finley's Halloween make-up. I hadn't thought a 5-year-old dressed like a jellyfish needed make-up, but what did I know? "And she didn't ask *any* of the other kids? She only said this to you?"

"Yup!" Finley repeated, clenching her eyes shut as my mom applied glitter to her eyelids. "I can't wait to meet Titus!"

I reread the text from Kendall, feeling like the middle-man in this arrangement. Why hadn't she mentioned this to me in person? I wished Finley could remember more details from their conversation, but trying to get more out of her would only waste my time. I sighed. "I guess we'll add another stop to our list."

My mom stepped back from Finley to admire her work before giving me the side eye. "I bet Ms. Devin's got a treat for both of you."

"What's that supposed to mean?" I could feel my face getting hot. Why the hell would she say that? She just peered at me over the top of her reading glasses before pulling a tube of shiny lip gloss from the basket on her vanity. I looked down at my phone and absentmindedly scrolled, trying to appear as casual as possible.

She quickly applied Finley's lip gloss and asked her to rub her lips together. "You better go get your shoes on," she said, lovingly swatting at Finley's butt as she skipped away, stopping to pick up her pumpkin bucket on the way out of the bedroom. I folded my arms and stared at my mom, awaiting some kind of explanation. She just laughed. "Don't look at me like that. I may be old, but my observational skills are still top-notch."

"I have no idea what you're talking about."

"Oh bologna," she said with a laugh, turning to face her mirror as she applied her own lipstick. "I know my son. And I know when he's trying to be sneaky."

"You think I'd really get involved with Finley's teacher?" Sometimes I hated her for being so observant. She had a knack for figuring out when I was up to something—like the time she came into my room with a basket of folded laundry when I had a girl hiding in my closet when I was fourteen. I thought I'd gotten away with it, too, until she was on her way out and turned around to say, *"And if she's not gone in the next five minutes, I'm calling her parents."*

Christine always knew.

"I'm sure you're just *really* passionate about volunteer work all of a sudden."

I shook my head and looked down at my lap, but I couldn't control the way my face softened into a smile. "There's nothing going on." I ran my fingers through my hair. "She can't date one of her students' parents, anyway."

My mom turned off the lighted mirror on her vanity and grabbed a jacket from the back of her bedroom door. "I imagine not. And it could really affect Finley if you start messing around with this woman and break her heart. She could pick on Finley—you know, single her out because she's got a vendetta against you."

"Mom. Kendall wouldn't do that."

She turned toward me with a few overdramatic blinks, tilting her head to the side, and it took a few seconds for me to figure out why.

"I mean—Ms. Devin." Whoops. I covered my eyes with my hands, knowing I'd just exposed myself. My mom laughed. "Damn it."

"Do I know my son, or do I know my son?" My mom asked, slipping into her jacket. "I'll see you at the trunk-or-treat."

* *

Finley and I may have overcommitted ourselves. We hit the two trunk-or-treats first—starting with my mom's church, and then Traci's church. Finley's bucket was already full after the first stop, and she had to dump her candy into a grocery sack in my backseat on the way to the next one. "Not even one freakin' Kit Kat," she grumbled.

"Hey! Don't say 'freakin'.'"

"It's a lot better than what *you* say," she muttered. She had me there.

I was dreading the trunk-or-treat at Traci's church the most. I thought about skipping it altogether, but I'd get an earful about that on Sunday. Still, I was feeling wary about it. Traci's behavior was so unpredictable, and this was outside of our usual, safe routine. When Traci saw us approaching her car—which was made to look like a monster with teeth around the open trunk— she clapped her hands together and yelled, "There's my jellyfish girl!"

"Trick or treat!" Finley held up her bucket.

Traci turned to the teenage boy wearing a black hoodie standing next to her. "Look, Finley! Say hi to Uncle Levi."

I wasn't aware Finley even had an Uncle Levi. Judging from the apprehensive look on her face, neither was she. "She's really shy," Traci said to him. I couldn't help but laugh in response— that may have been the first time I'd ever heard that word used to describe my kid.

She wasn't shy. She was uncomfortable.

I took a deep breath, gently nudging Finley closer to the plastic cauldron full of candy so we could get through this and move onto the next car. And that's when Traci turned to me and muttered, "She doesn't even remember her own family because you only let me have her a couple hours a week."

"Oh, is that the reason?" I stared into Traci's eyes. No—into her soul. She had nothing to say in response as she dropped a generous handful of candy into Finley's bucket.

"Wow. She really does look exactly like those old pictures of Whitney," Levi said, amplifying the awkwardness. Thankfully, Finley was too distracted by the Tootsie Roll she was attempting to unwrap that she didn't hear this comment. But to my utter horror, Levi lifted his phone like he was about to snap a picture of her.

"Don't do that," I blurted.

He lowered his hand and looked up with wide eyes. "I was just going to do a side-by-side comparison."

"Do *not* take a picture of my daughter." I grabbed Finley by the wrist because both of her hands were full and gently pulled her toward the next car. Maybe it was an overreaction, but I didn't know anything about this guy or what his actual intentions were. He could send it to Whitney, for all I knew.

Traci scoffed. "Now we can't even take pictures of her? You're ridiculous." She turned to her son. "See? I told you how he was."

I plastered the biggest, cheesiest smile I could muster onto my face and said, "Happy Halloween, Traci." This was quite a feat, considering I would have much rather flipped her off. But this was not the time nor place.

I was grateful for Finley's oblivion during that entire interaction. She moved onto the next trunk without even saying goodbye to Traci, too captivated by the bubble machine up ahead to look back. I sighed and trailed behind her with my hands in my pockets, trying not to let this Traci encounter put a damper on the entire evening.

Because both trunk-or-treats took longer than I expected, we had to skip trick-or-treating in our own neighborhood. Especially if we wanted to have time to make it to Kendall's house, which I anticipated being the highlight of the night for both of us.

We still made time to stop by Owen and Sarah's house, where toilet paper streamed from every tree and bush in their front yard. "I just don't understand," Sarah said with a frown, peering out at her yard as Owen dropped some candy into Finley's bucket. "They did this to the last principal, but why me? Don't the students like me?"

"I told her it's just tradition," Owen said.

"I'm sure they're just targeting Owen, anyway." I winked at them, taking Finley by the hand. "Science deniers, probably."

"That must be it," Owen agreed, but Sarah wasn't buying it.

"You guys are full of it." She bent over to get down to Finley's level. "I love your costume, Finley. Have you had a fun Halloween so far?"

"Yup. And now we get to go to Ms. Devin's house!"

Sarah straightened back up, and she and Owen stared at me with the same amused, inquisitive expression. "Uh," I said, taking a step backward on their porch. "She invited the whole class. I think. Probably."

"No she—" I covered Finley's mouth, but it was too late. Owen and Sarah knew exactly what was going on, and all I could do was shake my head. The two of them laughed as we said goodbye, and I had trouble explaining to Finley what she'd done wrong as I lifted her into the Jeep.

"It's okay, kiddo. I was just goofing off." She was still confused, but that answer seemed to satisfy her. By this point in the night, it was well after her bedtime, and she was yawning every couple of minutes despite assuring me she wasn't tired at all. I caught her nodding off as we pulled up to Kendall's house. "Better not fall asleep, Fin, or you might not get to meet Ms. Devin's dog."

That jolted her awake immediately. She unbuckled before the car even came to a full stop in front of the small white house in the middle of the block. At the edge of the porch sat three jack-o'-lanterns—a classic spooky face, a spider, and a jellyfish.

"Look, Dad! Do you think Ms. Devin did that for me?" Finley pointed at the jellyfish when she reached the porch.

"Yeah, Fin—I think she did." I swallowed, stepping up onto the porch with my hands in my pockets. Finley was already knocking on Kendall's front door and peering through the glass into the living room.

A dog yapped somewhere inside the house, and within seconds, there were three women at the door clamoring to look at us. The other two practically stepped on themselves to push Kendall out of the way. The one with short blue hair and a sucker in her mouth surveyed me from head to toe with a mischievous glint in her eyes. "Did you bring your hammer?"

"Jamie!" Kendall's eyes widened as she gave her sister a shove, keeping her eyes on me. I'd have to ask her to clarify the meaning of this "hammer" comment later.

"What do we have here?" the other woman asked Finley, standing between the other two with a bowl full of Kit Kats. She tucked her sleek, black hair behind her ears and smiled at Finley. "Are you a jellyfish?"

Finley nodded, but she was craning her neck to see past them. "Can I pet your dog?"

We all laughed, and Jamie pushed the door open wider and motioned for us to come inside. I glanced at Kendall as I stepped across the threshold. She wasn't in her costume anymore, I noticed—she was wearing black leggings with the fall festival t-shirt, and her hair was loosely hanging over one shoulder. "So, let's do quick introductions before we let the monster out," Kendall said. "This is my sister, Jamie, and her girlfriend, Daya—and guys, this is, um, Finley and her dad, Mason."

Jamie met my gaze, reaching out for a firm handshake. "We've heard *so* much about you," she said, and I couldn't help but notice the dimples in her cheeks as she tried not to smile. I could only imagine the kind of things Kendall shared with her sister about me. She probably knew everything.

"Great," I said with a sheepish chuckle, turning to shake Daya's hand. "I'm sure she told you all about my laminating and cutting skills."

"Oh, she told us about your skills, all right," Jamie said, pulling the sucker from her mouth. I knew it. I managed to laugh this comment off, but Kendall buried her face in her hands.

"Jamie," she grunted. "Why don't you guys show Finley where we keep the dog treats?"

Finley put her bucket down on their coffee table and followed Jamie and Daya into the kitchen. Daya opened a door off the kitchen to reveal the shaky white dog, who was wary of Finley until he smelled the treat in her hands. She knelt down with him on the floor and giggled as he licked every last crumb off of her fingers.

"Do you want to see Titus's room?" Daya asked.

Finley stared up at her with wide eyes. "He has his own *room?*"

With Finley preoccupied with the dog, Kendall nodded for me to follow her onto the front porch. "I've really got to get that girl her own dog," I said, letting the screen door swing shut behind me.

Kendall leaned against the porch railing and turned to me. While it had been warm most of the day, there was a chill in the air now—and she hugged her arms against her chest. "I was starting to think you guys might not come tonight," she said.

"Wanted to save this for last." I leaned onto the railing beside her, facing the road. "Thanks for inviting us."

Kendall turned toward me, furrowing her brows. "But Finley—" Her mouth gaped open, and she began to smile. "Wait, this wasn't your idea, was it?"

"My idea? No, Finley said you told her—" Suddenly, I understood the reason behind Kendall's grin. "That manipulative little… invertebrate sea creature."

Kendall leaned her head back and laughed. "She parent-trapped us."

"I guess she did. That girl is too smart for her own damn good."

"Did she give you the puppy dog eyes?"

"Not this time," I said, running a hand through my hair. "Believe it or not, it didn't take a lot of persuasion to get me to come here."

Kendall's gaze held mine for a moment, the warm glow of the porch light softening her features. It took everything in me not to close the gap between us and kiss her right then. But I knew I couldn't—not again. Not now. Especially not with Finley laughing and playing with the dog just on the other side of the door.

So instead of kissing, which I knew was on her mind as much as it was on mine, we talked.

We talked about Owen and Sarah, laughing at the image in our heads of them having to clean all of the toilet paper out of their yard in the morning.

We talked about her Halloweens as a child—how she and Jamie would trick-or-treat in nicer neighborhoods because they gave out better candy. The more she spoke, the more I realized the neighborhood she was describing sounded an awful lot like mine. I wouldn't point this out to her, though.

And we talked about the trunk-or-treat incident with Traci— which turned into a rant about all of my recent interactions with the woman. Kendall listened to every word, and by the end of it, I think she disliked Traci as much as I did.

We could have been out there for ten minutes or an hour—I lost all sense of time on that porch with Kendall. And as the temperature plummeted, we inched closer and closer together until we were standing shoulder-to-shoulder, the warmth of her body melding with mine. Just as I turned to face her, to ask if she wanted to go back inside, the door behind us opened.

"Um, your kid is totally passed out on our couch," Jamie said.

"You're kidding."

"What'd you guys do to her?" Kendall laughed as we followed Jamie into the house. Sure enough, Finley was curled up asleep on one end of their couch, still clutching an open bag of Kit Kats. Her jellyfish costume was crumpled up beside her on the floor.

"We tried to wake her up, but she's out cold," Daya said.

I shook my head, smiling at the sight of drool collecting on the couch next to Finley's mouth. "Yeah, she's a deep sleeper. She could sleep through a freight train, to be honest."

Jamie let out a loud, melodramatic yawn. "Speaking of sleeping—I think we're going to head to bed." She turned to Daya and widened her eyes, nodding her head toward the back of the house. "It was nice meeting you, though."

"Yeah, you too."

Jamie and Daya said goodnight and disappeared into their bedroom. And just as I prepared to scoop Finley up and say goodnight myself, Kendall reached for the fleece blanket draped on the back of the couch and covered Finley with it. Then, kneeling on the floor beside her, she gathered up the empty Kit Kat wrappers surrounding her and gently pulled the bag of candy from her hands, putting everything on the coffee table. Turning back to Finley, she tenderly brushed her hair out of her eyes, tucking it behind her ear.

"She's so peaceful when she's asleep," Kendall said, glancing up at me with a soft giggle. I sucked on my bottom lip as she continued to stroke Finley's hair. There was something about this tiny, nurturing gesture that tugged at my heartstrings—it came so naturally to Kendall. While I knew she would be this gentle and caring with any of her students, there was love in her eyes as she wiped chocolate from the corner of Finley's mouth with her thumb.

I was lost in a daydream, fantasizing about some imaginary future with Kendall completing our family, when I realized she was staring up at me. "Are you okay?"

Swallowing the lump in my throat, I said, "I'm fine."

Kendall rose to her feet. "I'm sorry, you probably need to go. It's already—"

"Can we talk?" I blurted these words before I was even aware of what would come next. I only knew I needed Kendall to understand how I felt—and why I couldn't be around her like this. "I've got just a few things I need to get off my chest."

chapter thirty-two
mason

Kendall's bedroom smelled like lavender and vanilla—just like her, but intensified. And much like her desk at school, her dresser top and bedside table were cluttered with books, notebooks, and all kinds of lotions and sprays. Next to a palm-sized amethyst stone on her dresser sat a wooden incense burner that still contained ashes from the last burn, which would explain the strong lavender aroma. As Kendall sat down on her fully made bed, I took a moment to take in all the details of her room—observing all the things that made her… her. The wicker hamper overflowing with clothes. A row of succulents along her windowsill that looked like they were in desperate need of attention. Pictures from her students taped all over her closet door.

"That looks familiar," I said, zeroing in on the heart-shaped neon light next to her mirror.

Kendall followed my gaze, turning to the light with the tiniest grin. "I bet it does. Do you want to sit?"

"No," I answered, perhaps too quickly. I couldn't risk being on a bed with this woman right now. "I should stand for this."

"Okay. What is it you want to tell me?"

I slipped my hands into my back pockets and stared into her eyes, almost forgetting the very reason we were in this room. Those eyes had a way of pulling me in and turning my brain completely off. She was so beautiful—which was going to make the words I was about to say even more difficult. "I have to stop volunteering in your classroom."

"Why, did Owen hire you?"

"No." I sighed. "I haven't heard about that yet. No, I'm saying that because of me and you."

Her shoulders slumped. "Oh."

"It's really difficult for me to be around you, knowing I can't be with you. And I—I hate that I put you in such an awkward position with one of your colleagues the other day. I think it's probably for the best if I step back."

Kendall slowly began to nod. I felt a twinge of disappointment that she was agreeing with me, but it was the mature thing to do. "I guess it was just a matter of time before we reached this conclusion, huh?"

"Yeah, and it—" I gave in and sat beside her on the bed, leaving at least a foot between us. "Sucks."

"I know." Kendall inhaled deeply, pulling her legs up onto the bed so she was sitting cross-legged, facing me. She looked down at her lap and said, "You'd be so perfect for me if you weren't one of my student's dads."

"*I'd* be perfect for *you*? You're kidding, right? Because I'm feeling like the universe just put this perfect, knockout of a woman in front of me just to tease me. It kills me not to be able to have you the way I want you." Fuck, that was probably too much.

"What would we do if I weren't Finley's teacher, Mason?"

Kendall likely assumed my mind was going to a dirty place—and admittedly, the memory of her naked body beneath mine flashed before my mind for a second. But it was quickly replaced by that silly fantasy I had of her becoming a more permanent fixture in my life. Finley's life. There was nothing I wanted more than for Kendall to be the missing piece to the puzzle—to fill the void in our hearts.

I hesitated, choosing my next words carefully. Choosing to be vulnerable. "I would've asked you to be my girlfriend a long time ago, for one."

Kendall's lips parted in surprise, and a soft blush tinted her cheeks. Goddammit, I wanted to kiss that woman. I had to look down at my folded hands to avoid losing control.

"And I wouldn't be sitting next to you twiddling my thumbs, I'll tell you that," I added.

Kendall let out the cutest giggle in response, and I had to restrain myself from looking up. I became hyperaware of her body on the bed next to mine, and though we weren't as close as we had been on the porch—this was a million times more intimate. For a moment, neither of us spoke, but the silence between us was the loudest thing I'd ever heard. It was probably time for me to go, but I couldn't get my feet to move. I let out a heavy sigh, preparing myself to say goodbye, when she said, "Can I be honest with you for a second?"

"Yeah. Honesty's good."

"The thought of not seeing you anymore is breaking my heart a little bit right now. And I know it's for the best, but I can't help but wonder if there's not… another option."

"How could there be?"

"Well, have you considered, you know—" Kendall flipped her hair to the opposite shoulder and glanced up at the ceiling with a deep inhale. And then, rolling her eyes like even she couldn't believe what she was about to say, she continued. "Just seeing how this plays out while keeping it secret?"

My heart pounded in my chest. I never thought Kendall would have been the one to propose the notion of dating in secret. All this time, I'd been worried I'd be the first to beg her for this. But here she was before me, saying the words I couldn't—and she was even giving me the puppy dog eyes.

Which were totally unnecessary, by the way.

"Are you saying you want to sneak around with me?"

"I think I am?" She raised her hands to the sides of her head in a mix of amusement and agony. "But only if you want to.

And if you don't want to, I take it back one hundred percent and we can forget I ever brought it up."

I twisted toward her, bringing one knee up onto the bed, and smiled. "So your feelings are completely contingent upon mine? I thought you were going to be honest with me, princess."

She laughed, sliding the palms of her hands down her cheeks. "God, you can't call me that."

"Why? You don't like it?"

"I like it too much—that's the problem." Kendall's hands went from her hair to her lap and back to her face. Her eyes focused on anything but me, and she was fidgeting so much that I took her hands in mine and held them still between us on the bed to ease her nerves.

"Hey. One-two-three, eyes on me." When she looked up, she flashed me a grin, but my own smile began to fade. "Kendall, you don't really want to risk losing your job. Not for me. I promise I'm not worth all the trouble this could get you into."

"That's where you're wrong," she said. "And I don't plan on telling anyone. Do you?"

My mom's *do I know my son, or do I know my son?* remark popped into my head. "No. I just don't want to—" Her eyes were distracting me now, and I wasn't even the one with ADHD. "I don't ever want to be the cause for any turmoil in your life."

"I think you're underestimating the amount of turmoil you'll bring to my life if you walk out of it now."

I swallowed, deciding right then and there that I never would. Walk away from her, that is. No force on earth could keep me away from this woman. Letting go of her hands, I placed my palms on her knees instead and leaned in to close the space between us. And, with my lips on hers, I made a silent promise to never, ever let her go.

I eased her back onto the mattress, showering her with slow, tender kisses on the way down. And then, wanting to kiss more of her skin, I tugged on the bottom of her shirt until she got the message and helped me yank it over her head. With her hands in my hair, she whispered, "Is it okay to do this now? With her here?"

We touched noses. "If people were never intimate while kids were under the same roof, there'd be a lot more only children." I kissed her along her collarbone.

"Right," she answered, letting out a little giggle—which may have been a reaction to my beard tickling her skin.

But God—that laugh—it destroyed me. I brought my lips back up to her mouth, the only mouth I ever wanted to kiss, as I ran my palm over the pale pink lace of her bra. Kendall used both of her hands to pull my shirt off, and just as I lowered myself back down, there was a single high-pitched bark on the other side of the door that jolted me back to reality.

"Let me check on her real quick," I said, fearing Finley was awake out there. But when I opened the door and peered into Kendall's living room, Finley was in the exact same position, curled up beneath the blanket. She was even snoring, which was a good indicator she wouldn't wake up for a while. The dog was standing on the back of the loveseat growling at something out the window. Trick-or-treaters, probably.

I turned back around and closed Kendall's door behind me, locking it this time. She was standing between her bed and her dresser with a look of concern on her face. "Is she okay?"

"Yeah, she's still out." I slipped my hands around her waist and tried to pick up where we'd left off—kissing her in the crevice of her neck. It was becoming my new favorite place to kiss her because of the way it made her tremble with pleasure. "But listen," I said between breaths. "Even though I said she could sleep through a freight train, we should still try to be quiet."

"It's easy for me to be quiet when my mouth is full," she said, reaching for a scrunchie atop her dresser.

Her words didn't quite register in my mind until her hair was pulled back and she was fumbling with the button of my jeans with a naughty grin. I cleared my throat. "Jesus." My pants were unzipped and sliding down my legs before I could say anything else. Kendall tucked her fingers beneath the waistband of my boxers, dropping to her knees as she tugged them down, too. "Oh, you don't have to—"

But she was already running her tongue along the length of my half-erect cock.

"Never mind."

The way she giggled as she wrapped her hand around the base of my cock made me go completely hard. With my back against her dresser, I held her ponytail in one hand as she slipped her mouth over the tip. She wasted no time at all, bobbing her head up and down as she took more of me into her mouth with each pass—all the while applying the perfect amount of pressure with her hand.

"Fuck, Kendall," I said, barely able to breathe. This woman was overqualified—she was about to bring me to my knees myself. I wanted to gaze into her eyes, but hers were closed— and as I looked down, I saw her free hand go into her leggings so she could play with herself. "You like this, don't you?"

Her eyes shot open. "Mmmm," she answered with a gargled hum, taking me even deeper into her mouth. Instinctually, I pressed my hand against the back of her head and pushed her even further onto my cock, essentially fucking her mouth. Kendall ate it up, too—quite literally—and I loved every fucking second of it.

But she was *too* good at this.

Too.

Fucking.

Good.

"Kendall, wait." I yanked on her ponytail, and she got the message, pulling away to gaze up at me. Her bottom lip and chin glistened with drool, and her eyes were watering as she took a couple of deep breaths. "This feels *so* amazing—it really does—but I had something else in mind."

"Do it, then."

Damn, okay.

Her bra was off within seconds—followed by my shoes and the rest of my clothes. I yanked down her leggings and panties in one fluid motion, not bothering to slow down or apologize when I heard a seam ripping somewhere. I pushed Kendall's naked body onto the bed horizontally and laid beside her, dropping my hand down to the warmth between her thighs. "You're gushing," I said, passing over her wet opening with one finger.

"That's what you do to me."

I kissed her mouth as I massaged her clit, taking my time. "And what do you think you do to me, princess?" She couldn't answer—I didn't take my lips off of hers long enough for her to speak. I slid two fingers inside of her with ease, thrusting them in and out and keeping my eyes open so I could see hers widen with pleasure. I fucked her with my fingers until she started to let out a few soft moans, tilting her head backwards on the bedspread. "Do you want to come on my hand?" I whispered.

"No," she rasped. "Please."

"Why, what do you want?"

"You know what I want."

Oh, yes, I did. And I was preparing to give it to her, maneuvering my body to climb atop hers, but Kendall took complete control. Before my mind had time to process, I was under *her*, and she was lowering herself onto my cock. I didn't have to give it to her—she was taking it. *All* of it. She let out a breathy moan as she started to grind, and I was too distracted by the sight of her bouncing up and down on me to remember we were supposed to be quiet. "Fuck," I grunted, squeezing her perfect hips. "You ride me so well."

Kendall folded herself in half on top of me so we could kiss. I held her ass in my hands to give her support as she gyrated on top of me. It felt incredible to relinquish control like this and let her do her thing. She was loving it—and I couldn't think of anything in the world I'd rather be looking at.

Kendall cupped her own breasts in her hands and sighed, arching her body backwards and working herself up. She picked up the pace, leaning farther and farther backwards and propping herself up with her hands on my thighs. I slid my hand down her lower abdomen to touch her just above where our bodies met. Massaging her clit with two fingers, I smiled as I watched her eyes roll back in her head. I loved seeing her like this—the woman who had been so in control just moments ago was losing it completely now, each moan and sigh louder than the last.

And as her muscles tightened around my cock, she began to tremble, folding herself forward again. She pressed her face against my neck to muffle the sound of her moans as she came. With both hands, I grabbed her rear end again and finished what she started—lifting her up and down while grinding my hips against her body. Kendall was completely spent and out of breath, so I was content doing all the work until I finished inside of her.

Our sweaty bodies remained exactly how they were, and it was hard to tell where mine ended and Kendall's began. I held her in my arms for a couple of minutes—God knows how long—as we both caught our breath. Some of her hair had come loose from her ponytail and clung to her sweaty forehead, so I brushed it away with my fingers, whispering, "You are the second-best thing that's ever happened to me."

Kendall smiled, closing her eyes—she'd understood exactly what I meant.

While I could have held her like that all night, my mind couldn't rest while Finley was alone on a couch in a strange house. I hurried to get myself dressed before asking Kendall for directions to her bathroom—more specifically, to the linen closet—so I could find a washcloth. I took special care to clean her up, and then I gathered up all of her clothes for her. Her underwear had a small tear at the waistband, which would explain the ripping sound from earlier. Whoops.

"Can you stay for a little while?" she asked, pulling her shirt back on.

"Stay?" It was well past Finley's bedtime, and it was a school night. "I don't know…"

"Maybe we could watch a movie out there with the volume turned down low. And I baked apple tarts, which—if you can believe it—actually taste fantastic, despite how they look."

"Yeah. Yes, I'll stay."

And so my Halloween night ended with Kendall by my side on the loveseat adjacent to the couch where Finley slept, a plate of apple tart crumbs on the coffee table in front of us. While she tucked her feet beneath my legs to keep them warm, I absentmindedly stroked her ankle with my thumb as we watched *A Quiet Place*. Finley's snores were louder than the movie, which made Kendall turn to me with an amused smile a couple of times.

That void in my heart was slowly beginning to fill.

chapter thirty-three
kendall

This wasn't my first rodeo with forbidden relationships. Two years ago, I was Owen Gardner's dirty little secret, and the novelty of illicit love eventually wore off—even faster when I realized it was all he'd ever want from me.

This time, I was the one whose job was on the line, and I was putting Mason in the same position Owen had with me, forcing him to keep us under wraps. But the most crucial difference in my relationship with Mason compared to that fling with Owen was that both of us would shout it from the rooftops if we could.

Still, there was some part of me that couldn't help but wait for the other shoe to drop. There was this nagging voice in the back of my mind telling me this was all just temporary. He was going to tell me he was in love with his best friend or decide my quirks were too annoying—it was only a matter of time, wasn't it?

With Mason, I decided to put all of my red flags on full display before he got too close. I'd let him see the annoying parts and decide for himself if this was truly worth it or not. "You might think my quirks are cute now, but you're going to lose patience with me eventually."

"I would never get upset with you over something you can't control," was Mason's response.

I told him more about my family's issues, even warning him that my mom and I averaged one major fight per year—usually around the holidays—which meant he should probably prepare himself for my impending tear-filled rants. "And don't even get me started on my daddy issues."

"Do you want to hear about mine?"

Mason countered every one of my red flag warnings with acceptance and understanding. The more I pushed him to find some fault in me, the harder he seemed to fall.

"If this becomes too much for you, I understand," I told him in his car Friday night. We'd ordered coffee at the Riverside drive-thru and parked near the river downtown. He left Finley at home to play board games with his parents so we could go on our first official date, if you could call it that. "I feel like I'm asking for a lot from you."

"Kendall," Mason said, rolling his eyes with a laugh. "I wouldn't be here if any of this were 'too much' for me. I'm not sure I've ever been this happy before."

I turned toward my window so he couldn't see my dorky smile. By now, I'd already listed all of my negative traits, none of which scared him in the slightest. After a moment, I thought of another one and turned back to him. "What if I told you I have an unhealthy obsession with Taylor Swift and call into work every time she releases a new album so I can listen to it on repeat until I have every lyric memorized?"

"Is that supposed to intimidate me?"

"It should."

Mason gazed out the windshield for a moment, watching a speedboat make its way down the river. Maybe dating an obsessive Swiftie was where he drew the line, and this would be the red flag he finally decided was too much for him to handle. "Okay. What if I told you my friends and I won our school's Battle of the Bands back in 2014 with our ironic cover of 'We Are Never Getting Back Together'?"

"Shut up. No you didn't."

"I would not lie about Taylor Swift," he said, holding his hand against his chest in an melodramatic manner. "And if you don't believe me, my mom's got a video of the whole thing—she'll probably show it to you someday."

I inhaled, trying not to overreact to Mason including me in his version of "someday." He saw me in his future, one way or another. Mason must have realized what he'd just implied with that statement, too, because he stared down at his cup with a tight-lipped smile. I decided to let it go so he wouldn't feel embarrassed.

"That's funny," I said, pausing to take a sip of my coffee, "because my sister calls you Kurt Cobain."

"Dave Grohl would be more accurate. I was on drums. But wait, why does Jamie call me that?"

"That's one of her many nicknames for you."

"You and your sister talk about me, huh?"

"Maybe. But I want to hear more about this band of yours. You were a drummer? I bet you had girls throwing themselves at you all the time."

Mason smiled and shook his head, but he didn't deny it. "Not as much as our lead singer."

"You know, you've never told me about any of your past relationships apart from Finley's mom." Maybe Mason had some red flags I should know about. "Who was your last serious girlfriend?"

Mason stretched his arms and grimaced, and I almost regretted asking. But at the same time—he knew more about my two most recent ex-boyfriends than I ever wanted him to, and it was only fair that he spilled the beans with me. "Isabel," he finally said, staring down at his gear shifter as he lazily ran his fingers down the side of it. "We broke up in January after dating for six months."

"Why?"

He sighed. "I had to keep canceling on her because stuff came up with Finley. At that point, I had Fin every weekend because Whitney was kind of starting to drift... and I wasn't always willing to give up my time with her. And when Isabel asked me to choose her or Finley—well, that was the easiest decision of my life."

"Wow—I bet it was."

"And it was probably for the best things ended when they did, because I don't think she would've handled everything that went down with Finley this year very well."

"Did Finley like her?"

Mason looked up at me. "She never met her."

"You dated this woman for six months and she never met Finley?"

"No. I've always been careful about the women I let into Finley's life. I don't want her getting attached to someone who's not going to stick around."

"That makes sense." There was a long, but comfortable, silence between us following this exchange. Mason asked if I thought it would be safe to go for a walk by the river since it was after dark and the weather was starting to turn cold—which meant nobody else was around. He slipped his hand in mine as we walked along the riverfront beneath the dim light of the streetlamps.

His phone was blowing up with notifications in his pocket. "Sorry, I can't ignore this," he said, pulling his phone out. For a moment, I worried something might be wrong with Finley, but judging from the smile on Mason's face when he looked at his screen, everything was good. "Look at this."

He turned his phone around so I could see a photo of Finley standing on a dining room chair in a unicorn nightgown, wearing what looked like a Candy Land gameboard as a hat. Beside her, her grandpa's head was buried in his hands in frustration. "I'm guessing she won the game?"

"She always does. Even when she… doesn't."

I laughed, and Mason squeezed my hand as he slipped his phone back into his pocket. As we walked, I couldn't help but notice the way his arms clung close to his side and he shivered every few steps. I was wearing a thick quilted jacket, but his hoodie looked a little on the thin side. So I dropped his hand and yanked the scarf from the collar of my coat, making him stop so I could drape it over his neck. I used the ends of the scarf to pull him in for a kiss.

Mason chuckled against my mouth. "I should be the one trying to keep you warm."

"Says who?"

"I don't know—the patriarchy?"

I resisted the urge to quote Taylor Swift as he rested his forehead against mine. He kissed me again, making me shiver when his cold hands slid down the back of my pants. I could almost guarantee his hands would find their way to my ass every time we embraced, and sure enough, there they were—grabbing a hold of my buttcheeks and not letting go. "Thanks, I'm getting warmer now."

I laughed, and we stayed just like that for a minute or two, all alone on that secluded riverwalk. But his phone buzzed a couple more times—this time, it was Owen.

"He wants to meet me for brunch on Sunday."

"That's a good sign, right?"

Mason sighed. "I almost feel guilty now. Like I'm forcing him to hire me."

"Mason." I pulled back and looked into his eyes. "Owen's not an idiot, okay? He didn't get where he is by making impulsive business decisions. Everything he does is… calculated. If he offers you this job, it's because he knows he needs you. You're not forcing him to do anything."

"Damn," he said, enveloping me in a hug. "I think you just made my insecurities about this melt away."

"You're welcome."

"Could've gone without all of the Owen praise…"

I tickled him, which was a mistake, because he tickled me back until I was shrieking and struggling to wriggle out of his grasp. Tickling turned into wrestling, which ultimately turned into the sort of fondling that could get us both in trouble for public indecency.

After walking along the river for a few more minutes, Mason turned to me with a frown, saying he needed to get home to put Finley to bed. "She doesn't like to go to sleep without me. And I know I should probably break her of that, but—"

"Don't."

"Don't what? Don't go?"

"Don't break her of it. Not yet. I used to get so lonely falling asleep by myself as a kid. And it got worse after the divorce. The house was so quiet at night, and it was just me with my sad thoughts. Sometimes I'd curl up on the rug in my sister's room just to feel less alone." I laughed at myself, suddenly feeling embarrassed about the way I was rambling. "God, I am so sorry, I don't know why I'm sharing all of this with you."

"I love it," Mason said, running his hands down my arms. "Share more. Share everything. Just—not now. I really do have to go. But—" He let go of me, pulling my scarf off his neck and draping it back over mine. With the sexiest grin, he said, "I'd better give this back to you before you write a ten-minute song about me."

My mouth dropped open, and Mason grinned, well aware of the effect this Taylor Swift reference was having on me. *Don't fall in love,* I thought—but I wasn't sure which one of us I was saying it to.

chapter thirty-four
mason

I had more than the usual amount of trepidations about taking Finley back to Traci after the confrontation on Halloween. I had let this woman look me in the eye and tell me how "ridiculous" I was for having boundaries, and I wasn't that thrilled to see her again.

But blowing her off would be unfair to Finley, who was looking forward to going to McDonald's that day. So when Traci muttered, "Wasn't sure if you'd even show up," as I got Finley out of the car, I kept my snarky comeback to myself. Finley was staring at my face, having heard Traci's comment. She was picking up on the animosity, which wasn't entirely Traci's fault. I could stand to be better about how I responded to her in front of my daughter.

"Here we are," I said, trying not to sound like an asshole.

Traci put a hand on her hip. "There's a luncheon after church, and it might go until about one or so. Would that be all right?"

I looked at Finley, gauging her reaction. "As long as it's okay with her."

"You want to have coneys and chips at the church with Mamaw, don't you, Finley girl?"

Finley just nodded, looking up at me in silence as I strapped her in. Knowing this child wouldn't touch coney sauce, I told her, "I bet she can get you a plain hot dog."

"Of course Mamaw can," Traci said, closing the car door after I kissed the top of Finley's head. "Thanks for being mature about this."

I inhaled. "Yup. Just call me when you're done."

As they pulled away, I stood outside of my car with my hands in my pockets for a moment, wondering if there would be other kids for Finley to play with at this luncheon. She was pretty good about finding ways to entertain herself—with the imaginary YouTube channel and all—but I felt a pang of worry in my chest when I pictured her sitting there surrounded by a bunch of people she barely knew—people I didn't know at all.

At least I had my meeting with Owen to distract me. He asked me to meet him at The Noshery, an old-fashioned diner downtown known for its pancakes. Kendall was surprised he hadn't asked to eat somewhere more "bougie"—but Owen was probably just trying to appear down to earth. And everyone knew The Noshery had the best breakfast food in town.

"Don't let me leave here without a to-go order of biscuits and gravy for Sarah," Owen said, speaking over the Van Morrison song playing overhead. "I promised her I wouldn't forget."

Biscuits and gravy sounded like a good idea. That's what I ordered, and as Owen talked to our server, I pulled out my phone to send Kendall a quick text.

Mason: "Brown Eyed Girl" is playing here and all I can think about is you

She'd probably heard that from a dozen other men—maybe even the one sitting across from me now. I tried not to think about it. If I was going to work alongside Owen, I'd have to stop imagining him with Kendall like this. A lot of questions about them lingered in the back of my mind, but I was afraid asking would annoy her. So I never did.

"You know our moms worked here together back in the day?" Owen asked before taking a sip from a little white coffee mug.

"Oh, I've heard all the stories." I shook my head. "My mom always says she was pissed at Michelle because she had to do everything she did."

"And now look at them. I swear they have a two-hour phone conversation every single day."

"Yup. 'What do you want? I'm on the phone with *Michelle!*'" I said in my best Christine voice—I'd perfected it so well, it almost made Owen spit out his coffee. "You'd think they'd run out of shit to talk about."

"There's never a shortage of family gossip." Owen said with a laugh, reaching for the messenger bag in the seat beside him. I rested my arms on the table, observing him pull out a piece of paper. He cleared his throat as he skimmed the document before looking up to say, "All right, you had your proposal for me last week. Now it's my turn."

I held my breath as he slid the paper across the table toward me, exhaling when I saw the words 'EMPLOYMENT OFFER' at the top. And below that, in a smaller font—CREATIVE DIRECTOR.

He'd included a list outlining the job duties seemingly related to the projects we'd discussed and all the included job benefits, but the words blurred together as my thoughts circled around the job title he was offering me. I hadn't asked for that, and "director" felt like too much. I opened my mouth to say something, but then I saw my proposed salary at the bottom. It was close to my earnings at the publishing house—suspiciously so—and more than I had imagined Owen could afford to pay me.

I was ready to protest all of this and tell him he was offering too much, but I could hear Kendall in my head reminding me Owen was no idiot and I wasn't forcing him to do any of this. While every instinct I had was telling me to reject his offer, I forced myself to graciously accept. "Fuck, Owen."

Okay, maybe not that graciously.

"So what do you say? Do I get to work with my baby cousin?"

"Not if you call me that," I joked. I paused to take a sip of coffee to bide myself time to collect my thoughts. "This sounds incredible, man. I mean, you've pretty much just outlined my dream job for me on this sheet."

"Yeah?" He crossed his arms against his chest. "And just so you know, everything on that list will change and evolve over time, especially as you get more and more comfortable taking control of certain things."

"Owen, I don't—" I stopped, taking a deep breath. I'd almost let my self-doubt spill out, and while I was sure Owen could tell from my body language I was nervous as hell, I was trying my best to appear cool. "Well—just—thank you. I accept."

"I should be the one thanking you. I can't even begin to tell you how excited I am about this. We—Sarah and I—have already been carving out a workspace for you in my office. Of course, you're welcome to work remote instead, if that's what you—"

"No," I interrupted. "I'll share digs with you. Probably be easier to brainstorm that way, and it beats being alone all the damn time."

"Exactly." When our food arrived, we stopped talking for a couple of minutes so we could eat. My mind wandered, envisioning all the ways this new job would change my day-to-day life. My hands were shaking as I ate, and I couldn't wait to tell Kendall and Finley.

Owen explained he wanted to wait until the first of December for me to start, since he was getting married over Thanksgiving weekend. That gave me time to wrap things up with my current clients, anyway.

After we finished, Owen paid for our breakfast and hugged me goodbye on the sidewalk in front of the diner. "I guess the next time I see you will be my bachelor party, cousin," he said, slapping me on the back.

"Sounds good, boss."

**

Finley seemed tired and cranky when I picked her up, yanking her shoes and socks off in the car. She pulled her hair out of the braid I'd spent twenty minutes on that morning, too, looking out her window with a sigh. "What's wrong, Fin?"

"I just want to go home."

"Me too. Hey—guess what?" I looked at her in the rearview mirror. "You know how Owen does all the science stuff with the podcast and the videos and books and everything? I'm going to start working with him."

She was silent. I'd expected at least some kind of reaction or response, but she just sighed some more.

"We'll probably be able to get our own house next year, kiddo."

Still nothing. Maybe she was just too tired. I decided to let her relax the rest of the way home. But as soon as I turned the music back up, I heard her say my name from the backseat. "Daddy?"

"What, baby girl?"

She took a big, deep breath. "How come you're not married?"

Well, shit. "Oh, uhhh…" That was a loaded question, and I didn't know how to answer it. "Because you're the number one girl in my life, Finley."

"But you could still get married."

"…Correct."

"Then why don't you?"

"Jeez, Fin. I don't know. I probably will one day. But not for a long, long time. What made you—"

"Can we go to the gas station?"

Well, that was the end of that, then. Though confused, I was relieved to not have to answer any more questions about my lack of a wife. "What do you want to go to the gas station for?"

"Because I want to get Ms. Devin some chocolate donuts."

I actually turned around to look at her instead of peeking at her in the mirror this time. "What?"

"One time I saw chocolate donuts in her desk, and I want to surprise her with some tomorrow."

Rather than ask any further questions, I immediately pulled into the Circle K parking lot, much to Finley's delight. She didn't even complain about having to put her shoes back on to go inside. She found the chocolate donuts right away, assuring me she knew it was the exact kind Ms. Devin liked. She sweet-talked me into getting her a slushie, too.

"Hey Fin," I said once we were back in the car. "Why don't you let me give those to Ms. Devin tomorrow when I get there? Because I always bring her a coff—"

"No!"

"But she could eat them during her—"

"No, I want to give them to her." She scowled at me from the backseat, holding her slushie with both hands. "It was my idea, not yours."

"You're right," I said with a laugh, conceding to her like I usually did. Arguing over which one of us got to surprise Kendall with a treat gave me a glimpse of a life that didn't feel as impossible as it once did.

I hoped this was the first of many arguments just like this.

chapter thirty-five
kendall

There wasn't a single day that passed without a "good morning" text from Mason. He asked me what time I woke up, and I could count on a message from him within ten minutes after my alarm every morning. Sometimes he had something perverted to say, like, "my hands are cold" (knowing I'd understand exactly where he wanted to put them.) Other times, he'd say something that would take the breath right out of my lungs, like, "Hope you have a good day, pretty girl. Wish I were waking up beside you."

And there was never a shortage of heart emojis.

I lay in my bed for a few extra minutes Monday morning, holding my blanket around me tight. Jamie and Daya hadn't turned the furnace on yet for the season, making me wish Mason's warm body was next to mine. My room was so cold, I was having trouble getting motivated to get up and get dressed, so I scrolled Facebook for a few minutes—a decision I regretted when I saw my dad's latest post.

My step-mom, Angie, had tagged my dad in a photo. There he was with his new family, all of them in coordinating plaid and puffy vests amid a picturesque fall landscape. His two new daughters (I could hardly call them "new" considering they were in middle school now) were on either side of him, and all of their smiles were obnoxiously fake.

He had taken zero family portraits like this with us, so to see him like this was as hysterical as it was infuriating. I almost reacted to the photo with a laugh emoji, but that was a little too on-the-nose. So I opted for the heart reaction, wondering if he was smart enough to understand the sarcasm behind it. I wanted him to know that I'd seen it, and I hoped like hell there was some part of him that knew how much it hurt.

I showed the photo to Jamie that morning as she filled her water bottle at the sink. "Gross. I need to bleach my eyes now." She walked over to the kitchen table and picked up a black jewelry box. "Hey, let me know what you think of this."

She opened the box, revealing a circular starry constellation pendant dangling from a white-gold necklace chain. I gasped. "That's gorgeous. Is it for Daya?"

"Yep," Jamie said, snapping the box shut with one hand. "It's our anniversary. That's what the night sky looked like the day we met. Is that stupid or cool?"

"Are you kidding me? It's the coolest thing I've ever seen. She's going to flip over it. So are you guys doing okay, then?"

Jamie shrugged with one shoulder. "I don't even know. Things are pretty weird right now. She knows I've got to move out of Woodvale eventually, but I don't think that's what she wants. I know she'll follow me like a lost puppy if I go, but I don't want to force her away from this job that she loves—or her family. She shouldn't have to sacrifice what she wants for me."

"You don't think *you're* what she wants?"

Jamie grunted in response as she reached for her water bottle on the counter. Before she could give me a real answer, my phone chimed. My heart nearly stopped when I realized who the Facebook message was from.

Troy Devin: Haven't heard from you in a while. Hope you're doing well

"Are you kidding me?" I blurted, laughing at the audacity of his implication that our lack of contact was in any way my fault. I flipped my phone around so Jamie could see the screen.

She read the message and rolled her eyes. "And that's exactly why I've had the dude blocked for the past year."

Smart.

* *

Finley Reed had something for me hidden behind her back, and she was insisting I guess what it was. "Is it a jellyfish?"

"Nope."

"Is it… an acorn?"

"Nope! Keep guessing!"

"Finley, I give up." We'd been at this for a few minutes now. She had been the first student to arrive that day, and the class was filled with students now. Everyone was in their seats and ready to start their day—except for Finley. She stood before me with the goofiest grin, awaiting my next guess. "Why don't you just show me?"

Walter, who was seated in his chair just behind Finley, couldn't take this anymore. "It's donuts."

Finley's face fell. I thought she'd respond with tears, but she chose violence instead—lobbing the little package of donuts directly at Walter's head. Her entire face turned red with rage. "You ruined the surprise!"

"Finley!" After giving Walter a quick glance to make sure the impact of the donuts hadn't actually hurt, I crouched before Finley and took her hands in mine. "Honey, I'm still very surprised. How'd you know I like those donuts?"

"He ruined it!"

"No he didn't. I'm so, so happy you brought those for me."

Her eyes were welling up with tears now. "I wanted it to be special."

"It is, sweetheart. It is." I leaned forward to pick the donuts up from the floor. A couple of them were smashed now, but other than that, they were fine. "You are so sweet and thoughtful to think of this. But you do need to apologize to Walter."

"He needs to apologize to *me*."

I bit my lip, trying not to laugh. She wasn't completely wrong. "I don't think he knew it would upset you so much, and we don't throw things at our friends. Please tell him you're sorry."

Finley's bottom lip quivered, and a few seconds later, her entire face scrunched up and she fell into my arms. Sobbing into my shoulder, she begged, "Please don't be mad at me."

I adjusted my position so I could sit on my feet and pull Finley down onto my lap. She shook as she sobbed into my shoulder, and I was beginning to get the impression this wasn't just about the donuts. "I'm not mad at you at all," I said, pulling her hair away from her face. "Everybody makes mistakes. You were feeling angry at Walter for ruining the surprise and you threw the donuts at him without thinking. Why don't you catch your breath, and then you can apologize." I looked over her head at Walter as I spoke—for someone who just had a package of donuts thrown at his head, he looked pretty calm. He was watching us closely.

Finley sniffled and pulled away from me, rubbing her eyes. "I'm sorry, Walter."

He glanced up at me before turning back to Finley. "I didn't mean to make you sad." That was almost an apology, and Finley seemed satisfied with it. She nodded in response before finding her seat so we could get started for the day.

What a morning.

**

"I told you I would let you know if I observed any changes in Finley's behavior," I said to Mason as he set my coffee down on my desk in front of me that morning. His eyes widened, so I quickly added, "She's okay, there was just a little incident this morning."

I waited for him to sit in his usual chair and pull it up to my desk before I told him about the donut incident—emphasizing how Finley cried when she worried I might be "mad" at her. "But are the donuts okay?" he asked when I was finished explaining what happened.

"Mason."

"I'm just kidding." He cleared his throat, leaning forward to rest his hand on my knee. "Yeah, I'm not surprised she reacted that way. This little gesture of hers was really important to her for some reason."

"I don't understand why she thought I would be mad."

Mason shook his head, staring down at his hand—the one lightly stroking the inside of my knee. "She likes to act tough, but she's sensitive sometimes."

"That sounds familiar."

He smiled, hooking both of his hands behind my knees to roll my chair closer to his. "I'm surrounded by sensitive girls trying to act tough."

"I was talking about you," I blurted, mustering up the best straight face I could manage as Mason leaned forward. His hands slid underneath my thighs where he gripped me tight, grinning devilishly.

"Must be the Gemini in me," he said.

"I'd like to have a Gemini in me."

Up until that point, Mason had been trying to play it cool—but those words broke him. He bowed his head and laughed into his chest, squeezing my legs even harder. It wasn't often I could make Mason squirm like this, but I enjoyed it immensely. When he was finally able to pull himself together, he said, "We're in a school, Ms. Devin."

Before I could quip back with something even dirtier, my phone chimed—and it was yet another notification from my dad.

"What now?" I muttered, picking up my phone to read the message.

> **Troy Devin:** I would love for you and your sister to come for pre-Thanksgiving dinner on Sunday. Grandma Deb will be here and it would mean so much to all of us if you could come. Miss you, kid

I swallowed. Something about the inclusion of the word "kid" tugged at my heartstrings, transporting me right back to my childhood. The version of my father that woke up early with me to eat Rice Krispies cereal and watch ESPN together flashed through my mind—the man who let Jamie and me sneak cans of Mountain Dew even though our mom said we weren't allowed to have it.

The nostalgic side of me longed to see him again, but the realist in me doubted the sincerity of this sudden invitation. He was probably just keeping up appearances. He'd get my step-mom to take a picture of us together so he could post it on Facebook and pretend like he was Dad of the Year, and just by sending this message he could say that he was *trying* to be a good father. If I didn't accept the invitation, it would be on me. I'd be the bad guy.

"Something wrong?" Mason asked, watching me close.

I let out a long sigh. "My dad wants me to visit on Sunday."

"Oh," Mason responded, his hand giving my knee a reassuring squeeze. A second, more pronounced, "*Oh*" followed once he understood the reason behind my heavy sigh.

"I haven't been there in years. And it's been even longer than that since I've seen my grandma. She'll be there, too."

He was still eyeing me closely. "Do you like her?"

I shrugged. "I barely know her. She sends me a card every birthday, every holiday. She's nice." Staring down at Mason's fingers tracing a circle on my knee, I chewed on my bottom lip. A lump formed in my throat. How many invitations like this had

I ignored now? When would the distance become my fault? "I have to admit, I'm a little curious. It's like showing up there would satisfy my inner child somehow. I know that probably sounds stupid."

"That's not stupid. I know my opinion here doesn't really matter, but I think you should go."

"No. Nope. I'm not going alone, and there's no chance in hell Jamie would go with me."

"Ah." Mason nodded, and for a moment, he was quiet. He stared down at my knees. The longer we sat in silence, ignoring the papers I needed stapled, the closer I came to saying something idiotic and impulsive.

"Um." *Oh God. Here it comes.* There was still a chance to turn back, but the words I knew I'd regret tumbled out anyway. "You wouldn't want to go with me, would you?"

I forced out a nervous laugh, trying to downplay the absurdity of what I'd just proposed. *Of course* I wasn't serious about asking him to meet my father. That was boyfriend behavior, and I knew as well as he did we weren't ready for that level of intimacy. And, thanks to our unique situation, we might never be.

"Sorry, I'm just—"

But before I could dismiss my own words, Mason said, "Sure, I'd love to go."

"You would?"

"Yeah," he said with a casual shrug, like he was unbothered.. "As long as you really want me to. It sounded like you were about to change your mind for a second there."

I couldn't keep anything from him. "It's probably going to be awkward, and it's, like, a half-hour drive. You don't have to do this, Mason."

"I can handle awkward. I'm really good at impressing dads." He grinned. "And I don't mind driving. Just tell me what to wear and when to pick you up." He was saying all the right things, and something in his smile told me he knew it. "There's a chance I'll be slightly hung over, though."

"Oh, right. That makes two of us." Owen and Sarah's bachelor and bachelorette parties were Saturday night. While I initially wasn't included in Sarah's plans, considering I wasn't in her bridal party, she insisted that I join them for a girls' night in. She hired a boudoir photographer to come to the house and photograph everyone in their lingerie, and she mentioned something about a tarot card reader, too.

As for Mason and the guys, they were going into the city for dinner and drinks. He said he was looking forward to it, having not had a night out like this in months. He promised Sarah he'd return Owen in one piece—joking that it wasn't in his new job description.

As I pulled out some booklets for him to cut and staple, I couldn't help but notice how distracted Mason seemed as I gave him instructions. His eyes were fixated on something behind me on my desk. I followed his line of sight past the stack of unfiled papers to the little painted acorn Finley had given me, sitting atop a stack of post-its.

"Still with me?" I asked him.

He cleared his throat, leaning forward in his chair. "I think I might have worked out why Finley got so emotional about the donuts."

"Why?"

"She's observant, you know—and I think there's some part of her that senses what's happening between me and you. Or she's at least hopeful. She wants to feel closer to you, and I think that little gesture was her way of... trying to win you over."

"Win me over? But she already has," I said with a chuckle. "I love that kid so much."

Mason's eyes shot back up to my face, and I felt a twinge of self-awareness, recognizing the weight of the words I'd just said.

It wasn't the first time I expressed love for my students, even individually as I just had. I loved all of them.

But Finley—well, Finley was special.

The affection I felt toward her was different, and Mason knew it, too. His Adam's apple bobbed as he took the packets out of my hands and reached for a pair of scissors. With an almost imperceptible trembling in his voice, he said, "Okay, can you repeat those instructions for me, princess? I wasn't listening the first time."

chapter thirty-six
mason

Saturday night kicked off with an aggressive game of Rock, Paper, Scissors against two of Woodvale's biggest assholes. "Fuck," I muttered when Jake's paper defeated the rocks Xander and I threw out. Angling my body toward Xander, I said a silent prayer, feeling Owen watching us over my shoulder. "Rock, paper, scissors, shoot."

I chose scissors. Xander picked rock.

And I could've punched the smirk right off his face when he said, "Ha, you were the one who suggested that game. How unlucky."

Owen stepped between us, dangling his keys in front of my face. "Sorry, cuz. It had to be one of you."

"At least you get to drive the Volvo," Jake said, pulling a little black baggie from his coat pocket. I reluctantly yanked the keys from Owen's hand, sighing as I watched my eldest cousin pull a gummy shaped like an orange slice from the little bag. He held it toward Owen. "Here. Take this, little brother."

Owen spent all of two seconds observing the edible in Jake's hand before tossing it into his mouth without question. "How many milligrams was that?" I asked, turning to Jake with wide eyes.

"Hmm, can't remember," Jake said, exchanging a grin with Xander.

"Don't worry," Owen said, turning to me as he swallowed. "I never feel a thing after eating these."

"Better take another one then, for good measure," Xander suggested. Jake agreed, pulling another orange slice gummy from the bag. Owen hesitated this time, searching for something in Jake's eyes—how much did he trust his brother? "If not now, then when?" Jake asked, and all I could think about were those D.A.R.E. videos I was forced to watch back in elementary school about scenarios just like this.

But Owen didn't remember them, apparently. I'd always thought of him as one of the smartest people I knew, so I watched in astonishment as he downed the second edible without really knowing what he was getting himself into. It wasn't exactly the brightest move. "Just don't let me do or say anything stupid tonight," he said.

"That wasn't in my job description."

Owen just laughed.

**

First on our agenda for the night was dinner at a steakhouse in the heart of downtown Indianapolis. It took well over an hour to get there, thanks to traffic on 465, and it felt like it took just as long to find parking. I'd circled the block three times before giving up and settling on a nearby parking garage.

"You good, buddy?" Xander asked, squeezing Owen's shoulder as we walked into the restaurant. The car ride up had been pretty uneventful, besides Jake's backseat driving and Xander reading aloud the results from his Google Maps search for strip clubs around the city. Owen was quiet for the second half of the ride. Maybe too quiet.

"I'm fine. I told you—I never feel anything with these gummies. Might as well have given me fruit snacks." He unzipped his leather jacket, and the rest of us watched as he proceeded to rezip it, glancing over his shoulder at the group of people who walked in behind us. "I don't feel a thing. They didn't work. I'm fine."

The way he was obsessively playing with his zipper indicated otherwise, but the rest of us just nodded, deciding to see how this played out.

"Where's your kid tonight?" Jake asked once we were seated.

"She and her grandma are having a sleepover in the living room," I answered, opening my menu. "She wasn't going to let me leave until my mom promised her they could make a blanket fort."

"What's the story with her mom?" Xander asked. I looked up at him in disbelief, wondering why he thought this was an acceptable question to ask someone he barely knew. He was so unbothered, though, staring me down as he awaited my answer.

I tapped my fingers on the edge of the table. "She…"

As my voice trailed off, Jake chimed in. "She ditched her kid to follow some dick down to Florida. Left our boy Mason here with full custody earlier this year so she could open up a goddamn food truck on the world's skankiest beach."

While my cousin's summary of events was both accurate and succinct, I probably would have worded it differently.

Xander nodded slowly, and if I wasn't mistaken, his features softened a bit. Maybe he expected a less dramatic answer. "Mom of the year," he said. I caught the slightest hint of compassion in his voice.

"Yeah," I responded, forcing a chuckle. "But it was ultimately the right choice for everyone involved." Something about trash-talking the mother of my child in such a public setting didn't sit right with me, despite her faults. I didn't want to delve into my personal life any more than we already had, anyway. So I turned to Owen, deciding a subject change was necessary. "How are you feeling?"

"I need to… wash my hands," Owen declared, and it took every bit of self-control not to laugh in the guy's face. It wasn't his words, necessarily—it was really more the slowness at which they came out and the paranoid look in his eyes that made me glad I hadn't just taken a drink. I'd be spitting it in his face.

"Okay?" I chuckled. "Go wash your hands, then."

"I don't think I can manage that… alone."

"Why not?"

"Because this place is a dark and complicated labyrinth, and I fear that if I leave now, I may never find my way back."

Well, we certainly didn't want that. Owen was no doubt feeling the effects of the edibles, so I decided to escort him to the bathroom—which was, admittedly, a long journey from our table. I stood outside the door and texted Kendall while he did what he needed to do.

Mason: So. Owen ate 2 edibles. And he's starting to feel a little paranoid.

Kendall: Maybe that's why he's not answering Sarah's texts.

Mason: I'm not sure he's capable of that at the moment. How's the boudoir shoot going?

Kendall: Wanna see? 😊

Mason: Is that a rhetorical question?

As I waited for Kendall's photo to load, I noticed the sink had been running for quite some time. I opened the door to peek at Owen, who was not washing his hands at all, but staring at his watch.

"We should probably get back to the—"

"It's been 7:28 for a really long time. Too long."

I laughed, letting the door swing shut behind me. "No, it hasn't. You're just high. And I bet you're even more starving than I am, so why don't we head out there?"

Owen ignored me, gazing at his watch a little longer before flipping his wrist over to remove it. "I think my watch stopped working." And then, to my horror, the smartwatch slipped from his uncoordinated hands into the slowly draining sink below. His reaction time was delayed, so I lunged forward and dropped my phone on the countertop before fishing his watch out of the water. "Oh nooo," Owen drawled.

I turned off the sink and reached for a paper towel. "Well, I've already let you down, boss," I said, drying off his watch the best I could. "You asked me not to let you do or say anything stupid tonight."

"You're fired," he said with a dazed grin.

His watch was still displaying the time, along with a notification from Sarah. "Look at that," I said, turning it around to face him. "It still works—and it's 7:30 now. Time is moving forward again."

"Fuuuuuuck," Owen said, slapping his hands to his eyes. I had thought this would give him some relief, but he groaned like he was in pain. "I was *not* meant to see that."

"See what?" I asked.

And then I saw it, too.

My phone was sitting on the counter, screen side up, with Kendall's latest photo on full display. It was a full-body selfie taken in Owen and Sarah's bathroom mirror, I assumed—and she was wearing nothing but lacy, black lingerie. The picture showed her entire face, so there was no denying who she was.

I scrambled to pick the phone up and held it against my chest. "Ah, no—you weren't meant to see that. But you didn't recognize her, right?"

Owen peeked at me from behind his fingers. "I wish I could say that I didn't. I'm sorry."

"Oh." Panic shot through my veins as I searched for some way to explain this. It was fine if he merely *suspected* Kendall and

I were involved—there was no risk there—but I'd just given him solid proof. "Not your fault."

The door swung open behind me and an older man nodded at us before stepping into a stall. Owen stood with his eyes clenched shut like he was trying to erase what he'd just seen from his memory.

With a heavy sigh, I said, "Let's head back out there, I guess." I opened the door for him so I could follow him out to ensure he made it back to the table without any other mishaps.

"Was David Bowie in there with a kidnapped baby?" Xander asked when we sat down.

It took a few seconds for the *Labyrinth* reference to make sense. "No," I said, reaching for my glass. "What occurred in that bathroom was even scarier." I didn't elaborate, and neither did Owen.

chapter thirty-seven
kendall

I was no stranger to posing in my lingerie.

I would need all of my fingers and some of my toes to count the men in Woodvale who had laid eyes on my nudes. Maybe I was a little too eager to share them, especially for a teacher, but I enjoyed taking them as much as they liked receiving them. It was freeing. Empowering.

So when Alex, the boudoir photographer Sarah hired, encouraged us all to disrobe and get comfy, I was the first to shed my clothes. I was wearing a lacy black bodysuit and four-inch heels, and I wasn't exactly feeling shy about it. Half the women in Sarah's living room were strangers when I walked in, but we were about to get to know each other a lot better. Sarah's sister, Samantha, cast a lingering stare in my direction, and I couldn't determine whether it stemmed from annoyance or admiration. I didn't know her well enough yet.

"You guys don't want to see my mom pouch," Vicki Santiago said, holding her robe shut. She and I weren't close, but we'd worked on a few projects together over the past couple of years at Grissom. I didn't know a lot about her personal life except that she had a lot of kids and always knew about the best sales.

"Wrong," I said, putting a hand on my hip. "That's like a badge of honor, girl. And I have a pouch, too, but mine's just from… carbs." I laughed at myself, hoping it would put her at ease.

Alex looked up from the light she was assembling. "Okay, I love this girl already," she said, nodding toward me. "That's the kind of energy we need!"

And that was the kind of energy that followed for the entirety of the night. We all had our turn posing for Alex's camera, starting with Sarah, who looked radiant in her white bridal lingerie and veil. Alex instructed her how to pose in the leather chair in front of the fireplace. Sarah was a little stiff at first, but after ten minutes of the rest of us hyping her up, she was draping herself across that chair like Leonardo DiCaprio was sketching her.

"Owen's going to shit when he sees these pictures," Samantha whispered to the rest of us, holding her wine glass against her chest.

"I still haven't even met Owen." Jenny—an old friend of Sarah's—had just flown into town for the week leading up to the wedding. "But it seems like he's a step up from Eli."

"They're soulmates if I ever saw any," Vicki said, shaking her head. "He was after her for years before she finally opened her eyes. I was there the night they first got together. It was at a conference up in—"

Sarah cleared her throat, shifting her eyes to me as she arched her back the way the photographer showed her. "You guys are talking about me like I'm not right here." She let out a nervous laugh, trying to hold her pose.

"It's not like we're saying anything bad," Jenny said, adjusting the straps of her bralette. "I want to hear the story of how the two of you got together." She turned back to Vicki. "What's this about a conference?"

"They kissed on an elevator at a teacher convention. She said he just grabbed her and went for it. I didn't think he had it in him, really. Everybody at the school knew he carried a flame for her for such a long time."

She glanced my direction like she expected me to comment in agreement, so I nodded. It wasn't news to me that Owen hooked up with Sarah 24 hours after I ended things with him—Heath heard them going at it through the wall, apparently, and he didn't exactly keep that information to himself. It became common teacher's lounge fodder for the rest of that school year. It was almost funny to watch the two of them scramble to get people to hush about it when I was in the room.

"I mean, you saw it—didn't you?" Vicki asked, clueless.

I forced a laugh. "We all did," I said, running my fingers through my hair. Some of us were just a little more in denial than others. Noticing how Sarah had gone rigid for the photographer again, I made every attempt to sound as casual as possible when I said, "You're so right about the soulmate thing, too. I mean, have you guys heard the way he talks about her on the podcast? It's adorable."

I hoped Sarah could hear the sincerity in my voice. We were never going to get past this awkwardness if we couldn't openly talk about it, right?

Thankfully, the conversation shifted to *STEM for the Win* and Owen's rising popularity as a science influencer, so I picked up my phone to check on the guys.

Kendall: How's the night going?

Mason: At the first bar now. Owen is crossfading into oblivion and he's one shot away from making friends with an inanimate object. Missing you.

Mason: I am

Mason: The one that is missing you I mean

Mason: Not oweb

Kendall: Not Oweb. Got it. Are you drunk?

Mason: Sadly no, just typing extremely fast

I giggled as I put my phone back on the end table. I was half-tempted to slip away and take more bathroom selfies, but I didn't want to take away from Mason's reaction when he got the photos from the actual photographer.

Sarah's mini shoot wrapped up, and Alex turned to the rest of us to ask, "Alright, who's next?" She was met with crickets and nervous giggles. Since none of the other women felt ready, I handed my wine glass to Vicki.

"I guess I'll go." It felt a lot like volunteering to give a book report—not that I'd ever given a report dressed like that. Alex expertly posed me on that leather chair and I thought of Mason when I said, "I really want to emphasize my butt."

"Oh honey—I assure you, your butt is going to be the star of the show," Alex said. Everyone laughed as the shutter kept clicking. Any lingering nervousness I had dissipated, and I noticed even Vicki was standing more confidently with her silk robe open at the front. It might've been the wine, though.

And then my gaze shifted to Sarah, who was watching me closely. The second our eyes met, she looked down at her wine glass and took a sip. I sighed, turning back to the camera, wishing I could do something about this wall between us. No matter how hard I tried, how far I bent backwards to accommodate Sarah's emotions about my history with Owen, the awkwardness was still there. Would she ever get over it?

My session didn't take as long as Sarah's—I was able to pretzel myself into a series of flattering poses pretty quickly. Jenny volunteered to go next, and Sarah excused herself to check on the buffalo chicken dip in the kitchen.

I followed her. "Oh, hey," she said, looking up as she pulled the lid off the crockpot. She was wearing an oversized Cubs t-shirt over her lingerie now—probably one of Owen's old shirts. "I can't wait for Alex to give us our sneak peeks, can you?"

"No, I'm dying to see them."

She finished stirring the dip and returned the spoon to the spoonrest on the counter. And then, staring down at the white marble, she took a deep breath. *Here it comes.* "Kendall, I'm sorry about all of that talk about Owen and me earlier."

"You have no reason to be sorry."

"I tried to steer the conversation a different direction, but it didn't work."

"I caught that. But it didn't bother me at all."

She turned to face me, pressing her hip against the counter. "We were selfish and impulsive and we weren't thinking about anyone else. It just happened."

"He and I weren't together anymore. It's fine."

"But it hadn't even been—"

"Do you *want* me to be upset with you?" I snapped. Sarah's lips parted in shock at the way I cut her off. My heart was racing. I couldn't see the other women, but I noticed their voices dying down in the next room—they were listening. That didn't stop me, however. "How many times do I have to tell you 'it's fine' before you believe me? I don't care how or when you two got together. This whole time, I sort of wondered if something physical happened between the two of you even sooner, anyway. So I mean, I'm obviously not holding a grudge."

She swallowed. "He never cheated on you, Kendall."

I fought the urge to tack the word *"physically"* onto the end of Sarah's statement—it would serve no purpose. Sarah's face was already beet red, and calling her out for participating in an emotional affair would only make it worse. "It was two years ago, anyway. I've moved on and—" I paused, fiddling with the charms on my bracelet. "If I could erase everything that happened between me and him, I would. I love you, and I love being able to think of Owen as a friend now, too. Can you just try to stop making things so—weird?"

I gave her a small a smile, praying my words wouldn't cause her to break down. Nobody liked being called out for their behavior, but at this point, it was necessary. To my relief, Sarah laughed at herself, drawing one hand to her forehead. "Jeez. Why do I always make things more awkward than necessary?"

"I don't know. I'm the one standing here half naked." It seemed a little absurd that we were having this much-needed conversation while neither of us were wearing pants.

"I don't deserve you as a friend," Sarah said, shaking her head. "But here you are. I wish it weren't too late to ask you to be in my wedding." She paused, gasping. "Wait, maybe it's not?"

"It is," I said before her thoughts spiraled out of control. "Don't get ahead of yourself—I'm perfectly content just being a guest."

"You're right. But speaking of that," Sarah said, maneuvering around the giant island in her kitchen to open the pack of whiskey shooters one of the other women had brought. "Did you find yourself a plus-one?"

"Uh, no. I think I'm just going to tag along with the rest of the Grissom crew. Abigail and the others—they're all riding together."

Sarah handed me a little bottle of whiskey. "Actually... Abigail caught me in the hallway yesterday afternoon—Heath asked her to be his date."

"Oh." I sighed, realizing Heath was going to watch me show up to this gig alone despite lying to him about having a date. Not that I wanted one now, anyway. My date was going to be on the altar beside the groom, and we were the only two who knew. The only two who *could* know.

Dammit, I would have loved to tell Heath. Rub it in his face a little.

"Guess I'm flying solo, then." I twisted the cap off the bottle and tilted it back, taking a long swig. Sarah drank hers at the same time, wincing as she swallowed.

"I wish the boys would get in touch," she said. "Owen sent me a cryptic text that just said the word 'sink', and that was at least a half hour ago."

"According to Mason, he's having a pretty good time. Maybe too good."

A devious smile crept onto Sarah's face.

"What?"

"Can you just admit you've got a thing for Mason already?"

"A—a *thing*?" I scoffed. "No I don't. I've told you this already."

"Look me in the eyes and tell me you don't think Mason Reed's good-looking."

I couldn't. I looked down at my bracelet instead, feeling a warmth spread across my cheeks.

"Exactly," Sarah said, giggling. "It's so obvious."

"Sarah. He's Finley's dad," I said, looking back up at her face. "I can't."

"Just because you're attracted to him doesn't mean you have to act on it."

Whoops. I tucked my hair behind my ears, glancing over my shoulder into the living room, where the other women were hyping Vicki up as she took off her robe. "Okay, yeah. Mason's… cute. And sweet. But I'm not about to get myself fired."

I awaited her reaction, internally urging her to assure me I wouldn't be fired. If she said anything at all to indicate a relationship with Mason wouldn't necessarily be that big of a deal, I was going to tell her the truth—or at least half of it. *Tell me I wouldn't get fired.*

"I know you wouldn't. I'm just saying—I wouldn't be the least bit surprised if you two got together." She attempted another sip of her whiskey, scrunching up her face again, before adding, "When you're no longer Finley's teacher, of course."

Of course.

The way she added those last words, like they were a warning, reminded me we needed to tread carefully. Sarah was still my boss, and I was still breaking district policy. If she knew about my relationship with Finley's dad and didn't report it, it could probably jeopardize her job, too, for all I knew. I couldn't ask her to cover for us.

"Yeah, maybe one day," I said, taking both of our empty bottles and throwing them in the trash.

If Sarah's hang-ups about my history with Owen hadn't driven a wedge between us, this certainly would. As I trailed behind her back into the living room, the weight of my secret had never felt so heavy. We had just had this productive heart-to-heart conversation, and then I proceeded to look her in the eyes and lie.

She was wrong—I didn't deserve *her*.

chapter thirty-eight
mason

"Are you trying to kill him? He's a lightweight."

"The only thing getting killed here is the vibe," Xander answered, dropping a five-dollar bill in the tip jar at the first bar of the night. Xander chose this place because it had a comically exorbitant number of one-star reviews, and he wanted to see what it was all about. "And you're single-handedly responsible."

I said nothing as I watched the other three guys tip back their shot glasses. It was their second round, and this came after we all shared the filthiest pitcher of beer ever poured.

We had taken an Uber here from the restaurant, which was a relief—it meant I could at least have a couple of drinks myself, and I wouldn't have to navigate through downtown Indy again until it was time to head back to Woodvale.

Owen and I were seated on stools at the bar while Jake and Xander stood directly behind us, debating whether we should stay here or move onto the next bar. "There aren't enough women in this place," Jake said, glancing over his shoulder. During the ride over, he had informed all of us his wife recently filed for divorce. It was so fresh, in fact, Owen hadn't even known about it yet. "I won't be getting any phone numbers here. Let's just go."

I took a quick survey of the room, noting we were some of the youngest people in this seedy sports bar. Not only that, the ratio of men to women was about 5:1. Jake and Xander's prospects weren't very good.

My eyes stopped on Owen, who was absentmindedly gazing at the color-changing rope light outlining the mirror behind the bar. At least he was having fun.

"On a scale of one to ten," Xander said in a low voice, putting his hand on my shoulder, "how inappropriate would it be for us to ask Mr. Volvo to pay our way into that nightclub with the cover fee?"

"Eleven," I said, just as Jake blurted, "Let's do it."

I shook Xander's hand off my shoulder. "What do you want to do, Owen?" I asked, since no one else was considerate enough to check with him. This was his night, after all, and though he had enthusiastically gone along with everything these guys suggested so far, maybe he had something else in mind.

Owen tore his eyes from the colored lights to look at my face. "What?"

"Where do you want to go?"

He blinked. "When?"

"Jesus Christ," I muttered, bowing my head as I listened to the guy with a master's degree in science giggle like a schoolgirl at my frustration. "And that's my boss, ladies and gentlemen." I picked up my frosty mug and took a drink, staring down at my phone on my lap. After that hastily-typed "Oweb" text, I was grateful Kendall changed the subject, describing the bachelorette party in great detail.

I didn't mention the incident with Owen finding out about us. I wasn't sure how to bring it up, and besides, I didn't want to ruin her night, too. It would probably have to come up sooner or later, however, because I wasn't sure how good my cousin was at keeping secrets.

At the rate these guys were all going, though, I was the only one who'd remember this night.

"Care to chime in, Mason, or are you going to keep staring at your crotch?" I looked up from my phone at Xander, and he continued. "Nightclub. You in?"

"Um." I glanced at Owen, who was concentrating really hard on the knots on the wooden bar top now. "That might be too stimulating of an environment for some of us."

"Can we at least get the fuck out of here?" Jake urged.

Ultimately, we all agreed—even Owen—that this bar wasn't our scene. And after twenty minutes of trying to get drinks in the crowded nightclub, we decided that wasn't our scene, either. By 10:30, we found ourselves in an alleyway beside the club, arguing about what to do next.

"This is why I should've listened to Sarah about the itinerary," Owen said, squatting against the brick wall. None of us were quite sure what he was doing, but we didn't ask.

"Bro, what the *fuck* are you talking about?" Jake paced for a couple of steps with his hands in his jacket pockets before turning back to his brother. "Tell me you did not just say 'itinerary.'"

"I did. Sarah drew us a map of all the best bars—I bet she can text it to me."

A map? No wonder she and Kendall got along so well. "Hey, that's not a bad idea," I said, placing my hand on the wall. "This stag night isn't going so well, and sorry, Xander, but you're zero for two. Text her, Owen."

Owen, still crouched on the ground like he was taking a dump, looked up at me with fearful eyes, dragging his palms down either side of his face. "I'm afraid if I touch my phone I'm going to accidentally call my mom or the police. Not sure which would be worse."

"Fuck's sake, someone take his phone," Jake muttered, kicking a piece of trash.

"You should just text Kendall," Owen said. *Damn it.*

"Who?" Xander turned to me.

"I've got—I have Kendall's number. The teacher. Because of the volunteer thing." I widened my eyes at Owen, who I could tell was trying desperately not to laugh upon the realization of what he'd almost revealed. I turned back to Xander, who still looked confused. "She's at Sarah and Owen's right now."

"Okay. Well, forward that number to me and let's have some fun, my guy."

Owen couldn't contain the laughter anymore. God, could this night be over already? I shook my head. "I'm about to take an Uber back to the Volvo and leave you all stranded here," I said.

"What the hell did *I* do?" Jake demanded to know. I ignored all of them as I texted Kendall to get this mysterious itinerary and map. And sure enough, Sarah still had it. We'd already fucked up the first half of the night she'd strategically planned out for us, but she had done her research—we now knew which bars to avoid and which were worth our time.

Our journey through the Indianapolis bar scene first took us to Swish, a sports bar on the fifth floor of a downtown hotel. Its expansive windows gave us a fantastic view of the city below—a sight I sort of missed. According to Sarah's notes, we all needed to try their signature cocktail, the Larry Bird. Jake promptly ordered one for Owen, unwilling to grant the guy a moment to sober up. His cheeks puckered after he downed the sour green concoction, but he still had his jokes. "Exactly how I imagined Larry Bird would taste."

Xander turned to me. "I love this guy."

Our second stop was a dive bar where the female lead singer of a blues band nearly had Jake declaring his love for her. We practically had to drag him to the next location.

Over the course of the night, Owen had transitioned from his quiet, introspective state to entertaining us with mostly coherent spiels about the history of Hoosier breweries or the science behind alcohol metabolism. I had half a mind to record his ramblings to play back for him later—maybe this would be good podcast material?

By the fourth stop in our bar crawl, Jake still hadn't obtained a single phone number—but Xander got two with absolutely zero effort. The shot girl at the third bar willingly gave hers up on a napkin, and one of the women Jake tried talking to asked for Xander's socials instead.

He was still unsuccessful in acquiring Kendall's number, however, and that gave me a small sense of satisfaction. Of course, we still had the wedding to get through, in which the two of them would inevitably meet. But I wasn't worried—especially after Xander tried to ask Owen twice if he knew whether or not Abigail had RSVPed.

I had other things to be concerned about, anyway. Every so often, Owen and I would exchange this look like we both knew we had an awkward conversation in our future. I wasn't sure which one of us would initiate it—or how—but it was inevitable.

Owen was probably high on Kendall's list of people she didn't want to know about us—for a number of reasons. And by extension, Sarah was going to know soon, too—and she was even higher on that list. The two of them would be married in a week, and I couldn't imagine they kept many secrets from one another.

On top of these worries, I had my own issues with Owen having seen the picture of Kendall. I'd gone through the trouble of preventing him from accidentally swiping on Kendall's phone and seeing one of her nudes only for my dumb ass to practically hand him one. Was he aware I knew they used to date? Maybe they just slept together a couple of times. I still wasn't sure of the extent of their relationship, but maybe it was time to start asking questions. Just get it all out in the open.

Some other time, of course.

"I'm freezing my fucking nuts off. It's cold as shit."

I nodded in agreement at Jake's astute observation as the four of us made our way down Meridian Street. The final destination in our bar crawl was only a block and a half from the last spot, so we opted to walk. Owen was the only one of us unaffected by the cold, but I noticed him starting to wobble on his feet. Twice, we had to direct him away from obstacles on the sidewalk—a traffic cone here and a pipe jutting out from a building there. It reminded me of the way I had to physically guide a half-awake Finley toward the kitchen table for breakfast some mornings.

We had almost reached the bar when we came upon a mound of leaves along the curb. Owen staggered toward them, and I shook my head, expecting him to leap into the pile or at least traipse through them. He had other plans, however, and the rest of us stood back and watched in awe as the six-foot-four giant curled up into the fetal position in the middle of the leaf pile. As Owen tucked his folded hands beneath his cheek, I glanced around, half-afraid someone on this crowded sidewalk might recognize him from SFTW and pull out their phone for a chance at a viral video. The secondhand embarrassment nearly killed me.

"We should probably–"

"Ahh," Owen sighed, closing his eyes. "Now I know why they call it a *bed* of leaves."

It was time to call it a night. I was completely sober, and the other two had accomplished what they'd apparently set out to do—get Owen fucked up beyond belief for his last weekend as an unmarried man. "That's it, I'm getting an Uber to take us back to Owen's car."

"What—now?" Xander glanced from me to Jake, who looked equally displeased. "The night's still young."

"Our groom-to-be is currently napping five feet away from traffic. It's time to go."

"Why do you get to decide?" Jake asked.

"I want Sssssarah," Owen moaned. "Or crêpes."

"See?" Xander motioned toward Owen. "He doesn't know if he wants his fiancée or breakfast food. Let's stop in this last bar real quick and then find this guy a Denny's."

By then, I'd already ordered us a car. "You guys are free to stay, but Owen, the Volvo, and I are heading back to Woodvale. Geoff and his–" I glanced down at my phone, "–Toyota Camry will be here in six minutes."

That got both of them to shut up. My next challenge was getting the three of them from the Uber to Owen's car in the parking garage. It was like wrangling a trio of toddlers. Two of them were pouting, and the other one was so sleepy he needed to be physically guided toward the car. "Why don't you lay down back there, cousin," I said, pushing Owen into his backseat.

He mumbled something about Xander being his pillow as I was closing the door. Up front, I had to deal with Jake reaching for the steering wheel as I maneuvered through the maze-like parking garage. He tried it again when I merged onto 465—and that time, I slapped his arm away. "You're going to cause us to wreck and Owen's going to break his pretty face and his bride will be very sad. Is that what you want?"

"I want you to stop driving like Grandpa."

"Grandpa's a perfectly sensible driver. So shut the fuck up."

Thankfully, that was the last comment out of him. The rest of the ride to Woodvale was relatively quiet, with only a few groans from Owen and some mumblings from Xander about how we should've gone to a strip club.

Jake and Xander lived outside of town, and I dropped them off at their houses first. They'd figure out a way to get to their cars in the morning. With Xander out of the backseat, Owen slumped over and rolled onto his back. "Unnngh."

"Hang in there, man," I said, trying not to laugh at the sight of his lanky body stretched across the entirety of the backseat with his squeaky-clean Converse propped up against the headrest. "We're eight minutes away."

This stretch of the two-lane highway was eerily empty, but I supposed that wasn't unusual for the middle of the night in a small town with a non-existent nightlife. It was quiet—too quiet. I fumbled with the buttons on Owen's dash until I found a radio station playing an early Green Day song to fill the silence. We pulled up to a red light and I drummed my fingers on the steering wheel, softly singing along. For it being so late, I was feeling pretty energized—and all I could think about was the fact Kendall would be at Sarah's house when we got there. Would the girls still be awake?

Owen stirred in the backseat. I heard him inhale, and then he spoke. "I'm sorry for what I did to Kendall."

My hand shot toward the volume button and my mouth went dry. "What—what do you mean?" I asked, turning the music down. I strained to see him, but it was too dark to even tell where his head was.

Another sigh from him, and I braced myself. I knew the next words out of Owen's mouth could affect the entire trajectory of our friendship and professional relationship. "I used her as a distraction after Sarah rejected me. I was—I wasn't good to her."

My grip loosened on the steering wheel. "Oh."

"I didn't handle it well," he slurred. "She—she was just there when I was feeling lonely and I just wanted someone who could, you know…"

I closed my eyes in a long blink, thankful he didn't finish that sentence. "I'm sure you've apologized, right?"

"Multiple times," he said quickly. "She should hate me."

"Well, she doesn't. She actually holds you in pretty high regard."

The backseat fell silent. I caught a glimpse of Owen's face in the rearview mirror as I drove beneath a streetlight. He was lying on his back staring up at the ceiling with his hands resting on his stomach. "She deserves someone good—like you."

I chewed on my bottom lip. "She's Finley's teacher. And if people find out we're seeing each other, she'll probably get fired." I glanced over my shoulder at him. "She will absolutely kill me if Sarah finds out. You can't say anything."

"I know," Owen said with a grunt. "I tell her everything, though."

I didn't like the sound of that. "Well, not this. Okay?"

He moaned, and all I could do was pray he'd forget everything about this night.

Except for taking a nap in a bed of leaves—I'd never let him forget that.

Desperate for a subject change, I asked him, "How are you feeling about being married in a week?"

Owen sighed, and I swore I could hear the smile on his lips when he said, "I… can't believe I get to call Sarah Lavely my wife."

"You are a lucky man, cousin," I said, turning the volume back up a little. "Sarah's a great person."

"She's the *best* person," he said with a yawn. He was quiet for a while, and I decided to let the man try to rest. I turned the music up some more and sang along as we neared the Woodvale city limits. And then, just when I thought he'd drifted off to sleep, I heard his voice from the backseat. "I just wish—just wish I could fix it for her."

I stopped singing. "Fix what?"

"'Dim-diminished ovarian reserve,'" he answered, like he was quoting something—a medical report, from the sounds of it. "It's the technical term for a low egg count."

I turned the music down again. "Oh. Are you saying Sarah can't get pregnant?"

"She can. It's just going to be—" He paused for a long, deep inhale, pushing the breath out with the word, "Hard."

"Aren't there treatments for that?"

"We're researching all our options. It's all so new. There's so much information out there. It's overwhelming."

"Yeah, I bet." I peered into the backseat, struggling to see his face in the darkness. "You know, Kristin and Spencer did IVF and now they have two kids." According to my mom's gossip, our cousin struggled with infertility for years before having twins.

"I know. I told Sarah to reach out to her, and she's going to."

I had to wonder if Owen would have been telling me any of this if he hadn't been inebriated. "That's good," I said, trying to sound upbeat.

The road curved, and Owen groaned again. "Can you slow down? Actually—" He attempted to sit up, clutching his stomach.

"Do you need me to pull over?"

No response. And that was enough of an answer for me to pull off the highway onto a gravel side road. The car barely came to a stop before Owen was tumbling out of the backseat. I unbuckled and hurried out of the car, too, just to ensure he didn't roll down the slope into the ditch—which was a possibility.

Owen stood at the edge of the grass with his hands on his knees and proceeded to throw up twice. Then, he lowered himself to a squatting position and buried his head in his hands. I quickly maneuvered myself in front of him in fear he might roll forward. With my hands in my pockets, my arms clinging tightly to my side in the cold November air, I asked him, "You good?"

"She's going to be devastated if it doesn't work," he answered, his voice muffled by his hands. I struggled to find some comforting words—what could I say? His body trembled as he continued, saying, "I just want to see her become a mom."

Fucking hell.

"You will," I said, with unwavering conviction. I took a deep breath, stepped forward, and squeezed him on the shoulder. "And you're going to be the best dad someday, too."

He lifted his head, wiping his mouth. "If I can be half as good as you, then I'm set."

I swallowed the lump in my throat. "Thanks, man."

This was one of the most heartfelt conversations I'd ever had, and one of its participants was squatting five inches from his own vomit. I doubted he would even remember this talk of ours in the morning.

I let Owen collect himself for another minute or so before helping him up and walking him back into the car. He laid down in the back again, closing his eyes the second his head hit the leather seat.

Just as I pulled back onto the highway, he said, "Don't tell Kendall about that. Sarah's not ready to talk about it yet."

"I guess we've both got secrets to keep, huh?"

He answered with an affirming grunt.

I looked at the clock. 2:13 a.m. Kendall and the others were probably sound asleep by now. My heart sank, because I hoped I could at least see her—maybe even sneak a goodnight kiss or something. We'd barely spoken in the last twenty-four hours, and I was beginning to miss her. And, since it seemed like the perfect night for confessions, I chuckled and admitted out loud for the first time, "I think I'm in love with Kendall, to be honest."

I waited for some kind of response. A reaction.

Finally, Owen snored.

"Nice talk." I grinned and shook my head, deciding it was probably best I tell him some other time, anyway.

I drove us the rest of the way home, the sounds of Owen's snores and the alternative hits of the 90s providing a backdrop to my thoughts. My heart ached for Owen and Sarah—I knew this was just the beginning of a long and possibly painful journey for them. And suddenly, I felt a pang of guilt for all the negative, jealous thoughts I'd been harboring for the last few months.

We all struggled—even Owen Gardner.

chapter thirty-nine
kendall

"I might just pump and dump."

It was getting late, and the night had delved into a breastfeeding discussion. I found myself sandwiched on the couch between two moms—Vicki and Samantha—who didn't seem to notice my discomfort as they compared breast pumps and debated over how much wine was safe for a nursing mom to drink.

"I promise you, by the time you're home tomorrow afternoon, your milk will be safe," Vicki assured Samantha. "Don't waste that milk, hon."

Sarah appeared just as bored with this conversation as me, staring down at her lap with another whiskey shooter in her hand. Expressionless. A few feet away, Jenny was shuffling her tarot cards. Since the photographer left, we had been sitting around Sarah's living room indulging in drinks and finger food while taking turns having our fortunes read by Jenny. So far, she seemed to be nailing it—Sarah's reading made her cry. Samantha's gave her goosebumps. And Vicki told her, "Shut the hell up. Keep going."

When it came time for my turn, I was a little reluctant. I had just posed in front of these women in my lingerie, but somehow, having my fortune read in front of all of them felt even more revealing. What if Jenny uncovered something too personal or unsettling?

Surprisingly, Jenny's reading focused on my dad—which made sense once I thought about it. I'd be having dinner with the man in less than twenty-four hours. Jenny homed in on my daddy issues pretty quickly, hinting that his heart might be in the right place this time. I was sure she was just telling me what I needed to hear, so I didn't read too much into it.

It was the last card she drew that stuck with me—the Empress. While every single one of the previous cards indicated some "masculine energy"—her words, not mine—the Empress symbolized a nurturing, almost maternal-like figure.

And she said that card represented *me*.

"That makes perfect sense," Sarah interjected, squeezing Jenny's arm in disbelief. "She's a kindergarten teacher."

But there was something in Jenny's lingering gaze, something she didn't voice out loud, that made me pause. I could tell she wanted to say more, but as though she could sense my unease, she just said, "Ah, I thought you might be a teacher."

I just nodded, absentmindedly twisting the drawstring of my pajama pants around my finger. I pictured Finley's sweet face, and then Mason's—and the way his voice trembled when he told me Finley was trying to "win me over." Just three months ago, I didn't know either of these people, but now they were... well, they were my entire *world*.

Across the coffee table from me, Jenny's eyes were twinkling. "Love just radiates from you, I can tell. Those students of yours are so lucky to have you. And this card is telling me that this is just the beginning—you're going to have a long and happy... teaching career. Where you are now is where you're meant to be."

I understood Jenny's message to be about Mason and Finley, not my students. And her words replayed over and over in my mind as we wrapped up our night and began to turn in, all spread out across Sarah's massive sectional couch.

They're "lucky to have you."

It was going to take more than a bachelorette party fortune teller to convince me that was true.

I settled into the cushy corner of the sectional, all curled up with one of Sarah's many luxuriously soft blankets, and checked my phone. The last I'd heard from Mason, the guys were about to leave Indianapolis. It had been almost two hours now.

A foot from my head, Sarah stirred on the chaise lounge. "Kendall," she whispered. I lifted my head to glimpse Sarah's face, lit up from the glow of her phone's screen. "I haven't heard from Owen in a long time. Do you think they're okay?"

"Of course," I said, avoiding sharing the extent to which I'd been texting Mason throughout the night. Getting updates on the status of Owen's wild night was one thing—that was mostly for Sarah's enjoyment. I couldn't let on that Mason and I kept up the conversation. "I bet they're on their way back."

She twisted her hair in her fingers, thinking this over. And just when I contemplated shooting Mason an ETA text, we both heard the unmistakable sound of car doors closing. We sat up at the same time, listening. Frozen. Was it just a neighbor?

"Easy there, boss." My stomach somersaulted at the sound of Mason's voice coming from the porch, and Sarah flew to the front door. Someone was fumbling with keys on the other side, but Sarah beat them to the punch, yanking the door wide open. Owen, wearing a sleepy smile, lunged forward to hug his fiancée—or, more accurately, fall into her—pushing her backwards a few steps until she found her footing and held him up.

Mason stepped inside the foyer, giving me a quick glance before shaking his head at the other two. He was trying not to smile. "You told me to bring your groom back in one piece, and well…"

Owen, still burying his face against Sarah's neck, murmured something that sounded like, "I tasted Larry Bird."

"There he is," Mason finished.

The other women were all sitting up on the couch now. "And that's my future brother-in-law," Samantha said with a giggle.

I stood up from the couch and caught Mason's eye. "How was the drive back?"

"Eventful." He was smiling from one side of his mouth, watching Sarah stand on her tiptoes to hold Owen's face in her hands. The sound of loud, sloppy kisses erupted from them, much to everyone else's disgust.

As though he didn't have an audience, Owen's hands drifted down Sarah's backside. Somehow, he managed to scoop her up in his arms to carry her up the stairs. Sarah shrieked, wrapping her arms tight around his neck. "I'll be back down in thirty minutes, girls," she called out between laughs.

"No she won't," Owen hollered over his shoulder. The two of them tumbled up the steps, making it about three-fourths of the way up before they dropped, deciding to make out where they landed. "I could take you right here on these stairs," Owen not-so-quietly told her.

"Um, please don't," Samantha insisted.

Mason covered his eyes. As for me, my hands went to my ears, but I could still hear Sarah's shrieking laughter as Owen scooped her up again, carrying her the rest of the way to their bedroom.

"That man is going to be asleep in five minutes," Mason said, pointing at the staircase. The other women laughed. I was still awkwardly standing between the couch and the coffee table, unable to remember why I'd leapt to my feet in the first place.

Mason reached into the pocket of his jeans and pulled out a set of keys before carefully placing them on the console table beside him. "My work here is done," he said, the sound of a thump above our heads pulling his eyes upward for a second. "Goodnight, ladies," he said, holding his hand to his forehead in a salute.

I resisted the urge to walk over to him, my eyes flickering toward the other women, who were all still sitting up on the couch. Mason's gaze lingered on my face, and I tugged at the bottom of my cotton shirt, trying to appear nonchalant. "Um—say hi to Finley for me," I blurted.

Mason ran his fingers through his hair, opening the front door with his other hand. "She'd better sleep in for me tomorrow," he said with a chuckle.

"How old is your daughter?" Jenny asked.

"Five—she's in Kendall's class,' Mason answered, nodding toward me.

"Oh!" Jenny said, giving me a sly look, like it was all clicking for her. I was blushing, but Mason didn't seem to pick up on any of the awkwardness.

"Yeah, she's a stinker," he said. With one final, lasting stare in my direction, he said goodbye another time before pulling the front door shut behind him. I lowered myself back to the couch, a pang of sadness striking my heart. It was always going to be like this—pretending Mason was nothing more than the father of one of my students. It would be a long time before we became that couple making out on the stairs, wouldn't it?

The other women got settled again, and I tried to get comfortable on the couch. I couldn't push thoughts of Mason from my mind, however—it had been too long since I'd touched him or held him close.

You'll see him tomorrow, I told myself.

But that wasn't soon enough.

Before I was even fully aware of what I was doing, I rose to my feet and headed toward the foyer. "I need to get something out of my car," I quietly announced, just before slipping out the front door. Much to my relief, Mason's Jeep was still parked near the end of the driveway with his headlights on. My heart leapt to my throat as I took off into a run, pulling open his passenger door and climbing inside.

He grinned like he was expecting me. "You're a sight for sore eyes. Get over here." Mason grabbed me by the hips and pulled me onto his lap. It wasn't easy to find a place for my knees on either side of him on that narrow seat, but we made it work. With a hand on the back of my head, he gazed into my eyes with a tired expression and said, "I knew you were going to run out here. That's why I took my time."

"I'm just that predictable, huh?" I leaned forward to kiss him. "Or you just know me too well."

"That's it," he said, pulling my hand toward his lips to kiss my fingers. Aside from the hum of the engine running and the air pushing through the vents, all was quiet. He rubbed his thumb along the side of my palm and absentmindedly stared down where my legs straddled his lap. I expected him to make some comment about my silly flamingo pajama pants, which I had initially purchased for pajama day to amuse the kids. But he was quiet for a long time.

"Everything okay?"

"Yeah, yeah. It's just been a long night. Lots of... talking."

"I wish I could have been a fly on the wall for some of those conversations."

He shook his head. "Trust me, you don't."

"You're probably right about that." I could only assume the guys' conversation topics differed quite a bit from the drunken talks I'd participated in that evening.

"Kendall," Mason said, his Adam's apple bobbing.

"What?"

His stare lingered. "I..." He hesitated, and my heartbeat picked up its pace. There was something in the look in his eye, something new, that made me wary with anticipation. At first, I wanted to believe he was getting ready to say the three little words that were in the back of my own mind, but his expression was too somber for that. This was something else. And the longer he waited before continuing, the more my panic began to settle in. Finally, he exhaled, saying, "I can't wait to meet your dad tomorrow."

"Oh," I said with a little giggle, knowing full well that wasn't what he initially wanted to say. Adjusting myself on his lap, I leaned in close to rest my head on his shoulder. "Don't remind me. I had to talk about my daddy issues with the tarot card reader."

"Did my name come up in that reading?" Mason asked, playing with my hair.

I let my eyes drift shut and sighed. "Wouldn't you like to know?"

"No. You don't have to tell me everything." Mason brought his hands to either side of my face, angling my head so he could kiss my lips. I kissed him back, opening my mouth to let him in. He circled my tongue with his, dropping his hands to my rear end—I should've known they'd find their way there sooner or later. And, pulling away from me with a gentle tug, he said, "Let's get out of here. Leave with me."

"Mason," I said with a chuckle. "I can't just leave. We're doing mimosas and facials in the morning."

A smile gradually spread across his face. "I can give you a facial in the—" I pinched his side before he could continue that thought, making him squirm beneath me. "Ow! I'm just kidding. I'm sorry. I shouldn't have suggested you bail on them. I just hate that I've got a night without Finley, and we still can't…"

"I know. But it won't always be like this."

"Maybe…" Mason idly kneaded my hips with his thumbs. "Maybe we could test the waters with certain people knowing about us."

"Like who?"

"Like… Sarah and Owen."

I pulled back. "My boss? Are you kidding me?" I waited for him to laugh, to indicate he was joking, but he remained stoic. "Mason, Sarah *can't* know. Because it puts her job on the line, too, if she knows and doesn't report it. And she *would* report it, you know. Sarah's a rule-follower, almost to a fault."

"Oh," Mason said, swallowing. "I hadn't really thought about that."

"I would love to tell our friends. We just can't."

Mason looked down, giving this some thought. I lifted his chin with my hand to force him to look at me. The sadness on his face almost broke me—it was killing him that we couldn't have a normal relationship. And it was all my fault.

"Mason, I'm sorry."

And then he softened like butter before me, and that familiar twinkle returned to his eyes as he wrapped his arms around me tighter. "You have nothing to be sorry for, princess. I'll take you any way I can get you."

I rested my head on his shoulder again and closed my eyes. I could have drifted to sleep just like that, with Mason's fingers delicately running through my hair, but I would need to head back inside before the others got too suspicious.

This was enough—for now. But it seemed like Mason was beginning to grow tired of having to sneak around, and it had only been a few weeks. Could he really do this for the remainder of the school year?

Or would he someday decide it wasn't worth it anymore?

chapter forty
mason

"Did you know somebody stole the Candy Land game?"

I yawned as I opened the car door for Finley and waited for her to climb in. "Somebody stole it?"

"Yup," she said, reaching for the seatbelt. "Grandpa and me looked all over for it last night, but it's gone. We had to play Go Fish instead."

I had a feeling my father knew exactly where the Candy Land game was, but I wasn't about to admit that out loud. Once she was buckled, I closed her door and got into the driver's seat. "So between the blanket fort and the banana split and Go Fish, it sounds like you had one heck of a good time last night, Fin."

Her hair was pulled up into two sloppy buns—not my best work. But after three hours of sleep, it was the best I could do. I was half-tempted to let her skip church with Traci so we both could sleep in, but I didn't want to risk pissing the woman off.

So away we went on that gray November morning to meet her at our usual spot. The closer we got to Wal-Mart, the quieter Finley became. She stared out the window as I drove, and it wasn't until about the fourth or fifth time I glanced at her in the rearview that I realized she was frowning. "What's wrong, Fin?"

She sighed. "Sometimes my belly hurts when I go with Traci."

"Probably from all the sweets she gives you," I muttered.

"No," Finley asserted. "It starts happening before I get in her car. My belly hurts right now."

As soon as she said those words, I pulled off the road into a random driveway and shut the music off. "Finley," I said, turning around to face her. "Is it your nerves?"

"I dunno," she said with a shrug.

"Does it make you nervous when you have to go with Traci?"

It took her a moment to answer, almost like she was afraid to tell me the truth. Finally, barely moving her lips, she mumbled, "Sometimes."

I inhaled, scratching my chin. "Do you want to skip going with her today?"

Her eyes widened. "I don't have to go?"

"No."

"But she's going to be mad."

"No, it'll be okay. And Finley, listen." I reached for her hand. "If going with Traci makes you so uncomfortable that your stomach hurts, you don't have to do it anymore. This isn't a requirement. If you want to stop, you can."

"She's going to yell, though."

My blood was boiling through my veins, and this reaction of hers further proved I was making the right decision. "She won't yell at you. I won't let her."

"She's going to yell at *you*, Daddy." She bit her bottom lip.

I squeezed her hand, taking a deep breath before I responded. "I can handle it." I threw the car in reverse and backed out of that stranger's driveway, mentally preparing for a fight with Traci. I briefly considered taking Finley home first just in case the argument got ugly, but we were already so close to our meeting point.

And if she threw a fit, I could simply turn around and leave immediately. I didn't have to listen to that.

"Just sit tight for a minute," I said to Finley as I unbuckled. Traci was waiting. "It's going to be okay."

With my hands in my hoodie pocket, I made my way around to the driver's side of Traci's car. She stepped out and stomped on a cigarette, giving me an apprehensive look. "Where's my girl?"

"Um, listen," I said, taking a step closer. I didn't want to have to talk very loud. "Finley isn't going to go with you today."

"What's going on? Is she okay?" She glanced toward the Jeep.

I cleared my throat. "Traci, Finley just told me that going with you on Sundays makes her uncomfortable. So I'm not going to m—"

"Uncomfortable? How? What do you mean?"

"It's affecting her nerves. She said it makes her stomach hurt."

"Well," Traci scoffed. "It's probably something you're feeding her for breakfast, then."

"No, it's my kid having a physical reaction to anxiety and finally being able to communicate it. She says she doesn't want to go with you—and I'm not going to force her."

Traci contorted her face into a scowl. "What have you been telling her?"

"Nothing. I've been trying to be mature about this, Traci. This was her decision, not mine."

She took a couple of steps forward. "Let me talk to her."

I planted my body right in front of hers—there was no way in hell I was going to let her get close to the Jeep. "No, that won't be necessary," I said, holding one hand up between us. I knew better than to let this woman manipulate and guilt my daughter into going with her anyway. Traci stared up at my face and blinked in surprise—and I think it was then that she realized I was serious about this.

"Well you can't just let a five-year-old call the shots. She doesn't get to decide this. She probably just gets bored at church. We could do something else if she doesn't like church."

"That's not the issue."

"So you mean I just never get to see her again?"

"I think just taking a break will be good, and we can reassess later, see where it goes from there. But for now, I'm putting the brakes on these Sunday meet-ups." I resisted the urge to glance away, instead forcing myself to maintain eye contact. I needed her to understand I meant my words.

"Well—I—you—" Tears welled up in the corners of Traci's eyes as she struggled to form a complete sentence. "I've lost my daughter already. And now I'm losing my granddaughter, too. But I don't want to make the poor girl's stomach hurt. I guess there's nothing I can do."

She used the collar of her shirt to wipe away her tears, and I shifted my weight on my feet, unsure of what to say. I'd expected anger. I'd braced myself for yelling and name-calling. Not this. My mouth became so dry it was a struggle to even swallow. I knew I was being manipulated, but I felt the urge to comfort her somehow—or to take back what I'd said.

Damn it, why did she have to cry?

I pinched the bridge of my nose, hardly able to believe the words about to come out of my mouth. "What if… the three of us went to church together?"

"The three of us?"

"Yeah. Me and you and Finley. I'll tag along with you guys this time." I had been a card-carrying agnostic for at least eight years, and I was half-afraid I'd burst into flames the second I stepped foot in a church. But this felt like a necessary compromise, and it wasn't about me.

Traci wiped her tears away and stared at me, as though trying to determine whether I was serious or not. "Maybe we could do something different. Could we go out for an early lunch? Or brunch, I suppose."

That sounded much better. "Yeah, okay. All of this is up to Finley, though." I paused to stare into her eyes. "If she doesn't want to go, we don't go."

To my surprise, Traci nodded and said, "Okay."

Finley was completely on board. Having me tag along, it seemed, solved the issue of her discomfort. So fifteen minutes later, I found myself at The Noshery seated across from Traci and Finley, who were doing a word search together on the back of the children's menu. Finley's stomachache was long gone.

As tired as I was, I forced myself to socialize for an hour for Finley's sake, and the three of us had a decent meal. We even laughed. Afterwards, as Traci walked us to our car, she asked, "What now? Could we make this a regular thing?"

"Sure." We arranged to meet a little earlier next Sunday so Traci could still attend church. She and Finley hugged goodbye, and she thanked me before getting in her own car.

This was not how I anticipated my morning would go, but I drove home feeling a sense of accomplishment. Traci and I had reached a truce. I knew she didn't like this arrangement any more than I did, but she was willing to sacrifice her comfort in order to keep Finley in her life. And for that reason, I felt the ice around my heart begin to crack. I could tolerate this woman an hour a week, couldn't I? And with me joining them, I'd be able to keep a close eye on their interactions—if Traci misbehaved or Finley seemed uncomfortable, I could intervene.

This could actually work.

**

Kendall: Look at this pie!! I've never been prouder of anything I've ever made.

Kendall's adventures in baking led her to make a pecan pie that afternoon, fearing it would be impolite to show up to her dad's house empty-handed. Though I tried to assure her a bottle of wine would be perfectly adequate, she still insisted on whipping something up.

And I had to admit, the pie looked like one of her best baking attempts. The multiple exclamation marks were more than justified.

It was funny—I almost preferred these kinds of pictures from Kendall over the sexy ones. Because being on the receiving end of messages like this, in which she excitedly shared her accomplishments, meant so much more. This was the real Kendall, a side of her I got the feeling she didn't show a lot of people.

And my responses to the texts were the same as if she'd sent me her nudes.

Mason: Damn, I'm drooling already.

"What's this your mom says about us taking Finley again tonight?" My dad asked, walking into the living room carrying his reading glasses and a book.

I'd been attempting to get some rest on the living room couch while Finley watched a movie, but Finley was simply too chatty that afternoon. And I could never fully relax with my dad prowling around. "Uh, yeah," I said, sitting up. "I'm having dinner with a friend."

While my mom had a dozen questions about this dinner with a "friend," I knew my dad wouldn't concern himself with the details. "I figured it would be another school function," he said, walking over to the window to watch the birds on the feeder. "You seem to attend a lot of those."

As though that were a bad thing. I couldn't remember my dad volunteering at my school a single time when I was a kid.

That kind of thing was beneath him—he had more important work. "Nope, just dinner," I said. "Sorry to put you guys out two days in a row."

"You're not putting us out. I was only curious." He turned from the window to look at me. "When does your work with Owen start?"

This question came as a surprise, considering I hadn't mentioned the job to my dad. Of course my mom would have brought it up to him by now, but his sudden interest in the job struck me as odd. "Not until they're back from Cancun."

He just nodded. "I'd love to know how much money he's bringing in annually." No congratulations. Nothing positive. Just obsessing over Owen's success and wealth, as usual.

I sat there twiddling my thumbs for a second, considering how I might respond to that. Ultimately, I decided I could no longer bite my tongue. "I'm not sure, Dad, but I'll be sure to ask him for you."

He blinked. "That won't be necessary."

Giving Finley a brief glance, I rose to my feet and started to walk out of the room. I suddenly had an unpleasant taste in my mouth and needed to get far away from my father.

"What's the matter with you?" he called after me.

"Nothing, Dad. Nothing." But I paused and turned around, taking a few steps toward him. "Actually—you've been hounding me about getting a 'real' job for months, yet when I manage to put myself out there and get one that I'm really excited about, you can't even congratulate me or throw a single 'attaboy' my way? All you want to know is how much the golden child of the family makes. No matter what I do—it's never going to compare, is it?"

He hooked his glasses to the collar of his shirt and stared at me, completely dumbfounded. "I'm sorry. I thought you were just doing this as an excuse to goof off with your cousin."

I cracked my knuckles. "Yeah. That sounds like me. A big goof-off."

"Son—"

"Save it." I didn't care to hear whatever excuses he had. It didn't matter that I was raising a little girl alone. Didn't matter that I was about to make a potentially life-changing career move, working in the very field I'd studied—which was more than I could say for a lot of my peers. Those weren't wins in his eyes. I didn't know what it would take to finally earn praise from the man, and quite frankly, I no longer cared.

Kendall: I think I might finally be ready to confront my dad today.

Mason: It's a good day for that kind of thing.

chapter forty-one
kendall

"Dude. Why are you torturing yourself? Are you a masochist or something?"

"I'm starting to think I might be," I said, carefully placing my pecan pie in its container. I snapped the rubber lid on top and looked at the clock on the stove. Mason would be here to take me to my dad's any minute now, and I still needed to find my boots.

I was questioning every decision, from the pie I'd made to the rust-colored jumpsuit I was wearing. It looked good on display at the boutique, but that mannequin didn't have curves like mine. It was too late to change my mind about my outfit, though. I had to commit.

"I can't believe you're doing this. And you're taking Fabio? You're out of your mind, Blondie," Jamie said. She was leaning against the counter and watching me like she was about to witness a sitcom play out. She'd probably like to be a fly on the wall for this entire encounter. But unfortunately for her, the only way she could witness this event would be to attend it herself— and that was out of the question.

"I just want to see what he has to say," I said, carefully wiping the sweat from my forehead with a folded paper towel. "And I don't know, I kind of miss the rest of the family. I mean, those girls are our sisters and we barely freakin' know them."

"Right. Send Anastasia and Drizella my love."

"That's mean." Rylee and Paislee had done nothing to deserve to be nicknamed after Cinderella's step-sisters. Before I could say anything else in their defense, the doorbell rang, and Titus started in on his yapping. "Shit. Where are my boots?"

I bravely allowed Jamie to answer the door while I searched for my shoes. A few minutes later, I emerged to discover Mason sitting on the couch with Jamie, scratching Titus's ears. He jumped to his feet when he saw me, taking the pie from my hands so I could grab my purse from the hook by the front door.

"Wow," he said, his eyes traveling down the length of my jumpsuit. "Never seen you wear *that* to school."

I gave him a half-grin. As for him, he looked handsome as ever in the outfit I told him to wear—a brown suede button-up over an olive green Henley. We'd Facetimed earlier in the day so I could assist him in picking out the perfect outfit. And he didn't complain once, which was more than I could say for Heath, who hated that kind of thing. Even Owen grumbled a little when I picked out his outfit for a convention once. Mason, though? He *wanted* my input.

"Good luck with Dad," Jamie said to us as we stepped out onto the porch. "And good luck meeting the family, Point Break."

Mason squinted, holding the pie against his chest as I closed the front door behind us. "Wait. Was she talking to me?"

"Well, she wasn't talking to me, was she?" I asked, fully enjoying his confusion. "Let's go."

**

My dad lived in one of those "blink and you'll miss it" small towns that made Woodvale look like a bustling city in comparison. My stomach was in knots the whole way over, and Mason could tell something was up. "You don't have to make yourself do this, you know," he said. "Just say the word and I'll turn around."

"I need this," I said. "It's hard to explain why."

"Okay," he said, resting his hand on my thigh as he drove. I swallowed, watching his face. If he was nervous about meeting my dad's family, he wasn't letting it show. Asking him to do this made me feel a little guilty, but at least he was taking it in stride.

Just like everything else.

Mason parked along the curb in front of my dad's place, a cute blue house on the corner. There were the same frog statues in the landscaping that were there a decade ago—Jamie tried to steal one of them one time, but I wouldn't let her. As we made our way up the walk, Mason's hand on the small of my back, I turned to him and said, "I'm feeling stupid about my pie and my outfit."

He tilted his head back and laughed at me—but in a sweet way. "Relax," he told me as I rang the doorbell. And as we waited for someone to come to the door, he squeezed my hand, which made my fears melt away. Halfway, at least.

What was I so nervous about? My dad should've been the one sweating right now.

One of my sisters—I could never remember who was whom—pulled open the front door. "They're here!" she announced, looking me up and down. And then she turned to Mason, staring at him with even wider eyes as we stepped into the house.

"Move out of their way and let them in, Paislee Ann," my grandma said from a few feet away. I hadn't heard that gravelly voice in ages. She made her way to us, her silver hair cascading in soft waves over her shoulders. "Get over here and give me a hug. It's been way too long."

The woman threw her arms around me, and Mason took the pie from my hands as I sank into her embrace. It was deeply comforting in an unexpected way—and she smelled just how I remembered. Like menthols and baby powder.

"Who do we have here?" she asked when we pulled away.

"This is Mason," I said, tucking my hair behind my ears as he reached out to shake her hand. "My boyfriend."

I wasn't even aware of what I'd said until Mason gave me a side glance. Were we labeling each other like that now? I guess I'd sort of decided that for us. He didn't seem to mind, though. My grandma took the pie from us, thanking me for it, and hollered at the rest of the family to come greet us. Paislee stood in the front hallway and continued to stare the entire time.

Finally, we were ushered into the living room, and my dad came down the stairs with the biggest smile on his face. "There's my girl," he said, and he looked as though he might cry as he reached out for a hug. It was a stiff, uncomfortable embrace, but he was trying. As he withdrew, I got a good look at his face—his brown eyes, now adorned with more wrinkles than I remembered, and a slender nose that reminded me of Jamie's. "How was the drive over?"

"It wasn't that bad," I said. "Um, Dad—this is Mason."

Mason shook hands with my father, making eye contact with him as he said, "It's great to meet you."

"I brought a pecan pie," I blurted. "Grandma took it to the kitchen. I hope that's okay."

"That sounds delicious," my dad said. "Angie will be relieved—she was worried we didn't have enough for dessert."

I exhaled, feeling Mason's hand on my lower back again. We continued to make small talk until dinner was ready. Mason shook my step-mom's hand, not even reacting when I referred to him as my boyfriend again. "The more the merrier," Angie told us as we took our seats at the table. I opened my mouth to thank her, but she turned to scream for Rylee over her shoulder. "We can't get that girl to come out of her room these days," Angie muttered.

"Isn't that just like Jamie?" my dad asked, taking his spot at the head of the table. "I almost forgot what she looked like because she spent the entirety of her middle school years locked in her room."

Angie hollered for Rylee another time, and finally, she joined us at the table with a scowl on her face. She was the older of the two girls, and I had to guess she was around thirteen or fourteen. She perked up when she saw Mason, I noticed, tucking her hair behind her ears and watching him closely as we filled our plates.

Paislee, on the other hand, had questions for us. "How long have you been dating?"

I sipped my sweet tea, taking a moment to formulate a response, but Mason beat me to it. "Since September fifth," he said. I shot him a quizzical look, and he grinned. And then it hit me. That was the day of that first PTO meeting, when we had our very first kiss.

He remembered, and I didn't. "That's right," I said.

"How did you two meet?" my grandma asked.

"Uhhh," Mason and I answered in unison, eyeing each other.

"I feel like there's going to be a good story there," Angie said with a wink. She and my dad exchanged smiles as I scrambled to come up with an explanation.

"Sorry, we've never been asked that before."

"We need to work on our story, don't we?" Mason asked, looking me in the eye. I felt his hand on my knee beneath the table.

I turned back to Paislee. "He volunteers in my classroom. Because I teach his daughter."

"Or the truth," Mason said with a laugh. "That works, too."

My grandma gasped at this latest tidbit of info. "You have a daughter? How sweet!"

"So she's a kindergartener, then?" Angie asked. "That's such a fun age."

Mason talked about Finley while we ate, spilling about her jellyfish obsession, the fake YouTube channel, and her tendency to cheat at Candy Land. He charmed them all with his stories—and even Rylee was smiling.

"We'd love to meet her, wouldn't we, Troy?" Angie asked, looking at my dad.

"We sure would. You should bring her sometime."

I held my breath, but Mason didn't even flinch. "Sure, she loves meeting new people." For all he knew, there wouldn't be a next time, but he was playing along, anyway. He sat through dinner and answered their questions like a champ, and if I wasn't mistaken, he was actually having a good time.

After dinner, we migrated into the living room for dessert. We sat around eating pie and Angie forced my half-sisters to talk about their recent athletic accomplishments. My dad seemed to have an active interest in their sporting events, a detail I couldn't help but notice. "She scored the winning shot just as the buzzer went off in their last game," he said, nodding toward Paislee, who was blushing. She couldn't take her eyes off of Mason.

"And I can't even dribble a ball and walk at the same time," I said. Everyone laughed.

Angie took everyone's plates to the kitchen, and Mason got comfortable on the couch beside me, interlocking his fingers across his abdomen. "So I have to ask—do you have any old embarrassing pictures of Kendall I need to see?"

My dad grinned, but his eyes were fixated on the floor. "Uhh… well, I'm not sure." It dawned on me that my dad probably didn't have many photos of me around. Why would he? My mom kept the old photo albums, and it's not like my dad took many pictures of me himself. Mason looked like he wanted to crawl into himself, likely sensing he'd struck a nerve. After a moment, though, my dad pulled his wallet out of his back pocket. "As a matter of fact, I do."

He handed a tiny photo of me to Mason, who immediately smiled upon viewing my crooked teeth and frizzy hair. "Oh, wow," he said, glancing up at my face.

"I know. It's a wonder what orthodontia and learning how to use a flat iron can do," I mumbled. My sisters giggled, craning their necks to see the picture in Mason's hand. He flipped it around so they could take in my awkwardness, too.

Angie returned to the room to ask the girls to help her and my grandma in the kitchen. I began to stand up, but my step-mom pushed down on my shoulder. "You're a guest, so don't you lift a finger. You stay here and visit with your dad, sweetie."

My dad angled his swivel recliner toward us, casually pushing it back and forth with one foot. I wondered if this felt as awkward to him as it did for me. He propped his elbow on the armrest and held up his chin. "There's this one picture of you on that overlook in Tennessee. Remember when we got up at five to watch the sunrise? God, you loved the mountains." He turned to Mason. "This girl was eight years old, but she outpaced me on that morning hike. She was afraid the sun was going to beat us."

"Didn't know you were outdoorsy," Mason said, eyeing me with a smirk.

"I was then."

"She sure was," my dad said. "I wish I could look at the pictures from that trip again. And," he said, pausing to clear his throat, "I wish I could see some pictures from your middle school and high school years, too. The years I missed."

I stared down at my shoes, surprised he was the one who brought up his absence. At least he could admit he missed out on a portion of my life. It gave me hope he wouldn't try to gaslight me into thinking he was the world's greatest dad.

But that hopeful feeling was short-lived.

"More than anything, I wish your mom hadn't convinced you and your sister I was the bad guy. She had both of you hating me without even understanding why."

My lips slowly parted. I fought the reflexive urge to defend my mom, instead focusing on the assumption my sister and I were too naïve to recognize what was really going on. "Jamie and I understood the situation perfectly," I said coldly.

My dad inhaled. "Can I have a chance to explain myself?"

I just shrugged. Mason's hand found mine on the couch cushion between us, and though I didn't turn my head, I could feel him watching me.

"Kendall," my dad started, shaking his head. "I'm not going to pretend like I was the perfect dad, or even a good dad. I'm aware of my shortcomings. Wish I could go back in time and change all of that. But there's a lot you're not aware of. There were countless times I tried to come see you girls, but your mom made excuses for not letting me pick you up. She would change plans at the last minute and keep crucial information from me. You had that, uh—that performance. Your award-winning dance routine?"

I furrowed my brows, remembering my first solo dance performance when I was ten. I came in first place at a regional competition, and my dance teacher put together a local showcase after. My dad was invited, but he didn't show. I could remember my mom shaking her head and telling me, *He used to break my heart, and now he's breaking yours.*

My dad sighed. "Did you know your mom texted me the wrong date for that? I tried to be there. She blamed it on me, saying that if I had a more active role in your life that I would have known the correct date without her relaying the info to me in the first place. But I couldn't have been the one taking you to and from your rehearsals. I worked second shift."

I didn't know how to respond, so I didn't.

"And working second shift meant I had to miss out on all your stuff. Your mom never gave me enough notice to request time off to see you dance, and when she did, she got the damn date wrong."

He was nearly seething—but so was I. "If all of this is true, Dad, then why didn't you tell me this ten years ago? Why am I hearing this for the first time?"

"Your mom had you and Jamie so brainwashed back then, you wouldn't have listened."

Without meaning to, I gave Mason's hand a hard squeeze— any harder and I think I would've broken his fingers. "Did you work the second shift seven days a week, then? Weekends and holidays, too?"

Mason squeezed my hand back.

My dad's jaw clenched. "I'm not saying I didn't screw up. I know I came around less and less as you girls got older. I didn't—I didn't know how to relate to you anymore. It was pretty obvious you would have rather been with your mom. I didn't want to force it."

"You find it pretty easy to relate to Rylee and Paislee," I blurted.

My dad opened his mouth to respond, but he stopped, bringing his lips together in a frown. "Well, like I said." His voice was cracking. "I wish I could go back in time and change it all. I know you and your sister deserved so much better than what I gave you. I'm sorry if it seems like I'm making excuses. I'm just—I needed you to understand that I *did* try."

Could've tried harder, I thought, but I couldn't stop thinking about the dance recital he'd missed. That incident really stuck with me as a child, and I'd never forget the way my mom ranted about him the whole way home afterwards. She complained about him a lot, actually, and when I tried to remember what my dad used to tell us about her, I came up with nothing.

In fact, the conversation we were having now might have been the first time he ever spoke a single negative word about her to me.

I loosened my grip on Mason's hand, deciding to be the one to break the long, awkward silence. "You know... I think we've got a video of that dance recital somewhere."

Without uttering a word, my dad stood up and walked over to the TV stand. He bent over and opened the long drawer at the bottom before pulling out a homemade DVD in a clear case. "You mean this?" Written on the disc were the words, "KENDALL'S SOLO."

"Yeah, that," I answered, swallowing.

Mason casually draped an arm over my shoulders. "Okay, I am dying to see this award-winning performance."

My dad grinned. "Should we watch it now?"

"That won't be necessary," I said, widening my eyes at Mason. "It's embarrassing."

"Hey," Mason said, squeezing my shoulder. "If you let me watch this, I'll let you see the video of my band's Taylor Swift cover."

I considered that for a moment. He gazed at me with puppy dog eyes, the same pleading expression I often wore with him. And, for the sake of easing the tension in the room, I rolled my eyes and said, "Fine."

The others returned just as the video began, both of my half-sisters sitting on the floor to witness my spirited dance routine to a Nelly Furtado song. I watched Mason's face as he stared at the screen, noticing the way his smile grew as the performance went on.

And I looked at my dad, who stood in front of his chair with his hands in his pockets, a solitary tear streaming down his cheek as he stared at the screen. The only time I could recall seeing my father cry was at his father's funeral—an eye-opening moment for a little girl who didn't know until then grown men were capable of such displays of emotion. Jamie and I both crawled onto his lap, which only seemed to make him sob harder as he clutched us against his chest.

The memory brought a lump to my throat, a sob that begged to escape—but I was too stubborn to release it. I bit my bottom lip instead, watching the end of my performance.

"Do you still dance?" Paislee asked me as my dad put the DVD away.

"Um," I said, sniffling. "No. I'm afraid I'm not as flexible as I once was."

Beside me, Mason stirred like he was trying to hold in a laugh or a perverted comment. Thankfully, he kept his thoughts to himself, and Paislee continued with the questioning. She wanted to know everything from how I got into dance to what kind of outfits I wore when I performed.

Soon, the conversation shifted to Finley's recent interest in tumbling, which Mason joked was partially my fault. My dad was quieter than he had been before, limiting his responses to the occasional smile and one-word interjections.

After a while, Rylee started complaining about wanting to go back to her room, which I took as our cue to get up to leave. Angie insisted on giving us leftovers, assuring me she didn't need any of the food containers back.

As we prepared to leave, I found myself face to face with my dad by the front door. The tension between us was almost palpable, but he reached out and placed a hand on my shoulder, saying, "Listen, kid."

There was that word again, that reminder of simpler times when I was still his little girl.

"I'll never be able to undo the mistakes I've made or the moments I've missed," he continued. "All the pain I've caused for you and Jamie. It's my deepest regret. I hope you know that. You being here today has just been—" He stopped to swallow. "It's been the highlight of my entire year. And I hope you come around again, because this has been really nice."

I stepped forward to put my arms around him, and he enveloped me in an embrace that was nothing at all like our awkward hug when I'd first arrived. Everyone else standing around fell silent. With a shaky deep breath, I brought my mouth close to his ear and said, "It's going to be hard for me to fully forgive you, but just give me time, okay?"

He squeezed me harder. "Take as long as you need."

"I think I would like to come around more often."

We let go of each other and my dad wiped a tear from his eye. "It would be wonderful if you could come for Christmas. You and Jamie both. We'll have stocking for you regardless—it would be great if you're here to open it."

I nodded, pressing my lips together. Jamie wouldn't go for that, but maybe I could. Maybe.

My dad turned to Mason. "We'd love for you to come, too— and your daughter."

He and Mason shook hands. "Bringing her might be a little tricky, but I appreciate the invite." He thanked my step-mom for a nice meal, even accepting a hug from her with a smile on his face.

And that was that.

The second we got in the car, I stared at Mason in stunned silence. "That went pretty well, huh?" he asked, shifting the car into drive and pulling away from the curb. He reached over and rested his hand on my thigh. "I'm so proud of you."

"I'm just grateful you were there with me," I said, letting out a deep exhale.

"Me too," he said. When we pulled up to a stop sign, he lifted his hand to grab my wrist. I stared at him in confusion as he fiddled with my charm bracelet, twisting it around until he found a certain one. The mountains. "Hmmm."

"What?"

"'For the aesthetic,' you told me." And that was all that was necessary for him to say to get his point across. Goddammit, he was too good at figuring me out.

I jerked my wrist away from him and crossed my arms against my chest, hiding the charm I'd once tried to downplay the significance of. "Shut up." Mason just laughed.

It was dark by the time we reached my house. Mason walked me up to the porch and wrapped his arms around me so tight I couldn't lift my own arms to return the hug. All I could do was lean against him and let him have this. "Thank you, again, for being there for me today," I whispered.

"Of course."

"Can you stay for a little while?"

He pulled out his phone to glance at the time before turning back to me with a sorrowful look on his face. "I really can't. I need to be home to tuck Finley in tonight. I'm sorry."

"That's okay."

"It's always going to be like this. I'm always going to have to run home to her. Fuck, I hate this. I'm so sorry."

"Mason." I grabbed the open flaps of his suede jacket and gazed into his eyes. "Don't ever apologize for putting Finley first. I understand." I kissed him on the cheek, just below his eye. Was it frustrating that we couldn't be alone together that night? Of course. But it wasn't like he didn't have a good excuse. I couldn't think of a better one, actually.

"You're perfect," he told me, his hands sliding down my hips. He rested his forehead against mine and we stayed on the porch just like that for a moment, enjoying each other's silent company. And we would have held each other even longer if it hadn't been for Daya yanking the front door open.

"Oh, sorry," she said, moving past us with Titus tucked beneath her arm. "Didn't know anyone was out here."

Even in the darkness, her eyes looked red and blotchy like she'd been crying. "It's fine," I said, taking a step back from Mason. "Are you and Jamie okay?"

"There is no me and Jamie," Daya muttered over her shoulder. And with that, she stepped down off the porch and got in her car before peeling away from the curb with Titus in tow.

I watched her car disappear down the street and turned to Mason, who was staring down at the porch with his hands in his pockets. "Yikes. Sounds like you probably need to go talk to your sister."

"Yeah, I do," I said, already feeling sick to my stomach. I hated it when Daya and Jamie fought, and this seemed like it might be more than that. This really could be the end.

Mason stepped forward to kiss my lips. "Today was fun. I—" He stopped himself short, deciding against saying whatever he was about to say. "I'll see you at school tomorrow."

chapter forty-two
mason

My sister and I found new and creative ways to torment each other after having kids of our own. As it turned out, involving the kids in our shenanigans only amplified the fun.

"Don't tell your dad," I heard Lesley whisper to Finley at the kids' Thanksgiving table at our grandparents' house. It took a minute for me to figure out what she could possibly be referring to—and it absolutely had to have something to do with the red cup in Finley's hands and her wide-eyed expression as she sipped the fizzy drink.

"Did you give my kid Mountain Dew?" I asked my sister as she walked past me toward the kitchen island to grab a divided Styrofoam plate.

"I have no idea what you're talking about."

Right. Two could play this game. I'd been contemplating getting my niece and nephew an obnoxious electronic drum set for Christmas, and after this Mountain Dew incident, I decided to pull out my phone and submit the order. I showed Lesley the receipt. "Can't wait for Christmas."

"Don't you dare."

"It's already ordered."

"I freakin' hate you."

"Your kids don't."

Lesley glared at me, but she smiled from one side of her mouth as we got in the buffet line behind our cousins. I hadn't realized how much I missed her until she came home for Thanksgiving. Normally, we only saw Lesley's family at

Christmastime—but since Owen's wedding was over Thanksgiving break, she decided to make the special trip.

I wished like hell Kendall could have met her. I had an inkling the two of them would get along—if anything, they could discuss my horoscope together. It killed me not to be able to mention Kendall's name. And when my aunts and uncles inevitably asked if I was seeing anyone, I had to lie and say I was focusing on Finley's well-being and didn't have time to date.

I caught Owen's eye from across the table as I spoke, and he didn't utter a single word. As far as I could tell, he hadn't disclosed my indiscretion to Sarah. Similarly, I hadn't mentioned his and Sarah's secret to anyone, either—and I played my part in swiftly changing the subject when my mom asked them if they were going to be the next in the family to have a baby.

"Personally, I think Lesley's going to pop out two or three more kids," I said, taking a bite of turkey.

"Really?" She raised an eyebrow at me. "Because I think Finley needs a baby brother or sister."

"Please," Jake said with his mouth full. "It's a miracle he got a woman to touch him the first time. The only way he's fathering another child is by visiting a sperm bank."

"How many numbers did you end up with the other night again, Jake?"

"Same amount as you."

I just smirked in response. I couldn't wait for the day I could reveal to these jerks I was dating the sexiest woman in all of Woodvale. If Owen told them right now, I doubt I'd even care. I would have loved to rub Jake's face in it.

One day, I would.

Once the meal was finished and the family was getting started on a game of charades, I excused myself and snuck away to my grandparents' bedroom, where everyone had thrown their coats on the bed. I pulled my phone out and called Kendall.

"Oh my god, it is *so* good to hear your voice," she said.

"Are you having a bad day?"

"Not necessarily. Thanksgiving at my mom's is just always so chaotic. Picture the most redneck event you possibly can—that's Thanksgiving with my mom's family. They're deep-frying the turkey in the garage, and one of my aunts is crying because my cousin came out as a vegetarian."

"Oh, how… devastating."

"On the plus side, they're all so focused on Jamie's break-up with Daya that they're not asking any questions about my love life."

"How are things between your sister and Daya, anyway?" On Monday, Kendall explained Jamie ended things with Daya after announcing she would be moving to Indianapolis at the end of the academic year. Daya said she couldn't leave her job, which put them at a stalemate. They each wanted the other one to make a sacrifice—and it looked like that wasn't going to happen.

Kendall exhaled into the receiver. "They're still giving each other the silent treatment, using me as their go-between."

"So," I said, lying back on my grandparents' bed. I pushed someone's puffy coat away from me. "If Jamie moves to Indy, what does that mean for you?"

"I'm trying not to think about life without Jamie, to be honest. To go from seeing her every day to…" Her voice trailed off.

"It'll be an adjustment. But we could visit her a lot, you know." I swallowed, realizing a second too late I was accidentally making long-term plans with Kendall again. Between that and the fact I'd almost uttered the L-word twice now, I was probably on the verge of scaring her off. *Pump the brakes, Mason*, I told myself. I didn't want to spook her.

"I guess I'm lucky it's just an hour drive. You said your sister lives six hours away, right?"

"And that's not far enough," I joked. "She's giving me hell today. Her and all my cousins. Except Owen, of course—he always leaves me alone."

Kendall was silent for a moment. "I think I just realized for the first time that spending holidays with you someday means spending them with Sarah and Owen, too."

I chewed on my bottom lip. "Yeah, but that's a good thing, right?"

"Of course. They'd be like… family."

That last word sent a warmth throughout my entire body. There I was worrying about scaring her away with my nonchalant mentions of a future together, and she was using a word like "family." That felt like a commitment. Kendall quickly laughed it off, though, saying, "Anyway, I need to go. I guess I won't see you until the wedding, right?"

"I'll be the hottest guy up on that altar."

"I'll be the judge of that."

I grinned. "Bye, Kendall."

**

Forty minutes from Woodvale, nestled between rolling hills and a tranquil pond, stood the White Pine Pavilion, a building that tried desperately to appear rustic despite being built within the last five years. Its enormous windows offered a panoramic view of the orange and red foliage down below, and I could understand why Owen and Sarah chose this location for their wedding.

The rehearsal dinner on Friday night was surprisingly casual, with a catered meal from a local barbecue place and plenty of beer to go around. The rehearsal itself was a cause of stress for Sarah, who was determined to get the timing of the procession just right. We walked through it no less than five times, with Jake and Xander getting rowdier by the minute. "Just to be clear, nobody's going to be carrying a beer down the aisle at the actual ceremony," Sarah warned my eldest cousin.

"Wanna bet?" Jake asked her, taking a swig as he linked arms with Sarah's sister.

Owen laughed until he saw the look on his fiancée's face. "Knock it off, Jake."

The second Sarah announced we'd nailed the procession, everyone scattered across the venue—putting together the table decorations or going back to the buffet for seconds. After helping my uncle carry an arch into the venue, I spotted Owen standing on the balcony outside by himself. He was staring down at the pond below with his hands in his pockets, and he looked lost in thought.

"I'll be back in a sec," I announced, slipping out the sliding doors.

"Hey, cousin," Owen said, angling his body toward me as I joined him at the railing.

"You okay?" I asked him.

"Yeah. Just soaking it in."

"This is the last night you'll go to bed as an unmarried man. How you feelin' about that?"

Owen stared down at the ground below, a smile stretching across his face. "If you would've told me two years ago that this is what I'd be doing, I wouldn't have believed you. Feels like winning the lottery. Tomorrow, I marry my best friend—and then it's off to Cancun for a week. And when I return, I get to start working alongside my baby cousin."

I decided to let the inclusion of the word "baby" slide, simply returning Owen's smile.

"I feel like my happiness is almost maxed out," he continued. "There's only one thing that could make this better, but I might be waiting a while for that."

My smile faded as I studied Owen's face, observing the crinkle between his eyebrows. As happy as he was, he still felt like there was something missing. I wished like hell there was something I could do about that. "It's going to happen for you, man. Your story's not over yet."

He just nodded. We stood at the edge of the balcony in silence for a few moments, watching a couple of mallard ducks waddle around the bank of the pond below. Laughter echoed behind us, where the rest of the wedding party was getting less sober by the second.

And in the spirit of confessing our innermost thoughts, I turned to Owen and blurted, "I'm in love with Kendall Devin."

His eyes shot my direction. "Damn. I didn't know it was that serious."

"I'm dead serious about that woman."

"And Finley loves her, too, right?"

"Yeah. She can't know about us yet, of course—but it's going to rock her world when she finds out. Ever since Whitney left, there's been this… incompleteness. And I think Kendall could be the one to fix that. For both of us. Eventually."

Owen gently elbowed me. "Guess your story's not over yet, either."

Just as I opened my mouth to reply, the door behind us was thrust open and Jake and Xander tumbled onto the balcony. "Jake's going to jump in the pond!" Xander declared.

My Aunt Michelle wasn't far behind, warning Jake that he'd better not get us all kicked out of the venue and ruin his brother's wedding. But Jake was already halfway toward the pond and removing his shirt, much to the amusement of the rest of the wedding party who had joined us on the balcony. The poor ducks scattered, making way for the madman swinging his belt over his head like a lasso.

"Maybe he'll get it out of his system and be on his best behavior by tomorrow?" I wondered aloud.

Owen sighed. "Don't count on it."

chapter forty-three
kendall

"I have an enormous favor to ask you."

Jamie sat on my bed early Saturday afternoon with a wary look on her face. I was painting my nails a shiny champagne color, which would offset the boldness of the dress I planned to wear that evening. "What is it?" I asked her.

"I'm heading out of town tonight, and Daya's going to be stuck here. I think she's depressed. And it's all my fault. Can you take her to that wedding with you?"

"Will she even want to go?"

"I think she'll go if you suggest it. Make it seem like it's a favor for you, and she won't be able to say no."

That seemed a little manipulative, but Jamie's heart was in the right place, at least. "It seems like you still care about her."

"Of course I care about her," she said, pulling her knee up onto the bed. "I love her, dude. I just don't see how this can work. We want different things."

"But you're not planning to move for what—six, seven months? You don't think the two of you could reach some kind of compromise before then?"

"She's not going to leave that job. So I'm not going to put the work into a relationship that's not going anywhere. Why waste my time?" She had a point.

"Well," I said, blowing on my fingernails. "I'll see if she wants to tag along tonight."

"Thanks, sis. Appreciate it." Jamie leaned back onto her hands. "You excited to see Prince Charming tonight?"

"Prince Charming?" I laughed. "That's one of your better nicknames for him."

"Just to be clear, I'm referencing Prince Charming from Shrek."

I rolled my eyes. "Of course you are. And yes, I can't wait to see him. But do you know what I'm most excited about?" I paused, biting my bottom lip. "I can't wait to hang with Finley and see her all dressed up. She told me she's got a new dress, and she's going to twirl for me. Isn't that the sweetest?"

"Jesus. You're in deep with these people."

"I know." I tightened the cap on my nail polish. It was true, I was "in deep" with Mason and Finley. They'd both woven their way into my heart right under my nose—I almost felt like I'd been tricked. I tried not to smile when I thought about how much my life had changed in just a matter of months.

Love had a funny way of sneaking up on you when you least expected it.

**

"I've never felt more feminine."

Daya stood before the mirror in my bedroom, gawking at her reflection. She was much skinnier than me, but I was able to find a navy maxi dress I hadn't worn in two years that fit her well enough. She had a tan cardigan to wear over it—it wasn't perfect, but it worked. "You look amazing," I said. She'd even let me apply a little make-up, which she said felt even more foreign to her than the dress. But I could tell she was enjoying it.

As for me, I was wearing a satin wine red dress with an exposed back, praying the built-in bra cups would hold my breasts in place. It was a daring choice of attire, but with two of my ex-boyfriends and my current boyfriend in attendance, I was okay with turning heads. I walked into the kitchen as I fastened one of my dangly earrings, finding Jamie throwing some granola bars into her overnight bag at the kitchen table. "How's my hair?" I asked her.

But she was looking past me. I glanced over my shoulder at Daya, who emerged from my room behind me. She and Jamie locked eyes, staring each other down as though I wasn't even there.

"Be careful tonight," Jamie said.

"We will," I answered cheerfully, trying to smooth over the tension between the other two as I put my second earring in.

"Daya."

"What?" Daya asked with a hint of annoyance in her voice.

"I'm telling you to be careful."

"I heard you."

"You look… beautiful," Jamie said in an almost whisper. Daya ignored her, but her cheeks tinged pink as she adjusted her cardigan. Standing between the two of them was almost unbearable.

"Well. Safe travels to Indy," I told Jamie before we left.

**

Sarah and Owen's wedding venue was enormous—and it was a good thing, too, considering they'd invited everyone they'd ever met. Heath was there with Abigail, and they sat in a row with a bunch of other teachers and staff from Grissom. Even my old boss, Cates, was in attendance with his husband. I sat directly behind the rest of my co-workers on the bride's side, noticing a moment later Finley and her grandparents were seated directly opposite us. She waved at me from her grandma's lap, beaming.

At exactly 3:00 p.m., the pianist began playing a beautiful rendition of "Invisible String" by Taylor Swift. "Why do I feel like crying?" Daya whispered in my ear. "I don't even know these people."

She wasn't the only one with a lump in her throat. I had to admit, the sight of Owen up there awaiting his bride affected me in an unexpected way—I was filled to the brim with happiness for him. And when Mason entered the room with Jenny on his arm, I held my breath. Dressed in a sharp black suit, his rust-colored tie perfectly complementing Jenny's dress, he looked effortlessly handsome. As he made his way down the aisle, Finley's excited voice pierced the air, declaring, "Daddy!" Laughter erupted around us as Mason gave Finley a fist bump.

A hush fell over the room as the double doors opened at the back of the venue and Sarah emerged in the most beautiful gown I'd ever seen—it was an ivory off-the-shoulder dress with billowing layers of lace and tulle. Her hair was pulled back in a sweet but elegant updo. I instinctively glanced toward the altar, where Owen was struggling to keep it together. The man beside him—whom I could only assume was his brother since they looked so similar—squeezed his shoulder as Sarah approached. My eyes found Mason's, and we exchanged smiles over the heads of the people in front of me. "God, he looks so good up there in his suit," I whispered to Daya, squeezing her arm.

"Please tell me you're not talking about the groom."

I shot her a playful glare. "Daya!"

As the ceremony unfolded, Sarah and Owen exchanged vows that were just as cheesy and adorable as I'd expected, with Owen mentioning something about the "teacher across the hall" being worth the wait. And as the preacher rambled on about the meaning of love, Mason's eyes found mine again, igniting a warmth that spread beneath my skin. He barely took his eyes off of me for the remainder of the wedding, turning to give Owen and Sarah his attention when they kissed for the first time as husband and wife.

Immediately following the ceremony, the entire wedding party headed outside for pictures. We made our way to the other side of the massive room, where there were dozens of round tables waiting for us. Finley found me and grabbed my hand, beckoning me to follow her to the table where her grandparents were already sitting. "Oh, there's probably assigned seats, Fin," I said, but Daya pointed at the seating chart on the table beside us—Sarah had put me at Finley's table, anyway. She must have known I wouldn't have wanted to be anywhere near Heath.

So we took our seats with Mason's parents and his sister, Lesley—really getting a head start on that whole "spending time with his family" thing.

"Are you Finley's teacher?" Lesley asked, flipping her auburn hair over her shoulder.

"Yes, I am," I said, grinning as Finley climbed onto my lap. Lesley turned to her mom, and the two of them exchanged a knowing glance—it was subtle, but I caught it. Did they know about Mason and me?

"We heard all about you on Thanksgiving," Lesley said, unwrapping a Hershey kiss for the little boy beside her. "We all went around and said what we were thankful for, and Little Miss Finley here said she was thankful for her teacher."

Finley looked up at me with a sheepish grin. "You said that, Fin? How sweet. I'm thankful for you, too, kiddo."

Lesley smiled. "So what's it like having my butthead brother volunteer in your room?"

"He's..." I wasn't sure how to answer that. Just a few feet away, Mason's mom was facing her husband, but I could tell she was listening closely. "He's very helpful."

"That's surprising."

I laughed. "He really is—and the kids adore him. I'm going to miss having him around when he gets too busy working for Owen."

"Oh, that's right," Lesley said, raising her eyebrows. "I can't picture the two of them getting any actual work done together. They'll probably just... build a robot that can jerk them off, or something."

Beside me, Daya almost choked on her water. Finley raised an eyebrow at her aunt, asking, "What does that mean?"

Thankfully, Lesley didn't have to explain, because the lights dimmed and the DJ announced the wedding party was ready to get the night started. They danced into the room one couple at a time to the song "I Gotta Feeling" by the Black Eyed Peas—which was a little cheesy, but also very... them. Owen's brother and Sarah's sister took turns sling-shotting each other as they entered the room, and some dark-haired guy leap-frogged over Vicki, who proceeded to crawl through his legs. And then Mason and Jenny danced into the room like they were doing a waltz, him with a flower from her bouquet in his mouth. "My daddy looks so, so handsome," Finley said, wiggling around on my lap.

"You're right, he does." The words sort of slipped out—I only hoped the rest of Mason's family couldn't hear.

"And now, introducing for the very first time—Mr. and Mrs. Gardner!" the DJ boomed. Owen and Sarah came through the door hand-in-hand, and he dipped her backwards to kiss her, pumping one fist in the air like Sarah was a prize he had a won. And in a way, I guess she was.

Daya and I were absolutely ravenous by the time the meal was served. After clearing about a fourth of her plate, Finley asked me if she could be done—as though I had some kind of authority. "Yeah, I guess so," I told her. She decided there were some balloons on the dancefloor that needed popped. Mason's mom wandered off to talk to someone at a nearby table, and the second she was gone, the groomsman with the brown hair took her empty seat.

He had piercing gray eyes and a chiseled jawline, and he carried himself like he knew he was attractive. "You look familiar," he said, scooting his chair closer. He was clutching a bottle of beer to his chest. "Have we met?"

"No, I don't think so."

He held out his hand. "Xander."

"Kendall," I said, shaking his hand. His grip on me lingered a bit too long for my comfort, but the way he stared at me was even more unsettling. "So, um… are you a friend of Owen's?"

"I'm his *best* friend," he said, a bit too confidently. "And you—you're a teacher at Sarah's school, aren't you?"

"Is it that obvious?"

"Well, you've just got this inherent warmth about you, this 'educator' vibe—I could sense it right away."

Daya touched me on the shoulder. "I'm going to go get a drink," she said before getting up. I tried to beg her with my eyes to stay, but she didn't get the message. I was stuck with this guy.

"I'm a writer," Xander said as he set his beer down, giving the impression he planned on sitting here for a while. He had somehow inched closer without me noticing.

"Okay. What do you write?"

"I'm a journalist. I strive to, you know, take the mundane and turn it into a captivating story. Reveal the hidden gems within the everyday occurrences of small town life. That kind of thing."

I almost laughed. "You're a reporter for the Woodvale Times, you mean?"

"Uh, yeah," Xander said, blinking a couple of times. And then he cleared his throat, wrapping his fingers around his drink. "So tell me, Kendall, what's *your* story?"

Oh, God. I couldn't take it anymore. Luckily, Mason swooped in behind me at that very moment, placing one hand on the back of my chair. "I see you've met Xander."

"You two know each other?" Xander asked.

"Oh, you don't remember the conversation we had when you pulled her pic up on the Grissom website and asked if she'd be at this wedding? Or what about when you tried to get her number from me last week?"

If looks could kill, Mason would've dropped dead. Xander looked like he wanted to strangle him. I pressed my lips together tight to hold in the laugh that threatened to escape. Mason's other hand found its way to the back of my chair, and his closeness suggested a more-than-platonic relationship between the two of us. Right now, though, that didn't seem to matter to him. He just wanted Xander to back off.

"That doesn't ring a bell?"

Xander sighed. "We were having a nice conversation until you interrupted us." He looked at me. "Weren't we?"

I didn't take my eyes off of his when I said, "Is that what that was? I thought you were just listening to yourself talk."

A couple feet away, Mason's sister let out a hearty laugh. And Xander, deciding he'd had enough, snatched his beer off the table and rose to his feet. And though he had a mischievous grin on his face, he pointed a finger at Mason, saying, "Fuck you."

"You wish," Mason muttered as Xander walked away.

I joined Lesley in laughing as we watched Xander return to his spot at the head table. "I knew I liked you," Lesley said, tossing an ice cube into her mouth.

Mason leaned over my shoulder and brought his mouth to my ear. "I didn't mean to get all 'touch her and die' just now, but that guy pisses me off," he whispered. He placed one hand on the table beside me, the other still on the back of my chair. I could only imagine what his sister was thinking about the way his body hovered over mine.

When I turned to face him, our mouths were dangerously close. "You've never been sexier to me than you are right now," I said, just loud enough for him to hear. I watched his eyes drop to my cleavage.

"I want to tear that dress off of you and do unspeakable things to you," Mason said, his voice low and husky—the way I loved it.

Exactly one second later, his mom approached him from behind, touching him on the shoulder in a greeting.

"Oh hey, Mom," he said, standing up straight. "Where's my kid?" As though she'd been summoned, Finley appeared at my side, instantly climbing up onto my lap again. "Ah, there she is. Have you been having fun with Ms. Devin, Fin?" Mason adjusted his tie.

"Uh huh. How come you can't sit with us, Daddy?"

"Because I've got to hang out with the wedding party. But we can dance later, okay?" One of his hands remained on my chair, his thumb grazing my bare back. Mason didn't seem to mind that his family could see this. Then again, from the way his mom and sister were behaving, they already suspected something, anyway.

Mason was pulled away by Owen's brother, who needed his attention up by the head table. I turned around and scanned the room for Daya, spotting her near the bar throwing back a shot with Abigail, of all people. And then Abigail leaned in close to whisper in Daya's ear, saying something that made her laugh. Were they flirting?

I wasn't the only one observing them. Heath was sitting two tables over, watching them interact with furrowed brows. I wondered if he knew his date was bisexual. But with the flirty way she touched Daya's arm as she spoke, it was pretty obvious.

This was going to be a long night.

chapter forty-four
mason

Once all the typical wedding rituals were out of the way—the cake-cutting and bouquet toss and speeches—the energy in the room shifted. With the dancefloor open and free beer flowing, people were starting to get rowdy. I ditched my suit coat and rolled up my shirt sleeves, getting comfortable as I downed my second beer. I needed this night.

I kept close tabs on Kendall, who seemed to be having a good night herself. She took to the dancefloor with Finley, Daya, and Abigail. I almost dropped the beer bottle from my hands as I witnessed her take a shot with my sister. The two of them were hitting it off, just like I suspected they one day would—it was just happening sooner than I predicted.

Relatives confronted me all night, eager to ask about my new venture working for Owen. Thanks to both of our mothers, word had spread pretty fast. The first few times I spoke about it, I downplayed the job like it was just some temporary thing until I found more serious work. But my confidence grew as the night went on. "I'm Owen's new creative director," I declared with confidence, pushing my dad's voice out of my head. And most of my cousins and aunts and uncles seemed genuinely happy for me—maybe even jealous. After all, they were stuck at 9-5 jobs they hated while I got to work alongside my favorite cousin. My best friend. They *should* be jealous.

The night was perfect.

I had a decent buzz going.

I just watched Kendall reject Xander.

Finley was having one heck of a good time.

Owen just sealed the deal with the love of his life.

And on top of everything, Kendall looked absolutely ravishing in that dress.

I tugged on her arm on the dancefloor and brought my mouth to her ear. "Meet me in the groom's suite at the end of the corridor in five minutes." I didn't wait to see the reaction on her face before slipping out of the reception hall. Whistling, I made my way down the corridor to the room where Owen and the rest of us got dressed earlier in the day. It was a spacious room with every accommodation imaginable—brown leather seating, a wardrobe rack, a refreshment bar, and a private bathroom with a basket of all the essentials—deodorant, toothpicks, a lint roller, and some aspirin. And condoms, which Jake and Xander had ambitiously stuffed in their pockets that afternoon. I smiled as I reached for one, knowing what I was about to do. If those guys only knew.

Kendall didn't wait five minutes. She slipped inside the door soon after I did, closing it behind her and leaning against the frame. "Jeez, this room is bigger than my bedroom."

I reached around her to lock the door. "Did anyone see you come this way?"

"No," she said, swallowing as I put my hands on either side of her body, effectively pinning her against the back of the door. It felt like it had been so long since I'd touched her. *Too* long. I was getting hard already.

"Good," I said, brushing my lips against hers. Slowly, I brought my hand to her throat, curling my fingers around her neck. Her lips subtly curved upwards, letting me know she liked where this was going. "Now take off your panties."

Kendall obeyed, sticking her hands up her dress to pull her underwear all the way past her high heels. She kicked them aside before bringing her hands to my chest.

"That's a good girl," I murmured, pushing her dress up with one hand. I slipped my fingers between her thighs until I felt the heat of her, stopping before I got too close. I wanted her to yearn for it. So I focused on the way I kissed her along her collarbone, listening to her sigh when my beard tickled her skin. "What should we do in here?"

"I think you know what I want to do, Mason."

I slid my hand a little higher up her leg, my thumb just grazing her warmth. "Really? I'm not sure."

Kendall responded by lowering herself onto my hand—and just in case I wasn't getting the message, she enclosed her fingers around my wrist, forcing me to touch her along her slit. I let out a laugh—this woman wasn't subtle at all. Slowly, I rubbed my middle finger between her lips before slipping it inside her. Kendall moaned against my mouth. "Oh!"

Another finger found its way inside of her, and I pulled both of them in and out to get her good and ready for me. Just when her breathing started to pick up, I grabbed her by the arm, nudging her toward the leather chaise lounge in the middle of the room. Kendall didn't roll over onto her back—she remained upright on her knees while I knelt behind her, kissing the back of her neck as I cupped her breasts over the satin fabric of her dress.

"What if someone tries to come in here?" she whispered, reaching around to run her fingers through my hair.

"Let them try." I kissed her shoulder just before pressing my hand to the back of her head, forcing her onto her hands and knees. She smiled as she went down, even letting out a little laugh. Fuck—if she kept giggling like that, I'd be finished in no time.

I ripped open the condom as fast as I could. Its purpose was to contain the mess—the last thing I wanted to do was ruin that pretty dress for her. And Kendall didn't complain as I pulled down my pants to slide it on. I pushed her dress up her back and took in the sight before me. Goddammit, her body was magnificent. Before I entered her, I had to get a little taste. I lowered myself, slowly licking the full length of her slit like she was some kind of dessert. There was nothing sweeter. I flicked my tongue against her clit, relishing in the way it made her squirm. I could have devoured her all night, but we needed to make this fast before we were caught. I grabbed her by the hips and slowly slipped the end of my cock inside of her. "Oh God, Mason," she whined as I pushed all the way into her.

She felt amazing from that angle—and it gave me the best view, too. I hooked my hands onto her hips as I thrust again and again, the sound of skin clapping against skin echoing through the room. Kendall lowered herself onto her elbows, lifting her butt even higher for me. I gathered her hair into a ponytail in my fist and gave it a good tug, pulling her head backwards so I could see the look on her face as I fucked her. Kendall responded with a grin that nearly killed me. "Goddamn. When am I going to learn to stop calling you a good girl?"

Kendall closed her eyes with her face pressed into the brown leather, and I could tell from the way she moaned she was nearing completion. Which was a relief, because so was I.

I squeezed Kendall's thighs as I thrusted faster. If anyone happened to be wandering the halls, they'd definitely hear the sounds of our passion—and that chaise lounge was rocking back and forth on the hardwood floor. When I slapped Kendall's ass hard enough to leave behind a crimson handprint, she screamed in pleasure, turning her face against the leather. I could feel her clenching around my cock, and that was enough to send me over the edge right after her. I folded my trembling body over hers, pressing my chest against her back. "Fuck," I whispered, sweat collecting along my brow. I wrapped one arm around Kendall's torso, bringing my palm to the center of her chest. Her heart was pounding.

The words "I love you" were on the tip of my tongue, but this didn't feel like the right time.

And then Kendall turned her head to look up at me, saying, "Will you hold me for a minute?"

As if she even needed to ask. I took a moment to clean up and zipped my pants back up before joining her on the chaise lounge, which was just wide enough to hold the two of us. I spooned her from behind, wrapping my arm around her waist. Kendall took my hand in hers, bringing it to her mouth to kiss my fingers. "I wish we could stay in here all night," I said.

"People are probably wondering where we are."

Some people probably knew. I didn't express that concern aloud, however—there was no need to worry her. I just held her in silence for a few minutes, soaking in every bit of this moment—the smell of her hair, the way her body seemed to align perfectly with mine. The dim light from the single lamp on the other side of the room cast a soft glow on her face, and though she wasn't smiling, she looked satisfied. I pressed a gentle kiss on her jaw. "You know, this is only the second weirdest place we've had sex."

Kendall giggled, and I gave her a squeeze before sitting up. We would need to get back out to the dancefloor before people started getting suspicious. I brought her panties to her and watched in amusement at the way she shimmied them up her legs. "I'll sneak out there first," Kendall said. But before she could slip away, I grabbed her by the wrist and pulled her against me for one more kiss.

The second she was gone, I already missed her. I went into the bathroom to wash my face and took advantage of the complimentary bottle of mouthwash. Just as I was patting my chin dry, I heard the door open again. As I lowered the towel, I was disappointed to find Xander slithering into the room. He would have seen Kendall in the hallway—I just hoped he couldn't discern which room she'd come from.

I attempted to nonchalantly pick up the condom wrapper from the floor without him noticing, but Xander watched me like a hawk as he fumbled with his coat. He pulled a vape pen from one of the pockets. "You want in on this?" he asked, throwing himself onto a regal-looking leather chair.

"I'm good."

Xander shrugged. "Suit yourself." I adjusted the sleeves of my untucked shirt, carefully rolling them up so I didn't look like such a sloppy mess when I returned to the dancefloor. Before I could leave, however, Xander snapped his fingers and pointed at me. "I've got it."

"Got what?"

"My next headline."

I inhaled, knowing I wasn't going to like whatever he had to say next. "Oh yeah? And what's that?"

An arrogant grin spread across his face as he took a hit from the vape. He held one hand up in a dramatic manner and said, "'Local teacher fucks student's father at wedding.'"

I tried to maintain a calm demeanor, though I was panicking on the inside. Xander was definitely bluffing, but who knew what he could do with this information? I cleared my throat and attempted to regain my composure. "Are you open to critique?"

"Always."

"Good," I said, taking a step toward him. "Because I've got a better idea for that headline."

"Well, let's hear it, then."

"How about something like, 'local reporter rejected by teacher; student's father predicted this months ago'?"

Xander made a face like he was giving this some consideration. "I don't know," he said, taking another hit from the pen. "It might be a little wordy."

"I'll work on it," I retorted, sticking my hands in my pockets. Xander just stared at me, and it was all I could do not to punch the smug look off his stupid face. "But it's true, isn't it? And I know how important it is for you to maintain your journalistic integrity."

"Hmm. My headline wasn't a lie, though, was it?" he asked, studying his fingernails. He licked his lips and inhaled deeply. "Doesn't smell like I'm wrong."

My face felt warm. I couldn't deny the way the smell of sex still lingered in the air.

"Besides," Xander continued. "I think my buddies on the school board would be more interested in the one I came up with."

Maybe he wasn't bluffing after all. After being rejected by Kendall, who knew what he might do? And considering his evident dislike for me, I felt inclined to take him seriously. I swallowed. "As a journalist, you should know making accusations without evidence could tarnish your credibility. And we wouldn't want that, would we? Who else would give us the scoop on the… Woodvale bridge league?"

Xander's face fell. While I had no idea whether Woodvale had a bridge league or not, or if he would ever report on such a thing, I could tell I'd struck a nerve with the guy. He wasn't exactly doing any kind of award-winning reporting in this backwards town, and we both knew it.

Wanting to have the last word, I pulled the door open and walked out without giving him another glance. I couldn't let this asshole put a damper on my mood. I made my way down that long corridor, the sounds of "Party in the USA" echoing from the dancefloor. And that's where I found Finley dancing in a circle with Kendall, Sarah, my sister, and some of my nieces and nephews. Even a couple of my drunk aunts were out there with them—Owen's mom included. Jake and Owen were not far away, seemingly having a beer-chugging contest by the DJ booth.

The sight of Kendall surrounded by my family immediately turned my mood around. Because this was it—this was exactly what had been missing from my life. Our lives. I stood back, watching Kendall take Finley's hands and twist her around and around, both of them laughing hysterically. I could have cried at the sight.

And as though the universe was on my side for once, the Miley Cyrus song faded out and a slow Shawn Mendes song began playing. I was feeling pretty bold, so I walked right up to Kendall and grabbed her by the elbow as she started to leave the dancefloor. "Dance with me," I demanded.

Her eyes widened as she glanced toward my mom. "But—"

I yanked her toward me, unwilling to give her a choice. "Just a couple of friends dancing. No one will think a thing of it." At that point, who the fuck cared? Owen knew. My mom knew. Xander knew. Who were we trying to hide this from, anyway?

Kendall still had a look of concern on her face, but she draped her hands behind my neck, anyway. I slipped my arms around her waist, maintaining just enough distance to not arouse too much suspicion. Kendall's eyes were still darting around.

"Eyes on me, princess," I said. "Nobody's looking at us."

But that might have been a lie. With a quick skim of that reception hall, I observed a lot of eyes pointed in our direction. My entire family, for starters. A disgruntled looking Heath scowled at us from a nearby table. Xander was back in the room now, too, looking just as dejected as Heath—but he was staring at Abigail and Daya, who were talking close at the edge of the dance floor. I wanted to believe he was rejected by one or both of them, too.

And directly behind Kendall, I spotted Owen dancing close with his new bride. He smiled warmly in our direction, flashing me a subtle thumbs up behind Sarah's back.

My eyes found Kendall's again, and she responded with a sweet grin. "You are the most beautiful woman in this room," I told her.

"I think Sarah's more deserving of that honor tonight."

"Well," I said, glancing toward Owen and Sarah again. "She *does* look stunning, I'll give her that. But she still comes in second, even tonight. Nobody can hold a candle to you."

Kendall giggled. "You already got into my panties tonight, Mason. Stop trying to flatter me."

"I'm just being honest," I said, letting go of her waist so I could twirl her. When she came back to me, I drew her in even closer. It took every bit of strength I had not to kiss that woman right then and there.

Before the song reached the second verse, Finley excitedly wedged herself between Kendall and me. "Twirl me, Daddy!" she squealed. I shot Kendall an apologetic smile before taking Finley by the hand and twirling her, just like I had with Kendall. She laughed the entire time. I motioned for her to step up onto my shoes with her bare feet so we could dance together. Then, I brought her hands to the belt loops on my hips, freeing my own hands to reach for Kendall's waist again. And the three of us danced just like that, with Finley tucked between us. I almost apologized to Kendall for the interruption, but it was unnecessary—her smile was as big as mine must have been.

And if people weren't looking at us before, they sure were now.

My heart broke when the song came to an end and both of my girls pulled away from me. I had half a mind to request another slow song, just to relive that perfect moment.

Just then, one of my cousins came up behind me and clapped his hand against my shoulder. "Hey man," he said, "what's Whitney doing in town?"

My heart skipped a beat, and I suddenly felt dizzy. It was as if a fog descended on the dancefloor, narrowing my focus until everything around me faded to black.

I found it difficult to even swallow.

"What?"

chapter forty-five
kendall

I danced with Finley in an attempt to distract her from the conversation unfolding two feet away from us. Thankfully, she hadn't heard the mention of her mom's name. But I eavesdropped on the conversation, too curious about it to give Finley my full attention. "Yeah," the guy talking to Mason said. "We saw her at the gas station earlier."

"And you're sure it was her?"

"Unless she's got an identical twin, it was *definitely* her. I sat behind her in homeroom for four years. I know what she looks like."

Mason appeared to go shaky at the knees, and his face was paler than I'd ever seen. He darted off the dancefloor and disappeared into the dark corridor near the bathrooms. My stomach was in knots. What did this mean? What was Whitney doing back in Woodvale?

"I'll be back, Finley," I said, leaving her with Lesley and Sarah. I needed to check on Mason. He had to be panicking out there. I assumed he probably returned to the groom's room at the end of the hall, but he was standing in a dark corner by a row of tall windows overlooking the balcony—and he was looking at his phone.

"Mason," I said, coming up beside him. He didn't look up. "Is she really in town?"

"She is. She really is," he said. His hands were shaking. "I usually keep tabs on her online, but I haven't thought about it in a long time. Her last photo was taken at Poppy's earlier today."

"Oh," I said. I touched Mason's arm. "Well, maybe she's just in town for Thanksgiving?"

"She and her mom have been on the outs since March, at least according to Traci. I'm so—*fuck*, I'm so afraid she's moving back here." Mason was shaking so much I nudged him toward a nearby bench, motioning for him to sit so he wouldn't pass out. "How can I prevent Finley from seeing her if she's here? Woodvale's a small town. We're going to run into her."

I put my hand on his knee. "Just wait and see what she does. You don't know that she's going to stay."

Mason shook his head, chewing on his bottom lip. "I'm so scared she's going to reach out. Make contact. But at the same time, half of me is pissed that she's here, she's so close, and she doesn't care about her daughter. It doesn't make any sense."

"You're right, it doesn't." I didn't know what else to say other than validate his feelings.

Both of Mason's knees were bouncing rapidly. "What do I do if she asks for a visit?"

I wasn't the right person to answer that. "I don't know."

"I can't keep the girl from her mom. Can I? Who am I to deny her of that? Here I've been trying to practically erase Whitney from that kid's memory, never expecting her to show up here again. I should have known better. I've fucked my kid up."

I took Mason by the hand and gave him a squeeze. "No you haven't. That girl is thriving. Look at how happy she is tonight."

His bottom lip quivered, and he began to rapidly blink. "But what's going to happen if Whitney wants to see her? Then what? Do I let her hurt my kid all over again? It's just one hard decision after another—it never stops. And I never know if I'm making the right one. It's too much, Kendall."

I slid my arm around Mason's back.

"It's too much," he repeated, trembling.

With my other hand, I cradled Mason's head, pulling him against my chest. I expected some resistance, but he collapsed against me, breathing shakily as he clung to my body. I wished I could absorb every ounce of his pain and worry, but for now, holding him while he cried was the best I could do. My heart shattered for him. For Finley. I hated a woman I'd never even met for causing so much havoc in their lives.

"I'm sorry," Mason said, his words muffled by the fabric of my dress. "I just—I just can't do this alone anymore."

I pulled away, placing my palms on either side of his face to make him look at me. And with unwavering sincerity, I said, "You're not."

Mason took another deep, shaky breath. And then, with an exhale, he finally spoke the words I knew he'd been aching to say for some time. "I love you."

It felt like my heart stopped and the entire world froze in place. I knew that couldn't be true, though—I was still alive, after all, and Dua Lipa's voice still boomed from the reception hall. But right there in that dim and abandoned hallway, time seemed to stand still.

I'd never felt more undeserving of those words. We were only supposed to have a one-night stand, and now I'd gone and entangled myself in his and his daughter's lives. I made him fall in love—or at least think that he had.

Mason was too sweet. Too... pure. And he and Finley deserved so much better than anything I could offer either of them.

I opened my mouth to begin to explain this when another couple burst through the double doors into the hallway, clinging to each other and laughing.

It was Daya and Abigail.

I slid away from Mason on the bench just as the two of them pulled apart, having spotted us at the same time. "Oh—oops," Abigail said, looking from me to Daya. And just as I'd witnessed her almost kissing my sister's ex a second ago, she had undoubtedly seen Mason and me embracing.

Daya clutched her chest as though she were just coming to her senses. "Oh my god. I am so not myself tonight."

"Um," Abigail said, playing with the locket around her neck. "I'm going to go back in there and get a drink. Maybe see what… Heath is up to."

She disappeared back into the reception hall just as quickly as she'd sprung through the doors. Daya stood still before us, shaking her head at herself. "Kendall, I think I need to go home. Now."

"Oh, okay," I said, springing to my feet. I turned to Mason, who was staring down at the floor with his hands folded between his knees. "I need to take her."

"It's okay," Mason said with a shrug. "Go. We'll talk tomorrow."

"Are you going to be okay?"

"I think I got it all out of my system," he said with an embarrassed chuckle. "I'm fine. Don't worry about me."

"I'm sorry," I said, holding his gaze. Could he understand what I was apologizing for?

Mason stood up and touched my hair, giving me a reassuring smile. "You have nothing to apologize for." But there was something in his expression that signified there was pain behind that smile. It might have just been due to this situation with Whitney, but I was sure my refusal to reciprocate his feelings was weighing down on him, too. He brushed it off, though, leaning in for a quick kiss. "Tomorrow."

I followed Daya back through the double doors so we could both get our things from our table. I needed to say goodbye to Sarah, of course—and I found her on the dancefloor talking amongst co-workers. "Congratulations," I told her, giving her a hug. After her, I hugged Owen, who seemed a little wobbly on his feet.

Finley ran up to us as we made our way toward the exit. "You're not leaving, are you?" she asked, sticking her bottom lip out.

"I have to, Fin. But I'll see you on Monday, okay?"

She lurched forward to hug my legs, and I bent down to squeeze her. She was more than a little reluctant to let go, so her grandma came up behind her to pry her off of me.

"This little girl really loves you, you know," Christine said, taking Finley by the hand.

I sighed as they walked back to the dancefloor. "There sure is a lot of that going around," I mumbled to Daya as we left.

chapter forty-six
mason

As eager as I was to see Traci and ask about Whitney's intentions, I knew there was no way I could get Finley to wake up in time to have breakfast with the woman. So I canceled, telling her we'd both had a rough night and looked forward to seeing her in one week.

I couldn't sleep in, however. Thoughts of Whitney infiltrated my mind, and I imagined about twenty different scenarios playing out—the best case being that Whitney quickly found her way back out of town without either of us having to see her. How likely was that to happen, though?

By mid-morning, my curiosity got the best of me. Instead of waiting for Whitney to make a move, I decided I'd go directly to the source and find out why she was really here.

Mason: I'm not trying to be rude but I'm just curious... are you just in town for the holidays or is this going to be a permanent thing? Just need to know so I can prepare Finley.

It took Whitney so long to reply, I questioned whether she still had the same phone number. For all I knew, she got on her boyfriend's phone plan in Florida or something. But halfway through breakfast with Finley, my phone finally lit up with a reply from her.

Whitney: Here for thanksgiving but I have been having a difficult time being so close without seeing her

Whitney: I miss her. can we meet up?

My heart sank as I watched Finley slurp the milk from her cereal bowl. This was exactly what I'd been afraid of. On one hand, I knew this could potentially be the best news ever for my little girl. She'd probably be so excited to finally see her mom that she'd cry happy tears. I could only imagine their reunion after all this time apart.

But then what?

A million questions swirled in my mind. What was Whitney's game plan? Considering she was only here for the holiday, it meant we probably couldn't count on seeing her again for a while. Would she want to stay in touch now? Had she truly had a change of heart? Or was it just the proximity to Finley that was making her nostalgic for the way things used to be?

How long would it last?

Mason: Can you meet at 1?

I had a plan, or at least part of one. Before I made any kind of decision, I would talk to Whitney first by myself and gauge her true intentions. If her heart was truly in the right place, I'd allow her to see Finley. But if she couldn't prove to me she'd had a change of heart, I couldn't let this reunion happen.

When I sent Kendall a screenshot of the messages and explained my plan, she offered to come along just in case I needed her support.

Mason: I can handle it. But thank you for offering. Just knowing that you'd be willing to come along means a lot.

I told her I'd text her after the encounter to let her know how it went. Finley, finished with her cereal, hopped down from the kitchenette barstool and dragged her jellyfish stuffed animal to the couch, where it looked like she was minutes from falling back to sleep. As for me, I stayed in my seat, my thoughts shifting from Whitney to Kendall and her lukewarm response to my love proclamation.

It was more of a non-reaction, really. But why? I could tell she loved me. I saw it in her eyes. Felt it when we danced. Heard it in the way she laughed. But something had prevented her from saying it back to me, and I was determined to discover what that might be.

I'd have to deal with that later.

**

I met Whitney at our usual spot and paced beside the Jeep while I waited. She arrived just a few minutes after me in a car I didn't recognize with Florida plates. I held my breath as she stepped out, watching her closely as she approached. She was tanner than I remembered, but her once gaunt face had filled out more. She looked healthy.

"Where is she?" she asked, peering toward my backseat.

I took a few steps forward, holding up both of my hands in a calming manner. "Whitney. Let's be realistic for a second here."

Her mouth dropped open. "You didn't bring her? You tricked me into coming and she's not even with you?"

I nodded toward the picnic table in the grass where I'd seen some employees take smoke breaks. "Let's sit down and talk."

"Why'd you lie?" she screeched. I tried not to let the fury in her eyes intimidate me as I made my way over to the picnic table myself.

"Come sit down," I repeated, pulling myself atop the table to rest my feet on the bench.

"Do you know how manipulative this is? I can't believe you—"

"Sit. Down."

I didn't have time for her games. I tried to keep my judgmental thoughts at bay as I waited for her to listen. Finally, she took a seat at the opposite end of the picnic table and stared at me in disgust. "You're such a dick."

I closed my eyes for a second, silently counting to three before I opened my mouth. "So, Finley started therapy again recently," I began. "She's made a lot of progress, but she's still not fully healed from you leaving."

"So let me see her. What the fuck are we doing here?"

"It's not that simple, Whitney. If she sees you today and then doesn't hear from you again, it's going to tear her apart. It'll be like starting back at square one. And I know you don't care, but the first couple of months after you left were a total nightmare. It was traumatic."

Whitney took a deep breath. "Don't act like I don't care. I kept away because I knew that was what was best for her."

"Exactly," I blurted. Whitney looked down at the ground, watching a grocery sack blow past us. She'd walked right into the point herself—a lot quicker than I had anticipated. "I need to know what your plan is here. Are you going to keep in touch? Will you be here on her birthday and every holiday? Do you want to help me support her? Raise her? Or were you planning to give her one good day before disappearing again?"

Whitney continued staring straight ahead.

"Tell me." I kept my tone calm. Level. "What's your plan?"

"I didn't have one," she said, rolling her eyes. "I just wanted to see my daughter."

"Well, for seven months, you didn't really care whether you saw her or not. So it's all or nothing. Either be in her life or don't. None of this inconsistent bullshit. I'm not about to let you reopen the wounds we've been working so hard to patch up after you abandoned her the first time."

The way Whitney scowled reminded me of Finley. I swallowed, feeling sick to my stomach. This shouldn't have been something a person needed to think about. It should have been an instant, "yes, I will be here." But it was never like that with Whitney.

Her silence went on for a long time. By then, I'd figured out her answer—but she was too proud to say it. So I decided to coax it out of her.

"If you want to go back to whatever life you've created down in Florida, that's okay, too. If you truly want to do what's best for Finley—that's probably it."

"I mean, I don't want to keep hurting her," Whitney mumbled. She leaned forward, hugging her knees. Her eyes were welling up with tears. "That's all I can seem to do."

"Then allow her to heal from losing you once instead of prolonging the pain."

She was breathing hard, running her fingers along the seams of her jeans—silently making a decision. It was all I could do not to sit there and yell at her. Jesus Christ. Either choose to be a mom or don't—it shouldn't have been so hard. "You know," she said after a couple of minutes, "you weren't always there for her, either."

That felt like a slap in the face. I wondered if that might come up, so I was prepared with a response. "And I wish I could change the past, but I can't. I hate myself for it. But I'm doing everything I can to make sure Finley's life is full of love and stability now."

Whitney nodded, and a tear rolled down her cheek. Damn it. It was simply too hard for me not to fold when people cried in front of me. Whatever Whitney had going on with her mental health, maybe it was too complex for me to understand. I started to wonder if I had perhaps been too harsh.

And then Whitney said, "I'm going to get it right this time."

Panic ran through my veins as I considered what this meant. My mind raced with thoughts of everything that would have to happen now—how would I tell Finley? Was this really going to work out? Would we have to get the courts involved again? How would this affect Finley long-term?

But then I noticed the way Whitney cradled her lower abdomen in her hands. For the first time in that conversation, it dawned on me she was pregnant. She couldn't have been far along, from the looks of it, but there was definitely a bump there.

My mouth fell open.

Whitney hadn't meant she was going to get it right with Finley.

She was going to get it right with *this* child.

That realization nearly knocked the wind out of me. I immediately thought of Kendall and all of her qualms about her dad's "new" family and the pain it caused. One day, Finley was going to find herself in a similar situation. I couldn't even begin to fathom the heartbreak she'd feel upon learning her biological mother had essentially replaced her with another child.

The expletives on the tip of my tongue threatened to spill out, but I resisted. It wasn't worth it. Deciding I'd had enough of this conversation, I shot up from the picnic table. "Good luck with that," I muttered before turning around and walking back to my car.

"Mason!"

I didn't look back. As soon as I got in the Jeep, I blocked Whitney's number from my phone. I didn't want or need to hear anything else she had to say. Not now. Sometime in the future, we'd likely have to deal with her again—especially if I was going to allow Finley to maintain a relationship with Traci. But for now, I could do my best to shield Finley from the inevitable storm Whitney would bring into our lives. Whatever it took—I'd do it.

**

Finley was helping my mom fill the bird feeder in the yard when I got home. Without a word, I scooped her up and held her against my chest. She giggled uncomfortably, raising one eyebrow at this inexplicable gesture, but she hugged me back, anyway. "You are such a weirdo, Dad."

"Runs in the family," I responded, kissing the top of her head.

My phone buzzed in my pocket. I braced myself for a call from Traci—or perhaps Whitney had found a different way to reach out. But to my surprise, the call was from Owen, who was supposed to be leaving for his honeymoon at some point that day.

I set Finley on the ground. "Hello?" I answered warily.

"Hey, cousin. I've got to warn you about something. Um…"

I sighed, assuming he'd heard through the grapevine Whitney was in town. "Wait, aren't you on your honeymoon?"

"We're at the airport now. Waiting at the gate. But listen, you know how our moms like to gossip, right?"

"Uh huh," I answered, watching my mom lift Finley so she could pour birdseed into the feeder. Maybe this wasn't about Whitney, after all.

Owen sucked air through his teeth. "My mom may or may not have confronted me and Sarah about you and Kendall last night. She wanted all the details, but Sarah obviously didn't have any. She's a little upset with me for not spilling the beans with her, actually." He laughed.

I grimaced. I couldn't risk my mom or Finley overhearing this conversation, so I walked around to the other side of the house. "So. Sarah knows."

"Yeah, Sarah knows, and she's very excited. It's all I can do to keep her from texting Kendall about it. But I wanted to give you a heads up first."

"I appreciate it. But I mean, I guess we weren't exactly trying to hide it last night."

"Yeah, I saw you dancing with her and Finley. That was pretty awesome, man." I could hear Sarah rambling in the background. Owen laughed, adding, "Sarah says it was the most disgustingly adorable thing she's ever seen."

I chuckled. "Tell her I said… thanks?"

Their flight was announced over the speaker, so Owen had to hang up. I slipped my phone back in my pocket and put my head in my hands. At some point, I was going to have to tell Kendall her boss knew about our not-so-secret relationship.

And her ex-boyfriend.

And my mom.

And Xander at the Woodvale Times.

Fuck.

chapter forty-seven
kendall

My anxiety was through the roof the day after the wedding. When Mason told me he was going to talk to Whitney in person, I caught myself pacing back and forth through the house, worrying what she might have in store. I even tried to distract myself by baking brownies I was too anxious to eat.

Finally, in the late afternoon, Mason sent me a message.

Mason: Could we meet at our spot by the river? I'll bring coffee.

Something about the formality of the message made me feel uneasy. I knew he'd fill me in on the Whitney situation, but I couldn't help but wonder if he was going to bring up my refusal to return his "I love you" last night. This conversation would be about me and him—not Whitney. I just knew it.

Daya was in the living room, frantically tying her shoes, when I started to leave. "Where you headed?" I asked her, picking my purse up from the coffee table.

"Indianapolis."

I whipped around to face her. "You are?"

"Yes," she said, pulling her shoestrings tight. "I can't let Jamie slip through my fingers. I've just been passively watching her drift away from me and I have to stop it before it's too late. Maybe it already is—I don't know—but I have to at least try. You know? I could live in the city. And I will."

I stared at her in stunned silence, thinking this was exactly the kind of passion Jamie needed from her. Daya hurriedly gathered her things, taking her jacket off the hook by the front door. "Good luck," I said, and I meant it.

But when Daya tugged open the door, Jamie was standing on the other side of it with her key out. They stared at each other for a few seconds until Daya said, "What are you doing home?"

"I'm not going to move," Jamie said, stepping inside.

Daya took a step back to give Jamie some room. "What? Why not?"

"Because it's not worth it. I realized it's not that important to me. I'd rather stay here, with you—*you* are my future."

"But—but—that's stupid." Daya shook her head. "You've had this career goal for so long, and—"

"You and I both know it's like the fourth time I've switched career goals. But my life goals have never changed. They always involve you. And if it means staying in Woodvale, well, I guess then that's the plan."

"No. That is *not* the plan. We're not staying here."

Jamie blinked. "Excuse me?"

"I'm not letting you give up on this just because of my stubbornness. We're going to get a house in Indy where you're going to be a pharmacist and I'll find a job as a vet tech somewhere—literally anywhere. And we're getting another dog. That's our new plan."

I'd never heard her sound so… decisive. Jamie smiled and took a step forward, placing a hand on Daya's waist. "Okay," she submitted.

They were about to kiss, but my excited clapping interrupted them. "Oh! You guys are going to make me cry!"

Without taking her eyes off of Daya, Jamie said, "You might want to find somewhere else to be for the next couple of hours, Blondie."

Hours? Jesus. "I'm leaving now," I said, draping my purse over my shoulder. "You kids have fun."

**

Mason and I pulled up next to the river at the same time. He carried a coffee over to me, and we walked to the closest swinging bench together. "I hope nobody sees us," I said, glancing over my shoulder. It was a relatively mild day, and we weren't the only people with the idea of heading to the riverwalk.

"I wouldn't worry about it," Mason said as we sat down. He was wearing a forest green flannel over a Nirvana t-shirt—but it ironically featured a picture of Hanson instead. Jamie would've had a heyday with that.

"How did it go with Whitney?" I asked, holding my caramel macchiato on my lap.

"If it's okay, I'd rather not talk about her yet. I know you're curious, but I just need to think about something different for a little bit. Is that okay?"

"Of course." I was dying to know, but I squeezed his hand to let him know it was okay. "Just tell me when you're ready."

Mason nodded, sipping his coffee. He stared straight ahead at the river and leaned forward, resting his forearms on his knees. Something was bothering him. I never would have predicted the next words out of his mouth, though. "Sarah knows about us," he blurted.

My skin prickled with dread. "What?"

Mason looked down at the ground. "And Owen. His mom told them."

This was a lot of information to process in a matter of seconds. "Wait, what? His mom? How did—"

"My mom told her."

I knew it. I knew his mom was aware of our relationship—it would explain the looks she and Lesley exchanged the night before. "Oh… my god."

"That's not all." Mason clenched his eyes shut. "Owen knew a week ago. He sort of… saw a text you sent me. I—I wasn't going to tell you, but you deserve to know that. I kind of confessed everything to him."

My face and neck felt hot. "What text did he see?"

The inner corners of his eyebrows lifted in an apologetic expression, and though he didn't say a word, I already knew. Owen must have seen one of the pictures I sent Mason. If I had to guess, it was the one from the night of the bachelorette party. Owen would have been with Mason when he received that message.

"Mason," I said, a hint of shame in my voice. "This happened a week ago? I feel so—God, I hugged him last night. They watched us dance. I'm so embarrassed right now." I covered my face with my hands. "I can't believe Sarah knows I lied to her face about us. She's going to be so upset."

"She's not upset at all," he rushed out. "The opposite, actually—she seems thrilled about it."

"But she's still the principal—it's her duty to report this. I warned you about this. Oh god, everything I feared is actually happening."

"It's not that bad, Kendall. I think you're wrong about Sarah. I doubt she'll run to the school board about this. Although…" He took a deep breath.

"What?"

Mason ran a finger along his bottom lip, contemplating his next words. He stared down at his coffee cup, unable to look me in the eye. Whatever he was about to say, I could tell it might be the worst news yet. And I was right. "Xander at the Woodvale Times may know, as well, and he *might* have also threatened to report us."

Xander. That smarmy asshole. "Are you serious?"

"He came in the room right after we had sex, and he figured it out."

"But you denied it, right?"

"Well, I—there wasn't anything I could say. He wouldn't have believed me, anyway."

"So you just went along with it?" Of course he did. He *wanted* Xander to know—wanted to make him jealous after he hit on me. "What did you say when he threatened to turn us in?"

Mason hung his head in shame. "I sort of just… made fun of his writing. That was pretty much it."

"You insulted the guy who holds our fate in his hands? Great."

Mason rolled his eyes. "Come on."

I scooted away from him. "Why are you minimizing all of this like it's not a big deal? Nobody was supposed to find out about us, but now your entire family knows? And my boss? And the Woodvale Times? Half the town might know by now."

I paused long enough to watch his eyes widen in panic.

"And don't *ever* roll your eyes at me," I continued. I almost stood up and walked away right then, but there was a lot left to discuss.

Regret was written all over Mason's face. "I am so sorry. I won't. I—I swear it wasn't because of you. It was merely a reaction to the thought of Xander having any kind of control over us."

His apology seemed genuine, but I was still fuming. Heath used to roll his eyes at me all the time, and it made me feel like my concerns were silly. Deep down, I knew Mason was nothing like Heath—it wasn't fair of me to compare them. "Okay. Well, maybe he's just bluffing. Owen could probably convince him to keep his mouth shut."

"Probably. And if Sarah can have some grace, we'll be fine. We can continue dating behind closed doors like we have been until summer. It'll be okay."

I rested my elbows on my knees and buried my head in my hands. "It's not even December yet."

Mason fell silent as I envisioned how the next few months would play out. Our inner circle of people who knew about our relationship had more than doubled, and it was only a matter of time before the rumor reached the wrong person. We'd already been so careless. Staring down at his coffee cup, Mason said, "If you want to play it safe and keep away from me, I'd understand. If I have to wait until June to touch you again, I will. It won't be easy, but it would be worth it."

I stared at him in bewilderment. "What are you saying?"

"I'm giving you an out. I can see that I've caused you so much stress already, and I don't want to keep upsetting you." He shook his head with a frown. "You could lose your job because of me. I don't want to wait, but I will."

"I'm not that worried about losing my job," I admitted. It was the truth. "I would hate to leave Grissom and Sarah, but it's not like there aren't other teaching jobs all over the place."

"Then what *are* you worried about?"

"Finley," I stated, like it was obvious. "We don't know who they'd replace me with. Who would become Finley's teacher if I got fired? She needs stability more than anything right now, and that would shake everything up."

"You're worried about… Finley." It wasn't a question. Mason blinked at me a few times, and the corners of his mouth subtly curled upward.

"Well, yeah. That would be a rough transition for her."

"You're right," he said. "And I have to admit, I hadn't even thought about that as a possibility. But if it happens, we'll get through it, just like we've gotten through everything else. The three of us—we're in this together."

Mason's gaze was intense. *The three of us,* he'd said. He was once again referring to us like we were a little family or something. I thought of how he, Finley, and I danced together at the wedding, and how happy he looked. The nagging guilt I had felt when he told me he loved me returned.

"I don't know if I'm the one, Mason," I said quietly, holding his stare. "You're searching for someone who can step in as some kind of maternal figure for Finley, and I'm just—I'm terrified that I'm not the right person to one day fill that role in her life. To be someone she looks up to in that way."

Mason's face softened into a gentle smile. He set his coffee cup on the ground and angled his body toward me on the bench, reaching up to pull a few loose strands of hair away from my eyes. "But Kendall," he whispered, sliding his fingers down my jawline to lift my chin. "You already are."

My eyes welled up with tears. He was right, wasn't he? Finley cared about me so much already—and it was mutual. "I really love her, Mason," I said, my voice trembling. And there was that guilty feeling again. Only now, it was because I was so quick to admit I loved his daughter, yet I still couldn't make myself say the words to him. They were right on the tip of my tongue.

"I know you do," he said, playing with the ends of my hair. "And she loves you, too. We both do."

Now he'd said it twice. I leaned against his chest, feeling him wrap both arms against me tight. I inhaled, taking in the clean pine scent that had become so familiar to me. But it was the stupid Nirvana/Hanson t-shirt that brought a smile to my lips. I loved everything about this man—and I could say that out loud. "I love you, too," I said. Piece of cake.

His grip around me tightened. "There you go," he said, like he'd been expecting those words. He rested his chin atop my head. "Now we've got to figure out what to do."

"We need to tell Owen to convince his asshole friend to keep our secret."

Mason nodded. "I'll talk to him."

"And I'll talk to Sarah."

"Maybe we should wait until they're back from their honeymoon before pestering them with our drama," Mason said.

"Probably."

We held each other just like that for a few minutes, completely oblivious to the people walking past us. I was ready to ask about his interaction with Whitney, but I held my tongue—he'd bring it up when he was ready.

When he pulled away, I thought he might have been ready to spill what happened, but he held my face in his hands and said my name softly. "Kendall. I need you to know you're more than worthy of being loved. I think you've got these voices in your head telling you you're not good enough, and I'm going to make it my personal goal to get them to shut up."

I attempted a grin to cover my vulnerability, but my mouth involuntarily contorted into a half-frown, half-smile kind of a grimace. "They're really loud sometimes," I admitted.

Mason wiped away the tear rolling my cheek with his thumb. "I know. You just replace them with my voice now, okay? Imagine me telling you how perfect you are instead." He paused for a moment, smiling. "You are exactly what Finley and I have been waiting for."

I bit my bottom lip in an attempt to hold in a sob, but there was no use. And once I saw that Mason's eyes were welling up with tears, too, I was a goner. "If you keep talking like that, I might start believing you."

"All part of the plan, princess," he said with a chuckle, leaning in for a kiss.

A few months ago, Mason Reed was nothing more than pixels on an app—a potential one-night-stand to help me get over an ex. But now, he and his daughter had worked their way into my heart—and I couldn't be happier to hold them both there.

chapter forty-eight
mason

The day was an emotional rollercoaster.

Kendall cried again when I told her about the encounter with Whitney. I almost didn't want to share what happened because I knew she'd find the news disturbing. And because she loved Finley so much, she hated the thought of this new development reaching her ears. "That's going to break her, Mason."

"I know."

We parted ways because I had promised Finley we could make a Christmas paper chain countdown that afternoon. But before we got started on our project, I told her to wait for me downstairs. I asked both of my parents to join me in their room where Finley couldn't hear. They both sat on the edge of their bed, exchanging worried glances as I stood before them on the rug.

"I saw Whitney today."

My mom's mouth fell open. "Whitney's in town?"

"Yes," I confirmed, shoving my hands in my back pockets. "She wanted to see Finley. But after talking with her, I decided that's not in Finley's best interest right now. Whitney hasn't changed, unfortunately. She doesn't intend to stick around. Not only that—" I stopped, taking a deep breath. "She's pregnant."

"Oh, good God," my mom muttered. My dad just squinted in confusion, probably wondering why any of this was relevant to them. But I was getting there.

"And I know she lives several states away, but this is a small town. People have seen her this weekend, and people talk.

Word's going to get out. I would like to shield this piece of information from Finley as long as I can."

"She's going to hear it somewhere, Mase."

My mom wasn't wrong. "I know. But it's too soon. She's still healing from what Whitney already put her through. I just—I need you guys to support me in this. If you hear anyone mention it in front of her, shut the conversation down immediately. Please."

"Wouldn't you rather tell her now and get it over with?" my mom asked. "She should hear it from you before someone else spills the beans."

"The boy's right, Christine," my dad interjected. My mom and I turned to him in surprise. "This will destroy that girl. Let her be blissfully ignorant for now. She's been through enough."

I swallowed as my dad removed his glasses, staring up at me.

"You've had to handle so much as a father, things that most people could never fathom having to go through. The decisions you have to make…" He paused, looking down at the rug as he shook his head. "I don't know how you cope with it all. I'm tremendously proud of you."

I hadn't realized how badly I'd needed to hear my father say those words until he'd said them. "Thank you, Dad." He rose to his feet, reaching up to give my shoulder a hard pat as he leaned his body toward mine—the closest he'd come to hugging me in over a decade. And then he walked out of the room, leaving my mom and me to stare at each other in awe.

"Wow," she said. "That's the most emotion I've seen from that man in ages."

"Anger's an emotion," I couldn't help but remind her.

My mom laughed. "True. I agree with him though, son. You're doing a good job. I don't know how you haven't snapped from all the pressure." If she only knew how many times I'd come close. "I'm sure that teacher helps relieve some of that pressure, huh?"

My eyes nearly bulged out of their sockets. "Mom."

She held her hands up like she'd just said something completely innocent. "I'm just sayin'. We all saw you dancing with her last night. Coincidentally, you both disappeared at the same time, too."

"Stop," I begged, crossing my arms against my chest. I couldn't resist smiling, though.

"There is something there, isn't there?"

I shrugged with one shoulder. "There might be."

"But she *is* Finley's teacher. You're going to have to be careful with this. It'll devastate Fin if she gets close to that woman and then the two of you split up."

"I don't see that happening. Kendall's kind of the endgame for me." I wasn't entirely sure what I meant by that, but I felt those words in my bones. Somehow, I just knew things with Kendall would last.

"Well, hang onto her then," my mom said as she stood up. She took a couple of steps forward and placed her palm on my cheek. "It's your time to shine, Masey."

In any other circumstance, I would have pulled away from her or told her off for giving me that ridiculous nickname, but this time, it was oddly comforting. "I hope so," I said.

**

When I got downstairs, Finley had already dragged out all the red and green construction paper, as well as a package of Christmas stickers I didn't even know we had. "You cut the strips, and I'll staple," she said, climbing up onto one of the barstools. I wasn't sure this kid should be wielding a stapler, but I decided to give her a chance.

We were about a third of the way through assembling the paper chain at our kitchen counter when she announced, "I have some news to tell you." I momentarily panicked, fearing she somehow knew about Whitney's visit to Woodvale. But then she said, "Elijah asked me to be his girlfriend."

I blinked a few times, unsure how to take this information. "Uh huh. And what did you say?"

"Well. It happened at recess on Friday," she said, putting a candy cane sticker on one of the links. "He gave me an Indian bead, asked me to be his girlfriend, and then ran away before I could say yes or no."

"And… what's your answer gonna be?"

"I think I might tell him I'm not ready for a boyfriend until, like, second grade. At least."

"At least," I echoed with a nod. I was so amused, I couldn't even be mad. I'd have to resist the urge to ask Elijah about it the next day, but I'd certainly watch him more closely. That little Casanova—it's always the quiet ones. "Elijah's got more game than I do. Maybe he can give me some pointers."

"Don't worry, Dad. I know you'll get a girlfriend someday. And guess what? I know someone who says you're handsome."

"Yeah?" I set my scissors down, genuinely curious. "Who would that be?"

"Ms. Devin."

I grinned, folding my hands on the counter. "Oh, really?"

"Yup. She said you looked handsome at the wedding."

"Must've been the suit."

"Prob'ly."

I picked the scissors back up, tapping them against the counter. "Ms. Devin looked really nice, too, didn't she?"

Finley nodded. "I liked her dress. And she let me have two pieces of cake when Grandma wasn't looking."

I chuckled. "You like her a lot, huh?"

She nodded again.

"Me too," I said, watching Finley haphazardly staple another strip of paper to create another link for our chain. It was finished now, and I lifted her up so she could hang it from the nail on the wall where we always hung paper chains just like this one. "Good job. Thirty days until Christmas, Fin. Have you thought about what you want?"

Finley pressed her forehead against my chin, getting her fingers entangled in my hair—usually an indicator she was feeling sleepy. "I can think of one thing."

"Let me guess. A phone?"

She pulled back so she could see my face. "Never mind. It's impossible."

"No, what is it? Tell me. Maybe Santa can pull some strings."

"Nuh-uh," she refused, laying her head down on my shoulder. "It's not the kind of present Santa can bring."

It must not have been something tangible, then. I wracked my brain, trying to guess what she might be hinting at. And then it crossed my mind that after our conversation about me someday getting a girlfriend, she might have been hoping for a mom for Christmas.

I held Finley close, wishing I could tell her I was working on that for her. By next Christmas, she would have one.

By next Christmas, we could call ourselves a family.

"You deserve the world," I whispered, kissing her on the temple.

chapter forty-nine
kendall

The Gardners were back from their honeymoon, and they had gifts.

They invited us over for dinner Sunday evening, knowing we had some things we wanted to discuss with them. But Mason had to bring Finley, too—they had plans to go to the Christmas parade after dinner, and his parents were preoccupied. We drove separately, however, so Finley wouldn't get suspicious.

"Owen's making fettuccine," Sarah said, leading us through the foyer to the kitchen.

"Smells good," Mason said, letting go of Finley's hand so she could chase after Leia. We walked into the kitchen to find Owen stirring a boiling pot of fettuccine. His nose and cheeks were sunburnt, and Sarah looked like she'd fared even worse— she was a little crispy. Mason noticed this detail at the same time. "Did they not have sunblock in Mexico?"

"You should see his back," Sarah said, reaching for a white plastic sack on the kitchen island. "Who wants their gift first?"

Those words caught Finley's attention. "Is there something in there for me?"

"You think we'd come back from Mexico without something for you, sweetheart?" Sarah pulled out a small paper bag and handed it to her. "Why don't you see what's in there?"

Finley withdrew a package of Mexican gummy candy from the sack, her eyes widening in approval. She reached into the sack again, this time pulling out a tiny ukulele magnet. "That's a real, working ukulele," Owen said, taking a wedge of parmesan from their fridge.

"Just what she needs," Mason said, taking a seat on one of the barstools at the island as Finley plucked away at the tiny instrument.

I touched her shoulder. "What do you tell them, Finley?" For half a second, I worried I'd stepped on Mason's toes—was it really my place to remind her about her manners? He glanced at me with a close-lipped smile, like maybe he was relieved to have someone else jump in. It was such a small thing, a moment that must have seemed so insignificant to Owen and Sarah, but it made me feel the slightest bit more confident that I could—one day—be Mason's partner in this whole parenting thing.

That wasn't such a scary thought anymore, either.

"Thank you," Finley said, dropping the ukulele back in the sack so she could rip open the bag of candy. Mason warned her not to eat too many since we were about to have dinner. I sat in the barstool next to him at the island, where Sarah removed a leather handcrafted sketchbook from her sack and slid it toward Mason.

"We went to this street market where there were all these local artisans selling handmade goods," Sarah said, "and a man named Ernesto made that."

"Good job, Ernesto," Mason said, running a finger along the sugar skull design embossed into the leather. "Thank you guys. This is so cool that I almost don't want to draw in it."

"Aw, I hope you do," Sarah said. And then she reached into the sack one last time, pulling out a giant bottle of tequila.

"Good heavens," I said, taking the heavy bottle in my hands with a chuckle. "Thank you. I bet this really weighed down your luggage."

"Not as much as all the shoes she packed," Owen joked.

"You hush up over there," Sarah snapped, smiling in his direction. "Grate your cheese."

"Well, should we crack this thing open?" I asked. "Get out your margarita maker, girl."

Sarah laughed, pointing out how weird it seemed to have margaritas with Italian food. "This feels illegal," she said a couple of minutes later, pouring the blended mixture of tequila, ice, and juice into a margarita glass for me.

She offered Mason a glass, too, but he held one hand up in refusal. "Tequila's not my jam."

I noticed Sarah didn't make a drink for herself, which was odd, considering she loved tequila almost as much as me. "You're not drinking?" I asked, taking a sip.

"Uh, no. Not tonight. Tequila and pasta—it'll make my stomach hurt."

Sarah wasn't a very good liar. She couldn't look me in the eye as she cleaned up the margarita mess, rinsing the pitcher from the blender in the sink. Then she sidled up beside Owen at the stove and whispered, "I'm going to tell them, okay?"

He looked up at her and nodded. "That's up to you."

Sarah turned back around, shooting a quick glance at Finley, who was playing with Leia nearby. And then she faced me. "We've decided to begin IVF in a few weeks."

Until she uttered those words, I hadn't realized I had been anticipating her to announce she was pregnant. This was a total surprise, though—I never knew they were struggling to get pregnant in the first place. "Oh," I said, tucking my hair behind my ear. "IVF? Wow, that's huge."

"Yeah," Sarah said, glancing at Owen, who took a break from making the fettuccine alfredo to put his arm around her. "That's why I'm not drinking. We've been reading up on it, and it's probably better for my reproductive health if I avoid alcohol for a while."

"That makes sense."

"It's just a precaution," Owen explained. "She's cutting down on her coffee intake, too, which has been—"

"A nightmare," Sarah interrupted with a laugh. "Anyway, this is all pretty new to us. I was actually looking into having my eggs frozen so we could both focus on our careers and do some traveling before having a baby, but as it turns out, I have an abnormally low egg count for my age. So… change of plans."

"Life can be funny that way," Mason said.

"Very true," Sarah said. "It's been really eye-opening for both of us, I think. We weren't really sure this was what we wanted until we were told how difficult it might be to get it."

I observed the way Owen looked down into Sarah's eyes, and somehow I knew these two were going to get through this. And even if it didn't work out, at least they'd have each other.

"Well, I'll be here whether you need a shoulder to cry on or someone to celebrate with," I said.

"Same goes for me," Mason added, glancing over at Owen.

"We appreciate you guys," Owen said, rubbing Sarah's lower back. "It'll be a lot easier to get through this with good friends by our side."

And that's exactly what we were. Good friends. I saw a lot of nights like this in the future—the four of us having dinner together, with or without Finley in tow. Sarah and Owen were becoming something like family to me, too—which I never could have predicted.

We kept dinner casual, eating around the island and engaging in a garlic bread fight. Finley ate two bites of her pasta and disappeared into the dining room to play with the dog. With her out of earshot, I turned to Sarah and said, "So, I'm dying to ask. What's going to happen now that you know about—us?" I gestured toward Mason. "Now that you're an accessory to our crime, can't you get in trouble if you don't report us?"

"Report what? You guys being really close friends?" She winked, taking a sip of her water. "I won't say a word to anyone about it."

I blinked. "You won't?"

"Of course not," she answered with a laugh. "Besides, I feel like I owe you one."

"Owe me one? For what?"

She gave Owen a quick glance, and he looked down at his plate.

I sighed. "Because of what happened two years ago?"

"Hey, it's cool," Mason said, putting his hand on the back of my barstool. "Let her owe you one."

"Okay," I said, the relief beginning to settle in. "You don't 'owe' me anything, but I appreciate your discretion, anyway."

Mason gave my knee a squeeze, his hand hidden from Finley's line of sight. "Don't you feel better about this now?"

"I do," I said with an exhale. "But now we've got to deal with Xander."

"Xander?" Owen asked. "What'd he do?"

"He knows," Mason answered. "He caught us, actually, and he threatened to tell his 'buddies' on the school board. Do you think you could talk to him and, you know, make sure that doesn't happen?"

Owen snickered. "He doesn't have buddies on the school board. They despise him for some of the articles he's written, exposing their hypocrisy. Trust me, they're not going to listen to a word he says. He was just trying to get under your skin."

"Okay. Sidenote," Mason said, crossing his arms. "Can you please explain why you're friends with that snake?"

"We have a history," Owen said, shaking his head. Something about this made him smile. "He's my oldest friend, and I promise there really is a good person beneath that asshole exterior he likes to put out there. That's not the real him."

"Uh huh." Mason didn't seem all that convinced, and neither did I.

"Xander hasn't had the easiest life," Sarah said, exchanging a glance with Owen. "And because of that, he's got a big chip on his shoulder. But he's actually harmless. So don't worry about him, either."

"I hope you're right," I said. "Noah Sherman's daughter is in my class, and I'm worried about him finding out."

Mason stiffened. "Let him say something about it. I wonder how the rest of the school board would feel about him sexually harassing a teacher during the apple orchard field trip."

"What?!" Sarah and Owen exclaimed at the same time, both of them turning to me.

"He got a little touchy-feely," I admitted, "but it's not that big of a deal."

Mason scoffed. "Yes it was. You don't put your hand on someone's lower back and whisper in their ear if you're not trying to—" He glanced into the next room to make sure Finley wasn't listening before continuing, "—fuck them."

Owen nodded in agreement, while beside him, Sarah was shaking her head in disgust. "Well, whatever happens, I'll go to bat for you."

"And the school board loves her," Owen said. "So does the superintendent. You guys have nothing to worry about."

I was feeling much better about the situation after talking to them. If Sarah wasn't worried about it, I wasn't going to fret, either.

We helped them clean up, and Finley begged to be taken upstairs to see the robots. Owen agreed to go with her while we finished up, and Sarah smiled watching him take her by the hand and let her pull him toward the stairs. "He's going to be a great dad someday, Sarah." I told her.

"I know." She grinned even bigger. "Listen, all that's left to do is put leftovers away, so you guys can head up there too, if you want. I know Owen's eager to show you your new workspace, Mason."

I quickly finished off my margarita, giving Sarah the empty glass, and Mason and I made our way up the stairs. Finley and Owen had already made it to his office, so Mason slapped my butt on our way up. "Mason," I protested, turning around to give him a playful shove. He fought back by tickling my waist, making me double over in laughter as I tried to wriggle away.

"I could take you right here on these stairs," he said, parroting Owen's words from the weekend before. I threw my head back and laughed before Mason kissed my lips.

"That's probably not the best idea," I said, my voice barely above a whisper. I nuzzled my nose against his before going in for another kiss.

Just as our lips touched again, a voice interrupted us from the top of the stairs. "What the *hell?*"

We both turned in horror to see Finley standing above us with her hands on her hips and her mouth open wide.

She had witnessed everything.

chapter fifty
mason

"Finley! I thought you were in Owen's office." My cheeks were burning.

"Does anyone wanna explain to me what's goin' on here?" She was speaking like she had some kind of authority over us. And in that moment, she did.

"We were, uhh, acting out a play?" I offered, glancing at Kendall. She looked just as mortified as me.

"What play?"

"Um. What I meant to say was—we thought there was mistletoe on the chandelier up there. And you have to kiss if there's mistletoe, right?"

Finley just stared at us. She wasn't buying my lame excuses, and why would she? I was doing a terrible job at covering for us. I wracked my brain for a better explanation, but it was already too late. My kid could see right through my lies.

"Hey," Kendall said, gently touching my side. "Is it okay with you if I try to handle this?"

I waved one arm, motioning for her to give it a shot. "Please. I'm dying here."

Kendall walked up the remaining stairs, taking a seat next to Finley on the landing. "Can you sit with me for just a second?" she asked. Finley nodded, taking a seat. A few feet away, Owen was standing in the doorway of his office with his hands in his pockets, half-listening. I didn't turn to look, but I could hear Sarah breathing at the bottom of the stairs. Whether she realized it or not, Kendall had an audience.

"Why were you kissing my dad?" Finley asked, her eyes still wide, but now she looked more amused than shocked.

"Well. Because your dad and I like each other."

"Yeah, I could tell," Finley said with a toss of her head. So sarcastic—I saw so much of myself in her at that moment. "Are you his girlfriend, or what?"

"I would like to be," Kendall said, putting her hand on Finley's shoulder. "Would that be okay with you?"

Finley pondered this for a moment, as though trying to discern whether Kendall was telling the truth or not. Finally, she began to nod. Her lips curled upward in a smile, and for possibly the first time in her life, she was speechless.

"I really care about your dad, Finley, just like I care about you. But listen—this is really important, okay?"

Finley gave Kendall her full attention.

"It wouldn't be a good idea to brag about this to other kids. Do you remember how Trinity bragged about getting a phone and it really upset you?" Finley nodded. "Nobody likes a bragger. And, well, when your friends hear that your Mr. Reed is my boyfriend, they might feel like you're bragging about it. They could feel jealous. And we don't want that, do we?"

"Prob'ly not."

"So while it's not a *secret*, necessarily, it's not the kind of thing we want to talk about at school. We can talk about it at my house or your house or even here at Owen and Sarah's place, but at school, I'm still going to be the same ol' Ms. Devin. Does that make sense?"

Finley nodded.

"So it's okay with you if I go on some dates with your dad?"

"Can I go too?"

Kendall giggled. "Sometimes. I think that would be a lot of fun."

Finley bounced up and down excitedly. "Then can you come with us to the Christmas parade tonight?"

Kendall hesitated, chewing on her bottom lip. I could tell she hadn't expected to be put on the spot so soon, but she took me by surprise when she answered, "Yes."

I cleared my throat, taking a step up. "Are you sure? There's going to be a lot of people there. A lot of your co-workers, probably." I hadn't been to the Woodvale Christmas parade in years, but I knew it always used to draw an enormous crowd.

"It's okay," Kendall said to me before turning back to Finley. "It's going to be cold tonight, but I know the perfect place where we can park downtown and see the whole thing without even getting out of the car. Can we try that?"

"Okay!"

"And then maybe we can talk your dad into getting us some hot chocolate afterwards." Finley responded by dramatically licking her lips. Kendall winked at her before standing up, looking from me to Owen to Sarah. "Were all of you watching that?"

Owen stepped all of the way out of his office and placed his hands on the railing to peer down at his wife. "Babe, are you crying right now?"

Sarah covered her eyes. "It's just too sweet. They're like a little family already. My heart can't take it."

My heart couldn't take it, either—if it swelled any more, it might explode. I made my way up the rest of the steps, patting Finley on the head before wrapping my arms around Kendall. "You handled that a million times better than I ever could."

"She's too smart to fall for your lies."

"I should have known better," I said with a chuckle, going in for a kiss. I jokingly covered Finley's eyes with one hand, but she pushed me away, giggling as she watched me kiss her teacher.

We eventually made our way to Owen's office, where he let Finley play with some of his crane robots. He showed me my workspace, and we discussed our gameplan for the next day, my first day as a *STEM for the Win* employee. And then we had to leave if we wanted to snag the prime parking spot Kendall mentioned.

In the foyer, I watched Kendall zip up Finley's coat and help her put on her mittens, knowing everything that had happened between us had led us here—to this very moment. I took a chance by swiping right on the bombshell of a blonde I doubted would ever give a guy like me a chance. And now, whether she was fully aware of it or not, she had captured my daughter's heart, too—and that was more than I could ever hope for.

I wouldn't give Owen and Sarah a "happily ever after"
only to yank it away from them forever.
Their story isn't over yet.

Acknowledgements

First, I want to thank every reader who chose this book instead of all the others in your enormous TBR stack right now. Yeah, I see you.

I want to thank my whole family for showing up for me from the very start, each of you in your own way—whether it was beta reading, sharing posts, coming to book signings, helping me decide what Kendall should wear, or offering words of encouragement. I love you all!

I want to thank my readers & supporters in Vincennes, IN for reminding me how lucky I am to live in this community. I will never forget the local support I received after publishing *Lesson Learned.*

Shout-out to every single one of my beta readers for getting through the unhinged early draft of this and sharing your equally unhinged reactions. Your feedback has been invaluable.

Shelby, I appreciate every bit of insight you had to offer, especially in helping me turn one of Mason's red flags into a sexy yellow-green flag. Genius.

Lesley, thanks for being the inspiration behind Mason's badass sister. And Lori, thank you for being nothing like the Lori in this book!

Big thank you to my street team and the bookstagram community as a whole for shouting about my books.

I want to thank my editor, Sarah, and my cover illustrator, Lyssa, because even when you're an indie author, it takes a team to get something like this off the ground.

And lastly, I want to thank Victoria M., whose support and connection to my characters means more to me than words can express. You are the embodiment of strength, and I'm so thankful to have connected with you.